The **Girl** *from*
Paradise
Alley

To

Dearest Mag

With love

always

San

× × ×

ALSO BY SANDY TAYLOR

The Runaway Children
The Little Orphan Girl

BRIGHTON GIRLS TRILOGY
When We Danced at the End of the Pier
The Girls from See Saw Lane
Counting Chimneys

The **Girl** *from* **Paradise Alley**

SANDY TAYLOR

bookouture

Published by Bookouture in 2020

An imprint of Storyfire Ltd.
Carmelite House
50 Victoria Embankment
London EC4Y 0DZ

www.bookouture.com

ISBN: 978-1-78681-908-6
eBook ISBN: 978-1-78681-907-9

In memory of my dearest son Bo, who loved to read my books.
Forever in my heart.
Fly free, my sweet boy,
And follow the sun.
Love Mum

PART ONE

CHAPTER ONE

Ballybun, County Cork, 1924

Me and my best friend Kitty Quinn were sitting on the graveyard wall watching Mr Hoolahan's last journey to meet his maker. The mourners were led by Father Kelly as they followed the cart towards the poor man's final resting place. Kitty took the little jotter out of her pocket and licked the end of the pencil.

Me and Kitty attended as many funerals as we could and we marked them out of ten for…

1. The number of mourners.
2. How dignified they held themselves.
3. Whether they were wearing boots or good shoes.
4. How much weeping and rending of garments took place.

The rending of garments was my idea; I thought it sounded desperate and sort of romantic. Kitty wanted to add 'throwing themselves on the coffin', but I thought that was a bit overdramatic for Ballybun.

'They're all wearing clodhopping boots,' said Kitty, screwing up her nose.

'Except Mrs Hoolahan,' I said. 'She's still got her slippers on.'

'That'll be because of the chilblains,' said Kitty. 'She's a martyr to them.'

Mr Hoolahan was a miserable old man who'd done very little good in his life apart from adding to the population of Ballybun by producing thirteen children.

'Is Teddy over from America?' I said, scanning the line of mourners.

'I can't see him,' said Kitty, straining her neck to see over the crowd of people.

'That's a shame,' I said. 'It would have added some dignity to the proceedings if he'd shown up.'

'A mark of respect,' nodded Kitty, writing down 'Teddy' then crossing a line through his name.

We sat on the wall until the coffin was lowered down into the ground.

'Can you hear any wailing?' I said.

'Not a squeak,' said Kitty, 'and definitely no rending. I think it's time we got rid of the rending bit, Nora.'

'You might be right; I think we'd need to go into Cork City for that.'

'They might even throw themselves on the coffin in Cork City,' said Kitty, with a dreamy look on her face.

'Now, wouldn't that be the pinnacle of our funeral watching?'

'Jesus, Nora, what sort of word is that?'

'It means the height of stuff.'

'Where did you learn a word like that?'

'From Grandad Doyle. He's a fierce reader, Kitty, and he gives me a new word every week.'

'What other words do you know?'

'Well, last week he gave me "grandeur".'

'What in all that's holy does that mean?'

'I think it means posh.'

Kitty chewed the end of the pencil. 'Like the Honourables up on the hill?'

'Exactly,' I said.

We jumped down from the wall and watched the mourners drift away from the graveside. Me and Kitty made the sign of the cross as they passed us. Mr Hoolahan might have been a miserable old sod but in death he deserved a bit of respect.

'How many points, Kitty?' I said.

'Only two, it was a poor turnout and not one to be remembered.'

'What was the two for?'

'Biddy Quirk was carrying her good handbag.'

I nodded. 'That was worth a two alright, and didn't I see Patricia Hoolahan with a ribbon in her hair?'

'Did you?'

'I did, and it was black. I thought that was very dignified.'

Kitty crossed out the number TWO and wrote THREE in its place.

We walked across to the grave and watched Mr Dunne and Dooney the Unfortunate shovelling dirt onto the coffin.

'It makes a grand sound, doesn't it, Mr Dunne?' said Kitty, staring down into the hole.

'It does, Kitty, I always think there's a feeling of finality about it.'

'Well, we'll leave you to your business,' I said. 'Goodbye, Mr Dunne, goodbye, Dooney.'

We started to walk towards the gate when Kitty stopped and stared at me.

'What?' I said.

'I have something to tell you, Nora.'

'That sounds serious.'

'Not so much serious as—'

'Thought-provoking?' I said.

'Grandad Doyle?'

'The very man. It means, something that is yet to come, something mysterious.'

'I think it could be all those things.'

'Tell me then.'

We sat on the wall and I waited for Kitty to speak.

'Have you ever been to Bretton Hall, Nora?' asked Kitty.

'I'm not allowed, my mammy says I'm not to go near the place.'

'Why ever not?'

'I don't know, but I'm guessing that something bad happened when she worked there. Anyway, I'm not to go there. Why? Have you?'

'Not yet.'

'Are you intending to then?'

'If I tell you something, you won't tell a living soul, will you?'

'I won't even tell a dead one, Kitty.'

'I've found a way in.'

'Into the Hall?'

'Not the Hall itself, but I've found a way into the gardens. There's a broken-down bit of fence round the back that looks big enough to squeeze through.'

'And how did you discover that?'

'I was on my way to see my Aunty Pat when a fox darted out in front of me. It scared the bejeebers out of me, Nora.'

'It would scare the bejeebers out of me too, Kitty, but sure, he's one of God's creatures and has as much right to be going about his business as anyone.'

'You're right, he has. Anyway, I investigated where he'd come from and that's when I saw the opening. What do you think?'

'What do I think about what?'

'Will we see if we can get in?'

'I just told you I'm not allowed anywhere near Bretton Hall.'

'Did your mammy say anything about the garden though?'

I thought about it. 'I don't suppose she thought she had to, Kitty.'

'We could just take a peek,' said Kitty. 'What harm can a peek do?'

I had a mind to see the gardens of Bretton Hall as much as Kitty did. Surely Mammy wouldn't mind me seeing the gardens? 'Alright, we'll take a peek,' I said, 'but not today. If I'm to call in at the cottage to see Annie, I'll be late for my tea.'

'Tomorrow then?'

'Okay,' I said. 'Tomorrow.'

CHAPTER TWO

I felt bad about not telling Mammy that I was going to Bretton Hall with Kitty, but I had a fierce mind to go and, as Kitty had said, she hadn't mentioned the gardens.

Me and Kitty had just turned thirteen. Kitty was beautiful; she had black hair, pale skin and bright blue eyes. The Irish seemed to fall into two categories. Some had red hair and freckles and others, like Kitty, were blessed with exotic looks. Grandad Doyle said that was on account of the Spanish, who had invaded Ireland's shores and left behind them a whole pile of dark-haired children. I didn't fall into either of these two types, for my hair was brown and curly and I looked like no one else in my family. We went to school at the Presentation Convent and we were taught our lessons by Sister Mary Immaculata, who was very beautiful indeed. No one knew what colour hair she had, because of the black and white wimple she wore, but I had a feeling that she was dark-haired like Kitty, for her skin was like alabaster and her eyes were blue. She swept through the corridors, her black veil flying behind her like one of God's angels.

'Do you think she's an angel, Kitty?' I said, as we were walking towards our classroom the next morning.

Kitty was about to answer when Orla Mullan, who was walking behind us, started laughing.

'Jesus, aren't you a couple of eejits though,' she sneered.

'What are you blathering on about, Orla Mullan?'

'You're eejits if you believe in angels,' said Orla. 'Don't you know it's all just a fairy tale?'

'May the devil cut your tongue out, Orla Mullan,' shouted Kitty. 'It's you that's the eejit, for everyone knows that we all have a guardian angel looking down on us. Nora even knows the name of hers, don't you, Nora?'

'I do,' I said. 'And she's called Nora Foley and she's my namesake, so stick that up your bum.'

Orla was going red in the face. 'I'm going to tell Sister what you said.'

'And we'll tell her that you don't believe in God's holy angels and Father Kelly will read your name out at Mass on Sunday and shame your whole family,' I said.

That shut her up and she flounced away down the corridor.

'I think we won that argument,' said Kitty, 'but you'll have to confess the bum word to Father Kelly when you make your next confession.'

'It was worth it,' I said, grinning. 'And when I explain the circumstances, I'm sure he'll forgive me.'

'He's bound to,' said Kitty. 'You'll probably just get the one Hail Mary for your penance.'

I was thinking that Orla Mullan was probably still put out about the day before, when we'd had a lesson about the meanings of our names. Mine wasn't too bad – Doyle meant 'dark foreigner', which I thought sounded romantic. Kitty was delighted when Sister Immaculata said that Quinn meant 'wisdom'. But poor Orla Mullan was only mortified when Sister announced that Mullan meant 'bald'. We all had a great laugh at Orla's expense and were told off for being unkind. The biggest surprise was when we learned that the name MacDermott meant 'free from jealousy', when everyone knew that Brigid MacDermott was so jealous that she begrudged you your breath.

The afternoon dragged; all I could think of was sneaking into the gardens of Bretton Hall. I couldn't even eat my potatoes at lunchtime.

'You have to eat them,' said Kitty. 'My daddy's daddy lived through the Great Famine and it's a sin in our house to waste a potato, unless you're stricken down by some desperate illness. We all eat our potatoes and we give the skins to Henry.'

Henry was the Quinns' old pig, who lived his life very happily snorting about in their bit of a yard behind the cottage.

'Why do you have a pig?' I said. 'He's a grand feller alright but as my Grandad Doyle says, he's neither use nor ornament.'

'Daddy bought him as a wee small one, from a tinker who was passing through the town. The idea was to slaughter him and make him into rashers of bacon but little Breda got terrible attached to him and cried for a week and called Daddy a murderer, so he couldn't bring himself to do it. He's like one of the family now and sure, he does no harm to anyone, even though he smells like shite when the weather gets hot.'

When the bell went for home time, me and Kitty grabbed our coats and raced through the town to Kitty's house.

'May God bless all in this house,' we chorused, as we dipped our fingers in the holy water font.

'Amen,' said Mrs Quinn, smiling at us. 'Are you stopping for your dinner, Nora?' she said, kissing the top of baby Sean's fat little head and placing him in a basket by the fire.

'Just a sip of tea,' I said. 'Me and Kitty have a mind to go out the Strand.'

'Can I come with you?' asked Breda, crawling out from under the table.

'No, you can't,' said Kitty. 'Tell her, Mammy, she can't come with us.'

'Sure, why not?' asked Mrs Quinn.

'Because she can't keep up,' said Kitty.

'I can,' said Breda. 'Can't I, Mammy? I can keep up.'

'I'll tell you what, Breda,' I said. 'Next time we go out the Strand you can come with us and we'll walk all the way and buy you a grand ice cream from Minnie's.'

'Okay so,' said Breda, crawling back under the table.

'I don't know why you don't put her bed under there, Mammy,' said Kitty. 'She's under there more than she's in the room.'

'I like it under here,' said Breda from under the table.

'She likes it under there,' said Mrs Quinn, smiling.

I drank the tea, and we headed out towards the Strand. There was a cold wind blowing in off the sea, but the blood was pumping through my veins from all the running and I was as warm as toast. As we neared Bretton Hall, Kitty stopped.

'It's around here somewhere,' she said.

We walked along by the fence, looking for the broken bit.

'This is it,' said Kitty.

'What if someone sees us?' I said, looking around.

'Stop your worrying,' said Kitty. 'Okay, I'll go first.'

I watched as Kitty disappeared through the gap in the fence and I had no choice but to follow her.

'Jesus, it's dark in here,' she said.

Kitty was right: it was black as night, with tall trees blocking out the light. A small grey squirrel stared at us for a moment then raced up a tree. It stopped halfway, then stared at us again, as if to say, 'What are you doing here?' I was wondering that myself and I was all for turning back. I knew I shouldn't be here; I knew I was going against Mammy's wishes and I felt guilty, but there was a little bit of me that was excited.

We got down on our hands and knees and pushed through the thick brambles.

'Jesus, my knees are ruined,' cried Kitty.

'So are mine,' I said, pulling brambles out of my good coat. 'Mammy's going to go mad when she sees the state of me.'

'Your mammy never goes mad about anything, Nora, but mine's going to kill me.'

'She *is* not, but your father might.'

'Thanks, Nora Doyle, I needed to hear that.'

'You are very welcome, Kitty Quinn.' I grinned into the darkness.

After much scrambling about, we came out into the daylight and there in front of us was Bretton Hall, perched on the top of the sweeping lawns. I thought it was the most beautiful thing I had ever seen. It dazzled in the bright sunshine, making it look as though the bricks were made of gold.

I stared up at the house, at the rows of windows and the grand steps leading up to the front door.

'Isn't it mighty, Nora?' whispered Kitty.

But I didn't answer her. I suddenly wanted to be alone. It was as if this moment was mine alone and too precious to be shared with anyone, even with my good friend Kitty. As I gazed up at the house, I wondered what it would be like to live in such a place. I knew it would be grand – grander than any house I had ever been in – but I could imagine it as if I'd already been inside those rooms. There would be a sweeping staircase and a drawing room. The bed would have white sheets and plump pillows and a quilt and when you stepped out of bed, your bare feet would sink into a soft rug. There would be long drapes at the windows and when you drew them back, you would look out onto the beautiful grounds. Someone would cook your meals and launder your clothes; you wouldn't have to lift a finger for yourself, it would all be done for you without even asking. I loved Paradise Alley and the Grey House and had no desire to live anywhere else, but I couldn't help imagining what that other life would be like.

'Isn't it, Nora? Isn't it mighty grand?' Kitty went on.

I wished in that moment that I was invisible. If I was invisible, I'd take off my shoes and feel the cool grass between my toes, then I'd run through the yellow daffodils that tumbled down the hill like gold dust and I'd open the big door and walk through the rooms and up the staircase.

'Jesus, Nora, have you gone entirely deaf?' said Kitty.

'I was just looking at it,' I said.

'And why would looking at it render you speechless?'

'Gotcha!' said a voice behind us.

'Holy Mother of God,' screeched Kitty, falling against me.

I turned around to find myself staring into the eyes of a boy of about my own age.

'Run,' said Kitty, catching hold of my arm. 'Run for your life, Nora!'

We pushed back through the thick brambles, towards the opening in the fence.

'Wait,' called the boy.

'Keep going, Nora,' said Kitty, catching hold of my hand. 'He's trying to trick us.'

'Don't go, please,' he called again.

I stopped and looked back at him.

'For God's sake, Nora,' said Kitty, pulling at my coat.

'I'm not going to tell on you,' said the boy, coming closer.

'Why should we believe you?' shouted Kitty.

'Because I said so,' said the boy.

For some reason, I felt that I could trust him. Kitty grabbed hold of my hand again. 'I think it's okay,' I said to her. She loosened her grip and we both stared at the boy. He had brown curly hair that fell over his eyes like a dark curtain.

'We're doing no harm,' said Kitty.

'I never said you were.'

'We were just taking a peek,' I said.

'Well, there's nothing wrong with taking a peek,' said the boy, grinning at me.

'Do you live here?' asked Kitty.

The boy nodded.

'Are you an Honourable?' she said.

'No, I'm a Dishonourable,' said the boy.

'And very rude,' said Kitty. 'I asked you a simple question that called for a simple answer, not the words of an eejit.'

'My father is the groom. Happy now?' he said, grinning at Kitty.

'You're still being rude,' said Kitty, glaring at him.

'Please forgive me,' he said sheepishly. There was something about the look on his face that made me think that he wasn't sorry at all, but it seemed to satisfy Kitty.

'I accept your apology,' she said solemnly.

'Will you come again?' he said.

'We might, if the humour is on us,' she said.

As I followed Kitty towards the gap in the fence I looked back. The boy was still standing there. He brushed his curly hair back from his face and winked at me. I smiled at him, then pushed through the brambles after Kitty's retreating back.

CHAPTER THREE

Me and Kitty ran through the town and out towards the Strand. We ran everywhere, even when we were supposed to be walking. It was grand to feel the wind in our hair, and anyway, we got to our destination quicker. We raced past a few people but still found time to smile and say hello. Mammy said it took no time at all to wish people the time of day and it showed everyone that I had been brought up well. We ran as far as the lighthouse, then rested on the wall.

'Shall we go and say hello to Annie?' I said. 'As we are in the vicinity.'

'Is that another one of your grandad's fancy words?'

'It is. It means "in the area".'

'Your grandad must be a mighty clever man, Nora.'

'Oh, he is, Kitty, he knows everything. My daddy says he could have been a teacher.'

'Well, you should be very proud to be related to such a clever man.'

'I am, Kitty, I give thanks to God for him every day.'

'Do you think Annie will be there?' said Kitty.

'I'd say we're about to find out,' I said, taking Kitty's hand and running across the road to Minnie's café.

My mammy and Annie used to work up at Bretton Hall looking after the Honourables. Poor Annie was an orphan, with neither kith nor kin. Mammy told me that all Annie had ever dreamed of was a little cottage to call her own and a grand turf fire to sit beside. When we moved into the Grey House, she had given Annie the little white cottage in Paradise Alley, along with Mrs Foley, who'd taken care of her in the workhouse.

We opened the café door and the bell tinkled above our heads, bringing Minnie in from the kitchen. It was lovely and warm in the café and it smelled of cakes and biscuits and sausage rolls and meat pies, making my tummy rumble.

'Hello girls,' said Minnie, smiling at us. 'Have you come for some tea?'

'We've no pennies for tea,' said Kitty, looking longingly at the pink iced buns on the counter.

'We've come to say hello to Annie,' I said.

'Mrs Foley is sick to her stomach today, Nora, so Annie is staying indoors to look after her.'

'I'm sorry to hear that, Minnie,' I said. 'I'll call in on my way home.'

'Take this bread with you,' she said, reaching under the counter and wrapping a loaf in a sheet of newspaper. 'And here are a couple of buns for the pair of you. They are yesterday's, but I'd say you won't be minding that.'

'Not a bit of,' said Kitty. 'We'll be glad to take them off your hands.'

'Say hello to Mrs Foley for me, Nora, and tell her I'm sorry for her trouble. And be sure to tell Annie to stay at home as long as she's needed.'

'I will, Minnie, and thank you.'

We ran back across the road and down onto the beach, where we settled ourselves on some rocks.

'Aren't these the best buns you ever tasted?' said Kitty.

'They are indeed,' I said. 'And all the better for being yesterday's.'

'How old do you think Minnie is?' asked Kitty, licking the sticky icing from her fingers.

'I'd say she's a good age. My mammy used to come here when she was a young girl, so I'd say she must be fifty, if she's a day.'

'She doesn't look it though, does she?'

'Mammy says she hasn't seemed to age one bit.'

We sat in silence for a while, filling our mouths with the sweet pink icing and watching the sea running over the sand. I looked along the beach to the town. Rising above it was the tall spire of the church and, beyond that, the grey walls of the workhouse, where my mammy had been born.

We ran back through the town and parted company at the bottom of Kitty's lane. I carried on running through the town, past Biddy Quirk's sweetie shop and past the bottom of the hill that led up to the workhouse. Sometimes when I thought about my mammy living in that gloomy place I felt like crying. But Mammy says she had a great time in there, with her best friend Nora, and she wasn't to be pitied at all.

Suddenly I doubled over with a stitch in my side, which often happened when I ran too fast. I sat down on the wall outside Toomey's, the cobbler. I put the loaf of bread down beside me, then rubbed my side and took a few deep breaths.

Just then the Honourables' posh car went by, driven by Dooney the Unfortunate's uncle, Paddy Lamey. He winked at me and I winked back. I liked Dooney's uncle, who was a good man with no airs about him, even though he was the Brettons' chauffeur. Dooney lived in the workhouse and Mr Lamey often took him out for a spin. I thought that was decent of him, as poor Dooney hadn't a clue who he was and the ride in the posh car was wasted on him.

There was a lady in the back of the car – she caught my eye and seemed to stare at me. I stared back at her until she was out of sight. The stitch had passed, so I jumped off the wall and carried on running, past the undertakers and under the stone arch that led into Paradise Alley. I tapped on Annie's door and walked into the little room. I dipped my finger in the holy water font just inside the door. 'God bless all here,' I said, making the sign of the cross.

'Amen,' said Annie, smiling at me.

'Minnie said to give you this.' I passed her the loaf of bread. 'I think it's yesterday's, but there's still good eating to be had.'

'That was nice of her,' said Annie. 'And I'm sure we're glad of it. Mrs Foley likes to dip it in her tea and suck on it, as she has only one good tooth left in her head.'

'Where is she, Annie?'

'She's asleep in her bed; she's a martyr to her bowels.'

'Minnie said to tell Mrs Foley that she's sorry for her trouble and that you can take all the time off you need.'

'Minnie's a good woman,' said Annie, unwrapping the bread and folding the newspaper carefully into squares.

'Would you like to take the paper for your grandad, Nora? I know he likes to read about what's going on in the world.'

'I will, Annie. I'm sure he'll be glad of it.'

I looked around the little room that Mammy had told me so many stories about. She told her stories in such a way that I felt as though I lived them myself. I imagined her grandaddy sitting hunched over beside the fire and how my mammy had thought he was the devil himself when she'd first laid eyes on him.

'He was fearsome, Nora,' she'd said. 'And I was frightened to death of him. You see, he didn't want me there because I had been born in the workhouse, but we grew to love each other. It was him that gave me my little dog Buddy for Christmas. My happiest memories were walking the fields together, with Buddy running ahead of us. I missed him terrible when he was taken up to Heaven and I still miss Buddy, he was a lovely old dog. I like to think of the pair of them running around Heaven together.'

'I wish I'd known the grandaddy, Mammy,' I'd said.

'He would have loved you, Nora. Oh, how he would have loved you.'

I sat beside Annie's fire, and breathed in the smell of the turf that filled every corner of the room. This little cottage had always felt like another home and I loved it here.

'Were you and Mammy happy working at Bretton Hall, Annie?' I said.

'It was hard work, but I was lucky to have the job, for I had nowhere else to go.'

'And was my mammy happy working there?'

Annie got a knife out of the drawer and started to slice into the bread. 'Mrs Foley is going to love this,' she said.

'Was my mammy happy working there?' I said again.

'I'd say she was happy enough.'

'Was I born here, Annie?'

'Jesus, Nora, you're full of questions today,' she said, smothering the bread with thick yellow butter.

'Grandad says I have an inquisitive mind.'

Annie handed me the bread and then she rattled the turf with the poker. It settled with a hiss and a blast of heat.

'How would I know where you were born?' she said.

'Didn't Mammy tell you?'

'She might have done but sure, I've forgotten; it was a long time ago and anyway, what does it matter where you were born? You're here, aren't you?'

I bit into the bread, then wiped away the butter that dribbled down my chin. 'I am,' I said. 'but I've a mind to know how I got here.'

'I shouldn't be worrying yourself about it, Nora, you'll have your head mashed.'

I popped the last piece of bread into my mouth and stood up. 'I'd best be getting home,' I said. 'Please give my best to Mrs Foley and tell her I will pray to the Virgin Mary to fix her poor bowels.'

'I'll tell her, Nora, and I'm sure it will give her comfort.'

I walked slowly up Paradise Alley, towards the Grey House. I loved the alley; its very name made me smile. It was set apart from the rest of the town, and you had to walk through a stone arch to enter it. All the little cottages were joined together, six in total, three on one side and three on the other. There was a gutter running down the length of the lane where the dirty water from the washing was thrown. Apart from Mrs Buckle, who was a slovenly article of a woman, everyone tried to keep their cottages clean and cared for. There would always be someone whitewashing the stonework or planting little boxes of flowers on the windowsills. There was no water in the cottages and no toilets, just a bucket hidden behind a curtain. I knew how lucky I was to live in the Grey House, for we had a spring that produced clean water and a little wooden hut where you had some privacy. Yes, I was indeed lucky.

I didn't know why it mattered so much to me where I was born, but it did. I knew every single detail about the night my little brother Stevie was born. How it was wild and stormy and how Mrs Heher, who delivered all the babies in the town, slipped on some wet leaves and had to be carried into the Grey House and could only shout instructions to my poor daddy from the chair and how Daddy delivered Stevie himself. The whole town said that my daddy was the hero of the day and Father Kelly read his name out at Mass on the following Sunday.

'My mammy says it wasn't your father who was the hero of the day,' Kitty had said. 'My mammy says it was your mother who carried that lump of a child around in her belly for nearly a year – all your daddy did was pull it out.'

'My daddy was a hero long before that,' I'd said, glaring at her.

'Oh, I meant no harm, Nora,' said Kitty. 'I think your daddy is as fine a man as ever was born; I'm just telling you what my mammy said.'

'Well, in future, Kitty Quinn, you can tell your mammy to mind her own counsel and keep her opinions to herself.'

'Are you cross with me, Nora?' Kitty had said, looking sad.

I'd put my arm around her shoulder. ''Twasn't you who maligned my father's good name, it was your mother and I don't hold you accountable for your mother's views.'

Kitty had looked at me in wonder. 'I wish my grandad was as educated a man as Mr Doyle, for you know some very fine words, Nora.'

'I'll teach you some if you like,' I'd said, smiling at her.

'That would be grand,' said Kitty.

My mammy and daddy often talked about the night Stevie was born but there were no tales about how I was born. I wanted a story too. I'd even begun to think that maybe I was adopted. After all, I didn't look anything like either my mother or my father. Stevie had very fair hair like my mammy but my hair was brown and a mass of curls that were the bane of my mother's life. I mentioned it to Kitty, who said that I had my mother's eyes and I should be grateful that I had a mammy who was as beautiful as a film star, because her own mammy had recently run to fat.

I shut up about it after that. After all, no one wants to be reminded that they have a mammy who has run to fat.

CHAPTER FOUR

Mrs Hickey was the cook at Bretton Hall. She'd died in her sleep and I couldn't help wondering if the Honourables had to get their own breakfast that morning.

I was just about to meet Kitty at the graveyard. 'Will you be going to the funeral, Mammy?' I'd asked.

'I don't think so,' said Mammy.

I stared at her and I wondered why she didn't want to pay her last respects to her old friend Mrs Hickey, who Father Kelly said was a fine God-fearing woman and a great cook, who'd filled the Bretton's bellies for many years. Maybe it was Mrs Hickey she'd fallen out with and that was why she didn't want me going near Bretton Hall. If that was the case it was good news, because now that she'd been taken up to Heaven to cook for the Lord, I could go back and see the boy without Mammy minding.

'Did you have a falling-out with her, Mammy?' I said.

Mammy was bending over, hanging the wet clothes over the wooden horse in front of the fire. She stood up and rubbed her poor back. Mammy was heavy with child and I prayed every night to the Blessed Virgin Mary to intercede on my behalf and ask her son Jesus to send me a baby sister.

Daddy said I should be praying for an easy birth for Mammy and a healthy child. Of course, I wanted those things too, but what I wanted was a healthy sister – if it wasn't too much trouble.

'What makes you say that, Nora?' asked Mammy.

'I was just wondering if that's why you don't want to go to her funeral,' I said, 'because the pair of you have fallen out.'

Mammy smiled at me. 'We're not all addicted to funerals,' she said, laughing.

I loved to hear my mammy laugh. My mammy was the prettiest mammy in Ballybun and I loved the bones of her.

'No, I didn't have a falling-out with Mrs Hickey, Nora.'

'That's a shame,' I said.

'Why is it a shame, child?'

'Oh, no reason,' I said quickly.

She shook her head. 'You're a funny little thing,' she said, walking across and putting her arms around me. She smelled of wet washing and lemons and home.

'I love you, Mammy,' I said.

'And I love you, Nora,' she said, kissing the top of my head. I smiled at her and ran down the road to meet Kitty.

'Have you got your jotter ready, Kitty?' I said, pulling myself up onto the graveyard wall.

'Of course, I have,' she replied, taking it out of her pocket.

Just then the Brettons' shiny car pulled up, and Mr Lamey got out and opened the doors.

'I'd say this is going to be a mighty funeral,' I said. 'Father Kelly has on his good Sunday vestments. I suppose that's because the Honourables are here.'

'Well, it shouldn't matter who you are,' said Kitty. 'We are all God's children and we all deserve Sunday vestments at our funerals.'

'I agree Kitty – didn't Jesus himself fraternise with the poor?'

'Your Grandad Doyle?' said Kitty.

'The very man,' I said. 'It means "mix with". Are you going to give Father Kelly a point for his finery?'

'I am not,' said Kitty, writing 'Father Kelly' and putting a line through it.

I spotted Annie walking towards the grave; she gave me a small wave of her hand, as befitted a mourner.

'Give Annie a point, Kitty, that was a very dignified wave.'

Kitty wrote 'Annie' and put a one beside her name.

I looked back at the car and watched as the Honourables stepped elegantly out onto the lane. There were two women and two men, all dressed in black. The two women had veils over their faces and the men were wearing fine suits. They walked to the head of the line of mourners and some people bobbed as they walked past.

'Do they get points for bobbing?' asked Kitty, chewing the end of her pencil.

I thought about it. 'Give them a half,' I said. 'They should be concentrating on poor Mrs Hickey, not making a show of themselves bobbing.'

Kitty wrote 'bobbing' and put a half mark against it.

'Can you hear any wailing?' asked Kitty.

I listened. 'There's some muffled sobs,' I said. 'And I think they're coming from Annie.'

'Annie should be proud of herself this day, Nora, for she did a fine wave and now she seems to be the only one that's crying.' She made another note in the jotter. 'Isn't that the boy?' she said suddenly.

I stared at the line of mourners. A young lad with brown curly hair was walking behind the Brettons. 'Is it?' I said.

'It looks like him,' said Kitty.

We could hear Father Kelly going on about 'dust to dust' and 'ashes to ashes', but I kept my eyes on the boy. What was he doing walking with the Brettons as if he was somebody, when he was only the son of a groom?

'Write down "boy" and put a line through it, Kitty.'

'Why? What did he do?'

'I haven't decided yet,' I said.

Kitty wrote down 'boy' and put a line through it.

'That'll show him,' I said. 'Getting airs above his station.'

The mourners started drifting away from the graveside, the Brettons were the first to make a move. I watched the boy pass me. He looked up and caught my eye but kept walking.

'How many points, Kitty?' I said.

'Five and a half,' said Kitty, studying the page. 'Annie got two for the dignified wave and the sobbing. I gave a half point for the bobbing. I gave two points for the Brettons turning up and another point for Mrs Connell the baker's wife, who was wearing her good Sunday hat.'

'Not a bad do,' I said, jumping down off the wall.

I watched as the boy climbed into the Brettons' car. Maybe I was being a bit hasty in condemning him – after all, he was just a child, and when you're a child you have to do as you are told. He probably had no liking to be there at all. 'Maybe we will see him again, Kitty,' I said.

'Shall I rub the line out that I put through his name?'

'Do you have a rubber?'

'No,' said Kitty.

'Then there'll be no rubbing out this day, will there?'

'I don't suppose there will,' said Kitty, grinning and linking her arm through mine as we walked away from the graveyard.

CHAPTER FIVE

It was Saturday morning and after I'd helped Mammy around the cottage, I called for Kitty.

'God Bless all here,' I said, dipping my hand into the holy water, except that there was no water in the font. 'You've run out of holy water, Mrs Quinn,' I said.

'We'll call in at the vestry and get a refill,' said Kitty, running down the stairs.

'Good girls,' said Mrs Quinn. 'Where are you off to?'

'We're off out the Strand,' I said.

'Will you roll Sean out with you?'

'Ahh, Mammy,' said Kitty.

'Less of the "Ahh, Mammy",' said Mrs Quinn. 'Sure, he'll sleep all the way and he could do with the air.'

'We'll be glad to, Mrs Quinn,' I said.

'You're a good girl, Nora, and you could learn a lot from her, Kitty.'

'Well, as long as we don't have to take Breda,' said Kitty, glaring at me.

'Breda's next door, playing with the twins,' said Mrs Quinn.

'Makes a change from sitting under the table, I suppose,' said Kitty.

'She's probably under next door's table, and I wouldn't be surprised if she had the twins under there with her,' said Mrs Quinn, smiling now.

Kitty went into the yard to get the baby's pushchair.

'How is your mother, Nora?' asked Mrs Quinn, pushing Sean's fat little arms into his coat.

'As well as can be expected under the circumstances,' I said.

'It won't be long now – are you excited?'

'I am and I'm not, Mrs Quinn. I'm praying like mad for a baby sister but Daddy says I should be praying for a healthy child, whatever God in His holy wisdom decides to send.'

'He's right, Nora. We get what we are given. I was hoping for a boy when I got Breda but sure, I wouldn't swap her for the world, and it will be the same for you.'

'I know I'll love a baby brother, Mrs Quinn, I just think I'll love a baby sister a bit more.'

'This bloody pushchair is falling apart, Mammy,' said Kitty, dragging the old pram into the room. 'It makes an awful squeaky noise when I push it – the whole town will hear us coming and I'll be shamed.'

'There are worse things to be shamed for, Kitty,' said Mrs Quinn, laying Sean down in the pram and covering him with a blanket. Mrs Quinn went to the dresser. 'For the Holy water,' she said, handing me a small bottle.

Sean stared up at us with a dreamy look on his face. He was a lovely fat feller with bright blue eyes and a shiny old head. We said goodbye and started walking through the town. We kept getting stopped by people wanting to coo at the baby. 'Jesus,' said Kitty. 'We'll never get there at this rate.'

What with getting stopped by the townsfolk every five minutes and trying to manage the wonky wheel and the squeak, it took forever to get to the Strand.

'Once your mammy has her baby, we'll be pushing two bloody babies everywhere we go,' said Kitty.

'I won't mind, if it's a girl,' I said.

'What's the baby going to be named?' asked Kitty.

'Well, if it's a girl I would like to call her Marigold, but Mammy says it's too fanciful for Ballybun.'

'What does your mammy want to call her, then?'

'She wants to call her Mary, after a friend of hers who went down with the *Titanic*.'

'Mary's a good Catholic name.'

'It is, Kitty, but isn't half the town called Mary? She won't be standing out with a name like that.'

'There are worse names, Nora – what about poor Dymphna Duffy? Imagine being lumbered with a name like that!'

'You're right, that's a desperate name altogether.'

'What if it's a boy?'

'I have no preference on a boy's name.'

'Grandad Doyle?'

'The very man. It means I have no feelings on it one way or another.'

When we got to the beach, we dragged the pushchair over the sand and settled ourselves on the flat rocks. I took the blanket out of the pram and spread it out on the sand. Kitty lifted Sean into her arms and laid him down on it. He smiled up at us and kicked his little legs. If God was hell-bent on sending us a boy, maybe it wouldn't be so bad if he was like Sean.

It was a beautiful day and we sat in silence watching the little waves tumbling towards the shore and trickling over the wet sand.

'Wouldn't you love to go for a paddle, Nora?' said Kitty.

'I would, but we can't leave Sean on his own. You go, and I'll mind him.'

'Thanks, Nora,' said Kitty, tucking her dress into her knickers and running down the beach.

There was a warm breeze coming in off the sea – it lifted the little bit of hair on Sean's round head, making him giggle. 'Aren't you the nicest little baby in Ballybun?' I said, smiling down at him.

Sean grinned up at me. His cheeks were bright red, as if someone had spread rouge on them, and his chin was wet and shiny from the dribble running down it. 'Ahh, you poor little thing,' I said. 'Are you plagued with the old teeth coming through? Never mind, you'll soon be able to eat a good piece of meat once you have a fine set of gnashers.'

I lifted him up into my arms. I loved the feel of his heavy little body on my lap. 'Aren't you a lovely old slob of a boy?' I said, kissing his sweaty little head. 'Aren't you just a little dote?' I rocked him gently until his eyes started to close.

I watched Kitty paddling at the edge of the shore. She lifted the water up in her hands and it sprayed around her head, sparkling in the sunshine like a thousand stars.

'Hello again,' said a voice.

I looked up to see the boy from the Hall grinning at me. 'Hello,' I said shyly.

'Is he your brother?'

I pointed towards the sea. 'No, he belongs to Kitty, she's paddling.'

'He looks as if he's out for the count,' he said, smiling down at Sean.

'Would you put the blanket in the pram please?'

'Of course,' he said.

I watched him shake the sand from the blanket and put it in the pushchair. I stood up and gently laid Sean down on it.

'You haven't been back,' he said. 'I've been waiting for you.'

'Do you think we have nothing better to do than climb through broken fences?' I snapped.

His face went red and I felt sorry for being so rude. 'I'm not supposed to go near Bretton Hall,' I said, more gently.

The boy sat down beside me on the rock. 'Why not?'

'I haven't a clue, but I think that perhaps my mammy had a falling-out with Mrs Hickey, may God rest her soul.'

'I saw you and your friend at the funeral,' he said.

'And we saw you too, dressed to kill and walking behind the coffin like Little Lord Fauntleroy.'

I knew I was being rude again and I didn't know why. 'Sorry,' I said.

'That's okay,' he said, grinning. 'I felt a bit like him myself. That book is one of my favourites.'

'Mine too,' I said, smiling at him. 'But *The Secret Garden* is my most favourite of all.'

'You've read *The Secret Garden*?' he said, looking surprised.

I could feel myself getting cross again. 'And what makes you think I haven't read it? Do you think that it's only folk who live in Bretton Hall that read books?'

'Gosh, I didn't mean that,' said the boy. 'I only meant that I love that book too. Please don't think that of me.'

I stood up and tucked the blanket around Sean.

'I don't think anything of you,' I said, turning to face him. 'Because I don't know you, do I?'

He came and stood beside me. 'I think we've got off on the wrong foot,' he said gently. 'My name is Eddie. What's your name?'

'Nora Doyle, and that's my friend Kitty Quinn,' I said, pointing down the beach.

'Do you live near here?'

I nodded. 'I live in Paradise Alley, with my mam and dad and little brother, Stevie.'

'I wish I had a brother,' he said.

'He's okay, but I'd rather have a sister. How come I've never seen you in the town?' I said.

He shrugged his shoulders. 'I help my father.'

'But what about school?'

'I have lessons at home.'

'But don't you get lonely sometimes?'

'I get lonely all the time.'

I thought that was sad. I couldn't imagine what it must be like to never go to school and never have any friends. I looked down the beach and watched Kitty standing in the water up to her knees. I couldn't imagine not having Kitty.

'How old are you, Nora?'

'I'm thirteen.'

'Oh, I'm twelve.'

'You look older,' I said.

'I suppose it's because I'm taller than most boys of my age. My father is tall.'

'And your mother?'

He didn't answer my question, but said, 'Will you come tomorrow? To the Hall?'

'Maybe,' I said. 'But I have to go to Mass first.'

'I'll wait for you,' he said.

'I'm not saying I will – it all depends on Kitty. I'm not coming on my own.'

'Then I hope that Kitty is agreeable,' he said. 'Goodbye, Nora Doyle.'

'Goodbye, Eddie.' I said, and I watched him walking away across the sand.

CHAPTER SIX

'Are you sure you want to see him again?' asked Kitty as we squeezed through the gap in the fence.

'We don't have to stay if we don't want to,' I said. 'I'm just intrigued by him.'

'Grandad Doyle?'

I nodded. 'It means, um…' I didn't know how to explain it.

'What's the point of knowing fancy words, Nora, if you don't know what they mean?'

I could feel my face getting red and I was glad we were in darkness. 'I *do* know what it means, it's just a bit difficult to explain.'

'Well, try,' snapped Kitty.

'Well, it means that I have a hankering to know more about him.'

'Well, next time, Nora Doyle, say you have a hankering, then we'll all know what you're on about.'

Sometimes I thought that Kitty was jealous of my fancy words because she didn't have a Grandad who was as clever as mine. But then I looked at my good friend Kitty in the darkness and I felt mean and unkind. It wasn't her fault that her Grandad was a martyr to the bottle and wouldn't know a book if he fell over one on his way home from the pub.

'I'm sorry, Kitty,' I whispered. 'I fear I have committed the sin of pride. I am going to have to confess to Father Kelly next Saturday.'

'Don't worry about it, Nora. I have the head of a fishwife on me this morning. Breda took my good velvet ribbon and gave it to Sean, who dropped it in his porridge, and now it's ruined. I ate the face off her and made her cry and now Mammy is cross with me. I think I have a bit of confessing to do meself.'

'Well there you are then,' I said. 'We are both desperate sinners this day.'

'Did he give you a time to meet?' said Kitty.

I shook my head. 'No.'

Kitty sighed. 'So, he might not come at all? And we could be crouching here all afternoon?'

'He might not,' I said. But in my heart, I knew that he would.

Just then we heard a rustling noise close by, and Eddie's grinning face came poking through the bushes. 'You came, then?' he said.

'We did.'

The three of us stood awkwardly staring at each other.

'This is my good friend Kitty,' I said.

Eddie shook Kitty's hand. 'Pleased to meet you Kitty,' he said smiling.

I cleared my throat. 'It's a grand day, isn't it?'

'It is indeed,' said Eddie.

'For this time of year,' added Kitty.

Eddie looked down at his feet and kicked at the brambles, scuffing the toes of his boots.

'Do you want to see something?' he said suddenly.

'See what?' asked Kitty.

'If I tell you, it will spoil the surprise.'

Kitty still looked doubtful. 'How do we know you're not going to trick us?'

'Well,' said Eddie, scratching behind his ear, 'you don't, you're just going to have to trust me.'

'The way Jesus trusted Judas?' said Kitty.

'I'm not about to get you crucified,' he said.

Kitty looked at me and I nodded.

Eddie grinned. 'Follow me then.'

He lifted the branches of a tree back and we scrambled through the dense undergrowth. We followed behind him until the thick brambles gave way to a path, and we were able to stand. Eddie kept looking back at us and smiling. I felt a bubble of excitement in my belly and I had the feeling that a great adventure was about to happen. Eddie stopped in front of a high stone wall that was covered in ivy. He pushed the ivy away, revealing an old wooden door, then he bent down, lifted up a rock and retrieved a big rusty key.

'Are you sure you should be doing that?' said Kitty, looking around.

Eddie grinned and turned the key in the lock. 'You worry too much,' he said.

'How much I worry is no concern of yours,' said Kitty, glaring at him.

I couldn't help thinking that it was Kitty's idea to come here in the first place, and now she was awful snappy and a bit rude. Maybe she still had the fishwife's head on her over the ruined ribbon. I reached out and held her hand and she smiled at me. Eddie pushed open the gate and we stepped inside. For a moment I just stood there, looking around me.

I gazed in wonder at the pink and yellow roses that trailed over the old stone wall that surrounded the garden. Sunlight dappled through the branches of the tall trees and shadows threw patterns across the grass. The shadows and the sunlight danced together as the breeze moved the leaves. The dandelions nodded their heads. The bees moved amongst the gorgeous petals of the old roses. It felt as if the garden was alive. I looked up at the branches – a thousand different shades of green were in the leaves above my head, like a mosaic ceiling with light shining through the cracks. I turned around, staring up, and the branches swayed gently and the sunlight moved across my face. I saw a squirrel clinging to a tree, saw it dart along a branch, and as it ran the branch dipped. The squirrel leaped into a neighbouring tree and disappeared into the foliage, disturbing a leaf, which fell slowly through the light and shadow, spinning as it descended. I watched it fall into a little pond in the centre of the lawn. Its surface was covered in leaves that floated lazily about as if they were swimming in the sea. I'd forgotten about the other two as I walked over to the pond. I knelt down and dipped my finger into the cool water, causing ripples of sunlight to spread in circles across its surface.

There was colour everywhere. I recognised the pale blue of the cornflowers and the deep yellow of the marigolds, growing side by side amongst flowers I hadn't seen before. Creamy golds, purples and pinks, feathery grey leaves and bright oranges. I felt as though I had walked into the pages of *The Secret Garden*. I was the spoilt little orphan, Mary Lennox, and Eddie was the boy, Dickon.

The grass was a carpet of white daisies. I had a notion to just sit there and make chains like I did as a child. This garden made me feel like a child, this garden made me want to lift my arms up beyond the tall trees to the sunshine and giggle.

Kitty was still standing just inside the gate. I looked at her and smiled. I wanted her to feel what I was feeling. I beckoned her over and she knelt down beside me on the grass. It was so silent. The only sound was the swaying of the tall trees and the rustling of the leaves as a warm breeze drifted through the branches. It reminded me of the moment when Father Kelly turned the bread and wine into the body and blood of Christ. That was the bit when everyone bowed their heads in prayer. Well, you were supposed to be praying, but mostly me and Kitty were counting down the minutes to the end of Mass when we could escape and go about our business.

'Do you remember when we used to make daisy chains, Kitty?'

'Up at the graveyard?'

I nodded and smiled, thinking of Kitty and me sitting beside my namesake's grave, picking daisies and making them into garlands to lay beside the little wooden cross. I could sense Eddie staring at me. I looked up at him as he pushed his dark curly hair out of his eyes. I knew that he was proud of this garden. I knew that he wanted me to like it. He waited for me to speak.

I felt a lump forming in my throat; this beautiful place made me want to cry. I wished I had the words to tell him how I felt. I wished I could summon up one of Grandad Doyle's special words. I took a deep breath and smiled at him. 'I think it's magical,' I said.

The first thing I did when I got home was to take my book from the bottom shelf and sit on the floor, leaning my back against the old wooden bookcase. I opened the first page and read the inscription there:

Christmas 1919
To sweet Nora, who loves to read.
I think that every child should find their own secret garden,
whether in reality or within the pages of a book.
I hope you find yours, Nora.
With love from your Grandad Doyle.

Well I had found mine, but the garden was not the only secret. It was where the garden *was* that was the biggest secret of all.

CHAPTER SEVEN

It was the beginning of the summer holidays and the days stretched ahead of us, with nothing to do but enjoy ourselves. Mostly we went out to the beach or walked along the wood road or scrounged pennies to have an ice cream at Minnie's. I couldn't stop thinking about the garden, and kept hoping that Kitty would suggest that we went there again but she never did, even though I talked about it all the time.

'For God's sake, Nora,' she said. 'It's just a garden, have you never seen a garden before?'

Kitty said it as if we were surrounded by gardens, when all she had was a back yard full of Henry the pig's shite and all I had was a field.

'Not like that one,' I said. I wanted to mention the book to her but although I was a fierce reader, Kitty only liked the comic books and there were no secret gardens in comic books. 'Wouldn't you like to see it again, Kitty?'

'And do what? My clothes were ruined and Mammy was awful cross with me and I couldn't tell her where I'd been, because you weren't supposed to be there and I didn't want to give you away.'

'You're a good friend, Kitty,' I said. 'And I thank you for not giving me away.'

'That's what friends are for, Nora. Besides, I didn't take much of a liking to the boy. He has awful airs and graces about him for the son of a groom and he walked behind Mrs Hickey's coffin, done up like a dog's dinner as if he was family.'

'I think maybe he was obliged to go.'

'Grandad Doyle?' said Kitty.

I nodded. 'It means he had to.'

'Well maybe I'm judging him too harshly.'

'Shall we go back, then?'

'Well I suppose we might as well – we've nothing better to do. The whole town seems to be brimming over with good health, so I'm thinking there's not much hope of a funeral.'

'But isn't old Biddy Dunne on her last legs?' I said.

'Old Biddy Dunne has been on her last legs for years. I'd say she'll outlive us all.'

'I've been thinking, Kitty. Isn't it a sin to be wishing people dead?'

'I'd say if it was a sin, then God in His holy wisdom would have added an eleventh commandment. Thou shalt not wish your neighbour dead, just so you can attend their funeral,' said Kitty, grinning. 'And wouldn't Father Kelly have had something to say about it by now?'

'You're right, he would. I'll stop worrying about it.'

Later that day I was helping Daddy clean out Bonnie's stable. Bonnie was almost pure white except for a flash of black down her nose. She was a gentle horse who loved to be stroked. Whenever she saw me, she gave this soft whinny as if she was saying hello. We used to have a horse called Blue but he was taken up to Heaven. Mammy and Daddy cried a lot when he died and so did Grandad Doyle.

'Do you still miss Blue, Daddy?' I said.

'He was a very special horse, Nora,' he said. 'Your mammy was only a wee slip of a thing when they first met and she was mighty frightened of him. She used to come on the milk round with me and in time the pair of them became great friends. He was a gentle fellow, with a big heart. It was hard to say goodbye to him.'

I had loved Blue too, but I wasn't allowed to ride him because he was old and tired and deserved to spend his last days in the meadow eating the good fresh grass and enjoying the sunshine.

I liked to think that this was something me and Eddie had in common. Being the son of a groom, he would know all about horses. Maybe I would tell him about Blue and Bonnie the next time I saw him.

I scraped the big shovel across the hay and Daddy threw big buckets of water over the floor.

'Daddy?' I said.

'Yes, love?'

'Do you know why Mammy won't let me go near Bretton Hall?'

Daddy walked out of the stable towards the barn to get fresh hay for Bonnie's bed. I put down the shovel and ran after him. 'Did she have a falling-out with the Honourables?'

'You'll have to ask your mammy that, Nora, but not right now, for the baby will soon be born and I don't want you dragging up the past.'

'I won't say anything, Daddy. I was just wondering, that's all.'

'Well, it's nothing for you to be worrying your head about, Nora. It was all a long time ago and best left in the past, where it belongs. Bretton Hall is nothing special and should hold no interest for you. You have Paradise Alley and for now, that's all any of us need.'

'Right, Daddy, I was just wondering.'

'Talking about your mammy,' he went on, 'she needs your help now; she tires easily and I don't want her doing too much. I need you to be helping out more in the house.'

'What about Stevie? Shouldn't Stevie be helping too?'

'Stevie is only eight, and he is not strong. You're thirteen. Right now, your mother is more important than running the hills and lanes with Kitty Quinn and forever having your nose stuck in a book.'

'Are you cross with me, Daddy?' My eyes were filling with tears – his tone was harsher than I was used to.

Daddy threw down the hay and took me in his arms. 'Of course, I'm not, my darling girl. I'm just worrying about your mammy. I'm sorry if I sounded cross. I'm proud of your book reading and I know that your grandad is too, but I would like you to help out more.'

'I will, Daddy,' I said. 'I'll go and help her right away.'

'Good girl,' he said, ruffling my hair.

I started running back to the house, then turned around and smiled. 'I'm still praying for a healthy little girl with brown curly hair like mine,' I shouted.

CHAPTER EIGHT

Me and Kitty were down the quayside watching the lads jumping into the water.

'Look at that feller, Nora,' said Kitty, pointing across to the lads who were jumping into the water.

'Which one?' I said.

'The desperate handsome one with the fair hair.'

I looked at the boy – he was taller than the others, and looked a few years older than us. We knew most of the boys in the town but I'd never seen him before.

'Do you think he's visiting from England?' said Kitty. 'Or maybe America?'

'How would I know?'

'I was just asking,' she snapped.

I was in no humour today to be wondering where the boy had sprung from. I was doing my best to help out in the house and my arms were only hanging off my shoulders from dragging water from the pump into the house. Stevie was less than useless.

'Sorry, Kitty, I have no humour on me today. I'm worn out doing all the chores.'

'I can help,' said Kitty, putting her arm around my shoulder.

I smiled gratefully at my friend. 'Would you come out to the wood road with me? I have to gather sticks for the fire.'

'I will, of course,' she said. 'We can take Sean's pram so we won't have to carry the stuff back.'

'Thanks, Kitty.'

There were loads of people on the quayside. Women were sitting on the wall chatting to each other while keeping an eye on their little ones, who were playing chase around the boats.

Children were welcoming the fishermen back with their haul of fish. Seagulls flew above us, screeching and squawking, waiting for a good feed. I watched as the men stepped out onto the quay, dragging nets full of slippery fish that squirmed and slithered as they threw them on the warm stones. The seagulls swooped down, pecking at the poor things.

'Not much of a life, is it?' said Kitty, staring at the fish. 'I bet when they woke up this morning, they didn't know it was going to be their last day on earth.'

'I don't suppose any of us do, Kitty,' I said, staring at the shiny fish flapping and twitching on the ground, with their dead eyes staring up to the sky and their mouths open as if they were surprised to find themselves there.

'Do you think they've left family behind, Nora? Do you think there are mammy and daddy fishes crying their eyes out for their murdered children?'

'Murdered?'

'Well, aren't they?'

I thought about it. 'I'm not sure you can murder a fish, Kitty. Didn't Jesus himself feed the multitudes with bread and fishes? It would be blasphemous to accuse Jesus of murder.'

'I hadn't thought of that. Do you think I'll have to confess?'

'I'd say not, for you said it in all innocence.'

I looked over at the boy, who was laughing along with the others. His laughter was high and shrill, almost like a girl. The lads were play-fighting and pushing each other into the water. I watched as the fair-haired boy did a perfect dive off the quay, hardly making a ripple as he glided into the water.

Kitty grinned at me. 'We must find out who he is.'

We walked across to Tommy Nolan, who we'd known at school. He was a couple of years older than us.

'Who's yer man, Tommy?' asked Kitty.

'You mean Finn?'

'If I knew his name, Tommy Nolan, would I be asking who he is?'

'We're curious, Tommy,' I said. 'We've never seen him before.'

'His name is Finn Casey and he's over here from England to stay with his uncle.'

'And who is this uncle of his?'

'And why would I be telling you his business, Kitty Quinn?' said Tommy, winking at me.

Kitty rolled her eyes. 'Jesus, Tommy, will you just tell us.'

'His uncle is Pat Lamey, the chauffeur up at the Hall.'

'You mean Dooney the Unfortunate's uncle?'

'The very man,' said Tommy.

I watched as the boy pulled himself back onto the quay. The sun caught his wet hair, making it shine, and his body glistened with the beads of water running down his back.

'He's related to Dooney the Unfortunate?' I said, shocked at this piece of news.

'They're cousins, Norah.'

I thought about poor Dooney, locked away in the workhouse, and then I looked at the boy, so tall and strong and carefree. God played some desperate tricks on people. Maybe I'd ask Father Kelly what it all meant.

The next morning, I called for Kitty. The door was open so I walked in. 'God bless all here,' I said, dipping my finger into the holy water and making the sign of the cross.

Mrs Quinn was feeding Sean. She looked up at me and smiled. 'Amen,' she said.

'Can we borrow Sean's pushchair please, Mammy?' said Kitty. 'Nora must gather wood for the fire.'

'Of course you can. You're a good girl to be helping your mammy with the chores, Nora.'

Mrs Quinn made me feel guilty, because I didn't help Mammy with a willing heart. I was cross every time she asked for my help and I could see the disappointment in my daddy's eyes, but sure, it was the summer holidays and I had other things to do. I was not a good girl at all. I decided right there and then that I would find the finest sticks in the wood and bring them back to Mammy with a good heart and a smile on my face.

We wheeled the squeaky pushchair through the town and out the wood road. The sun had been shining when I left home but now there were dark clouds and mist rolling in over the hills and the first drops of rain were beginning to fall.

'We're going to get soaked,' whined Kitty, looking up at the sky.

'We have to pay no mind to the rain, Kitty. I must collect as much wood as I can. I've been awful moody about helping out.'

'I'm the same,' said Kitty. 'Mammy's threatening to tell Daddy when he next comes ashore.'

Kitty's father, like a lot of the men in the town, was in the Merchant Navy and spent a lot of time at sea – in fact, he spent more time at sea than he did at home. That's the way it was in Ballybun. Most of the men were working away, while the women took care of the house and the children.

'Let's make a pledge to do better,' I said. 'I can't imagine Jesus pulling a face every time the Blessed Virgin Mary asked him to help with the dishes.'

'Did they have dishes back then?' said Kitty.

'Well, they must have had something to eat out of,' I said.

Kitty nodded. 'The two of us have been selfish, Nora, but from this day we will be reformed girls. Jesus might even see his way clear to forgive me after calling him a murderer.'

We both felt better after that and happily filled the old pushchair to overflowing with the best sticks we could find. 'We'll split them between us,' I said. 'Then your mammy might think twice about telling your daddy that you're not helping her in the house.'

We pushed the pram back through the woods, delighted with our offerings. It was hard going as the wonky wheel was very contrary and felt the need to go in the opposite direction to the other three wheels. We were halfway home when we saw Stevie running towards us, shouting my name. When he reached us, he bent over, holding his side.

'What's wrong, Stevie?' I said urgently.

He straightened up, his face red and sweaty, and he could hardly speak.

'It's Mammy,' he said, his eyes filling with tears. 'She's having the baby and Daddy and Grandad are on the milk round.'

Mammy wasn't due to have the baby yet and I was afeared at Stevie's words. 'Is someone with her?'

Stevie nodded. 'Mrs Heher, who delivers the babies.'

'Did you fetch her, Stevie?'

'I did,' he said, wiping his eyes with the sleeve of his jumper.

'Then you are the best boy and Daddy will be very proud of you. Now, we must get back to Mammy.'

We abandoned the pushchair and started running – poor Stevie couldn't keep up. I shouted back to him to go find Daddy. I didn't know what time it was and where he'd have got to on the round. 'Try Pasley's, and if he hasn't got to them yet, go to Sweeney's and wait for him. Ask everyone you pass to look out for the milk cart and for them to tell Daddy that he has to go straight home.'

'What if he's already delivered the milk to Pasley's?'

'Then go to Mulligan's. As quick as you can, Stevie.'

'I will, Nora.'

'Good boy.'

Kitty and I continued to run for home.

'What can I do, Nora?' asked Kitty.

'Run back and get the pushchair. I'll let you know what's happening as soon as I can.'

When we got to Paradise Alley, Kitty put her arms around me. 'May God be with your mammy this day,' she said.

'Thank you, Kitty,' I said, running under the stone arch.

I could hear Mammy screaming as I got closer. There was a crowd of neighbours outside the house. They touched me as I passed and Mrs Collins pressed a string of rosary beads into my hand. I opened the door and ran upstairs, dropping the beads as I went. Mammy was on the bed. Her face was shiny with sweat and her eyes were glazed with the pain.

'I'm here, Mammy,' I said, kneeling down beside her. She turned away from me as another pain gripped her. I didn't know what to do.

'Will she be alright, Mrs Heher?' I asked.

'All we can do is wait, Nora. She's in God's hands now,' she said, laying a wet rag on Mammy's forehead. 'Your father needs to be downstairs; it will give your mammy comfort to know he's there.'

'I've sent Stevie to look for him,' I said.

Mammy started to scream. Her legs were open and her face was bright red.

'That's right, Cissy, push,' urged Mrs Heher. 'Push, girl, push.'

I held tight to Mammy's hand. She squeezed it hard, digging her nails into the soft flesh, but I didn't mind, I just wanted her to be alright. '*Dear Lord Jesus, have pity on one of your own and help my mammy in her hour of need,*' I said softly.

'One more push, Cissy,' encouraged Mrs Heher. 'Just one more push, that's it, you're doing great.'

I watched as Mrs Heher put her hands inside Mammy and helped the baby slither out onto the bed.

'It's over now, my love, it's over and you have a fine boy.'

I looked at the baby laying so still on the bed. It didn't move and it didn't cry. Mrs Heher started rubbing its grey little body, then she turned to me. 'Run for the doctor, Nora, run as fast as your legs will carry you.'

I ran down the stairs, pushed through the neighbours who were still outside and raced under the Archway and up the hill to Dr Kennedy's house. I hammered on the door and Dr Kennedy opened it. He had a cup of tea in his hand and he was smoking his pipe.

'What is it, Nora?' he said.

'Mammy's had a baby boy and it's dead. You have to make it come alive again, Doctor, you have to!'

Dr Kennedy went back into the house and came out again carrying his case. I watched him hurrying down the lane. I couldn't move; it was as if my feet were nailed to the ground. I didn't want to go back to the house, I *couldn't* go back to the house. This was my fault; this was all my fault. And I couldn't go back.

I ran and ran until my chest was so tight that I could hardly breathe. I was nearly there, nearly there. I kept going until I got to the gap in the fence. I squeezed through the brambles and stumbled down the path. I felt under the rock for the key but it wasn't there. I pushed at the door and it opened. I threw myself down on the ground and sobbed and sobbed until there were no tears left. I was gasping for air, I couldn't breathe, my mouth was open and I was clawing at the wet grass.

And then I felt someone helping me up and a gentle voice murmuring in my ear. 'It's okay, Nora, you're okay.'

I leaned against Eddie and my breathing started to slow down and my heart stopped racing.

'You're safe now,' he said gently. 'You're safe now.'

'But it's all my fault,' I said.

'What's your fault, Nora?'

I moved away from him. 'I killed my brother, Eddie. I killed my brother.'

'You killed Stevie?'

'Not Stevie. I prayed to God to send a healthy baby sister and to punish me, he sent a dead baby brother.'

'Your mother gave birth to a dead baby?' said Eddie, staring at me. 'When?'

'Just now. Oh, Eddie, what am I to do?'

'That's terrible, Nora, and I'm truly sorry for your family – but it isn't your fault. I don't know much about God, but I don't think that He would be so cruel as to punish you just because you wanted a sister.'

I wanted to believe Eddie; I really did. I knew in my heart that God was a good God but Father Kelly said that he was also to be feared. Perhaps Eddie was right, perhaps it wasn't my fault at all. I was cold and wet and I shivered. Eddie took off his jacket and put it around my shoulders. I looked at this boy who had the same curly hair as me and I felt comforted.

'We have the same hair,' I said.

'We do,' he said, smiling.

And there in the garden, as I listened to the rain dripping through the leaves and the soft breeze moving the branches, I knew that here, in this magical place, I would always be safe. But I couldn't stay in the garden forever, I knew that I had to go home.

Eddie had wanted to walk with me but I knew that if we were seen in the town, word would reach Mammy and I would have to lie to her about where I had met him. I walked slowly; there was no point in hurrying now, the baby was dead and whether it was my fault or not, the house would be a sad place indeed. People smiled at me as I passed. I suppose the terrible news hadn't got out yet. I didn't smile back, because once they found out about the baby, they would shame me by saying I passed the time of day with a smile on my face when I should have been in mourning.

I walked under the archway and up Paradise Alley to the Grey House. People called out to me as I walked. 'A blessed day, Nora,' said Mr Hurley. 'God is good,' called Mrs Barry.

I started running, I burst through the door and went up the stairs to the bedroom. I stood at the bottom of the bed staring at Mammy, propped up against the pillows. The baby was in her arms and Stevie and Daddy were either side of her. She smiled at me and I started crying.

'Come here, love,' she said.

I crossed to the bed and laid my head down beside her. She stroked my hair, so gently.

'I thought he was dead,' I said.

'Look at him,' she said, moving the shawl away from his face. 'Isn't he beautiful?'

I looked at my brother's face poking out between the folds of the shawl. He was tiny but he was perfect. His little hands were moving about like a little starfish and he was staring up at me. I gave him my finger and he held it fast. He was strong, my brother was strong and, in that moment, I knew that I would love him all my life and I would never swap him for a sister even if God changed His mind and sent one.

'Yes, Mammy, he's beautiful,' I said.

'You don't mind that he's a boy?'

I shook my head. 'I wouldn't mind if he was a bag of potatoes,' I said, grinning.

'I would,' said Stevie. 'I wouldn't be able to play hurling with a bag of spuds.'

We all laughed.

'What are you going to call him, Mammy?' I said.

'Your daddy and me thought Malachi, after my grandaddy.'

I stroked the baby's soft little face. I thought Malachi was a fine name and very befitting for my baby brother, whom God had decided to save.

'Hello, Malachi,' I said. 'Welcome to Paradise Alley.'

CHAPTER NINE

Malachi was growing stronger every day and I loved the bones of him. His birth was the talk of Ballybun and even though I loved him and I thanked God every day that we had him, I couldn't help being a bit put out that here was another baby whose birth would be talked about for years to come.

Mrs Heher was much in demand, as she told everyone who had a mind to listen how her quick thinking had brought Malachi Doyle back from the brink of death. She was the hero of the day just like Daddy had been when Stevie was born. She couldn't walk through the town without someone inviting her in for a cup of tea and a bite to eat. Her story grew more exaggerated as the weeks went on, till you got the notion that it was she who had given birth to the baby and not Mammy.

Father Kelly read her name out at Mass and when she'd walked down the centre aisle, the crowd had parted like the Red Sea. She'd sat in the front pew, sporting her one good hat with the feather. She'd had the hat for as long as I could remember. She wore it on special occasions and she loaned it out for two pennies a week. It was showing signs of wear and the green feather leaned to the left, but Mrs Heher said that she felt it gave her a jaunty air. Kitty's mother said that in her opinion the house of God was no place to be jaunty.

I wanted a hero of the day and I didn't mind who that might be, I just wanted a story of my own.

'Jesus, Nora,' said Kitty. 'What does it matter where you were born? It's hardly going to affect the rest of your life, is it? Sure, no one talks about my birth either.'

'But you know where you were born, Kitty. You were born at home, in the upstairs bedroom of your cottage. I haven't a clue where I was born because no one will tell me.'

'I expect you were born in the cottage that Annie lives in. Sure, where else would you have been born? If your mammy had given birth to you in the middle of Paradise Alley, I'm sure the whole town would still be talking about it.'

Kitty was right and I didn't know why it bothered me so much but it did. Every time I mentioned it, the subject was changed and I just knew that I wasn't imagining it. Sure, it was a simple enough question to ask, so why all the mystery?

'I should forget about it if I was you,' said Kitty. 'After all, I doubt it will ruin your future prospects in life.' Me and Kitty talked a lot about our future prospects and where we would work when we left school. We were both turning fourteen a few weeks after the summer holidays, so we had plenty of time to think about it. Kitty had a mind to work at Bretton Hall and I would have liked to have joined her, but I knew that Mammy would forbid it. My life seemed to be full of things that I didn't understand.

'What about the workhouse?' asked Kitty.

I shuddered. 'I have no mind to work there,' I said. 'I'd say it would be a desperate sad place to work.'

'What about the hotel?'

'I wish there was a bookshop in the town, I'd like to work in a bookshop. Imagine being surrounded by books all day.'

'I couldn't think of anything worse,' said Kitty, making a face.

'Oh, Kitty, I don't know what you have against books, for they are the most wonderful things. You can lose yourself in a book and you can be transported—'

'Grandad Doyle?'

'The very man. You can be transported to places that you can only dream about.'

'I'd rather visit them, Nora.'

I thought about all the books I had read. How I'd cried when Black Beauty was taken away from his mammy and forced to pull carts in London. How I'd walked beside Lorna Doone over the wild moors of Devon. How I'd laughed at Tom Sawyer and his good friend Huck, growing up beside the great Mississippi River. *Little Women*, where I wanted to be Jo, who loved books as much as I did. *The Water-Babies, Treasure Island, Tom Brown's Schooldays* and my favourite one of all, *The Secret Garden*. So many books, so many wonderful stories within those pages, and while I might never go to all those places, as soon as I opened a book I was there inside my head. And I could do it all without stepping one foot outside Paradise Alley.

'Anyway, you will have to make up your mind, Nora, or you'll end up working in the laundry.'

'I'm never going to work in the laundry, Kitty.'

'Perhaps you could become a nun,' said Kitty, grinning.

'I don't think I'm holy enough to be a nun and although I love God and all His saints, I have no mind to be praying for the poor departed souls, day and night.'

'It had better be the hotel then – at least you'd see a bit of life and you never know, you might meet some rich man who will whisk you away from Ballybun and give you the life of Riley.'

'I haven't a clue who Riley is, have you?'

'No, but it sounds as if he had a grand time.'

'I'm in no rush to grow up, Kitty, and I'm in no rush to leave Ballybun.'

'Neither am I, but I don't fancy being married to some feller who spends his life down the pub, while I have to stay at home looking after the babies.' Kitty grinned. 'Of course, if it was Finn Casey, I might make an exception.'

'That's a grand big word you just used, Kitty,' I said, surprised. 'Grandad Doyle?'

'Yes, I remembered it,' said Kitty, grinning even wider.

'Then I'm proud of you, Kitty Quinn, but I don't think it will be Finn Casey you'll be marrying. He's too old for you.'

'A cat can look at a king, can't he?' said Kitty, grinning.

'He can, but I doubt he'd be invited into the castle.'

'Maybe he'll wait for me,' said Kitty.

'Then all I can say, Kitty Quinn, is that you're in for a long wait. Besides, I couldn't help noticing the way Tommy was looking at you.'

'Really?'

I nodded.

'Let's go down the quay, Nora,' she said, grabbing my arm.

I'd told Kitty about the day I'd gone to the garden thinking Malachi was dead and how Eddie had comforted me. 'As long as we can go to the garden afterwards,' I said.

'You and that bloody garden,' said Kitty, rolling her eyes.

'You and that bloody Finn Casey,' I said, grinning.

Finn wasn't down the quay, so we sat on the wall for a bit to see if he might come. We sat there for what seemed like hours. 'Let's go to the garden,' I said eventually. 'I'm getting awful bored sitting here.'

'I suppose we might as well,' said Kitty, jumping down off the wall. 'We'll try again tomorrow. But let's have a cup of tea first. I'm gasping for one.'

'I could do with one meself,' I said.

The bell tinkled above our heads as we opened the door of Minnie's café.

'Hello, girls,' said Minnie, coming through from the back. 'How are the two of you?'

'We're grand, Minnie,' I said.

'And how is your mammy and Malachi?'

'They're both grand, Minnie, and thank you for asking.'

Minnie busied herself with the tea. 'I hear Mrs Heher is still living off the story?'

'She is, and I'd say she's going to live off it for a lot longer.'

'Been to any good funerals lately, girls?'

'Not really,' said Kitty. 'Funerals aren't what they used to be.'

Minnie nodded her head in agreement. 'I can remember when the men of the town would sit beside the coffin all night as it lay in the church and the next day, the whole town – men, women and children – would follow the coffin to the graveyard. It was all very dignified, even the paupers had a grand send-off.'

'We're thinking that maybe they do it better in Cork.'

'Or Dublin,' added Kitty.

'I have a sister who lives there. She works in a grand bookshop. In fact, she's the manager.'

'Your sister works in a bookshop?'

'She does. It's called Finnigan's.'

'Well, that's a name and a half,' said Kitty.

'Have you been to Dublin?' I said.

'I have, and it's like another world. There's fine big stores and carriages and cars and the houses are immense. Of course, there's the poor quarter too, but sure, that's to be expected. And do you know what, girls?'

'What?' we said, hanging on Minnie's every word.

'Even the poor aren't as poor as our lot.'

'Are they not?' I said.

Minnie shook her head. 'Not that I'd want to live there,' she said. 'Sure, you can't move for bodies and although the River Liffey is mighty fine, nothing beats our own Blackwater.'

I nodded. 'I agree with you, Minnie. I can't imagine not being able to walk by the river whenever the mood took me.'

'So, you wouldn't want to live in Dublin then, Nora?'

I shook my head. 'I don't think so.'

'I wouldn't mind living there,' said Kitty.

'But wouldn't you like to travel to places beyond Ireland, Nora?'

'She says she does all her travelling in her books,' said Kitty.

'Foreign parts are of no consequence to me, Minnie.'

'Grandad Doyle?' said Minnie, shovelling sugar into the two cups.

'The very man,' I said, grinning.

'That's where you get your book learning from, Nora, for your grandad is a clever man.'

'And I thank God every day for him.'

'I don't thank God for my old feller,' said Kitty, shovelling another spoon of sugar into her tea.

'Ah, Kitty,' said Minnie. 'He's more to be pitied than scolded, for he's a martyr to the bottle, God love him.'

'Do you know Finn Casey, Minnie?' said Kitty, quickly changing the subject.

'Dooney the Unfortunate's cousin?'

'That's him,' said Kitty.

'I've met him – he's been in with his uncle. Nice young man.'

'He's staying with his uncle up at the Hall,' I said.

'Mr Lamey doesn't live at the Hall, Nora.'

'Does he not?'

'The Lameys have a cottage out beyond the bridge, near your Grandad Collins's farm.'

Kitty and I grinned at each other and finished off the grand sweet tea.

'We'd best be off, Minnie,' said Kitty.

'Have a grand day then, girls.'

'We will,' said Kitty.

'I'm thinking we won't be going to the garden?' I said to Kitty once we were outside.

'You think right,' said Kitty, grinning.

We set off along the wood road. It was a fine day with a bright blue sky and not a cloud in sight. As we walked, we could see the bridge ahead of us spanning the Blackwater. I stopped for a moment to watch the river flowing gently by and to look across at the green fields tumbling down to the water's edge. I would never tire of this beautiful place and I said a silent prayer of thanks that all this beauty was but a stone's throw from Paradise Alley. I could never want for more than this.

'Jesus, Nora, will you stop your mooning and come on. Sure, the river will always be here but Finn Casey will have packed his bags and be on the next boat back to England by the time we get there.'

'I'm coming,' I said, smiling at her. 'But don't you think it's beautiful, Kitty?'

'I do, but I've been looking at it my whole life and now I have a mind to be looking at Finn.'

'We'll call in to my granny's first. If the Lameys' house is close by, they'll know where it is.'

We crossed the bridge and followed the track to the farm. It was only the start of summer and yet the leaves were already starting to fall from the trees, drifting around us as we walked. I could see the farm up ahead and started walking faster. I loved visiting the farm and I loved seeing my Granny and Grandad Collins.

'You're awful lucky, Nora, to have a grand place like this to visit.'

'I know I am, Kitty, but you can share it with me.'

'Thanks, Nora.'

Granny Collins was just coming out of the barn as we walked through the gate.

'Be sure to close it behind you,' she called.

Me and Kitty made sure the gate was firmly latched, then I ran up to my granny.

'Well, isn't this a grand surprise?' she said, hugging me. 'And Kitty too. Come inside, the pair of you, for I have a grand apple cake just out of the oven.'

'Thank you, Mrs Collins,' said Kitty. 'I'm desperate partial to a bit of apple cake.'

The three of us walked across the yard and into the house. Kitty and me both dipped our finger into the holy water font that was just inside the door. We made the sign of the cross and sat down at the long table that took up most of the kitchen. A grand fire burned in the grate. Tommy, their old dog, was stretched out in front of it like a big black rug. When I was little, he would run to greet me, but now he just wagged his old tail and went back to sleep. The kitchen smelled of turf and apple cake and Granny and Grandad and I loved it as much as the Grey House, for it had always been like a second home to me.

'And what brings you out this way, girls?' asked Granny, cutting the cake and giving us a big slab each.

'We're looking for someone,' I said, biting into the warm sponge.

'And who might that be?'

'Finn Casey,' said Kitty, wiping away the apple that had dribbled down her chin.

'He's staying with Mr Lamey,' I said.

'Oh yes,' said Granny. 'I heard that Paddy's nephew was staying for the summer.'

'Is it near here?' asked Kitty.

'The Lameys' cottage is just over the hill, so you'll find it easy enough. What is this great interest in the boy? Isn't he a bit old for you, Kitty?' Granny had a cheeky smile on her face.

'Finn is desperate handsome, Mrs Collins, and I've a mind to get to know him,' said Kitty.

Granny laughed. 'You do right, Kitty, for he is a grand-looking lad. If I was sixty years younger and you a few years older, I'd give you a run for your money.'

'Mammy said that you were a grand-looking woman in your day, Granny,' I said.

'And she still is,' said Grandad Collins, coming into the kitchen and wiping his muddy boots on the mat.

'Get away with you,' said Granny, but she was smiling at him and she'd gone a bit red in the face.

'They're looking to visit the Lameys' cottage,' said Granny. 'For they have an interest in the boy that is staying there.'

'If you finish your cake, I'll walk you to the top of the hill and show you where it is,' said Grandad.

'Thanks, Grandad,' I said, putting the last bit of cake into my mouth. 'That was a grand cake, Granny.'

'Oh, it was, Mrs Collins,' agreed Kitty.

'You're welcome. Now off you go and find your handsome lad, and may his nature be as pleasant as his face.'

'Oh, it will be, Mrs Collins,' said Kitty, 'for goodness only shines out of him.'

I looked at Kitty and made a face. 'You only saw him for five minutes, Kitty, how could you tell what was shining out of him?'

'I could just tell,' she said. 'God in His wisdom wouldn't give a face like that to a rogue of a feller. Don't you agree, Mrs Collins?'

'Ah now, I wouldn't like to say but I hope it all turns out fine for you. All I will say, Kitty, is don't be swayed by a pretty face.'

'Oh, I won't, and thanks for the cake, it was mighty fine.'

'Come and see us again, girls.'

I hugged Granny and we followed Grandad out into the yard and up the hill that rose high above the back of the farm. As we reached the top of the hill, Grandad pointed down the valley to a low white cottage that nestled between a row of tall trees. 'That's the Lameys',' he said.

'Thank you, Grandad,' I said.

'Oh yes, thank you, Mr Collins.'

'You're very welcome, girls. Now I think I'll away and help myself to a slice of your granny's apple cake.'

'You do right,' I said.

'It's as fine an apple cake as I have tasted,' said Kitty.

'Then I'm in for a treat,' said Grandad, smiling at us.

We watched him walk back down the hill to the farm.

'Your grandad is a fine man, Nora,' said Kitty.

'He is, but he's not my real grandad, you know.'

'Is he not?'

'My real grandad was a fine sailor, from a foreign land far across the sea, called Norway. One day he sailed into Ballybun and fell in love with my granny.'

'That's desperate romantic, Nora.'

'I think so too. His name was Stefan. That's why Mammy called my little brother Stevie, in memory of him.'

'That was nice, Nora, and a fine way to honour a man who sailed the seas and came from such a lovely place. Do you have three grandads then?'

I nodded. 'One delivers the milk, one farms the land and the other sails the oceans.'

'Then you are mighty fortunate. I only have one grandad and he doesn't even know who I am half the time.'

I put my arm round my friend and hugged her. 'You can share mine, Kitty, and welcome.'

'Thank you, Nora,' she said.

We sat on the grass and looked down at the cottage. There was no one about.

'What do you want to do, Kitty?'

'We'll just sit here a while and see if Finn appears.'

'Grand so,' I said, linking my arm through hers.

After we'd got bored staring at the cottage with no sign of Finn we lay down in the warm sunshine, staring up at the blue sky above our heads.

'I don't understand how you can have three grandads, Nora,' said Kitty suddenly.

'I don't understand it myself,' I said. 'Mammy says the best way for me to get my head around it is to liken it to the Holy Trinity and just accept that it's a mystery.'

'I've never understood the Holy Trinity, Nora.'

'And I was under the impression that you were two good Catholic girls,' said a voice behind us.

We both jumped up and saw Finn Casey coming up the hill towards us.

'Jesus Mary and Holy Saint Joseph,' said Kitty. 'You shouldn't be creeping up on people like that and frightening the bejeebers out of them. Sure, I nearly lost me apple cake.'

'I'm sorry, girls,' he said, smiling.

'So you should be,' said Kitty, smoothing down her dress.

I thought he had a lovely smile and I thought he had lovely eyes. I decided that Kitty was right – God in His wisdom wouldn't have made such a beautiful face and given him a bad heart.

'My name's Finn, I'm staying with my aunt and uncle at the cottage down there,' he said.

'We know,' said Kitty.

'Do you now?' he said, grinning.

There was something about this boy that I couldn't quite put my finger on. I got the feeling that maybe he was making fun of us, but I didn't mind because he was so beautiful to look at and he did it in such a way that you couldn't be cross with him. Kitty was staring at him saying nothing, which wasn't a bit like her, so I thought it was only polite that I should speak to him.

'My name is Nora Doyle,' I said. 'And this is my good friend, Kitty Quinn.'

'I'm very pleased to make your acquaintance, ladies,' he said, bowing as if we were royalty.

He spoke funny and I liked it. I'd read lots of books about England. The boy reminded me of Colin in *The Secret Garden*. I could have listened to him all day.

'And may I ask how you know my name?' he said.

'Tommy Nolan told us,' said Kitty, going a bit red in the face.

'Then I shall be forever in his debt,' said Finn, smiling.

Oh, I liked this boy. He looked a good deal older than us and I thought it was mighty good of him to pass the time of day with two slips of girls as us.

'My granny and grandad live on the other side of the hill,' I said. 'They have a fine farm.'

'Is your grandad Mr Collins?' he said.

'He is,' I said, smiling at him.

'Nice people,' he said.

I was mighty delighted that Finn Casey knew of my grandparents and that he held them in high regard. 'Oh, they are,' I said.

'We were just out for a stretch of the legs,' said Kitty.

'And you chose a fine day for it,' said Finn. 'I was out walking myself and it's given me quite a thirst. I'm sure my aunt would be delighted to offer you some refreshment if you have the time.'

I looked across at Kitty and she nodded. 'That would be grand,' she said. 'And thank you. We're awful tired from climbing the hill.'

We weren't tired at all. For we were young and used to walking, but I thought Kitty accepted the offer with dignity. Finn strode away down the grassy bank, with the pair of us stumbling along behind him, trying to keep up. I was hot and gasping for breath by the time we got to the bottom and Kitty's face looked red and sweaty.

'Jesus,' she whispered. 'I'm only worn out.'

'So am I, Kitty Quinn,' I said. 'I hope it was worth it.'

Kitty smoothed her hair back from her face and grinned at me. 'I'd run down a hundred hills for him,' she said.

I had a mind to tell her that she was too young to be running down hills for a boy she'd hardly met. In fact, the pair of us were too young to be interested in boys at all, even boys with fair hair and a grand way of talking.

The cottage was pretty, with a little garden in front of it and yellow roses trailing across the white stone. Finn pushed open the door and we followed him inside. Mrs Lamey was sitting at the kitchen table, drinking tea with Mrs Toomey, the cobbler's wife.

'God bless all here,' we chorused, dipping our fingers into the holy water.

'Aunty Mary, these two girls are in need of refreshment,' said Finn.

'Then sit down and welcome,' said Mrs Lamey.

'That's a grand holy water font you have there, Mrs Lamey,' said Kitty.

I agreed with her. The font was a statue of the Blessed Virgin Mary wearing a blue dress and a white veil. I'd never seen anything so lovely.

'My cousin sent it all the way from America,' said Mrs Lamey.

'It's a sight for sore eyes,' I said. 'But I never thought that you could get anything like that in America.'

'They're more Irish than the Irish over there,' said Mrs Toomey.

'With shops selling holy statues on every corner,' said Mrs Lamey, placing two glasses of water in front of us.

'Alongside Irish pubs on every corner,' said Mrs Toomey, laughing with her head thrown back, showing off a set of teeth as black as coal.

'Well, I think it's very beautiful,' I said. 'And I wish I could get one just like it for my mammy.'

'There's a kind girl,' said Mrs Lamey.

'I'd like to get one for my mammy too,' said Kitty, not to be outdone.

'Two kind girls who love their mammies,' said Mrs Lamey, smiling at us.

'Have you been down the quay, Finn?' said Mrs Toomey.

Finn smiled at her and I noticed that his teeth were as white as the driven snow, when poor Mrs Toomey didn't have one good tooth in her head. 'Just walking the hills,' he said. 'It's a great day for walking.'

'You'll miss the good country air when you get back to London, Finn,' said Mrs Toomey.

'I will indeed,' said Finn. 'But home is home, Mrs Toomey, and I miss my parents.'

'Of course you do, lad,' said Mrs Lamey. 'But we'll miss you when you've gone.'

'When's that?' asked Kitty.

'Soon,' said Finn.

'Isn't it an awful shame that you couldn't stay longer?' said Kitty.

'I have to go back to school,' he said.

I looked at Kitty and I could see that she was as surprised as meself to hear that Finn was still in school.

'Aren't you a bit old for school?' said Kitty, who didn't seem to have the ability to think before she spoke.

'I'll be starting at the university, Kitty, studying to be a doctor.'

'And we're all very proud of him,' said Mrs Lamey.

'I'm sure you are,' I said.

'When I think of poor Dooney up at the workhouse, I can't help questioning the ways of the Lord,' said Mrs Lamey. 'Especially when I look at Finn and the fine brain he's been blessed with.'

Mrs Toomey made a kind of clicking noise with her black teeth. 'It's not up to us to question the ways of the Lord, Mrs Lamey – he must have his reasons for making Dooney the way he is.'

'Well, I'd like to know what they are, Mrs Toomey, for it makes no sense to me.'

'How's Malachi, Nora?' asked Mrs Toomey.

'Oh, he's grand and strong,' I said.

'And the way I hear it, you have Mrs Heher to thank for that,' said Mrs Toomey.

'If you believe everything the woman says,' said Mrs Lamey.

'We should get going,' I said, standing up. 'Thank you for the water and conversation.'

'You have lovely polite ways, Nora,' said Mrs Toomey. 'Your mother must be very proud, after all she went through to get you.'

'God love her,' added Mrs Lamey.

I had no idea what Mrs Toomey was talking about. I mumbled my thanks again and then Kitty and I left. Finn followed us outside.

'So, you're really going to be a doctor?' I said, as we walked back up the garden.

'It's what I've always wanted to be.'

'I think it's a very worthy profession.'

'I think so too,' said Kitty, not wanting to be left out. 'I expect we'll see you around,' she added hopefully.

'I expect you will,' he said, smiling.

We said our goodbyes and set off up the hill.

'Don't you think that was very odd?' I said.

'What was very odd?' said Kitty.

'What Mrs Toomey said.'

'I shouldn't take any notice of that, old biddy,' said Kitty. 'She's as mad as a coot.'

'I expect you're right,' I said.

But as I walked, I couldn't help but wonder.

CHAPTER TEN

'This is a memorable day, Kitty,' I said, as we sat on the wall watching the mourners following Billy Buff's coffin towards the grave.

Kitty took the little notebook out of the pocket of her dress. 'Don't you think it's a bit sad though, Nora? Don't you feel as if it's the end of our childhood?'

'It's time to put childish things away, Kitty.'

'Grandad Doyle?'

'No, Kitty, the Bible. There's a bit more, do you want to hear it?'

'Why not? There's not much to hold the interest here. There's not a good hat or a decent pair of boots in sight.'

'Any ribbons?'

'Not a one,' said Kitty, standing up on the wall. 'Hang on, isn't that Billy's old dog, Sonny, following the cart?'

I looked across at the mourners and my eyes filled with tears. 'Oh, Kitty, did you ever see anything so dignified?'

Kitty licked the end of the pencil. 'What should I mark it?'

'Mark it a ten, Kitty, for that old dog has stayed loyal to his master right up till the end and I think that is a wonderful thing.'

Kitty wrote 'Sonny' and put a ten next to his name.

'I wonder who will look after him now that Billy's gone, for there's no Mrs Buff.'

'We'll ask Father Kelly, for if there is no one to look after the poor feller, I'm thinking I should take him home to the Grey House.'

'Won't your parents mind?'

I shook my head. 'I think they'll be glad to offer him some comfort. It would be an act of human kindness.'

We sat on the wall and listened to the 'dust to dust' and the 'ashes to ashes' bit. Billy Buff was a simple soul who hurt no one, even though as a child he frightened the bejeebers out of me with his wonky eye and his half a leg.

'So, what's the rest of that saying then?' asked Kitty.

I cleared my throat and began. 'When I was a child, I spoke as a child, but when I became a man, I put away childish things.'

'What about women?'

'What do you mean?'

'Well, it says "when I became a man". What about "when I became a woman"?'

'I don't think women were very important back then, Kitty.'

'Well, they should have been – I mean, if there was no Virgin Mary, there'd be no Jesus, would there?'

'That's true enough, Kitty.'

'And don't tell me Noah managed to get all those animals onto the ark on his own. I bet Mrs Noah had a hand in it. I bet she had to do all the cooking for the journey.'

'I'd say you're right, for there is no mention of Noah providing any food.'

'I think we should change it to, "when I became a woman".'

'I'm not sure you can alter the Bible, Kitty. It might be seen as blasphemy.'

'Who's going to find out?'

'God Himself will find out, for he sees and hears all things.'

'Best leave it as it is then. I don't want the wrath of God to come down on my head.'

'I think that's wise,' I said, putting my arm around her shoulder.

The mourners started to walk away from the grave. We waited until Father Kelly walked towards us, followed closely by Billy's old dog.

Father Kelly was a big man – not fat, but big. Grandad Doyle said he had a presence about him. He was the kindest and wisest man I had ever known and he was loved by everyone, even the Protestants. Grandad Doyle said that when a man was kind and non-judgemental, then folk were drawn to him whatever God they worshipped. Even people who had no faith at all came to Father Kelly for advice and he never turned them away from his door.

'Are you taking the dog, Father?' I said.

'I am, Nora, for he has nowhere else to go and I can't see the poor thing wandering around the town with no food or shelter.'

'That's good of you, Father.'

'Sure, it's little enough, Nora, and he is one of God's creatures.'

'Then I hope you'll be very happy together, Father,' said Kitty.

Father Kelly bent down and stroked Sonny's old head. 'I'd say we'll rub along fine, Kitty.'

'This is a momentous day,' I said.

'And why is that, Nora?'

'It's our last funeral, Father,' I said.

'We've decided to put away childish things,' said Kitty.

'Ah,' said Father Kelly, 'Corinthians. There comes a time in everyone's lives when they have to put away childish things; it's part of growing up. But never stop being children at heart, girls, because after all, we are all children of God.'

We nodded and jumped down off the wall.

'We'll see you at confession on Saturday, Father,' said Kitty.

'Do you have a need to confess then, Kitty?'

Kitty nodded. 'I nearly re-wrote the Bible, Father.'

Father Kelly looked as if he was about to choke and as he walked away. I could see his shoulders going up and down.

'Well,' said Kitty, 'I thought Father would be shocked but it looks as if he's laughing his head off.'

'I don't think Father Kelly is easily shocked.'

Kitty closed the little notebook for the last time and we left the graveyard, leaving a little bit of our childhood behind us.

CHAPTER ELEVEN

The next morning, I helped Mammy with the chores. Ever since we'd nearly lost Malachi, I'd changed my ways. Malachi was getting grand and fat and I thanked God every day that he'd found it in his heart to spare him. I changed his little bottom and put the dirty nappy in the bucket to soak. I tickled his little tummy and he laughed up at me. I couldn't have loved a baby sister any more than I loved my little brother.

'Are you seeing Kitty today, love?' said Mammy.

'I am, Mammy,' I said. 'We're going down the quay to watch the boys.'

'That's a strange thing to be doing, Nora,' she said.

'It's not me that wants to watch the boys, Mammy, it's Kitty. She has a desperate admiration for one of them.'

Mammy raised an eyebrow. 'Isn't Kitty a bit young to be admiring boys?'

'I think so too, Mammy, but there's no telling her while she has the humour on her.'

'You have all the time in the world for boys, Nora, just enjoy being a child for now.'

'I will, Mammy.'

I kissed Malachi and Mammy goodbye and went off to call for Kitty.

As I got to the bottom of Paradise Alley, I spotted Eddie leaning against the archway.

'Jesus, Eddie, what are you doing here?' I said.

'Waiting for you,' he said, grinning.

I looked around. 'You can't just wait for me, Eddie, people will talk.'

'Talk about what?'

'About me being seen with you,' I said.

'I'm not a mass murderer, Nora.'

'I know you're not,' I said. 'But I'm not allowed to have anything to do with the Hall and if someone tells my mammy that I have been seen with a strange boy, she'll be asking who you are. I can't lie to her, Eddie.'

'I'm clearing the garden ready to plant up for spring and I thought you might like to help.'

A feeling of pleasure filled my tummy. I thought about the little garden all the time and I wanted to go back there, I wanted to help Eddie. I'd never had a friend that was a boy before – boys weren't for making friends with – but ever since that awful day, when I thought that Malachi was dead and Eddie had comforted me, I felt like I had made a friend. I just wished he didn't live in Bretton Hall.

'I'm on my way to call for Kitty,' I said. 'And if she's in the humour to come to the garden, then I'll meet you there. Now be on your way before we're seen.'

'Okay, Nora,' he said, smiling at me. 'I'll wait for you.'

'I didn't say I'd definitely be there; it all depends on Kitty.'

'Then I hope that Kitty is in the humour.'

I watched Eddie walk away and made my way up the hill to Kitty's house.

'She has a cold in her tummy, Nora,' said Mrs Quinn when she opened the door. 'She lost her good breakfast this morning and she's in her bed now, feeling sorry for herself. Go on up, she'll be pleased to see you; she's only fed up of Breda chatting to her.'

I kissed the top of baby Sean's old head and went up the narrow staircase to see Kitty. I could hear her going on at Breda. 'You have me head ruined, Breda, with all your talking. Will you go downstairs and let me have a rest?'

Breda's response was to say, 'Can I go under the bed then, Kitty?'

'No, you can't, I want you out of here, I need some peace.'

I walked into the room. 'Best go downstairs, Breda,' I said. 'While I visit with poor Kitty.'

Breda grinned at me. 'Okay, Nora, I'll go under the table in the kitchen.'

'You do that,' I said, smiling at her.

'I swear there's something wrong with that child, Nora, she's never right.'

'I expect she'll grow out of it,' I said. 'Like we grew out of the funeral watching.'

'Well, she can do it any time she likes,' said Kitty, hoisting herself up in the bed.

'So, how are you feeling?' I said.

'I thought I was going to die, Nora. I was terrible sick.'

Kitty isn't very good at being ill. If she has a headache, it's a brain tumour. If she has a pain in her belly, it's an appendix that's about to burst and actually being sick is her very worst thing. She was looking very pale and sorry for herself, so I thought I'd take her mind off it.

'Eddie was waiting for me at the bottom of Paradise Alley,' I said.

'When?'

'Just now.'

'Well, wasn't that very brazen of him, Nora? To be waiting for you at the bottom of Paradise Alley for the whole town to see.'

I couldn't help thinking that if it had been Finn Casey waiting at the bottom of the hill to see her, she wouldn't be up on her high horse about it.

'What did he want?' she said.

'He asked if I wanted to help him in the garden.'

'Did he now?' said Kitty. 'And does he intend paying you for your work?'

'For God's sake, Kitty, I don't need paying. I'd be only too glad to help. I like being in the garden.'

'I know you do,' she said more gently. 'But mind you don't get caught, or you'll have your mother to answer to.'

'I know,' I said. 'And that worries me. I feel as if I'm doing something bad behind her back.'

'You need to get to the bottom of why she wants you to have nothing to do with Bretton Hall, for it is indeed a mystery.'

'I don't think she'll tell me, Kitty, just like she won't tell me where I was born.'

'Has it ever occurred to you that the two things might be linked?'

I stared at her. 'How could that be?'

'I don't know, but it makes you wonder, doesn't it?'

I left Kitty's house feeling thoughtful. Could the two things be linked? If they were, I couldn't for the life of me think how.

It felt strange scrambling through the undergrowth without Kitty by my side. For some reason, I felt like I was betraying Mammy more by being here on my own. Maybe it was because creeping into the gardens of Bretton Hall had been Kitty's idea and I could tell myself that I'd just gone along with her, but I couldn't kid myself today. I was here because I wanted to be.

After the usual crawl on my hands and knees, I eventually came out into the sunshine and was able to stand up. I brushed the bits of twigs and leaves off my dress and walked down the little path.

I pushed open the old wooden door and was once again in the garden. Eddie was kneeling down, digging in the soil.

'You came,' he said, looking up.

I smiled at him, 'I did.'

He stood and wiped his hands down his trousers. 'I didn't think you would,' he said. 'But I'm happy you have.'

'Kitty's sick,' I said, shrugging my shoulders, 'so I thought I'd come anyway.'

'I'm glad,' he said. 'Oh, not because Kitty's sick, you understand, but because you came.'

I breathed in the smells that were all around me. A mixture of newly turned soil, the sweetness of roses, even the little pond had its own smell, a bit like cold tea. I sat down on the grass and watched Eddie clearing the last of the summer flowers.

'I need to dead-head the roses now,' said Eddie, 'so that they can bloom again. Do you want to have a go?'

I nodded.

'I'll show you how.'

We walked across to the old stone wall, where the roses were beginning to die. There was still one rose in full bloom – it was the palest orange, with a pinkish stain at the edge of its petals and still quite perfect. Eddie cut it. 'The last rose of summer,' he said, handing it to me.

I held it up to my nose and breathed in the sweet, warm scent, 'I can't keep it,' I said.

'How about if I press it? Then you can put it between the pages of a book.'

I knew just what book I would keep it in. 'Yes, please,' I said.

Eddie showed me how to cut the roses at just the right point so that they would flower again. Time seemed to stand still as we tended the small garden. It was so peaceful, the silence broken only by the gentle movement of the branches as the breeze moved through the tall trees and the twittering of the birds as they darted here and there above our heads. I looked across at Eddie and watched as he turned the soil and pulled away the dead leaves. He'd rolled up the sleeves of his shirt and every now and again he wiped away the sweat which glistened on his forehead. I was getting hot myself and my arms had begun to ache as I stretched up to clip the roses higher up the stone wall. All of a sudden, I let out a yelp. Eddie leaped to his feet and ran over to me.

Blood was seeping between my fingers and dripping down onto the grass.

'Let me see,' said Eddie.

I held out my hand and he gently pulled out a thorn, then took a white handkerchief out of his trouser pocket. It was a perfect square, as if it had just been pressed. He shook it out and wrapped it around my finger like a bandage.

I'd never met a boy who carried around a handkerchief before. Even us girls only used rags and that was only when we had a cold in the head. The boys wiped their noses on the sleeves of their jumpers. Yet here was this boy who took a handkerchief out of his pocket as if it was of no consequence at all.

'Look, it's ruined,' I said, as the blood seeped through the white cotton.

'Don't worry about that, it will soon wash off.'

Oh, I liked this boy, who cared about my sore finger and who talked about pressing a rose between the pages of a book. I wished I could take him home to Paradise Alley to meet Mammy and Daddy, Stevie and baby Malachi and Grandad Doyle. I had a feeling that Eddie and my grandad would get along fine, for they both had a love of books and had the same gentle ways about them.

'Are you hungry, Nora?' he said.

I'd been so busy with the roses that I hadn't thought about food, but suddenly I was ravenous. 'I am,' I said.

Eddie walked across the garden and picked up a bundle from beside the wall.

'I packed a bit of food,' he said, coming back, smiling. 'In the hope that you would come.'

We sat down on the cool grass and Eddie undid the bundle and laid the cloth on the ground between us. There was bread and cheese and a handful of red plums.

It was lovely sitting there in the afternoon sunshine, eating the delicious food. The bread was soft and the cheese melted in my mouth, like nothing I had ever tasted before. After I'd finished the bread and cheese, I bit into a sweet red plum and giggled as the juice ran down my chin. I unwrapped the hankie from my hand and wiped it away.

Eddie lay back on the grass and I leaned on my elbow, watching him. A fly landed on his face and he brushed it away but it kept coming back so he sat up.

'I fear that flies have very little brains,' he said. 'For nothing deters them, even when you swipe them away.'

'They're annoying alright,' I said. 'But sure, they're God's creatures all the same.'

'You're Catholic, aren't you?' asked Eddie.

'Of course I am,' I said. 'Aren't you?'

Eddie shook his head.

'You're not Catholic?' I said, shocked.

Eddie picked away at the grass. 'Not everyone is a Catholic, you know,' he said.

'Everyone *I* know is.'

He stared at me. 'Does it matter?'

I thought about it and couldn't see why Eddie not being a Catholic made any difference at all.

'I suppose it doesn't,' I said.

His whole body seemed to relax; it was if he had been waiting for my answer, as if it was of the utmost importance to him.

'After all, you're still Eddie,' I said, smiling at him.

'I am,' he said, laughing.

We worked happily away until the sun sank behind the tall trees and the shadows in the garden changed their pattern.

'I have to go,' I said. 'Mammy will be wondering.'

'You'll come again?'

'I will, of course,' I said, handing him the stained hankie. 'Thanks for the loan.'

'You're welcome.'

As I walked towards the gate, Eddie called me.

'Nora?'

I stopped and turned around. 'Yes?'

He was staring down at the ground and scratching at his ear. 'Are we friends?' he said.

I smiled at him, standing there so seriously, with a smudge of dirt on his nose.

'Yes, Eddie,' I said. 'We're friends.'

He grinned, a grin so wide it almost split his face in two. 'I'm terribly glad.'

'Eddie, has anyone ever told you that you're awful odd for a boy?'

He shook his head. 'Does it matter?'

'Not a bit,' I said. 'For I'm inclined to like odd.'

We smiled at each other and then I left the garden.

CHAPTER TWELVE

Me and Kitty were tending my namesake's grave.

'Are you still seeing the boy?' she said.

'I am.'

'In the garden?'

I nodded.

'I don't know why you are so set on it,' she said. 'It's just a bit of soil, sure, it's nothing special.'

'I think it is,' I said.

'And what would your mother say if she knew? With her so dead set about you not going to the Hall?'

'And what would *your* mother say if she knew you were running all over Ballybun after Finn Casey?'

'Well, at least Finn Casey is a living, breathing thing, not just a patch of weeds.'

I glared at her. 'The garden is a living, breathing thing, Kitty, and it will be there long after Finn Casey has taken himself and his handsome face back to England.'

'Don't you like Finn, Nora?'

I looked at my best friend's sad face and softened. 'I like him alright, Kitty, and I can understand your fascination for the boy, it's just that I think we have plenty of time for all that.'

'But Eddie's a boy,' she said.

'Eddie's different, he's more like Stevie.'

'Are you going to confess your secret to Father Kelly?'

'I suppose I'll have to.'

I sighed and looked at my namesake's little wooden cross. I brushed away the leaves and read her name: NORA FOLEY 1895–1909.

'She died awful young, didn't she?' said Kitty.

'She did. She was only a slip of a girl, not much older than we are now.'

'That's a terrible shame. God must have wanted her desperate bad to have taken her so young.'

'Mammy said that Nora was never strong, so I'm thinking that God must have wanted to end her suffering and take her into the arms of the angels, so that she could get better.'

'Well, that was good of him anyway.'

'They grew up in the workhouse, Kitty, both thinking they were orphans. They were looked after by Mrs Foley, who loved them and was very kind to them.'

'Well, that's a blessing anyway,' said Kitty. 'I've heard terrible tales about the place.'

'Well, Mammy said that they were both very happy there, because they had each other and were like sisters.'

'But your mammy's not an orphan, Nora.'

'That's the best bit of the story, Kitty. One morning, my Granny Collins took my mammy out of the place and they lived happily ever after in Paradise Alley.'

'That sounds like a fairy tale.'

I nodded. 'I think maybe it was.'

'And what about poor Nora? She was still stuck in there, so it wasn't much of a fairy tale for her, was it?'

'Well, when Nora died, it was then that Mammy discovered that Nora had a mammy all along.'

'Why didn't her mammy come for her?'

'Because it was Mrs Foley. Mrs Foley was Nora's mammy.'

'That's an awful complicated story, Nora.'

'Life is complicated sometimes, Kitty.'

Just then we saw Father Kelly walking towards us between the rows of wooden crosses.

'Good morning, girls,' he said, smiling.

'Good morning, Father,' we said, and stood up as a mark of respect for the Cloth.

'Visiting your namesake, Nora?' he said.

'I am, Father. It pleases my mammy.'

'Ah. It would, Nora.'

'God in His wisdom took her awful young, didn't he, Father?'

'He did, Nora, God love her,' said Father Kelly.

'And why would he be doing that?' asked Kitty. 'He must have had a pile a people up there already.'

Father Kelly nodded his old head. 'Who are we to know the workings of the Lord, Kitty?'

Kitty nodded her head very seriously, as if she knew everything there was to know about the workings of the Lord, when I knew for a fact that she struggled to remember the first page of her Catechism.

Father Kelly started to walk away and I called after him. 'Can I have a private word, Father?'

'Of course, Nora,' he said, smiling at me.

Kitty took an old pair of scissors out of her pocket. 'I'll tidy up a bit while you're gone,' she said.

Father Kelly and I walked away and sat down under a tree at the far end of the graveyard. He leaned back against the tree and I sat facing him, with my back to the workhouse that stood at the bottom of the hill like a dark grey prison.

'So, what is on your mind, child?' he said, smiling gently.

'It's a very convoluted story, Father,' I said.

'Grandad Doyle?'

'The very man. It means confusing, but I expect you already know that.'

He smiled and nodded briefly. 'I'm listening, Nora.' His voice was kind, like a friendly nudge to keep me talking.

'If I was doing something that someone I loved didn't approve of, would that be a sin, even though I didn't lie about it?'

Father Kelly scratched his old head, making his bit of hair stand up at an odd angle. 'Now that's a difficult one, Nora.'

'That's what I'm thinking, Father, and it's playing desperate havoc with me head.'

'Is what you are doing, a sin against God?'

'No, Father, I don't think so, for I'm a good girl and I respect my mam... I mean the person in question.'

'What we have here, Nora, is the sin of omission.'

'So, it's still a sin, then?'

'I'm afraid it is.'

'Isn't that desperate annoying, Father?' I said, pulling a dandelion out from the grass.

'Could you not stop doing it?'

'Oh no, Father, I've a mind to keep doing it.'

'Then you will have to make an act of confession.'

'I thought as much.'

'Let me ask you a question, child. If the Lord himself looked down on you, as you were doing this thing you shouldn't be doing, would it cause him pain?'

I thought about the garden and the flowers and birds and squirrels, all of them God's creations. 'No, Father,' I said. 'I think it would make him smile.'

Father Kelly nodded his head. 'Then I don't think that what you are doing can be all that bad.'

'Well, that's a relief.'

'I can hear your confession now, if you like,' said Father Kelly.

'That would be grand,' I said, 'for if I die now, I'd be in a state of sin and end up in purgatory and I don't like the sound of the place at all.' I closed my eyes and bowed my head. 'Bless me, Father, for I have sinned,' I began. 'It's been two days since my last confession. Do you want all my sins, Father, or just the omission one?'

'Well, we might as well do the whole lot while we're at it, Nora.'

'Right you are, Father,' I said. I took a deep breath and started.
'I moaned about dragging the water from the pump and it made
my daddy cross. I told Orla Mullen to stick something up her bum
when she said she didn't believe in God's angels – I meant to tell
you that weeks ago, Father, but I forgot and anyway, I thought
you'd understand.'

'Go on,' said Father Kelly.

I searched my brain for what I'd done wrong but sure, I'd only
been to confession a couple of days ago and I hadn't had time to sin
since. 'I think that's about it, Father,' I said. 'I'm not a great sinner.'

'I'm glad to hear it, Nora, but what about the sin we just spoke of?'

'Oh, yes, and I'm sorry about the omission thingy.'

Father Kelly laid his hand on my head. 'I forgive you in the
name of the Father, the Son and the Holy Ghost. Go in peace,
your sins are forgiven.'

'What about me penance, Father? And could you see your way
clear to making it short as I have Kitty with me?'

'I think that one Hail Mary and one Glory Be should do the
trick,' he said.

'Thank you, Father,' I said, standing up. 'My head feels a lot
lighter now.'

'Glad to be of assistance, Nora,' he said, smiling.

I ran back over to Kitty, who was clipping away at the grass on
my namesake's grave.

'You'll have to amuse yourself for a bit, Kitty,' I said. 'For I have
a Hail Mary and a Glory Be to get done.'

She looked confused. 'You've been to confession?'

'He heard my confession under a tree.'

'Are you sure that counts?'

'Sure, he wouldn't have heard it if it hadn't counted.'

'I suppose he knows what he's doing, Nora.'

'Of course he knows what he's doing, he's a priest, for God's
sake.'

Kitty didn't look convinced. 'I suppose so,' she said begrudgingly.

I closed my eyes and said my Hail Mary and my Glory Be.

'Do you feel better now, Nora? Now that you have been forgiven?'

'I do, and I'm sorry for what I said about Finn Casey.'

Kitty smiled at me. 'And I'm sorry for what I said about your garden. Finn will be gone soon and you'll tire of the bit of soil and things can get back to normal.'

I nodded, but in my heart, I knew that I'd never tire of the garden, not ever.

CHAPTER THIRTEEN

I had been feeling guilty about spending more time with Eddie than with Kitty and was mightily relieved when she palled up with Aoife Coyne, who had as much fascination for Tommy Nolan as Kitty had for Finn Casey.

'She hasn't replaced you, Nora,' said Kitty. 'For you are my best friend, it's just that…'

'Our priorities have changed.'

'Grandad Doyle?'

'The very man, it means that right now we are wanting different things and I think that is alright.'

'So long as it's not, um—'

'Permanent?' I said.

'Exactly,' said Kitty.

I took hold of Kitty's hand. 'Our friendship is far too important for a boy or a garden to get in the way,' I said, smiling at her.

'Anyway, Aoife has an awful habit of sniffing. She sniffs all the time, as if she has a lifelong bloody cold in the head, but she's company and I would be ashamed to go down to the quay on my own.'

'We'll go to Minnie's on Saturday for a grand cup of tea.'

'And I can tell you all about Finn and you can tell me all about Eddie.'

But fear of hurting Kitty wasn't the only obstacle to visiting the garden: Stevie was poorly. He was often poorly – it seemed that the stronger Malachi got, the weaker Stevie became, and Mammy was always up at the church lighting candles and asking the Blessed Virgin Mary to intervene on her behalf and ask her son Jesus to restore him to good health. He was laying on the couch now. His face was the colour of a beetroot and he was fast asleep, when he should have been running about the place and having a great time. I hated to see Mammy looking so worried.

'I'm off out again,' I said.

'Will you take Malachi with you, Nora? I'm going to take Stevie up to see Doctor Kennedy.'

I was just about to go and meet Eddie in the garden. How could I go to the garden with Malachi and the pram? And then I looked at Mammy's worried face. Wasn't I a terrible selfish girl for putting my own wishes ahead of Mammy's?

'Of course I will,' I said.

'Thank you, Nora,' she said, smiling at me. 'I've just fed him but I'll give you a bottle of water and a rusk; that should see him alright for a couple of hours.'

Malachi was a very beautiful baby, with wisps of white hair on his round head and eyes as blue as the sea. Everyone said that with his looks, he should have been a girl and I often wondered whether the Lord had taken into account my great hankering for a sister when He made him. Either way, I wouldn't have changed him for the world, just like Mrs Quinn wouldn't have changed Breda, even though she was wanting a boy.

I was thinking of calling for Kitty again, so that we could take our little brothers out together, but I'd told Eddie that I was coming today and we were going to discuss the planting of bulbs for the spring.

Malachi was sitting up now, with the help of a few pillows, and he was smiling at everyone we passed. He was a happy baby and I was proud to push him through the town for everyone to admire. We walked out to the Strand and I stopped to show Malachi the ocean. It was a bit choppy, with white foam tipping the tops of the waves. If I hadn't been in such a hurry, I would have carried him down the beach to dangle his fat little legs in the water. There was a chilly wind coming in off the sea and it kept taking Malachi's breath away, which he found very funny.

As soon as we got to the broken piece of fence, I knew that I could never pull the pram through. I lifted Malachi into my arms and left it where it was, which wasn't a great idea, because anyone passing might think it was abandoned and up for grabs and how would I explain that to Mammy when I arrived home without it?

It was even harder trying to crawl through the brambles with Malachi in my arms but bless him, he thought the whole thing was highly amusing and laughed his little head off all the way through. I parted the bushes and looked up at the Hall. 'That's where the Honourables live, Malachi,' I said. 'But don't tell Mammy where we've been, or she'll eat the head off us.' Malachi grinned at me and shook his head as if he knew exactly what I was saying.

I was relieved when we came out into the sunshine and hurried down the path to the garden. I pushed open the gate and Eddie came towards me, a big smile on his face.

'And who have we got here?' he said, brushing a twig off Malachi's head.

'This is my baby brother Malachi,' I said.

'The little feller you thought was dead?'

'The very one.'

'Well, he looks like a fine strong boy now.'

'I couldn't get the pram through the gap in the fence,' I said. 'And I don't want to leave it out in the lane for all to see. Do you think you could haul it through? If you can't get it through the brambles, leave it just inside the fence. But I will need his blanket, his bottle of water and his rusk.'

'Consider it done,' said Eddie.

After he'd gone, I sat down on the grass with Malachi beside me. 'What do you think of this then?' I said, smiling at him. Malachi looked up at the tall trees and waved his little arms about as if he was waving hello.

'It's a secret garden,' I whispered, 'and when you're a big boy, I'll read the book to you. Oh, you'll love it, Malachi, for it's my favourite story.'

Malachi picked at the daisies with his chubby little hands, then with a big grin on his face he shoved them into his mouth. I grabbed them off him and he began to howl like a demented banshee, as if I'd done him some terrible injustice. 'Holy Mother of God,' I said, 'you can't be eating daisies! You'll get terrible sick and Mammy has enough to worry about with Stevie.'

Then, with a sinking feeling in my stomach, I realised that Malachi was making too much noise and at any second, we could be discovered. I picked him up and started to walk around, with him hanging off my hip, but he wouldn't give up with the yelling. Just then a squirrel ran out from behind a tree.

'Look, Malachi,' I said, pointing to the little animal.

Malachi took a big gulping breath and stared at it, reaching out his hands and giggling. The squirrel stared back, then started to scratch its head with a tiny paw. Malachi was delighted and all thoughts of the daisies were forgotten.

Just then Eddie came back into the garden and the squirrel darted up a tree. I thought this would start Malachi off again but thanks be to God it didn't. Eddie looked worried and I knew that it was because of the noise.

'I'm sorry, Eddie,' I said.

'It's just that I don't want anyone to discover this place,' he said, handing me the things I'd asked for.

I laid Malachi down on the blanket and gave him his rusk. He looked very contented lying there, sucking away and staring up at the patch of blue sky between the tall trees.

'I'm sorry, Eddie,' I said. 'He's usually such a good baby but he was mad at me for stopping him eating the daisies.'

Eddie sighed. 'I wish everything wasn't so complicated, Nora.'

I'd been thinking the same thing. We were just spending time in a lovely little garden and doing no harm to anyone. 'Who are you scared will find out, Eddie, is it the master of the house?'

Eddie sat down on the grass, his thin knees pulled up to his chest. I sat beside him, with Malachi between us.

'Not really,' he said. 'It's just that everything will be ruined and it won't feel like my garden anymore.'

'Where do you get the bulbs from?' I asked.

'Corny the gardener. It was him that showed me the garden.'

'And you're not worried that he'll let on to anyone?'

Eddie shook his head. 'He's just glad that I've got something to do.'

I couldn't make Eddie out. He never seemed to help his father with the horses and he never seemed to have chores to do and here was Corny the gardener giving him his very own garden. I couldn't work it out.

I looked down at Malachi, who had fallen asleep with the rusk halfway between his tummy and his mouth. The rays of sun shone down on his fair hair, making it shine like gold. I wished Stevie could be here too, I wished I could tell Mammy about Eddie and I wished that everything wasn't such a mystery.

As Malachi slept, Eddie and I did some more clearing. 'We'll plant for the spring in October, Corny says that's the best time.'

'What will we plant?' I asked.

'Tulips and daffodils and crocuses,' said Eddie. 'We'll have a great show come the spring.'

'I'll be back at school by then,' I said sadly. 'And I won't be able to come so often.'

'But you can come after school, can't you? And on the weekends?'

'I don't know, Eddie. I'm deceiving my mammy by coming here and it makes me feel awful guilty.'

Eddie went quiet and then he said, 'I've never had a friend before, Nora. Working in the garden with you has been better than being here on my own.'

'Why don't you ask your father if you can go to school in the town?' I said.

Eddie shook his head. 'I will never be able to go to school in the town.'

'But why not?'

'I just can't, alright?' he snapped.

'Excuse me for asking,' I said, feeling a bit put out.

'Oh, I'm sorry, Nora, don't be mad at me. it's just the way it is.'

I softened. 'It's okay,' I said gently. 'It's the same with my mammy. We'll work it out, and Eddie?'

'Yes?'

'I'll still be your friend.'

Later, Eddie helped me push the pram into the lane and I headed for home.

As I walked through the town, I noticed that people were staring at me and I couldn't think why.

Mrs Tully called across the road. 'Get yourself home, Nora,' she said. 'You're wanted.'

As I passed Pasley's, Mrs Hurley put her hand on the pram. I thought she was going to admire Malachi, but she didn't even look at him. 'Hurry now, child,' she said. 'Your mammy is looking for you.'

I started running, causing people to jump out of my way. Something had happened and I felt sick to my stomach. I'd never known the road home to be so long. More people urged me along as I ran towards Paradise Alley, under the arch and up the lane. There was a crowd of people outside the house and the doctor's car was in the yard. Father Kelly walked over to me as I was about to go inside.

'You can't go in, Nora,' he said.

'Why can't I?'

Just at that moment, Dr Kennedy came out of the house carrying Stevie in his arms. Mammy was walking behind him and her eyes were red as if she'd been crying. I went to walk over to them but Father Kelly put his hand on my arm, as if to pull me back.

'Stevie has the scarlet fever, Nora. You can't go near him and neither can Malachi.'

I felt my eyes filling with tears.

'We'll pray, Nora, we'll pray like we've never prayed before.'

Dr Kennedy placed Stevie in the back seat of the car and Mammy went to follow him. 'Mammy!' I shouted. She turned and hurried across to me. 'We couldn't find you,' she said. 'We had the town out looking for you.'

'I'm sorry, Mammy.'

'You can't come back into the house, Nora. Your father is going to take you and Malachi up to Granny and Grandad Collins. You must stay there until the house has been scoured and it's safe for you to return.'

'But where are you taking Stevie?'

'To the fever hospital in Cork. Father Kelly has arranged for me to stay with the nuns until Stevie is well again.'

Tears were rolling down my cheeks and I brushed them away with the back of my hand. 'Stevie's not going to die, is he, Mammy? He's not going to die?'

Mammy pulled me into her arms and held me tight but she didn't answer my question. 'I want you to be a good girl while I'm gone and help Granny with Malachi. Will you do that for me, Nora?'

'I will, Mammy, I'll help all I can. Will you give Stevie a kiss for me?'

'Of course, my love,' she said, letting go of me.

'Cissy,' called Dr Kennedy, 'we must go.'

Mammy kissed Malachi and he reached out his arms to be picked up. His little face crumpled as he watched her walk away from him.

It was a sad journey and Malachi's sobbing matched my own as we made our way out of town towards the farm. Granny and Grandad were waiting for us as we turned into the yard. I got out of the car and ran up to her, while Grandad lifted Malachi into his arms.

'Oh, Granny,' I sobbed, 'Stevie has the scarlet fever and he's desperate sick.'

'I know, my love,' she said, holding me tightly. 'I know.'

'He's gone to the fever hospital in Cork and Mammy is staying with him.'

My grandma nodded. 'And they will make him better, Nora.'

This was what I wanted to hear. 'Of course they will,' I said.

But what if they didn't? What if God decided that He needed Stevie more than we did? *Well, He better not*, I thought, *because if He does, I shall never speak to Him again and I won't light any candles to Him, or the blessed Virgin Mary and I won't sing in the bloody choir. Oh, Stevie, please don't die!*

A week later, me and Kitty were sitting on the flat rocks at the beach eating sandwiches.

'What's it like living at the farm?' said Kitty.

'It's not so bad, but I miss my family and I worry about Stevie.'

'Have you heard anything?'

'Not a peep, but Granny Collins says that's a good sign, for if it was bad news we'd soon be told.'

'Are we singing in the choir on Sunday?' asked Kitty. 'I told Father Kelly we would.'

'I'm waiting to see if Stevie gets better before I commit to it, Kitty.'

'I wish you wouldn't use such big words, Nora. There are times when I think that your Grandad Doyle does you no favours at all.'

'You might be right, Kitty, but I have a fierce desire to learn new words. And I wish *you* hadn't said I'd sing in the choir without asking me first.'

'I know you do, Nora, and your words are grand, it's just that I don't know what the bloody hell you're talking about half the time. And as for the choir, when else will we get to wear a red costume with a grand white ruffle around the neck? We'd be eejits to turn down the opportunity.'

'I'll bear all that in mind, Kitty.'

'I'd be glad of it, Nora.'

We sat in silence for a few moments, but neither of us could ever keep that up. 'How is Finn?' I said, to change the subject.

'Sure, he'll be gone soon and I'll be desperate sad. What about Eddie?'

'I haven't seen him, Kitty, because I promised Mammy I'd help my granny look after Malachi. He'll be wondering why I haven't gone to the garden.'

'He'll trust there must be something stopping you.'

'I'm not so sure, because when he told me that he wasn't a Catholic he could see that I was shocked. He might think I don't want to be his friend anymore.'

'Eddie's not a Catholic?' said Kitty, looking as shocked as I'd been at the news.

I shook my head.

'Is he a heathen, then?'

'He didn't say, but then I don't know what a heathen looks like.'

'Neither do I,' said Kitty. 'But I hope he's not planning on going to Heaven when he dies, because he's going to be sorely disappointed. As a good Catholic yourself, it might be your duty to convert him to the true faith.'

'Well, if God in His wisdom decides to take Stevie to live with him, I've a good mind to become a bloody heathen meself.'

'Nora Doyle!' said Kitty. 'You'd better get yourself down to confession mighty quick, before God in His holy wisdom decides to take the pair of you.'

'Perhaps I'll sing in the choir on Sunday, that should keep Him happy.'

'Good idea,' said Kitty, linking her arm through mine.

CHAPTER FOURTEEN

I had very little freedom living at the farm – I was used to roaming the hills and lanes with Kitty. But I was well taken care of and loved. Granny Collins was a great cook, and she seemed to have made it her mission to send me home fatter than when I'd arrived. And I did all I could to help take care of Malachi, just like I promised Mammy. I took him to look at the pigs and the cows but he was getting to be such a lump of a child, my arms were only hanging off me from carrying him. He seemed happy enough. Daddy visited as often as he could and Malachi was delighted to see him but I think he missed his mammy. Well, he missed his mammy's titty and had to drink the milk from the cows. He didn't like it at first and yelled fit to bust but once he cottoned on to the fact that it was the only drink on the menu, he reluctantly gave in.

'It's a shame for your mother though,' said my granny. 'For she loved feeding him herself.'

'Did Mammy feed me?' I said.

Granny suddenly got very busy, bustling about the place and managing to ignore what I'd just asked her.

'Granny?' I said again. 'Did Mammy feed me?'

Granny looked at me and made a sort of tutting sound. 'What sort of silly question is that, Nora?' she said. 'Now go and see if there are any eggs to be gathered.'

I stomped out into the yard and decided that I had definitely been adopted and wondered who my real parents might be.

One Saturday morning, I was so bored that I took a walk over the hill to see if Finn Casey was at home. Any company was better than none. I rested at the top and looked down at the Lameys' cottage – there was no one in the yard and I considered going back home, but just then Finn walked around from the side of the house. I ran the rest of the way down the hill and into the yard.

Finn walked towards me. 'It's Nora, isn't it?' he said, smiling.

I nodded.

'Where's your little friend?'

He made it sound as if Kitty was a child. 'She's not so little,' I said. 'And neither am I. We'll both be out working soon.'

'Sorry,' he said, grinning.

'That's alright,' I said, softening.

We didn't say anything for a while and I was beginning to feel awkward and wondered why it had been such a good idea to visit a boy I barely knew. He seemed to be at a loss for what to say to me too, perhaps for the same reason.

'Do you want to see the new horse?' he said suddenly.

'Yes, please,' I said.

We walked around the back of the cottage to the field and there, standing as still as you like, was the prettiest horse I had ever seen.

'Isn't she lovely?' said Finn.

I nodded.

'Hey, girl,' called Finn.

The horse walked towards us and rested her head on the fence. She was pale brown, with a white flash down her nose.

'She's very beautiful,' I said, stroking her soft coat.

'My uncle is going to teach me to ride her. Can you ride, Nora?'

'I've been riding since I was four years old,' I said, with more than a hint of pride.

'And what a lovely place to learn. It must be great to live somewhere like this all your life.'

'It's all I've ever known, and I couldn't ever think of living anywhere else.'

'I live in London,' said Finn, picking up some grass and feeding it to the horse. 'I shall miss this place when I go back.'

'When are you going?'

'In a week's time. I have to get ready for university.' I didn't know anyone who went to a university and I was mightily impressed. 'I'm going to have to study hard if I'm to become a doctor.'

The horse pushed her nose into my shoulder and I patted her. 'That's a fine thing to be, Finn,' I said.

He smiled. 'Thank you, Nora. I think so too. That's why I've enjoyed being here so much – my last summer of freedom.'

'Well, you couldn't be in a better place,' I said.

'Are you hungry? Because I was just going inside for a bit of lunch.'

I thought it was funny, the way the English called their dinner, lunch.

'I am a bit,' I said.

'Wait for me here and I'll get us something to eat,' he said, smiling.

I watched him walking towards the house. It was funny – I hardly knew this boy and yet I felt comfortable with him. I wondered what Kitty would say if she saw me now. Perhaps I'd keep it to myself, for I had the feeling that she wouldn't be over the moon about it.

Finn came back, carrying a plate. I followed him over to a tall, shady tree and we both sat down on the grass. 'It's just ham sandwiches,' he said. 'I hope that's okay?'

'That's grand,' I said, taking one and looking across at the mare. 'What's her name?'

'She doesn't have one yet. My uncle said that I could name her.'

'She needs a name as beautiful as she is.'

'What would you call her, Nora?'

I looked across at the horse. She was standing very still, watching us. The sun shining on her back had turned the brown of her coat to a pale orange; it reminded me of the last rose of summer that Eddie had picked for me.

'I'd call her Rosie,' I said.

Finn nodded. 'Good name.'

I stood up and walked across to the fence. I rested my face against her soft head and she nuzzled into me. 'Would you like to be called Rosie?' I whispered. Suddenly she threw her head back and whinnied. It sounded for all the world as if she was laughing. I turned around and smiled at Finn. 'She likes her name.'

'Rosie it is then,' said Finn, smiling at me. 'Rosie it is.'

A few weeks later, Father Kelly came up to the farm to tell us that Stevie had turned a corner and would soon be well enough to come home.

'Is he going to be alright?' I said.

'He will need to take it easy for a while, but yes, I'm assured that he is going to be alright, Nora.'

'Does that mean that I can go home?' I said.

Father Kelly laughed. 'Don't worry, I'll come and let you know when they are back. I'd say that you are missed in Paradise Alley and they will all be delighted to see you and Malachi home again.'

That last week of the summer, I walked across the hill to the Lameys' cottage almost every day. Sometimes, I'd find nobody home, but on other days, Finn would be reading in the garden or tending to Rosie. He'd be welcoming and kind, and would answer my questions about London or university, and ask me about horses and books I read. I knew that he would soon be leaving and that I would probably never see him again but that was alright, it was the way it was meant to be. I kept our meetings to myself, I didn't tell anyone, especially not Kitty. If I'd told Kitty, she would want to join us, of course she would, and I didn't want to share our time with anyone else. It seemed I was getting very good at sinning by omission.

I taught Finn to ride Rosie. Every time he fell off the horse, I made him get back on again. We laughed a lot; I couldn't remember the last time I had laughed like that. Every day I got to know him better, I felt like I'd found a friend and I think that Finn felt the same. He told me about his dream of becoming a doctor and how worried he was that he wasn't clever enough.

One day we were sitting on the top of the hill eating sandwiches that Mrs Lamey had given us. Finn started talking about his family. He told me about his parents and his younger brother David, who he adored.

'David is special,' he said. 'He's not like other boys his age. He will never be a doctor, or a scientist, or a teacher, he will always remain a child.'

'What's wrong with him?' I said.

'It's called mongolism. He has a certain look about him but he has a smile that would light up the darkest of days.'

'I think I know what you mean,' I said. 'I think that maybe there are boys like that at the asylum, up at the workhouse.'

'That's where my cousin is,' said Finn.

I had forgotten for a minute that Dooney was Finn's cousin.

'My mother was afraid that it might run in the family, so my parents decided not to have any more children.'

'That's sad,' I said.

'It is,' said Finn. 'Because I know she would love to have had a daughter. That's why it's so important that I do well – I feel like that would somehow make things up to them.'

'But wouldn't they be proud of you whatever you did?'

'Yes, of course they would.'

'Well, as long as you are doing it because you want to and not because your parents want you to.'

'I've thought of that too but no, I really do want to be a doctor.' He smiled at me. 'What's your dream, Nora?'

'Mine?' I said, laughing.

'Yes, yours, everyone should have a dream.'

'It costs money to have that sort of dream, Finn.'

'I'm sorry.'

'What do you have to be sorry about?' I said.

'Sometimes I don't think things through.'

'There is one thing I'd like to do, though.'

'What's that?'

'I'd like to work in a bookshop and be surrounded by books all day. That's my dream.'

'And a fine one it is,' he said, smiling.

We sat in the sunshine and looked down on the cottage and the rolling hills behind.

'I'll miss this place,' he said.

'What made you come to Ballybun?' I said.

'My father was born in Ireland; my aunt is his sister. He left when he was seventeen, to make his fortune, he said.'

'And did he?'

'I guess he did. He worked his way through school to become a lawyer. My father is a very determined man.'

'What about your mother?'

'They met at college; they were on the same course but my mother gave it all up when she had me. I think she would have gone back to it but then she had David and that changed everything.'

'Could you do me a favour, Finn?' I said.

'Of course.'

'Before you go back to England, will you go down to the quay?'

'Why would you want me to do that?'

'Because my friend Kitty likes you,' I said, grinning.

Finn laughed. 'What's that got to do with going down to the quay?'

'She goes down there every day with her friend, Aoife Coyne, hoping to see you.'

Finn stared at me, then his face started to go red.

'Well? Will you do it? Will you go down the quay?'

'Well, I was planning to meet the Nolan brothers for a last swim anyway, so I suppose I'll be there.'

'Would you mind passing the time of day with her?'

He sighed. 'Well, if it's that important to you, I'll be happy to say hello to her.'

'Thank you.'

Finn stood up and I scrambled to my feet beside him. He was a good head taller than me and I felt like a child as I looked up at him. The sun was in my eyes and Finn's blond hair seemed to shine like gold. And there at the top of the hill, Finn reached down and gently kissed my cheek.

'Goodbye, Nora Doyle.'

'Goodbye, Finn Casey.'

CHAPTER FIFTEEN

It was lovely to be back home. Stevie was still pale and weak but as the days went by, he became more like his old self. When the weather was warm, Mammy would put a chair outside the kitchen window and cover his knees with a blanket. I tried not to think of what our lives would have been like without him.

'What was it like up in the hospital, Stevie?' I said one day, as we walked slowly round the yard.

'It was scary at first, but everyone was kind. I just wanted to come home, Nora. There were days when I thought that I'd never see any of you again. There were days when I thought I'd never see Paradise Alley again.'

'I felt a bit like that at Granny and Grandad's.'

'There was a window on the ward that looked down on the city and once I was feeling better, me and Connor used to stand there and watch the people coming and going. Cork is a desperate busy place, Nora, with everyone rushing about, it made me miss home even more and Connor felt the same. Neither of us had any desire to walk its streets.'

'Who's Connor?'

'He was the lad in the next bed, I think I would have gone mad if it hadn't been for Connor.'

'I'm glad you had a friend, Stevie. Will you see him again?'

Stevie shook his head. 'He never made it, Nora, he never got to go home.'

I stopped walking and put my arm around his shoulder. 'I'm terrible sorry about that, love, I'm terrible sorry that you lost your friend.'

'He died during the night and I didn't even wake up. I wished I'd been awake, I could have sat beside him, so that he knew he wasn't alone.'

'I'm sure he knows that, Stevie, and sure, he's in the arms of the angels now and I bet he's having a great old time.'

Stevie didn't answer me. I took his hand and we walked across the field and sat down under a tree.

'Is there something wrong, Stevie?' I said gently.

Stevie leaned back against the tree and frowned. 'I don't think I'll ever be strong like you, Nora.'

'Of course you will. You've been ill and it will take time for you to get better, you just have to be patient.'

Stevie shook his head. 'Even before I got sick, I wasn't able to do the things that you do. I wasn't able to help Daddy around the place because I tired too quickly. I don't think I'm the son that Daddy would have chosen.'

I could feel hot tears stinging behind my eyes. I hated to think that my little brother felt like this. 'Oh, Stevie,' I said. 'You're wrong. Daddy loves the bones of you and he wouldn't change you for the world.'

'I just want to make him proud.'

'But you do, my love, you make him proud every day. You make all of us proud.'

Stevie sighed. 'Do you know what, Nora?'

'What?'

'I don't think that I will ever leave this place. I don't think that I will ever travel beyond this town.'

'Ah, but that's where you're wrong, Stevie.'

'What do you mean?'

'There is a way to travel beyond this town. Sure, I've been all over the world without stepping one foot outside Ballybun.'

Stevie smiled. 'And how did you manage that?'

'Books, Stevie, books. You can go anywhere you want. You can sail the seas in a great big boat. You can be the hero in any adventure, you can stand on the very top of a high mountain and look down on the world below you. You can go anywhere you like and all within the pages of a book. Will you give books a try?'

'I suppose I'm going to have to,' he said, grinning.

'Let's go and find one then,' I said, standing up and helping him to his feet. 'As long as you learn to love books, I won't ask for anything else.'

'It's a deal,' he said and we linked arms and walked back to the house.

It was the last weekend of the holidays, and it was time to go back to the garden. I had to explain to Eddie why I'd been away. It didn't bother me squeezing through the gap in the fence anymore. I was smiling as I ran down the path and pushed open the gate. Eddie was in the far corner of the garden, painting a bench. He jumped up when he saw me.

'You came back then?' he said, grinning.

I pushed the gate closed behind me. 'I was staying at my granny and grandad's farm. I expect you've been wondering where I was?'

'I knew where you were, Nora.'

'You did?'

'This is a small town and even at the Hall, I get to hear the gossip.'

'So, you knew about Stevie?'

Eddie nodded. 'And I've heard that he is on the mend.'

'He is, but we could have lost him, Eddie.'

Eddie balanced the brush on the tin of paint and stood up. 'It must have been hard on you all. I thought about you, Nora. I missed you, and I hoped that you were okay.'

'I missed you too,' I said, smiling.

'I'd say the garden missed you as well.'

'Do gardens have feelings?' I said.

Eddie looked around him and smiled. 'I believe this one does.'

'Where did you get the bench from?'

'Corny gave it to me; it was rotting away and he was going to burn it. He showed me how to sand it down and now all it needs is a coat of paint. I thought it would give us somewhere to sit when the grass is wet.'

'I like the colour.'

'Irish green,' he said.

'Give me your hankie, Eddie,' I said, smiling again. 'You have a blob of paint on your nose.'

Eddie laughed and handed me a perfectly ironed white square of linen. He seemed to have no end of them. I spat on it and gently rubbed the paint from his face. 'Can I help?'

'I'll get another brush,' he said.

I watched Eddie disappear through the gate and sat down beside the pond. I dipped my fingers in the water, stirring the leaves that had fallen from the trees and making them spin around as if they'd just woken up. I looked up at the tall trees swaying above my head. I'd missed this place and I'd missed my good friend. The last time I'd seen him, we'd been about the same height, but he'd grown over the summer and was now a good head taller than me, even though he was a year younger.

I'd felt drawn to this boy from the moment he'd burst through the brambles and frightened the life out of me and Kitty. He'd felt familiar to me, even though we had never met. He seemed to understand me. He never commented on my fancy words, because they were the same words that he used. I supposed that living at the Hall and having his schooling there had lifted him out of the class that he had been born into.

I looked up as Eddie came back through the gate, carrying a paintbrush and a pair of gloves.

'Wear these,' he said, handing me the gloves. 'Then you won't have to explain the green paint on your hands.'

I took the gloves. 'Thank you.'

'Come and have a look around,' he said.

We walked round the garden together. It looked completely different to the last time I'd seen it. Grass that had been young and bright green at the beginning of the summer was older and browner now, littered with fallen leaves; red and gold and brown.

Where there had been bare patches of soil in the flower beds, now every inch was taken up with flowers and plants. Most of the flowers were over, but there were slashes of pink and purple, where the tough little geraniums still kept producing blooms and Michaelmas daisies were nodding their raggedy little blue heads up against the old brick wall.

'They're a bit wild,' Eddie said, as if apologising for the flowers.

'Oh no,' I said, 'they're just happy. Look at them! Look at their happy faces!'

He laughed.

Plants that had barely begun to grow the last time I was here were now tall and the flowers had turned into seedpods, ready to start making the next year's flowers. Eddie showed me the little dry bells at the tops of the long stalks of the granny's bonnets. He told me that *aquilegia* was their proper name, and that they'd self-seeded all over the garden. He shook the stalk and held his hand out flat beneath the bell and dozens of little black seeds fell into his palm.

'That's how they do it,' he said, 'that's how they spread. They grow beautiful flowers in the summer to attract the bees and in the autumn, they wait for the breeze to come and shake out the seeds. Clever, eh?'

I agreed that it was.

He'd pulled up some of the flowers that had 'gone over', as he put it. The compost heap was high, but anything that still had a bit of life left in it was allowed to have its last moments in the sun.

The air was cool with that smell of autumn, a smell I'd always loved. Spiders had spun their webs in the shrubs – funny how you only ever noticed the webs at that time of year – and there were still a few late blackberries on the brambles in the wild area.

The fruit trees had done their work too. Eddie said there'd been a grand crop of pears in the late summer. The apple tree was still bearing apples even as its leaves were turning from green to red. The fallers had been raked into a pile where the thrushes and blackbirds could come and eat their fill.

As we walked, a light wind sprang up and it lifted some leaves from the trees. They danced in the air for a moment and then began to spin down to earth.

'Catch one!' Eddie cried. 'Catch a falling leaf! It's good luck!'

'That's an old wives' tale!'

'No,' he said, 'it's true!'

I reached out for a leaf that was spinning towards me but as I grabbed for it, it spun away.

'It's harder than it looks!' Eddie said.

We spent the next minutes chasing after falling leaves and soon we were both laughing and I was breathless and warm.

CHAPTER SIXTEEN

Me and Kitty were back at school, but we both knew it would not be for long, for things were about to change. We would soon be fourteen and no longer children.

We were sitting on top of the hill above the town looking down on the river.

'It's awful boring now that Finn has gone back to England,' said Kitty.

I hadn't told her about my meetings with Finn Casey up at the farm; I didn't want to hurt her feelings or make her feel jealous.

'He said he'd write to me though,' she said.

'Did he?'

'Well, he didn't exactly say he would but I asked if he would write to me and he didn't say no, so I took it as a yes.'

'I hope he does then, Kitty,' I said.

'Well, I'm not holding my breath, Nora. I find that boys are very fickle and I doubt that Finn Casey is any different to the rest of them, even though he does look like a god.'

'I suppose that even gods can be fickle, but maybe Finn will be the exception to the rule.'

'Grandad Doyle?'

I nodded. 'It means that he might turn out to be different to the rest.'

'I've a feeling that he'll forget me once he's back with his own kind.'

'How could anyone forget you, Kitty Quinn?' I said, putting my arm around her shoulder. 'For you're the biggest catch in Ballybun.'

'I don't know about that, Nora, but thank you for saying it.'

'The pair of us will be working soon,' I said, 'and who knows what the good Lord has in store for us.'

'Are you going to ask at the hotel about a job?' asked Kitty. 'You should do it soon, before anyone else gets in before you.'

'I suppose so,' I said.

'You don't sound too keen,' said Kitty.

'Well, it's better than the workhouse.'

'I have an appointment up at the Hall, Nora.'

'Since when?'

'Since you were staying up at the farm and Father Kelly wrote to them about me.'

'Are you scared?' I said.

'I'm bloody terrified. Oh, I wish we could work there together, Nora. Couldn't you ask your mammy? Maybe she's had a change of heart.'

'I doubt it and she's had enough worry with Stevie without me asking a question that I already know the answer to.'

'It'll have to be the hotel, then. Shall we go there now? We could go to Minnie's and see Annie and treat ourselves to a grand cup of tea. Minnie might even have an old bun that we could take off her hands.'

'Annie won't be there,' I said.

'Is she ill?'

'No, but Mrs Foley is and Annie needs to work closer to home so she can keep an eye on her.'

'She'll have a job finding work near Paradise Alley.'

'She already has, Kitty. My mammy needs help with Stevie and Malachi and she's offered her a job.'

'Isn't that grand? She'll be just up the lane from Mrs Foley,' said Kitty.

'I know, it's great, isn't it?'

'I think your mammy is kind, Nora.'

'I think so too.'

I stood up. 'Come on then,' I said. 'We might as well get it over with.'

'Let's go the long way around,' said Kitty. 'It will put off the inevitable.'

I stared at my friend. 'Oh, Kitty,' I said, 'where did you learn such a refined word? Is it one of Grandad Doyle's?'

'It is not, Nora, it's one of my own.'

'And where did you learn it?'

'I was in Biddy Quirk's shop getting some sweets when mouth almighty Mrs Toomey came in.'

'God, she's an awful gossip,' I said.

'She was talking about Maureen Barrie's new baby, who as you know, God love him, looks like a suet pudding in a bonnet. Well, anyway, she said that it was inevitable that the baby was the size of a house, with the amount of food Maureen shovelled down his throat.'

'I'm proud of you, Kitty, for not only did you remember the word but you used it in the right place. It would be very dignified if you could manage to slip it into the conversation when you go for your interview at the Hall. I'd say that they would be mighty impressed.'

'I'll give it a go, Nora.'

We walked quickly down the hill. We had decided not to run everywhere, at the same time as we decided not to go to any more funerals. It was all a part of leaving childish things behind us.

We made our way round the back lanes. The cottages were very humble in this part of the town. Women were gathered in huddles, leaning against the walls, their cross-over pinnies looking as if they needed a good wash. Small children swarmed around their feet; one child was sailing a paper boat along the gutter. Everywhere smelled bad and I was beginning to wish we hadn't come this way.

We walked further down the lane and turned into Baggot Row. I stopped and stared at the last cottage. On the side of the wall, in white chalk, was written, DYMPHNA DUFFY LIVES HERE.

'What are you staring at?' asked Kitty.

'Isn't that the most dignified thing you ever saw, Kitty?'

Kitty stared at the wall and shook her head. 'What in God's name are you on about?'

'Can't you see?'

'See what?'

'Dymphna Duffy is proud of who she is.'

Kitty was looking at me as if I'd gone mad. 'And how do you work that out?'

'Don't you see, Kitty? Dymphna Duffy has been saddled with a name that would make a saint curse, and she's lumbered with it until the day she marries.'

'*If* she marries.'

'Not only has she got a terrible name but she has no friends and people call her pie face.'

'Well, her face is a bit pie-like, Nora.'

'But that's not Dymphna's fault, is it? It's the way God made her.'

'That's the bit I don't understand. It says in the Bible that God made us in his own image and likeness and I don't know about you, but I've never seen a picture of him that resembles a pie.'

'You're missing the point, Kitty. Dymphna has all that to put up with and yet despite it all, she is proud of who she is. Proud enough to let the whole town know that her name is Dymphna Duffy and that this is where she lives. There is a kind of nobility in that, Kitty.'

'Nora?'

'Yes?'

'I'm beginning to think that you read too many books. It's making you desperate fanciful.'

I laughed. 'Come on, let's see if there's any jobs going at the hotel.'

I couldn't get Dymphna out of my head as we headed out along the Strand. I had the feeling that there was more to Dymphna Duffy than met the eye and was determined to try and get to know her better if the opportunity should present itself.

As we walked towards the Green Park Hotel, I wished that I was wearing my good coat.

'I'm not dressed for an interview, Kitty. I'm not going to make much of an impression in these old clothes.'

'You'll be grand, Nora.'

We pushed open the glass doors and walked into the lobby. Theresa Duggan was sitting behind the desk, made up to the nines. She'd only left school a year ago and she was acting as if she was a woman of the world.

'What?' she snapped.

'Well, that's a nice way to talk to a customer,' said Kitty.

'Well, my guess is that you're not customers,' said Theresa, examining her nails as if she'd only just discovered she had them.

'I've come about a job,' I said. 'Are there any going?'

'Well, you can't just walk in off the street and expect to be given a job,' said Theresa.

'How else was she supposed to get in here?' said Kitty. 'Down the chimney?'

'Don't be saucy,' said Theresa. 'Anyway, there are procedures, you have to fill in a form.'

Theresa was talking as if she'd swallowed a plum.

'What's with the English accent?' said Kitty, giggling.

Theresa went red in the face. 'I haven't got an English accent,' she snapped.

'Have you a problem with your teeth then?'

'My teeth are perfectly fine, thank you very much.'

I was beginning to feel a bit sorry for Theresa. 'How about this form then?' I said.

Theresa rummaged under the desk and took out a sheet of paper. She licked the end of a pencil and stared at me. 'Name?' she said.

'For God's sake, Theresa, you've known me all your life, why are you asking my name?'

'I have to ask you what's written on the form.'

'My name, as well you know, is Nora Doyle.'

'Middle name?'

'Why do you need my middle name?'

Theresa sucked on her teeth and glared at me. 'Because it's on the bloody form.'

'Okay, Theresa,' said Kitty. 'Cop on to yerself. Her middle name is Mary, after her mother's friend, who went down with the *Titanic*. Happy now, dear?'

Theresa took a deep breath. 'Where do you live?'

'She lives in the same alley as you, ya eejit,' said Kitty.

Theresa ignored her. 'What sort of work are you looking for?'

'Anything, I don't mind what I do.'

'Right,' she said, folding the sheet of paper in half.

'I'll wait to hear then, shall I?'

'Don't build your hopes up, Nora Doyle. The manager is very selective about who he takes on.'

'He can't be that selective,' said Kitty. 'Or I doubt that you'd be sitting behind the desk, posing mad and talking like one of the British royal family. Come on, Nora, I can't abide the smell of cheap perfume.'

We were giggling as we went to Minnie's.

'Isn't Theresa Duggan an awful gobshite?' said Kitty.

'You're right she is, but I think she'll have the last laugh, because I have a feeling that that form will be going nowhere but into the nearest bin.'

'I think you're right, Nora. It will have to be the laundry then.'

'Hello, girls,' said Minnie, as we stepped inside the café. 'You look as though you lost a shilling and found a penny.'

'It's worse than that, Minnie,' I said. 'I was hoping for a job at the hotel but the pair of us have just blown my chances with that stuck-up little madam, Theresa Duggan.'

'She has airs alright,' said Minnie. 'Her mother was the same.'

'So, I'm going to have to work in the laundry and I have no mind to work there.'

'I'm going for a job at the Hall, Minnie,' said Kitty, 'but Nora's mammy won't let her anywhere near the place.'

'Is it tea you're wanting?' asked Minnie, changing the subject. I nodded.

'And any old cakes you might want taking off your hands,' said Kitty.

Minnie laughed. 'Well, I suppose if you don't ask, you won't get and as it happens, I do have a couple of buns that are past their best.'

'That's good of you, Minnie, and we'll be glad to do you a favour,' said Kitty.

'Sit yourselves down then and I'll bring them over.'

Minnie always had a fire going in the hearth whatever the weather – she said that folks found it welcoming after the sea breeze.

'It's very rude of you to be asking Minnie for old cakes,' I said, sitting down.

'Well, if I hadn't asked, they would probably have been thrown away and then no one would be getting the benefit of them. My father says that wasting food is a sin against God.'

'Well, we don't want to be upsetting God, do we, Kitty? We've upset enough people for one day.'

'You're right, girl, we have.'

Minnie came across with the tea and buns and then sat down with us, which was pretty unusual for her.

'Nora,' she began, 'would you have a mind to work in a café?'

I stared at her. 'This café?' I said.

Minnie nodded. 'You know I'll be needing someone now I've lost Annie.'

'Oh, Minnie,' I said, 'you're a gift from God as I've no mind to be working in the laundry. I can start any time you like.'

'You'd leave me there on my own?' said Kitty, looking disgusted.

'Sure, you'll be fine.'

'I won't be fine,' said Kitty, glaring at me.

'No rush, Nora,' said Minnie. 'It's only a few months and I'm sure that is what your mother and father would want you to finish school. The summer is behind us and customers are few – I can manage until you're ready.'

'There you are,' said Kitty, looking relieved. 'You won't have to leave at all.'

Minnie went back into the kitchen and left us to eat the tea and buns. 'Well, at least I won't have to work in the laundry.'

'Nora Doyle, you could fall into Henry's shite and come up smelling of roses.'

'Well, aren't I the lucky one?' I said, biting into a bun.

CHAPTER SEVENTEEN

Stevie wasn't yet strong enough to go to school and he was being taught at home by Grandad Doyle. I spent as much time with him as I could.

'Do you miss school, Stevie?' I asked one day as we were leaning on the fence, watching Bonnie.

'I miss the lads but I think I'm learning more from Grandad than I ever did from the Christian brothers.'

'Then you'll be top of the class when you go back.'

We stood together looking out over the fields. I wanted more for Stevie than the life he had. He was loved, but he had no freedom.

'If I tell you something, Stevie, can you promise not to tell anyone else?'

He nodded.

'I've found a secret garden.'

'In Ballybun?' he said.

I nodded. 'The thing is, Stevie, I'm not really allowed to go there.'

'Why not?'

'Because it's in the grounds of Bretton Hall and Mammy has forbidden me to go anywhere near the place.'

'You're disobeying Mammy?'

'I am, but oh, Stevie, I have to keep going there, I just have to.'

'How did you get into the grounds?'

'Kitty found a gap in the fence and persuaded me to go in. It was just a laugh to start with but then we met this boy and he showed us the garden. I wish you could see it.'

'Will you take me there?'

'It would be too far for you to walk.'

'I could manage it.'

I shook my head. 'I don't think you could, love, it's way out beyond the Strand.'

Stevie's pale little face looked sad and for a moment I wished I'd never said anything. 'I suppose we could borrow Malachi's pushchair,' I said.

'If you think I'm going to be rolled through Ballybun in a baby's pushchair you can think again.'

I laughed. 'I suppose not,' I said.

'Tell me what it's like,' said Stevie.

I thought about the garden and smiled. 'It's the loveliest place. You enter through a wooden gate. There are lots of birds. I don't know the names of all of them yet but Eddie is teaching me.'

'Eddie?' said Stevie.

'He's the son of the groom up at the Hall – we've become great friends. He knows all about the flowers and the trees and the wildlife. He knows what flowers to grow and when to plant them.'

'What else?'

'It's surrounded on all sides by an old stone wall that's covered in roses, hundreds of them. In the middle is a pond and the trees above the garden are so dense that you feel as if you are in a secret room.'

Stevie closed his eyes. 'Are you getting tired, love?' I asked.

'No,' he said, smiling. 'I'm just imagining it; I'm imagining your garden, Nora.'

'When you are strong enough, I'll take you there, Stevie, and that's a promise.'

'I'll hold you to that, it will give me something to look forward to.'

'Have you had enough?' I said.

Stevie nodded and together we walked slowly back home.

Me and Kitty were sitting on the wall in the playground. We'd been looking forward to leaving school but now the day had come, the pair of us were far from happy.

'Jesus, Nora,' said Kitty. 'Why in all that's holy are we in such bad humour? Haven't we been waiting for this day for years?'

'I think it's because it's the end of our childhood, Kitty – we're adults now and responsible for our own destiny.'

'You don't have to explain,' said Kitty quickly. 'I know what destiny means.'

I watched the little kids running around the yard and I envied them their freedom. Our freedom was about to be brought to an abrupt end. I sighed. 'When's your interview up at the Hall?' I said.

'In a couple of days, and I'm only terrified.'

'You'll be grand,' I said.

'But I know no one there; if I get the job I'll be wandering around the place like a lost soul.'

'You'll know Eddie,' I said. 'And anyway, I'd say you'll be too busy to be wandering anywhere.'

'I wish I could be working at Minnie's. You're mighty lucky to have landed that job.'

'I know I am and I'm grateful. But you can come and see me on your days off and I'll be sure to keep any stale buns for you.'

'That's good of you, Nora, but I'd say I'll be in my bed on my days off.'

I laughed. 'You'll get used to it, and just think of all the posh people you're going to meet if you work there – you never know, you might even meet an Honourable willing to marry you and never have to work again.'

'Wouldn't that be great altogether?' said Kitty, grinning.

I noticed Dymphna Duffy standing on her own, and called out to her.

'Why are you calling Dymphna over?' said Kitty.

'Because this is a momentous day.'

'A what day?' said Kitty.

'You know, it's significant.'

'Holy Mother of God, Nora, would it be too much trouble to speak English?'

'I'm sorry, Kitty. I just mean that today is special and that no one should be on their own.'

Dymphna walked slowly towards us.

'What?' she said, looking suspicious.

'I just thought you might like to join us,' I said.

'On this momentous day,' added Kitty.

'Why?' snapped Dymphna.

'Because it's our last day at school,' I said. 'And it bothered me that you were on your own.'

'Well, that's mighty big of you, Nora Doyle, but isn't it a pity that it's taken you nine years to notice?'

I could feel my face going red, because I knew that she was right. 'I'm sorry, Dymphna,' I said. 'I truly am.'

'It's because we've always had each other,' said Kitty.

To my shame I could see Dymphna's eyes filling with tears. 'Well, aren't you the lucky ones?' she said.

'Please forgive me, Dymphna,' I said.

'And please forgive me too,' said Kitty.

'We can be friends now, can't we? It's not too late.'

'I think that maybe it is, Nora.'

'I'm going to be working in Minnie's,' I said, smiling at her. 'Perhaps you could come in some time for a cup of tea.'

'I'm afraid that won't be possible,' she said. 'I'm leaving Ballybun.'

'And going where?' asked Kitty.

'To Dublin,' said Dymphna. 'To train as a nurse.'

I couldn't believe what I was hearing. 'You're going to be a nurse?' I said.

'In Dublin?' said Kitty.

'Don't look so shocked, ladies,' said Dymphna. 'Even girls with faces like pies can be nurses.'

If I hadn't been feeling bad before, I was feeling terrible now.

'So, thank you for your offer of friendship, but I'm going to be far too busy at college in Dublin to be worrying about you two in this God-forsaken dump.' And with that, she walked away.

'Well, I hope it stays fine fer ya,' shouted Kitty after her retreating back.

I was paralysed with shame. I'd thought myself a fine girl indeed to be feeling sorry for poor Dymphna and thinking I was doing her some kind of favour by asking her to join us. Dymphna Duffy was going to drag herself out of Baggot Row and head off to Dublin to train as a nurse and I had the distinct feeling that as she walked away, it was *her* that was feeling sorry for *us*.

'Well, I wouldn't want her nursing me,' said Kitty. 'She has hands like plates of meat.'

'But she's going to make something of herself, Kitty, and that's something to admire in a person.'

'But don't you think she was awful puffed up about it?'

'Don't you think we were being a bit puffed up ourselves?'

Kitty banged her feet against the wall and didn't answer.

CHAPTER EIGHTEEN

I'd been working at Minnie's for almost two weeks and loving it. I was so glad that me and Kitty had upset Theresa sour-faced Duggan and blown my chances of a job in the hotel.

I was learning to bake in the little kitchen at the back of the shop.

'You have a light touch, Nora,' said Minnie. 'Unlike Annie, bless her.'

'She's happy working with Mammy,' I said. 'She's great with Stevie and Malachi – they both love her. And she's such a help in the house. Mammy said she doesn't know how she managed without her.'

'I'm glad,' said Minnie, 'for she's a lovely girl and she's now able to keep an eye on Mrs Foley, which must be a blessing to her.'

When I wasn't learning to bake cakes, I worked in the shop serving the customers, who were glad to come in from the cold and sit by the roaring fire that I lit every morning. I knew most of the people that came into the café and it was great to have a chat with them and ask about their families. Sometimes a stranger came in on their way to Cork and I enjoyed passing the time of day with them and asking about the city. I was a happy girl and I hoped that my dear friend Kitty would be as happy working at Bretton Hall.

It was too dark after work to go to the garden, so the only time I could go there was Sunday, which was my day off. There wasn't much planting to be done because the ground was too hard for digging, but the garden was even more beautiful in the winter than it had been in autumn.

One Sunday, after I'd been to Mass, me and Eddie were huddled up on the bench, freezing cold but happy to be together. The bare trees looked magical in the frosty morning; their bony twigs silhouetted against a pale, cold sky. A hoar frost had settled over the pruned-back roses, turning them into an intricate pattern of silver threads that spread like a spider's web across the old stone walls. Holly and ivy leaves still showed green beneath the white, and the holly berries looked as if they'd been dipped in sugar.

A friendly little robin perched on a twig close to us, his puffed-out red breast like a jewel against the whiteness of it all. He hopped about our feet, on ground so hard that we could see the tiny imprints of his claws amongst our own footprints.

We sat together, rubbing our cold fingers, our breath made little clouds in front of our red cheeks and noses before it dissolved into the cold air.

'Are we mad altogether, sitting here freezing to death?' said Eddie.

'I wouldn't want to be anywhere else,' I said.

Eddie smiled at me. 'Neither would I.'

I breathed in the cold air; it caught the back of my throat, making me cough. 'You've never mentioned your mother, Eddie,' I said, clearing my throat. 'Is she a maid at the Hall?'

Eddie stared down at the ground. 'My mother died giving birth to me,' he said.

I thought of my own mother and how much I loved her and how much she loved me; I couldn't imagine not having her. 'Oh, I'm terrible sorry, Eddie,' I said.

'I never knew her, so I can't say that I've missed her. I mean, you can't miss what you've never known, can you? I've seen pictures of her though, and I think that she was very beautiful. I believe that she loved gardens too.'

'That's where you'll be getting it from then.'

Eddie smiled, a sad smile. 'I like to think so,' he said.

'Your dad's alright, though, is he?'

Eddie didn't answer right away, and then he said, 'Sometimes when he looks at me, I get the feeling that he blames me for her dying.'

'Not at all,' I said frowning, 'you're all he has, I bet he loves you to bits. I think that sometimes men have a hard time showing it.'

Eddie shrugged his shoulders. 'It's just a feeling I get.'

I shivered and Eddie put his arm around my shoulder. 'You're going to be seeing my friend Kitty soon,' I said, trying to lighten the mood. Kitty's interview had gone well, and she'd been offered the position.

'Who?'

'Kitty, my friend who found the gap in the fence.'

'Oh yes,' he said. 'But why will I be seeing her? Are you bringing her to the garden?'

'She's starting work at the Hall; you're bound to come across her.'

Minutes went by and Eddie didn't say anything; the silence began to feel awkward. 'Don't worry,' I said. 'She won't say anything about the garden, she won't give your secret away.'

Eddie stood up and walked across to the pond. Something was wrong. He had his back to me but I could see that his shoulders were hunched and he'd wrapped his arms around his body, as if he was protecting himself. He still hadn't spoken. I walked across to him and touched his arm.

'What's wrong, Eddie?' I said. 'Is it because we were talking about your mother?'

He shook his head and turned to face me. He had a kind of desperate look on his face. I'd never seen him look like that before.

'I'm sorry, Nora,' he said, rubbing at his eyes.

I was feeling worried now. Was this about Kitty? And if it was, why was he so upset?

'Tell me what's wrong.'

Eddie stared into the pond. 'I don't know how to tell you.'

'Sure, it can't be that bad,' I said.

'I've been lying to you, Nora; I've been lying from the very beginning.'

'About what?'

'Everything,' he said, so quietly that I could hardly hear him.

He took a deep breath. 'My name is Edward.'

I laughed. 'Is that all?'

'Edward Bretton.'

I stared at him. 'I don't understand. Your father's a groom. You said that your father's a groom.'

'I know what I said, Nora, but I lied to you.'

'Why?'

'Because I thought that if you knew who I was, you wouldn't be my friend. I've wanted to tell you so many times but I was so scared that you would run away and never come back.'

I stared at the ice that had formed on the top of the pond, floating around like a broken mirror. I wasn't sure what I was supposed to feel. I wasn't angry that he'd lied to me because I knew that he wasn't a liar. Yes, even though he had lied, I believed him to be an honest person. Nothing had changed, really – he was still the same boy who had shown me a garden and taught me about birds and flowers and nature. He was still Eddie; he was still my friend. Maybe he was right, maybe I would have run, but not now, not now that he had become so precious to me. I could feel his tall thin body beside mine and it was hard to think that one day he would be the master of Bretton Hall, a title that might prove too heavy for his narrow frame and gentle nature. I slipped my cold hand into his and felt his fingers close around mine.

We stayed beside the pond, holding hands. I felt blessed to be here with my friend on this beautiful day. I looked up at the crystal branches above our heads and let the garden work its magic. I was where I wanted to be and it felt like home.

CHAPTER NINETEEN

Kitty came bursting into Minnie's, bringing a blast of cold air with her. 'Jesus, I'm frozen,' she said. 'Let me get to the fire, quick.'

Kitty had started training for her job at the Hall but I'd hardly seen her since the interview and I was dying to know all about it. There was no one else in the café so Minnie said I could sit with her.

'I wouldn't be surprised if it snowed, Nora,' she said, holding her hands out to the flame. 'It's like the North Pole out there. Give the fire a poke, girl.'

I picked up the poker that was leaning against the side of the fireplace and rattled the turf. A gust of warm air blasted out into the room. 'Heaven,' sighed Kitty, turning around to warm her back.

We sat at a table close to the fire. 'Come on then, tell me all about it,' I said.

'I was like a blabbering eejit,' she said. 'I could hardly string two words together; I was that nervous.'

'But you got the job, you must have done something right.'

'I'm thinking they must have been desperate.'

'Of course they weren't. Did you manage to fit in your fancy word?'

'I did. Mrs Britton asked me why I wanted the position.'

'And what did you say?'

'I said that everyone wanted to work at the Hall and it was inevitable that I wanted to as well. Did I put it in the right place?'

'You did, Kitty, and I think that is what made you stand out from the crowd. I'm proud of you.'

'I was a little proud of meself, Nora.'

'What's the place like?'

'Oh, Nora, it's like a different world up there.'

'Describe it to me.'

'Well, you could fit the whole of our cottage into the hallway alone. The floor is so shiny you can see your face in it and there's a sweeping staircase that rises up to the floor above, with beautiful pictures in golden frames hanging on the walls.'

'What's the mistress like?'

'She's just as you'd expect an Honourable to be.'

'Did you have to curtsey?'

'Mrs Tittle, the housekeeper, showed me how to bob.'

I grinned. 'Mammy told me about the first time she went to the Hall to see Mrs Bretton. She said she tried to bob and nearly fell over.'

'I'd forgotten that your mam worked there.'

'So did Annie.'

'And now it's my turn,' said Kitty.

'Which room did she receive you in?'

'The best room, Nora, the drawing room. I wonder why it's called the drawing room; do you think people used to draw in there?'

'I suppose they might have done; I'll ask my Grandad Doyle – there isn't much he doesn't know. What was the room like?' I said.

'I can only remember bits of it, because I was terrified.'

'Try and think,' I said.

Kitty frowned, the tip of her tongue came out of her mouth and she licked her lips. 'The carpet was blue, yes, I think it was blue. The windows were long and I think that maybe the curtains were a darker blue. There was a big fireplace, with a grand fire burning, not a turf fire but coals. And books, lots of books, in cabinets that went right up to the ceiling.'

I closed my eyes, the better to visualise it all. This is where Eddie grew up, amongst all those beautiful things. Perhaps he'd sat in a chair beside the fire with a book on his lap. Maybe he'd stood by the long windows looking out over the lawn that fell away in front of the house, knowing that beyond the tall trees was a secret garden. He must have run up and down that grand staircase, taking no notice of the paintings on the walls because he'd run past them all his life.

I'd thought it didn't matter; I'd told myself that Eddie was the same Eddie but suddenly I felt like the boy I thought I knew had gone. My Eddie lived above the stables and helped his father with the horses. I'd thought that this was something we had in common, a love of horses, but I'd been wrong and I felt cheated and a bit silly.

'Oh, I wish you could see it all, Nora,' said Kitty, breaking into my thoughts.

'I know you do, but it's out of the question.'

'Because of your mammy?'

I nodded. 'But I'm happy here, Kitty, and I'm grateful for the job. When do you start?'

'Tomorrow morning at six o clock. This is my last day of freedom, Nora, and I've been in bad humour since the minute I woke up.'

Minnie brought the tea and a couple of apple cakes over to the table and me and Kitty sat down.

'Oh, thank you, Minnie,' said Kitty. 'That's awful good of you.'

'You look in need of sustenance, child,' said Minnie.

'She's starting at the Hall tomorrow, Minnie.'

'And I've a mind not to go,' said Kitty, pulling a face.

'You'll be grand, Kitty,' said Minnie. 'There's a whole new life waiting for you up there, you need to grab it with both hands. If you work hard, you could rise through the ranks and become a lady's maid and then, Kitty Quinn, the world will be your oyster.'

'It sounds quite exciting when you put it like that, Minnie,' said Kitty, grinning.

Minnie smiled and left us alone. I leaned across the table and held Kitty's hand, 'You'll be fine,' I said. 'They'll love you.'

'Will they?'

'Of course they will, you'll have all the lads after you.'

'Well, as you said, at least there'll be one friendly face up there.'

'And who would that be?'

'Eddie, the groom's son, ya eejit.'

'Mmm.'

'Mmm what?'

'There's something I need to tell you, Kitty.'

'That sounds serious.'

'I'm not sure how serious it is, but I think I need to let you know.'

'Well, out with it then.'

'Eddie isn't the son of a groom.'

'But isn't that what he told us?'

'It is, but he lied.'

'And why would he be doing that?'

'His real name is Edward, Edward Bretton.'

'Holy mother of God, Nora. Have you spent the past year gardening with an Honourable?'

'It would seem so, Kitty.'

'Aren't you terrible mad at him? Lying to you like that and pretending to be something he isn't.'

'I'm not mad at him, Kitty. He thought I wouldn't want to be his friend if he told me who he really was and I can kind of understand that.'

'Well, I'd be mad at him.'

'Would you be mad if it was Finn Casey who'd lied to you?'

Kitty grinned and bit into the warm apple cake. 'You have me there, Nora Doyle, but doesn't it feel strange to be passing the time of day with the master's son?'

'He's my friend, and I don't mind whose son he is. It doesn't change who Eddie is.'

'Does that mean I'm going to have to call him Master Edward?'

'I suppose you will.'

'What if I slip up and call him Eddie?'

'I'd say you'll be out on your ear.'

Kitty sighed. 'Is there another bit of apple cake going spare?'

'You'll be fat as a house at this rate, Kitty Quinn.'

'You and I are from the bogs, Nora, we can't afford to be fat.'

CHAPTER TWENTY

It was a week until Christmas Day and instead of going to the garden, me and Kitty were going out to the woods to gather holly and mistletoe to decorate the Grey House and Kitty's cottage.

'You'll need to wrap up, Nora,' said Mammy as I was getting ready. 'You'll freeze to death out there.'

The cold didn't really bother me that much but I didn't want to worry Mammy. 'I will,' I said.

Stevie was sitting beside the fire. 'I wish I could go with you, Nora,' he said sadly. 'I'd love to go to the woods.'

I felt terrible sad for my brother, who spent most of his days inside the house. 'Mammy,' I said, 'if we just went to the beginning of the woods, do you think Stevie could walk that far?'

'I think I could,' said Stevie, looking hopeful.

'I don't want you catching cold, love,' said Mammy, smiling at him. 'You are still not strong enough. Maybe come the spring, you'll be able to get out more.'

'Sorry, Stevie,' I said.

Stevie shrugged. 'I wish it was spring, Nora.'

'It soon will be,' I said, 'and then we can go all over the place, just like we used to.'

Mammy handed me a woolly hat and gloves that she had warming by the fire and then she took Daddy's scarf from behind the door. 'Wrap this round your neck and you'll be nice and toasty.'

I thought about poor Eddie, who had never known a mother's love, who never had a mammy that loved him so much that she warmed his clothes by the fire. 'I love you, Mammy,' I said.

'What brought that on?' asked Mammy, smiling at me.

'I'm just glad you're mine,' I said.

Mammy tied the hat under my chin and kissed the top of my head. 'And I'm glad you're mine, I'm so very glad you're mine.'

I looked out the window and there was Kitty, pushing Sean's old pushchair up Paradise Alley. I opened the door and waited for her.

'Bloody pushchair,' she said as she reached me. 'I swear to God that the squeak is getting worse.'

Grandad Doyle walked around the side of the house. I wasn't sure how old my grandad was, Granny Collins said he was a very upright man that belied his years. He had a full head of white hair and his eyes were brown like Daddy's but much paler, they reminded me of the acorns that fell from the trees in the garden. 'Let me get a bit of oil for that, Kitty,' he said, laughing.

'Thank you, Mr Doyle,' said Kitty. 'I'd be mighty pleased if you could do something about it. I felt a right eejit walking through town with the bloody thing. The Dolan boys were running after me and mocking me.'

'The Dolan boys would have mocked Christ himself when he rode through town on a donkey,' said Grandad. 'Go inside out of the cold while I fix it.'

Kitty came into the kitchen and crouched down in front of the fire. 'It's desperate cold out there, Mrs Doyle,' she said. 'It would take the nose off ya.'

'Then I suggest you get the holly as quick as you can and not dally in the woods, Kitty.'

'Oh, we will,' said Kitty.

Mammy put a parcel wrapped in cloth into Kitty's hands. 'A bit of a picnic,' she said, smiling. 'Gathering holly can make a girl hungry.'

'I'm always hungry, Mrs Doyle,' said Kitty. 'I'll be glad of a bite to eat.'

Grandad came into the kitchen rubbing his hands together. 'The chair is grand now, girls,' he said, smiling. 'I've fixed the squeak and mended the wheel, it's as good as new.'

We built up a grand sweat running through the woods till I was so hot, I could hardly breathe. I unwrapped the scarf from around my neck and went to put it in the chair.

'Give me that,' said Kitty. 'I feel the cold more than you do.'

We pulled the icy-cold holly from the trees and filled the pushchair with the bright red berries and the green ivy and then sat down to eat our picnic. As we were eating, soft flurries of snow began to swirl around us. It settled on the branches of the trees, turning the woods into a winter wonderland.

'Isn't it too beautiful for words, Kitty?' I said, looking around me.

Kitty shivered. 'I'm too cold to admire it.'

She had the scarf wrapped so tightly around her mouth that her voice was muffled and kind of snuffly, as if she had the start of a cold.

'You sound as if you have a cold,' I said, laughing.

'I'll be getting a cold if we don't get home soon,' she said.

'Kitty, do you see much of Eddie at the Hall?'

'I see him every day.'

'And do you remember to call him Master Edward?'

'I do, but it's hard, as I've always called him Eddie. I feel sorry for him, Nora.'

'Why?'

'Because no one really seems to care for him. He has his breakfast in the kitchen, then he gets his lessons from some crotchety old feller who looks as if he's not long for this world and then he disappears for the rest of the day. It's as if he's no one's responsibility. It's no wonder he was so desperate for a friend.'

'Then I'm glad he has the garden, for I know he is happy there. But I fear that for all his wealth, he has a sad kind of life.'

We sat in silence, eating the bread and cheese that Mammy had packed, and I thought about the garden and how beautiful it would look on this magical day. Oh, how I wanted to be there now, sitting on the green bench beside Eddie with the snow falling about our shoulders.

It snowed all week, covering the town in a blanket of silence. The school had closed and the children were dotted around the hillside, building snowy little men, pelting each other with cotton wool balls and sliding down the hills on bits of tin. Ireland didn't get much snow, so the whole place was alive with the sheer excitement of it.

I decided that I would get Eddie a little present for Christmas. I wanted him to know that someone cared about him, but it had to be something that he could keep without arousing suspicion. I got to work early the next day and walked across to the beach. The sea and the pebbles were bright white in the dark morning, as if someone had taken a pot of paint and thrown it over everything. I walked up and down, my head lowered, my eyes searching until I found it – a pale grey pebble in the shape of a heart, as perfect as if an artist had lovingly carved it and placed it there for me to find. I put it in my pocket and ran across the road to Minnie's.

Minnie had started to teach me how to make the bread and I was loving it. 'It's a living thing, Nora,' she'd said. 'You can feel it changing and coming alive beneath your fingers. I take all my frustrations out on it, so be as violent as you like – it won't bear any grudges.'

Minnie was right – I found it soothing and exciting in equal measure. The sharp smell of the yeast filled the little kitchen as the dough changed from a sticky mass that stuck to my fingers and pushed underneath my nails to a smooth plump mound that changed shape and consistency under my touch. Once Minnie was happy with my pressing and pummelling, she'd cover it over with a damp tea towel and place it on the shelf in the cupboard to rise.

'Now we have to let it rest for a couple of hours,' she'd said.

'A couple of hours?' I'd said. 'But that's ages.'

'If something is worth making, then it's worth waiting for.'

That morning, Minnie was showing me how to slide the proved dough into the hot oven. The smell as it baked made my mouth water and filled the room, drawing passers-by into the little café. Minnie said the waiting was like giving birth, because you never knew whether you were going to get an old lump of a thing or the perfect article.

Later on, Minnie called me into the kitchen, and there on the table was a pale brown crispy loaf of bread. 'Well done, Nora,' said Minnie, pulling off a chunk and handing it to me. 'The perfect article.'

Minnie had given me Wednesday afternoon off so that I could go Christmas shopping with Kitty. I was earning my own money now and I couldn't wait to choose gifts for my family, although there were very few shops in Ballybun. There was the baker's and the butcher's, Pasley's that sold groceries, Toomey the cobbler, the undertaker's and Mulligan's that sold shoes. The only decent shop in town was Merrick's, which sold just about everything, so that's where we would be heading. I helped with the washing-up as I waited for Kitty to come into the café. The bell tinkled and I dried my hands and went into the shop expecting to see her, but a man I had never seen before was standing by the counter.

'Could I trouble you for a cup of tea?' he said, taking off his hat.

'You can, of course,' I said, smiling at him. 'And would you like a cake to go with it? They were freshly baked this morning.'

'Well now,' he said, smiling back at me, 'I've never been one to turn down a freshly baked cake.'

'Sit yourself by the heat, and I'll bring it over.'

I watched him walk across to the fire – he didn't sit down immediately but stood with his back to me, spreading his hands out towards the flames. I'd never seen him before, maybe he was on his way to Cork, or perhaps he had business at the Hall. He was tall and handsome with dark hair that curled around the collar of his coat. I thought he looked like a film star.

I wanted to tell Minnie about him but when I went into the kitchen, she was fast asleep in her chair. I made the tea and placed a slice of sponge cake on one of our best plates, then I carried it across to the gentleman, because there was no doubt in my mind that was what he was – a gentleman. He looked up and smiled at me.

'Thank you, Miss…?'

'Doyle,' I said. 'Nora Doyle.'

He stared at me. 'And you live in the town?'

I nodded. 'Paradise Alley,' I said.

'Please join me,' he said. 'Is that allowed?'

I thought it was an awful odd request but he seemed alright. 'Well, there's no one else in,' I said, 'and Minnie's asleep, so I suppose I could, just for a minute.'

'Get another cup,' he said. 'I don't like to drink tea alone.'

I took another cup from the shelf. No one had ever asked me to join them for a sup of tea – he must be desperate lonely.

As I poured the teas, I was aware that the man was looking at me. I pushed a stray curl behind my ear and I could feel my face going red.

'Do you live with your parents, Nora?'

'Yes, sir,' I said.

'And they are both well?'

'They're grand,' I said.

He nodded. 'I'm very pleased to hear that.'

I wondered why he was pleased to hear that Mammy and Daddy were well. 'Are you?' I said.

'I am indeed.'

We drank our tea in silence, the man seemed to be lost in thought and I was feeling terrible awkward. Then he stood up, but made no move to leave the café. 'It's been wonderful meeting you, Nora,' he said. I didn't know what to say to him as we stood facing each other. Eventually he moved towards the door. As he opened it, he turned back. 'Are you happy, Nora?' he said.

'She's happy,' said Minnie from the kitchen doorway. 'And now I suggest you get about your business, sir.'

I had never known Minnie to speak to a customer like this – the whole thing was strange.

'I just wanted to know how the girl was,' said the man politely.

'So now you know. I bid you a good day, sir.'

The man tipped his hat at Minnie and left.

'That was the oddest thing, Minnie. He wanted to know all about me; now why would anyone want to know about me?'

'Don't be worrying your head about it, Nora,' said Minnie, going back into the kitchen.

I started to clear the table and as I picked up the saucer, I could feel the colour drain from my face. Underneath were two one-pound notes folded in half. I'd never seen so much money in my life. 'Minnie!' I shouted.

Minnie hurried back into the room and I held out the notes for her to see. 'Why would he leave me all this money?' I said.

Minnie didn't answer me.

I moved towards the door. 'I'll have to give it back, he can't have gone far.'

Minnie held out her hand. 'Give it to me, Nora.'

'But I can't keep it.'

'Yes, you can. But you're not to tell your mother. Promise me that you won't tell your mother.'

'I promise.'

'I'll keep it safe for you. There may be a time when you will need it.'

'Who was he, Minnie?'

'He was no one, Nora, no one at all.'

*

'You're awful quiet, Nora,' said Kitty as we walked through the town. 'Did you have a hard morning?'

'I had a terrible strange morning, Kitty.'

'What happened?'

'I don't know if I should tell you.'

'Jesus, Nora, you can't be telling me that you had a terrible strange morning and then not tell me why.'

'It's just that Minnie said I wasn't to tell Mammy.'

'Do I look like your mammy?' said Kitty.

'I think that what she meant to say was, don't tell anyone.'

'You're a mind reader now, are you?'

'Well, I need to talk to someone about it or I'll burst.'

'Well, don't burst in the middle of Ballybun, or you'll be the talk of the town.'

'Do Mulligan's still serve teas?'

'They do, but the girl who serves them is an awful baggage.'

'Do we know her?'

'Rumour has it she's old Mr Mulligan's niece from Cork.'

'But didn't Bernie Daley have that job?'

'She did, but then the baggage turned up and Bernie was out on her ear.'

'Ah, that's a shame for Bernie.'

'To be fair, Bernie managed to make a simple cup of tea taste like Henry's shite.'

'Did she get another job?'

'She's down the laundry.'

'Not making tea, I hope.'

'No, Mammy says she's up to her elbows in the town's undergarments and happy as the day's long.'

'I'm glad, Kitty, for Bernie's a lovely girl.'

'Shall we take a chance on the baggage, then?' asked Kitty.

'You're on,' I said, slipping my arm through hers and heading for Mulligan's.

We'd been sitting at a table for a good few minutes, listening to the baggage giving out to anyone daft enough to listen about how wonderful Cork was.

'If it's that wonderful, what's she doing in Ballybun?' said Kitty, trying to catch her eye.

'I haven't a clue.'

'If she doesn't hurry up, I'll make the tea meself.'

'She's coming over,' I said.

'About bloody time,' said Kitty.

The baggage stood in front of us, licking the end of a pencil. 'What can I get you, ladies?' she said.

'Two teas and a couple of buns,' said Kitty.

The baggage licked the pencil again and started writing. 'Two teas and two buns?' she said very precisely.

'Sometime today,' said Kitty, under her breath.

Once she was gone, Kitty leaned her elbows on the table. 'So, tell me about your strange morning, Nora.'

'A man came into Minnie's.'

'A stranger?'

I nodded.

'Well, that's not so unusual, is it?'

'No, but he asked me a lot of questions.'

'What sort of questions?'

'He asked me my name and where I lived and he asked if my parents were well.'

'That's mighty strange, Nora. Why would he want to know that?'

'I don't know.'

'And you've never seen him before?'

'Never,' I said.

'Well, that was very odd indeed.'

'That's not the oddest thing, Kitty. When I went to clear his table, I found two one-pound notes folded up under the saucer.'

Kitty looked as if she was about to fall off her chair. 'Jesus, Nora, that's a fortune. Are you sure it was meant for you?'

I thought about the way the man had looked at me. 'Yes,' I said. 'I think it was meant for me.'

'But things like that don't happen in Ballybun.'

'Things like that don't happen anywhere, Kitty.'

'You're a woman of fortune now, Nora.'

'I don't feel like a woman of fortune.'

'What are you going to do with it?' asked Kitty, shovelling sugar into her tea.

'Minnie says she'll keep it for me, in case I might need it one day.'

'But didn't Minnie think it was strange?'

'Minnie was pretty strange herself and really quite rude to the feller. I've never known Minnie to be rude to anyone.'

'Well, you've taken the breath out of me, Nora, for I've never heard the like of it in all my life.'

'Neither have I. I was all for running after the feller and giving him the money back, but Minnie stopped me and that's when she said she would mind it for me.'

'Well, if you go to work tomorrow and find that the place is bolted up, you'll know she's done a runner.'

I grinned. 'Minnie would never do that, Kitty.'

'Money can do funny things to people, Nora; it can turn a person's head.'

'Not Minnie's,' I said.

'You're right, I don't think that Minnie is a head-turning kind of woman.'

'So, what am I to do, Kitty?'

'There's not a lot you can do, unless he comes in again.'

'I don't think he'll be doing that; I think Minnie scared him off.'

'I wonder why she didn't want your mammy knowing about it.'

'Do you think I might be adopted, Kitty? Do you think that man was my real daddy? Do you think that's why I don't have my own story?'

'Did he look like you?'

I thought about the man, I thought about the way his hair curled over the back of his collar.

'He had curly hair, Kitty, just like mine.'

'I'd say half the men in Ireland have curly hair, that doesn't mean they're your father.'

'No, you're right. But why would someone give a complete stranger all that money?'

Kitty shrugged her shoulders. 'Maybe he's one of those do-gooder types.'

'What would you think if it happened to you?'

'I'd be only delighted and I'd go down to the church and thank God for me bit of good luck.'

'Maybe that's what I should do.'

'It might put your mind at rest, then you can forget about it and get on with your life.'

'I think that's good advice, Kitty.'

'He could be an angel, Nora; I've heard angels come in all shapes and forms.'

'If he'd been an angel, he would have known my name and he'd know all about Mammy and Daddy without having to ask about them.'

'The Devil then,' said Kitty. 'Come to tempt you away from the chosen path by making you a woman of fortune. Or it could be that God was testing you to see what you would do with the cash.'

'Jesus, Kitty, you have my head mashed with your theories.'

'Grandad Doyle?'

'The very man, it means you're suspicious.'

'Have you ever done someone a good turn? Or saved someone's life?'

I thought about it. I'd carried Mrs Toomey's shopping home for her once when she'd turned her ankle and I'd taken baby Sean out for a spin in the pushchair when Kitty was in bed with the belly ache but sure, they were both as poor as church mice and not in a position to be handing out one-pound notes. I shook my head.

'Then we will just have to leave it there and put it down to an act of kindness, like the Good Samaritan in the Bible.'

'I agree, and I thank you for your counsel on the matter. I feel better, having spoken to you about it.'

'That's what friends are for. Now, shall we go Christmas shopping?'

I smiled and nodded.

'You're in a great position this day, Nora Doyle, to be buying your family mighty fine presents altogether.'

'Minnie has the money, Kitty, and anyway, I'd have the whole town talking if I went around throwing pound notes all over the place.'

'But just think, Nora, if you ever find yourself out on the street, you'll have the boat fare to England and as I'm your best friend in the whole world, you might have a mind to take me with you.'

I laughed. 'What would I do without you, Kitty Quinn? What on earth would I do without you?'

'I have one more thing to say on the subject, and then I'll hold my tongue.'

'I'm listening.'

'If you thought that man was your father, aren't you smearing your mammy's good name?'

'You're right, Kitty, and I feel ashamed to have thought such a thing. Confession?'

'The very place,' said Kitty.

CHAPTER TWENTY-ONE

I couldn't stop thinking about the gentleman and the money – it made no sense and it worried me. I knew without a doubt that the money was meant for me. Maybe it was the way he'd looked at me or the fact that he'd wanted to know so much about me. When Kitty had asked me to describe him, the only thing that had stuck in my mind was the way his hair curled over the collar of his coat. I couldn't remember the colour of his eyes or whether he had a large nose, or whether his lips were full or thin. If I'd known that he was going to leave me a fortune I would have taken more notice. I wished I could have shared it with Mammy, she would have known what to do, but I'd promised Minnie that I wouldn't tell her and a promise is a promise. In my heart I knew that it was wrong to keep all these secrets from her, because she was the one person who would have taken the burden from my shoulders. My mammy was the wisest person I knew and the one person I respected above all others. Not telling her about the garden or Eddie and now a pile of money from a stranger was wearing me down.

Come Sunday, I was back at the broken piece of fence. As I pushed through, I was surprised to find that the brambles were nearly all gone and I could actually stand up. Eddie was in front of me, grinning, his arms full of the stuff. When he saw me, he tossed the lot onto a huge pile in the corner.

'I wanted to surprise you,' he said, grinning.

'You have,' I said, grinning back, 'it's grand altogether.'

'I have another surprise for you, Nora.' He held out his hand.

I took it and we ran down the path like a couple of excited schoolchildren. As we got to the gate, Eddie stopped.

'Close your eyes,' he said.

I did as he asked and let him guide me into the garden.

'Okay, you can open them now.'

I wasn't sure what I was supposed to be seeing. The garden looked the same as the last time I'd been there.

'Over by the tree,' said Eddie.

My eyes filled with tears as I stared at the swing hung between two stout branches.

'It's like the story,' I said, smiling.

'That's why I made it,' said Eddie.

I walked across and sat down on the smooth wooden seat. Eddie came and stood behind me. 'Ready?' he said.

I nodded and he began to gently push.

'Higher!' I yelled. 'Higher!'

Eddie laughed and pushed harder. 'You mad girl!' he shouted.

'I feel mad,' I shouted back, as I rose up into the sky, my two legs soaring over the pond and my hair flying about my face. I startled a grey squirrel, who stared at me suspiciously and then disappeared into the undergrowth.

We took turns on the swing, giggling and laughing as we pushed each other higher and higher. I felt like a child again, my heart bursting with the simple pleasures of childish things. I felt free and full of joy, and quite mad. I wanted to dance around the garden and not give a care, for I knew that Eddie wouldn't think me silly. I had never felt so completely safe with someone. I had never felt so completely alive.

'Thank you, Eddie,' I said, flinging my arms around him.

He didn't answer. Our breath drifted between us like a white mist. I could feel my heart beating against my chest and although it was cold, icy beads of sweat prickled my skin. I rubbed my forehead and stared down at the frosty grass. I didn't know what I was feeling and it frightened me. The silence was broken only by the sounds of the garden; the swaying of the tall trees as the cold wind moved the bony branches, the ice as it crackled and floated across the pond and the scurrying of creatures in the undergrowth. My senses became heightened as we stood there in the silence. The musty smell of the damp earth, the rotting vegetation, the fat robin ruffling his feathers against the cold and the thump of my heart, taking my breath away.

There was something between us but I didn't know what it was. He had felt familiar to me from the day we met. I didn't want to kiss him, not the way grown-ups kiss, but I wanted to hold him with the innocence of our tender years. I wanted to hold him close and never let him go. We were standing so close that we were almost touching. And yet we were worlds apart and we always would be.

I put my hand into my pocket and handed him the pebble.

He didn't speak for a minute, then he looked at me and smiled. 'It's the best present I've ever been given,' he said.

'It's only an old pebble,' I said.

He shook his head. 'I shall keep it forever.'

He reached out and gently pulled me into his arms. I felt the roughness of his jacket and the beating of his heart beneath my cheek and I was full of love for a young boy who felt like one of my own. I felt confused; something wasn't right and I didn't know what I was supposed to be feeling or what was expected of me. I looked at Eddie and something in his face told me that he was feeling the same and then I started to laugh, really laugh, at how foolish we had been. I could hardly catch my breath, I was laughing so much and then Eddie was laughing and our laughter filled the little garden and echoed around the stone walls, because in that moment, we knew that we were friends, the best of friends, and that was all we would ever be, or want to be. We would be the best of friends forever and from now on things would be different, easier – we could just be ourselves and being ourselves was enough.

'Happy Christmas, Nora,' said Eddie, grinning.

'Happy Christmas, Eddie.'

PART TWO

CHAPTER TWENTY-TWO

December 1927

A lot had happened in the last three years. I was still working for Minnie, I had turned into a pretty good cook and I enjoyed meeting all the people who came into the café. Malachi had grown into the sweetest little boy – he made us all laugh with his sunny nature. He was very close to Stevie, who he looked up to and followed everywhere. I suppose it was because Stevie had never been well enough to go to school and was at home all the time. Malachi was going to be stronger. He would run faster, he would go to school, he would find his way in the world in a way that his brother never would. Stevie's life was still restricted by his health but he helped Daddy as much as he could and continued to go on the milk round with him. He had also turned into a great reader and the stories took him away from what could have been a lonely existence. It was lovely to see him and Grandad Doyle discussing the books they had read. I loved being with my family, but my happiest moments were working alongside Eddie in the garden. I never tired of being there, because with every season there was change, nothing stayed the same. There was always new life pushing through the soil, life that we had planted and nurtured. I learned everything that Eddie could teach me and I loved it.

Christmas at the Grey House was magical that year. Everyone was there and it was full of laughter and love. I forgot my worries and just let myself enjoy the special day. The fire burned brightly and, above the hearth, the red holly berries shone in the glow of the flames. Stevie and Mammy had placed the wooden nativity figures on a bed of hay. The baby Jesus lay smiling up at us in a tiny wooden manger that Grandad Doyle had made. Daddy had taken Bonnie and the trap down to the little cottage and brought Mrs Foley and Annie up the lane, as poor Mrs Foley's legs were too weak to walk and her bowels were tormenting her. Granny and Grandad Collins brought a fine big turkey from the farm and the house was filled with the mouth-watering smell of the good meat, mixed with the sweet smell of pine from the Christmas tree that sparkled in the corner of the room.

Malachi was beside himself with excitement. I wondered why on earth I had thought a sister would be better, for I loved the very bones of him. Stevie watched wide-eyed from his chair beside the fire, where he spent most of his days. It reminded me of the stories that Mammy would tell me about her grandaddy, but her grandaddy was old and Stevie was just a child who should have been running the hills and lanes with his friends.

After dinner we exchanged our presents. I gave Stevie a new jotter and some pencils and he was delighted. I gave Malachi a little tin tractor, which he immediately started pushing around the floor, and for Mammy, a blue glass brooch which she pinned on her dress.

'Now, this is for you,' she said, handing me a parcel. 'I hope you like it.'

Mammy had bought me a new red coat and I couldn't wait to show it off to Kitty. Granny Collins had knitted me a white hat and scarf and gloves.

'You look like Father Christmas,' said Stevie, laughing, as I paraded around the room.

Grandad Doyle handed me a square parcel, which I knew was a book. Grandad Doyle gave me a book every year and I read and re-read all of them until I got a new one. The room fell silent as everyone watched me peel off the brown paper. As I pulled off the last piece, I stared at the book.

'*The Railway Children* by E. Nesbit.' I ran my fingers over the cover – there were three children running towards a train, waving flags. I opened the first page and breathed it in. When I was little, Mammy had asked what I was doing and I had said that I was smelling the story. Each of my books had its own smell. *Treasure Island* smelled of excitement and adventure, *Just William* smelled of laughter and mischief, and *The Secret Garden* smelled of sunshine and flowers.

'Well?' said Grandad Doyle, winking at me.

I inhaled the printed pages of the book and closed my eyes.

'It smells of…' I began, 'it smells of…' I looked across at Stevie, who was smiling at me. 'It smells of hope,' I said. And everyone clapped.

Grandad Collins left the room and came back, carrying a box. He walked across to Stevie. 'For you,' he said, placing the box on Stevie's lap. Stevie lifted the lid and two little brown eyes peeped out.

Stevie's eyes filled with tears. 'For me?' he said.

Grandad Collins nodded his head.

'To keep?'

'To keep,' said Grandad.

Stevie lifted the little puppy onto his lap and buried his face in the soft brown fur. 'I c-can't,' he stuttered, 'I can't…'

'You can't what, my love?' said Mammy, kneeling down beside his chair.

'I can't speak,' said Stevie, softly, wiping away the tears that were running down his cheeks.

'Take a deep breath, Stevie,' said Daddy.

Stevie took a deep breath. 'Thank you, Grandad, oh thank you.'

'You're welcome,' said Grandad, who looked as if he was going to burst into tears himself.

Malachi had toddled across and started pulling at the puppy's tail.

'Gently,' said Mammy.

'Doggy?' said Malachi.

'Yes, doggy,' said Mammy. 'Stevie's doggy.'

'What are you going to call him, Stevie?' I said.

Everyone was looking at him, he put his head on one side and smiled. 'Can I call him Buddy-two?'

'You can call him any old thing you like,' said Mammy.

'Hello, Buddy-two,' said Stevie very solemnly. 'You're mine now and when I'm strong again, I'm going to take you for walks over the fields.'

None of us knew what to say, because none of us knew if Stevie would ever be strong again.

'That's my boy,' said Daddy. 'Let's work on those legs of yours, shall we?'

Stevie looked around the room. He wasn't smiling; he was looking very serious. 'I *will* get strong,' he said. 'And I *will* take Buddy-two over the fields.'

And in that moment, I think we all believed him.

As evening fell, Father Kelly and some of our neighbours came to join us. Billy Hogan brought his squeezebox and Paddy Sullivan brought his bodhran. Mrs Tully sang 'Down by the Salley Gardens' and Mrs Toomey did some step dancing. Then Father Kelly put his pint of Guinness on the floor and started reciting 'The Lake Isle of Innisfree', his favourite poem. His clear, rich voice filled the room and the sheer beauty of the poem filled our hearts.

I will arise and go now, and go to Innisfree,
And a small cabin build there, of clay and wattles made;
Nine bean-rows will I have there, a hive for the honey-bee,
And I will live alone in the bee-loud glade.

And I shall have some peace there, for peace comes dropping slow,
Dropping from the veils of the morning to where the cricket sings;
There midnight's all a glimmer, and noon a purple glow
And evening full of the linnet's wings.

I will arise and go now, for always night and day
I hear lake water lapping with low sounds by the shore.;
While I stand on the roadway, or on the pavements grey,
I hear it in the deep heart's core.

There was silence in the room as he finished the poem, and then we all started clapping.

I'd let the words wash over me; they made me think of the garden and the peace that I had found there, and the boy that I had grown to care for. I looked around the room at my family and friends and felt blessed and I hoped that Eddie had felt as loved today as I had.

Grandad Doyle said that he believed that all great writers were also great readers, who had learned their craft from the best. Maybe I could write a poem – maybe I could write a poem about the secret garden.

The following Sunday was Kitty's day off and so I called for her on my way to Mass. I knocked on the door and walked into the little room. I dipped my finger in the holy water. 'God bless all here,' I said.

'Amen,' said Mrs Quinn.

'Amen,' said Breda from under the table.

I'd worn my new red coat to show Kitty and I had on my hat and scarf that Granny Collins had made me.

'Well, look at you, Nora Doyle,' said Mrs Quinn, smiling. 'Don't you look the business in your lovely outfit?'

'I got them for Christmas, Mrs Quinn,' I said.

Kitty came running down the stairs. 'Jesus, Kitty,' she said, 'you look like a film star. Doesn't she, Mammy? Doesn't she look like a film star?'

'She does indeed,' said her mammy.

'Stevie says I look like Father Christmas.'

'How is the poor boy?' asked Mrs Quinn.

'He's about the same,' I said. 'Grandad Collins got him a puppy and he says he's going to get strong, so that he can take him over the fields.'

'I shall pray to Saint Jude to intercede on his behalf and grant Stevie a return to full health.'

'I'd be grateful, Mrs Quinn,' I said.

'I wouldn't bother with that feller,' said Breda, poking her head out from under the table. 'I was down on my knees for weeks asking for a little kitten but I didn't bloody get one.'

'He was probably busy,' said Mrs Quinn.

'Or he didn't hear you,' said Kitty. 'On account of the fact that you were probably under the table when you asked him.'

'What difference does that make?' snapped Breda. 'He has God's ears, doesn't he? You're talking out the back of your fat head, Kitty Quinn.'

'Will you take Breda to church with you, Kitty?' said Mrs Quinn.

'No, I won't, Mammy, she has a mouth on her like a sewer.'

'And you have a nose on you like Henry's snout,' said Breda, going back under the table.

'Go fry yer head, Breda Quinn,' said Kitty. 'Let's go, Nora, or we'll be late for Mass and Father Kelly might read our names out from the pulpit.'

We hurried up the lane to the church, passing the time of day with our neighbours as we ran past. We took a seat by the side altar in front of the nativity scene and I lit a candle for Stevie.

'Do you think he will get well again?' whispered Kitty.

'We live in hope, Kitty,' I said.

After Mass we sat on the graveyard wall. 'Do you think that Eddie had a good Christmas?' I said.

'I think he did, Nora, for he was given a grand horse and all the staff were allowed to stand on the steps and watch him riding round the drive.'

'Oh, I'm glad,' I said. 'For I feared he might be lonely.'

'I think he was happy, he looked happy. But then again, who wouldn't be happy after being given a horse? Do you fancy a walk out the Strand?'

'I'm sorry, Kitty, but I have a mind to go to the garden,' I said.

'Alright,' said Kitty, sadly.

'I'll tell you what, I won't stay long and I'll call for you on the way back.'

'That would be grand,' she said, smiling.

We said goodbye and I headed for the garden. There was a cold wind blowing in off the sea and I was glad that I had on my new hat and scarf. I squeezed through the gap in the fence and hurried down the path. The gate was open and I walked into the garden, expecting to see Eddie, but it wasn't Eddie that was standing there, it was a lady. The one I had seen at Mrs Hickey's funeral a few years back and in the back of the posh car being driven by Pat Lamey. We stared at each other. I couldn't move, my feet seemed frozen to the grass that I was standing on. I felt sick in my stomach. She was wearing a green woollen cloak that came down below her knees and a hood that hid most of her hair except for a few curls that framed her pale face; they were the colour of gold and they shone in the thin winter sun that filtered down through the tall trees. She was indeed beautiful, but the sneer on her lips as she glared at me made her ugly.

'What is your business here?' she snapped.

I tried to speak but my mouth was as dry as sawdust.

'I asked you a question and I expect an answer.'

My heart was racing out of my chest and my legs were shaking so much that I feared I would fall to the ground. The lady's mouth curled downwards, she looked at me as if I'd crawled out from under a stone. This woman hated me for some reason and I was scared. I stared at the little pond and the swing that Eddie had made for me and they no longer felt safe. Every bone in my body screamed at me to run.

'Well?' she demanded.

I swallowed. 'I came to see Eddie,' I stuttered.

She glared at me. 'Eddie, is it? He's Master Edward to you, missy.'

Something in the way she said it made me feel angry, and I stopped feeling scared. Eddie was my friend and it was Eddie who had invited me into the garden. I lifted my chin and straightened my back.

'He's Eddie to me,' I said, glaring back at her.

We stood facing each other, neither of us speaking, and then she smiled, a cruel smile that didn't reach her eyes.

'You're the Ryan girl, aren't you?'

'No, I'm not,' I said.

'Don't lie to me.'

'I'm not lying.'

For a moment she looked confused and then she laughed, a mean horrible laugh that echoed round the garden. 'Of course,' she said. 'Your mother married the milkman, didn't she?'

'What's it to you if she did?' I shouted.

'You'd be surprised,' she said, taking a step towards me.

I stepped back; I didn't want to breathe the same air that she was breathing. There was something repulsive about her. Her sickly perfume invaded the little garden, overpowering the sweet smell of the earth and poisoning its innocence. It filled my nostrils and clung to my new red coat.

She took a step closer, her eyes narrowing and her lips seeming to disappear into her mouth.

'Now listen to me, girl, and listen well,' she snarled. 'You will leave this place and you will never return. You will neither see, nor speak, to my nephew again. Do we understand each other? You will never see Edward again. Now go, or I will have you up in front of the judge for trespass.'

I turned from her and ran. I didn't know where to go, I didn't know what to do. I longed for comfort, but I didn't know where to find it. I ran blindly through the town and up to the graveyard; I had to tell someone. I knelt down in front of my namesake's grave and cried as if my heart was breaking in two. I would never see the garden again; I would never see it change as the seasons changed. I wouldn't be there when the daffodils and crocuses and tulips that we'd tenderly planted together burst from the soil. I would never see Eddie again.

'Oh, Nora,' I cried, 'you must have seen what happened. Tell me what to do, for I am lost. Send me a sign so that I can go on, for I need comfort at this time.'

But as my words drifted out into the silence of this cold grey place, I knew that no sign would come, I knew there were no miracles here.

I looked across the field at the rows and rows of wooden crosses that tumbled down the hill to the workhouse and thought this to be the saddest place in the world. I ran my finger over the lettering scratched into the little wooden cross. *Nora Foley.* The young girl that I had been named for. Mammy's little friend, who had been taken up to Heaven when she was still but a child.

I shivered as an icy wind blew through the trees and across the field but I didn't move, for I had nowhere to go that would bring me any comfort. Maybe I even welcomed being in this loneliest of places, maybe love and laughter had no place in my heart this day. I lay my head on Nora's grave and sobbed. I don't know how long I remained there but the sky had grown dark and suddenly the place scared me.

I could hear footsteps behind me on the frozen ground but I didn't turn around and then I felt a familiar comforting arm around my shoulder. I leaned into Mammy and cried.

She didn't ask me what was wrong, she just held me against her as we sat there on the cold ground and as the light faded from the sky, I told my story.

CHAPTER TWENTY-THREE

I waved to Daddy until he was out of sight. Mammy had gone into the warmth of the bar but I'd stayed at the railings, watching the last of the green hills of Ireland disappearing into the mist.

Me and Mammy were going to England and I didn't know why; I didn't want to leave home but Mammy said she wanted to visit some old friends and she thought the change would do me good. I stared at the grey choppy waters that were taking me further and further away from Paradise Alley. Maybe Mammy was right, maybe it would do me good to get away from the garden and the memory of Caroline Bretton's ugly face, for now I knew who she was.

It had been four weeks ago that Father Kelly had spotted me lying beside Nora's grave and it was him that had run to fetch my mammy. It had felt good to tell her about the garden and about my friend Eddie. The more I talked, the calmer I felt and the burden I had been carrying round for so long seemed to fall from my shoulders. Mammy had listened to my story. She hadn't scolded me, she had just held me in her arms and it was shortly after that she had talked about going to England.

As the boat sailed into the harbour, we joined a queue of people waiting for it to dock.

'Is this London, Mammy?' I said as we hauled our cases down the gangplank.

'No, this is Wales. We have to get on a train now, it will be late when we get to London.'

'Are we being met?'

'We are, some friends of mine will come to fetch us.'

'Why have you never mentioned your English friends before?'

'Oh, it was a long time ago, Nora, and I was too busy with you and Stevie and Malachi to be reminiscing about all that.'

'I suppose you were,' I said.

The train journey seemed endless, but it was exciting too. I had never left Ireland and it began to feel like an adventure. It was dark outside so I couldn't see much of this new country that I had found myself in, just my own ghostly reflection staring back at me through the window.

Mammy was asleep as we pulled into Paddington Station. She looked so peaceful that I didn't want to wake her, but people were pulling cases down from the racks above our heads and putting on their coats. I knew that we had arrived in London. I shook her gently and she stirred.

'How long have I been sleeping?' she said, rubbing her eyes.

'Most of the journey,' I said, grinning.

'You should have woken me up.'

'I hope your friend has a comfy bed, Mammy,' I said, yawning. 'For that's all I'm good for.'

We stepped down from the train, lugging the cases behind us. The sharp smell of burning coal and the white smoke billowing in front of us reminded me of *The Railway Children* – the bit where Bobbie's daddy emerges from the mist and she runs into his arms. I missed my own daddy already and I hoped our stay in England wouldn't be too long. I looked up at the glass ceiling above my head and it felt like I had stepped into another world; everyone seemed to be in such a hurry. No one hurried in Ballybun unless they were late for Sunday Mass. Porters were rushing along, pushing trollies loaded with cases, and overtired children were screaming. The excitement I had been feeling as we'd crossed the sea was rapidly disappearing. It was all so different to the life I knew in Ireland. I had a fierce desire to be tucked up in my own little bed in Paradise Alley and not here amongst all these strangers and all this noise.

Someone was shouting Mammy's name and then I saw a nun hurrying across the platform. She was laughing and crying as she held her arms out towards Mammy.

'Sister Luke,' Mammy said, hugging her.

'And don't tell me that this beautiful young girl is Nora?' said the nun, smiling at me.

'It is, Sister,' said Mammy.

The last person I was expecting to see in this heathen country was a nun, but she looked kind and I allowed myself to be enveloped in her ample bosom.

'Come on, then,' said Sister Luke. 'I have a taxi cab waiting outside.'

Mammy put her head on one side and smiled. Sister Luke laughed.

'I know what you're thinking, Cissy Ryan, but I can assure you it is completely above board this time. I haven't deprived the poor of it. The Bishop in his wisdom has allocated us an emergency fund to use as we see fit, and I think it is perfectly fitting that we should ride home in a cab.'

'I thought that perhaps Sister Mary would be here too,' said Mammy.

'We lost her, Cissy, about a year ago; it took a lot of prayers and a lot of tears to get over that one.'

Mammy looked sad. 'She was lovely,' she said.

'She was a harridan most of the time but I loved her, Cissy. It's been very hard. Remember her in your prayers.'

'I will, Sister, oh, I will.'

I hadn't wanted to come on this journey, I hadn't wanted to do anything but stay in my room. But I'd hardly eaten a thing since my confrontation with Caroline Bretton and I knew that everyone was worried sick about me; maybe that's why Mammy decided to take me here for a bit of a holiday. I leaned forward in my seat and looked at the lights of London, reflected in the inky black river, as we drove over a bridge.

'This is Vauxhall Bridge, Nora,' said Mammy. 'Isn't it lovely?'

It was grand alright, but not as lovely as our own bridge over the Blackwater.

Sister Luke was sitting up in front with the driver and I could hear her chatting away to him.

'What's with the nun?' I said. 'Is she the friend you've been telling me about?'

'She is, Nora.'

'I don't understand, Mammy.'

'I know you don't, love. I know you don't,' she said, reaching across the seat and holding my hand. 'But I'll explain soon, I promise.'

We eventually pulled into a long drive and as we got closer, I could see that the building in front of us was a convent. What were we doing at a convent? In fact, what were we doing in this country at all?

When I opened my eyes the following morning, the first thing I saw was Mammy, standing at the window, looking out over the gardens.

'Have you been awake long?' I said, pulling myself up in the bed.

Mammy turned around. 'Not long,' she said. 'Sister Luke came in earlier but she didn't want to wake you.'

'I must have been dead to the world.'

'You were,' said Mammy, coming across and sitting on the bed.

'What are we doing here, Mammy?'

She reached out and held my hand, 'I will explain everything soon.'

'Ah, you're awake,' said Sister Luke, coming into the room. 'Now before you see Mother, Cissy, let's get some breakfast down you, the pair of you must be in need of sustenance.'

We'd hardly eaten since leaving Ireland and even though I was still feeling confused about why we were here, I realised that I was starving.

'Sister Monica is cooking up a storm in the kitchen, and don't worry, Cissy, she's a better cook than she used to be,' said Sister Luke, laughing. 'She wouldn't be out of place in a grand hotel these days.'

'We all survived,' said Mammy, smiling.

'We did, we did,' said Sister Luke.

After we'd eaten, Mammy went off to see the Mother Superior and I went into the garden with Sister Luke. It was so peaceful here. The garden was beautiful, with statues of our Blessed Lady dotted about the lawn. It made me think of home. I was in a strange country but I was amongst my own kind. We passed two nuns on their knees, tending to the plants.

Sister Luke introduced me. 'Welcome home, Nora,' said one of them, standing up. 'I'd give you a hug, but I'm covered in soil.'

She spoke to me as if she knew who I was, but that was ridiculous, as we'd never met. And why had she said 'Welcome home'? This wasn't my home. I'd never been here before. We continued to walk across the lawn. I stopped and looked back at the convent. 'Was my mammy a nun, Sister Luke?'

She laughed. 'Good gracious, child, what put that into your head?'

I shrugged my shoulders. I didn't understand any of this. Everyone seemed to know my mammy, so if she hadn't been a nun, then she must have worked here and if she had, then why was it never mentioned at home?

We turned around and started to walk back. I saw Mammy standing on the steps leading up to the big wooden front door. She waved to me and I ran over to her.

'Sister Luke is lovely,' I said. 'And she's so funny. She speaks very highly of you, Mammy.'

'They are all lovely, Nora, and you're going to love Iggy.'

'Who's Iggy?'

'She's the mother superior. Her real name is Mother Ignatius but we all called her Iggy.'

'How do you know them, Mammy?'

She linked her arm through mine and we walked down the frosty lawn to an old bench. 'This is where I used to sit with my friends, Nora,' she said.

'I asked Sister Luke if you had once been a nun.'

Mammy laughed. 'No, love, I was never a nun. I don't think they would have taken me – I was far too opinionated.'

'I don't understand any of this.'

Mammy took hold of my hand and held it in her lap. 'What I am about to tell you, my darling girl, is going to come as a shock, and I hope that once I have told my story, you won't hate me.'

'I could never hate you, Mammy, why would you say such a thing?'

She closed her eyes and took a deep breath. 'This is where you were born, Nora, here in this convent.'

'I was born here? In England? And not in Paradise Alley?'

Mammy nodded.

'But why? Why was I born here?'

'Because I fell in love with a boy when I worked at the Hall.'

'Was it Daddy? When he delivered the milk?'

'No, love, it wasn't your daddy. It was a lad with brown curly hair and blue eyes, who could charm the birds off the trees.'

'Curly hair like mine?'

'Just like yours, love, exactly like yours. I was a foolish girl, Nora, and I thought he loved me. I found myself pregnant with you. I was young and I was scared. I couldn't shame my family and I couldn't hurt Colm, your daddy, who I'd realised too late was the boy I truly loved.'

I could feel hot tears stinging behind my eyes. 'So, Daddy isn't my daddy? And Grandad Doyle isn't my grandad?'

'Your daddy *is* your daddy, Nora; he always has been and he always will be. He couldn't have loved you more if you had been his own child and it's the same with your grandad – why, you're more like him than his own son. There was never any question but that you belonged to them both. It isn't just blood that makes a family, Nora – it's being there for that person, it's wanting the best for them, it's caring more for them than you care for yourself. It's love, Nora, and they have always loved you. Your daddy didn't want me to bring you here. He was scared that once you knew who your real father was, you wouldn't love him anymore, but he knew in his heart that you had a right to know the truth.'

'How did you end up in London?'

'Father Kelly arranged for me to come to England, to come here to this place. I told your granny and Colm that I had a job here. I left everyone I loved and travelled to a strange country. I didn't know what lay ahead of me and I was lost but I knew it was the only thing I could do. I was planning to have you adopted, Nora, and then return to Ireland and marry Colm but when I looked into your sweet face, I knew that I could never let you go. I would stay in England, get a job and keep you by my side.'

'But you didn't?'

'I went to work for a woman called Mrs Grainger, who gave me a position in her house and promised to take care of you until I got back on my feet and was able to care for you myself. I believed her, Nora, so did the nuns. I trusted her, but she tricked me and stole you away.'

I couldn't take in what Mammy was saying. 'I was kidnapped?'

'I thought you were lost to me for ever, I thought that I would never see you again, so I went back to Ireland and told Mammy and Colm the whole story.'

'How did you get me back?'

'My friend Mary was emigrating to America.'

'The girl that went down with the *Titanic*?'

Mammy nodded. 'Me and Colm and Father Kelly went to Queenstown to see her off. It was there that I saw Betsy, a young girl who had worked in the house with me. She had spotted me and was waving from the deck and calling my name. I knew immediately that she was with Mrs Grainger and that they were about to sail to America.'

'So you saved me?'

'I would have turned the boat upside down to find you, Nora.'

'What happened to the woman who tried to steal me? Did she drown like your friend Mary?'

'I never knew what her fate was, Nora, and I had no mind to find out.'

I turned to Mammy and she held me in her arms. We were both crying now.

'My poor mammy,' I said. 'My poor, brave mammy.'

'You forgive me, Nora?'

'There is nothing to forgive. You kept me and you saved me and I love you for it.'

Mammy smiled her sweet smile and wiped away her tears. 'I thought you would be ashamed of me.'

'I'd never be ashamed of you, Mammy; you were brave and strong and you found me and you brought me home.'

We sat side by side looking up at the convent where I had been born. My mammy must have been so scared and so lonely when she had left her home and everyone she loved. She had been just a young girl, who had no idea what lay ahead of her. I'd heard of places in Ireland where the girls were treated badly and made to feel ashamed of what they had done. I could see that this place was full of love and that made me so happy.

'There is one more thing that you need to know, Nora,' she said.

'Is it about my real father?' I said, softly.

Mammy nodded. 'His name is Peter Bretton.'

Now I knew why Mammy never wanted me to go anywhere near Bretton Hall.

'Does he know about me?'

'That is something I have never been sure of. I married the boy I loved; I had my family. I was happy, living in Paradise Alley, I had everything I wanted and thought could never be mine. Whether Peter knew about you or not didn't seem so important.'

I started to cry, great heaving sobs, my whole body shuddering.

'Talk to me, Nora,' Mammy said, gently.

'Eddie is my brother?' I said, when I was able to speak.

'Edward Bretton is your half-brother. That is why I had to tell you the truth, Nora. That is why I had to bring you here, because of your friendship with him.'

'I want to be alone for a while, Mammy, do you mind?'

'Of course I don't mind.'

I walked away from her. I had so much to think about. I had always been confused about my feelings for Eddie and now it all made sense. He was my brother, just like Stevie and Malachi. I smiled to myself; I had three brothers now and I loved them all.

I remembered how I'd felt the first time I'd laid eyes on Bretton Hall. It was the day that Kitty and I had squeezed through the broken fence and into the grounds and there at the top of the sweeping lawn sat the house, bathed in sunshine, as if the bricks were made of pure gold. I remember that it felt strangely familiar, as if I knew the place, as if I'd walked through those rooms; I remember wanting to be alone.

I had my story now, and it was more dramatic than Stevie's and Malachi's had ever been. I didn't just have one hero, I had a convent full of them. And I had my family.

CHAPTER TWENTY-FOUR

We had stayed in England for a week and now, as the boat sailed slowly into Cork harbour, I scanned the crowds waiting on the quayside, searching for his face. And then I saw him – he was smiling and waving. I thought we would never get off the boat, I felt like jumping over the side and swimming to him, but I joined the queue of people dragging their cases and edging their way down the gangplank. And then I was in his arms and we were both laughing and crying. He took my face in his hands and looked into my eyes, searching for the words that he had been waiting for.

'I love you, Daddy,' I said. 'I love you.'

There on the quayside, surrounded by people, I let him know that he was still my daddy and the only daddy that I would ever need.

'Let's go home, Nora,' he said. 'Let's go home.'

The three of us held hands and walked towards Father Kelly's car, that would take us back to Ballybun and the Grey House.

As the car turned into Paradise Alley, my heart was full of joy. This is where I belonged; this is where I would always belong. I might have Bretton blood in me but I was the girl from Paradise Alley and I always would be.

They were all there waiting for us. Granny and Grandad Collins and Stevie and Malachi. Buddy-two was barking and jumping up at us as if we'd been gone a year. I looked around for my Grandad Doyle but he wasn't in the room. Why wasn't he here to welcome me home? Hadn't he missed me? And then he came in from the kitchen, carrying a cake with candles on it, put it down on the table and walked towards me. He held me in his arms and I breathed in the smell of him. He smelled of pipe smoke and hay. He smelled of my beloved grandad.

'Happy birthday, Nora,' he said, smiling.

'But it isn't my birthday, Grandad,' I said.

'And what do we care about that? I don't think we'll be hung for it.'

I put my arms around him. 'I've missed you, Grandad,' I said.

'And I've missed you too, my little Nora.'

Stevie was sitting by the fire and I walked across to him.

'I missed you,' he said.

'And I missed you too, Stevie, but I'm home now.'

'What was England like, Nora?'

'It was full of people and cars and carts and noise, and there was a grand big river called the Thames. When you looked along the length of it, there were lots of bridges and boats and tall cranes that reached up to the sky.'

'That must have been a fierce sight, Nora.'

'It was, but I had no mind to stay there, I was desperate to come home and anyway, the river looked dirty and grey, not like our own Blackwater.'

'You'll never guess what I did while you were gone,' said Stevie.

'And what was that, love?'

'I walked around the yard with Buddy-two,' he said. 'And I did it on my own.'

I looked over at Daddy. 'He did, you know,' said Daddy. 'He walked all on his own.'

Mammy knelt down beside me and put her arms around Stevie. 'My brave, clever boy.'

'I told you I'd do it,' he said, grinning. 'And I did.'

'Yes, you did,' said Mammy, laughing.

We ate the cake and we laughed, and we talked and I felt blessed to have my family around me.

I was determined to go back to the garden and not give a care who saw me. Eddie had as much right to know the truth as I did. Miss Caroline had said if she saw me there again, she would have me up in front of the judge for trespass, but I didn't care. I was going to see Eddie, with or without her approval.

The next morning, I called for Kitty. We walked down to the quayside and sat on the wall and I told her my story.

'Jesus, Kitty,' she said. 'I can't believe it, you're really an Honourable?'

'I'm half an Honourable,' I said.

'And Master Edward is your brother?'

'My half-brother.'

'Never mind that, girl, you're an Honourable alright. Maybe I should be bobbing to you.'

I grinned. 'Try that and I'll push you off the wall.'

'How does it make you feel?'

'How does what make me feel?'

'Being an Honourable?'

'I don't feel any different, Kitty. Mammy says it takes more than blood to make a family.'

'I'd say she's right about that, but it doesn't change the fact that their blood runs through yours.'

'I'm trying not to think about it, for it doesn't change who I am.'

'Does Eddie know?'

'I don't think he does and that makes me kind of sad.'

We sat on the wall and watched the fishing boats coming in and out and the fishermen emptying their catch onto the stones and the seagulls circling overhead and I thought again how happy I was to be back in Ballybun.

'Do you think Master Peter knows that he is your father?'

'I think he does, Kitty, for I believe it was him that came into the café and left me the money. But I have a daddy who I love and I don't need another one.'

'I'd be up there hammering on the door and demanding a share of what was rightfully mine.'

'No, you wouldn't,' I said, grinning.

'Do you realise that you are now in a different class to the rest of us?'

'Half a class,' I said, smiling.

'What are you going to do about Eddie?'

'I'm going to go to the garden and hope to God that he's there.'

'When do you intend going?'

I hadn't really thought about it, but suddenly I knew. 'Now,' I said. 'This very minute.'

'I'll bring a grand sandwich to the jail, so that you won't go hungry.'

'I have a feeling that even if Miss Caroline does find out that I've been there, she won't do a thing about it.'

'What makes you so sure?'

'Because she won't want the town to know that she is related to a girl from Paradise Alley.'

'I think you're right, for she's a terrible snob. My mammy says she's a baggage and she doesn't think that her bodily functions smell like those of the rest of us.'

'Your mammy cracks me up.'

'She cracks me up as well, Nora.'

We said goodbye and I walked out towards the Strand and turned down the lane that ran alongside the Hall. The closer I got, the more nervous I became, but I held my head high and kept walking. As I turned the corner, I stopped. At first, I couldn't make out what I was seeing. I rubbed my eyes and looked again: the fence had gone and in its place was a high wall.

CHAPTER TWENTY-FIVE

Father Kelly came to see me every day. He sat by my bed and read out joyful passages from the Bible.

'This is a favourite of mine, Nora,' he said. '*May the God of hope fill you with joy and peace, as you trust in Him. So that you will overflow with hope by the power of the Holy Spirit.*'

I closed my eyes and I let his words wash over me. I felt nothing; not joy or hope, not even sadness. I felt nothing and there was a strange kind of peace in that. I was a child again; I was being taken care of like a child. I didn't have to worry about anything, I just had to be.

Grandad Doyle read to me every evening. He had chosen to read *Anne of Green Gables*, which was perfect. I loved the feisty little orphan, who was always getting into trouble without meaning to. Her friendship with the sweet Diana Barry, who she called her bosom friend and kindred spirit, made me think of Kitty.

I overheard Dr Kennedy telling Mammy that I was suffering from exhaustion of the mind.

'I shouldn't have taken her to England,' said Mammy. 'It was too much for her, I brought this on.'

'I don't think you did, Cissy. I saw Nora when she came back from England and she seemed fine. She seemed to have accepted what she had learned about her birth. No, I believe there is more to this than we know about and Nora isn't able, or willing, to tell us what it is.'

'What are we to do, doctor?'

'Be patient, give her time, don't demand anything from her. For now, that is all you can do.'

I hadn't cried and I hadn't spoken a word. The words were there alright; my head was full of them. They sat on my tongue, they hovered on my lips, but the effort of speaking them was too much and so I stayed silent. It seemed I couldn't voice how that wall had made me feel. It had shut me out, it had put me in my place and it meant I could never see Eddie or the garden again. Even the worry on the faces of the people I loved didn't bring the words from my mouth.

Most days, I sat in the yard and sometimes, if it was warm enough, Stevie would sit next to me. Mammy wanted him to get as much fresh air as he could. Although there was no conversation between us, it was a comfortable silence. Stevie, more than anyone, seemed to understand and demanded nothing from me but my silent company.

As the weeks went by, I began to feel a change inside me. I didn't want to be here, doing nothing and saying nothing. And yet the thought of being anywhere else frightened me. One afternoon, me and Stevie walked slowly across the yard to Bonnie's field, with Buddy-two running ahead of us. I leaned on him as he had once leaned on me. I took baby steps; my legs weren't used to walking. I rested on the fence and watched Bonnie galloping around. The sun was shining, I closed my eyes and lifted my face up to the sky. I opened my mouth and breathed in the warm air and felt it seeping through my body, wrapping itself around my frozen heart. Then I saw the crocus, a small little flower that had bravely pushed through the soil to welcome in the beginnings of spring. It made me think of the garden and the bulbs that me and Eddie had planted. I knelt down and touched the soft purple petals and then I was sobbing, great shuddering tears that seemed to come from the very depths of my soul. All the tears that I had been keeping inside were released in a torrent so wild that I could hardly breathe. I was gulping for air, I was clawing at my throat. Stevie screamed for Mammy, who came running across the yard, and then I was in her arms and she was whispering words of comfort and rubbing my back and brushing back the hair that was sticking to my face. We stayed like that until I was calm. I closed my eyes and lay quietly in Mammy's arms. Stevie held my hand and Buddy-two licked my wet cheeks. I felt safe and loved.

'You're going to be alright now, my love,' said Mammy, gently. 'You're going to be alright, my Nora.'

Slowly, I began to feel better. Father Kelly brought Holy Communion up to the house and neighbours left stews and cakes on the doorstep. Minnie brought fresh bread every evening and it was lovely to see her. I didn't feel strong enough to go back to the café – I wasn't sure when I could ever go back, or even if I had a mind to.

Kitty visited me on her days off and even though I was poor company, she continued to come. She didn't seem to mind that I said very little and I didn't mind her ranting on about her job at the Hall.

'I'm sick of it up there, Norah, and I'd give anything to leave, but there's no work in this Godforsaken town, so what am I to do?'

I just smiled gently at her but I was unable to offer any advice. I was poor company indeed. I loved Ballybun, but Ballybun was home to the Brettons, and every time I thought about them, I could feel myself slipping back to that dark place and it frightened me. Something had to change, but I didn't know what. All I knew was that I couldn't stay in this town. I prayed every night to Saint Therese, who was the patron saint of flowers. I prayed for her wisdom and guidance. I asked her to find me a place where I would be at peace.

One morning, I sat at the kitchen table with Mammy and I told her about the wall.

'They must be very frightened of you to do that,' she said.

'But why would they be frightened of me? What harm can I do them?'

'They have a reputation to uphold, Nora, and it seems that they consider you to be a threat.'

'I'm no threat to them, Mammy, and I want nothing from them. I just wish I could see Eddie again.'

'I know, love, but I'm not sure that's wise.'

'I'm not feeling very wise, Mammy.'

'What would make you happy, Nora?' she said, reaching across the table and holding my hand. 'I just want you to be happy.'

'I want to be somewhere else, Mammy; I want to be away from this town.'

'You want to leave us?' said Mammy, frowning.

I nodded. 'I'm sorry.'

Mammy stood up and walked over to the window. I knew I'd hurt her, but she had to know what I was feeling. She turned around and smiled at me. 'If that is what you want, Nora, then we will all have to put out heads together and make it happen, for your happiness is more important to me than the thought of you leaving us.'

As I grew stronger, I was able to help Mammy a bit more. I took Malachi for walks. I pointed out the flowers that were now springing up all around us. The bright yellow daffodils, the tulips, the pretty white hawthorn wrapping itself around the hedgerows, the sweet crocuses in all their delicate glory and beautiful colours and the yellow spiky flowers of the forsythia. I taught Malachi the names of the flowers, just as Eddie had taught me.

I never walked beyond the boundaries of my home, not even down Paradise Alley. I wondered if I ever would – until the afternoon Minnie came to the Grey House.

We all sat around the table and listened to what Minnie had to say.

'I've spoken with your mother, Nora,' she began. 'And she tells me that you are looking for a bit of a change.'

'What sort of change?' demanded Stevie.

'A change for the better,' I said, gently.

'You're not going away, are you?' he said.

I shrugged.

'You can't.'

'Didn't you go away, Stevie?' I said.

'But that was because I was ill.'

'And maybe, in a way, I am too.'

We were all looking at Minnie. 'You remember that I told you about my sister?'

I nodded.

'Well, there is a vacancy in the bookshop she manages, and she is looking for a girl. I immediately thought of you, Nora. Is it something you would be interested in?'

I could feel something inside me, like a weight slowly lifting from my shoulders.

'Oh, it is,' I said, smiling at her.

'Where is this bookshop, Minnie?' asked Mammy.

'It's in Dublin, Cissy.'

Mammy frowned. 'Dublin? That's a long way away.'

'But there are trains, Mammy, and I could come home for visits.'

'I don't know, Nora,' she said, shaking her head.

'A bookshop, eh?' said Grandad Doyle.

I smiled at him. 'A bookshop.'

'Now, wouldn't that be something?'

'It would, Grandad, it would really be something.'

'Then I wish you all the luck in the world, girl.'

'But what about the café?' I said, looking at Minnie.

'You know, Kitty came into the café while you were in England and she was going on about how she hated working at the Hall and would rather work in the laundry than spend another day there.'

'I remember her saying that she was unhappy there,' I said.

'Well, she was going on, you know, the way Kitty does. So, if you're interested in going to Dublin, I'll ask her if she would like to work for me. Are you interested, Nora?'

I looked around the table at the people I loved. I didn't want to hurt them but I had to get away and what better place to go than a bookshop? 'I'm interested, Minnie,' I said. 'Oh, I am.'

I looked across at Mammy – I needed her blessing. I couldn't leave my home without it.

'If that is what you want, Nora, then I won't be standing in your way,' she said.

'Neither will I, love,' said Daddy. 'I shall think of you in your grand bookshop in Dublin.'

'I'll try to make you proud.'

'You have always made us proud, Nora,' said Grandad Doyle. 'Stevie?'

'Will you come back and visit us?' he said quietly.

'The first chance I get, Stevie.'

'Promise?'

'I promise.'

'I shall go to the rectory this evening and phone Berry,' said Minnie.

'Berry?' I said.

'My sister's name is Bernadette but she's never liked it, so she calls herself Berry.'

I stood up. 'Do you mind if I walk for a bit?' I said.

'You go ahead, love,' said Mammy.

I stepped outside and walked across to the meadow. I was going to Dublin. I was leaving Paradise Alley.

CHAPTER TWENTY-SIX

Dublin, 1928

As the train took me further and further from my home, the calmer I became. I felt as though all the anxiety and worries of the past few months were disappearing behind me, along with the fields and villages, streams and rivers that rushed past the window. It had been hard to leave and I was scared of what lay ahead of me but I knew without a doubt that I was doing the right thing and the opportunity that Minnie had given me was like a gift from God. I was going to miss my family and I was going to miss Kitty, but I had to get away. The town that I had loved so much had become a kind of prison. I felt as though everyone knew my story and I felt like a fool. I'd tried to explain how I felt to Kitty.

'Well, *I* didn't know it,' she'd said. 'And why do you care what anyone else thinks?'

I was standing at my window, looking out over the field, and Kitty was sitting on my bed. 'I just do,' I'd said, turning around. 'It's like I've had something taken from me, something that is mine alone, that has been talked about and chewed over. Minnie knew, Father Kelly knew and God only knows who else has gossiped about it over a cup of tea. It was *my* story, Kitty, and I was the last to know about it.'

'But leaving Ballybun isn't going to change anything, is it?'

'Not for the people who live here, but for me it will.'

'And what am I to do without you?' she'd said, softly. 'You're my only real friend.'

'I'm sorry, Kitty,' I'd said, 'but this is the only way that I am going to get better. I want to stop feeling like this.'

'Promise you'll write,' she'd said.

I sat down next to her and put my arm around her shoulder. 'Of course, I'll write and I'll visit. And you can come visit me too. You'll be sick of hearing from me.'

'I want you to be happy, Nora. I'm just being a selfish girl, for I'm jealous of all the grand new friends you are going to make in Dublin.'

I'd smiled and held her hand. 'None of them will be as grand as you, Kitty Quinn, and none of them will ever replace you. I promise.'

'I'll just have to let you go then, won't I?'

I nodded. 'But there is something I need you to do.'

'Ask away.'

'I want Eddie to know about the two of us; I want him to know what we are to each other.'

'Are you asking me to scale the wall and go to the garden?'

'Nothing that dramatic,' I'd said, laughing.

I'd taken a letter from under my pillow. 'I want you to give him this. Will you do that for me, Kitty?'

'I will, of course, Nora,' she'd said.

We sat in silence, with tears in our eyes, before we said our goodbyes.

I hauled my cases off the rack as the train pulled slowly into Dublin. I'd been told that I would be met at the station but I didn't know by whom. My tummy felt like it was full of frogs, but there was excitement too. I hadn't expected this to be easy but that was all part of it and I was going to meet my fears head-on. Maybe I was stronger than I thought.

There were people everywhere and noise and new smells; it reminded me of when me and Mammy had arrived in London. I stood looking around. How was I supposed to recognise someone I had never met before? I knew no one and no one knew me; what would I do if no one turned up? I had never felt more alone. Had I just made the biggest mistake of my life? Just as I was considering getting the next train home, I saw a girl tearing across the station towards me. She had a mop of red hair and a smile that warmed my heart and took away my fears.

When she reached me, she bent over double and held her side. 'I thought I was going to be late and you'd be all alone and wondering where the hell I was and wasn't this a desperate welcome for one who had come so far. But the heel of me bloody shoe is falling off and flapping all over the place and it's a wonder I didn't fall over and break me bloody neck.' She stared at me. 'You *are* Nora Doyle, I hope,' she said.

'I am,' I said, laughing.

'Thank God for that. I'm Josie Rafferty.'

'Pleased to meet you, Josie Rafferty,' I said, grinning.

'You look as if you could do with a cup of tea and a bun. I'd treat you, but I haven't a penny on me to call my own.'

'In that case,' I said, 'I'll be glad to do the treating.'

'I can see we're going to rub along a treat, Nora Doyle,' she said, picking up my case.

We walked across the station to the tearooms. 'You grab a table,' she said, 'and I'll get the tea.'

'Thanks,' I said, handing her some pennies.

I found an empty table by the window and sat down. The little tearoom was noisy and busy. People were queuing at the counter, where the cakes were displayed beneath glass domes. Women lifted up their children so the little ones could have a look at the range of buns, tarts, fruit and cream cakes. The waitresses were rushing between the tables, all of which were covered with red and white gingham cloths. As soon as one table emptied, it was occupied again, mostly by families. There was a great deal of laughter and chatter, and sighs of appreciation as plates were set down on tables, napkins unfolded, and forks picked up. I heard the chink of china; cups being set back onto saucers, the lip of the milk jug kissing the rim of a cup and then the gurgle as tea was added straight from the mouth of a pot.

A woman laughed, her voice loud and raucous as it rang out across the tearoom. I loved the bustle of it all; I loved the feeling of movement, people going places and people coming home, and I wondered about their stories and whether they were happy or sad. The café was bigger than Minnie's and a lot busier. As I looked around, it felt strange not to know one single person in there, for most of the people who frequented Minnie's were from the town and there was always someone that I knew. When people came into the café who we'd never seen before, we would call them strangers and it suddenly occurred to me that it was me who was now the stranger.

I smiled at the girl who came to clear my table, straightened my back, and waited for Josie to return. She came back carrying a tray with two teas and two buns on it. 'I hope you like currants,' she said.

'I do,' I said.

'So where are you from?' she said, spooning sugar into her cup.

'County Cork,' I said. 'A little town called Ballybun.'

'I'm from Kerry. My father has an antiques shop and the house is full of the bloody stuff. You can't move for stuffed birds in glass boxes, clocks that don't work and furniture from the Dark Ages. He was expecting me to work in the shop after I left school but I told him I'd rather be boiled in oil than work in that mausoleum of a place. He said I was an ungrateful girl, after he'd raised me and fed me and given me a good home. I told him that I was off to Dublin to see a bit of life and that was that.'

'And have you?' I said.

'Have I what?'

'Seen a bit of life?'

'I have and it's grand and I wouldn't want to be anywhere else, thank you very much. Now if you've finished your tea, we'll catch a bus to the digs. I hope you don't mind sharing a room with me.'

'Not a bit of it,' I said.

'Right then,' said Josie, standing up. 'Your future awaits.'

I liked what she said, because somewhere out there, in this strange new city, on unfamiliar pavements that I was yet to tread, lay my future. I couldn't wait to walk towards it.

CHAPTER TWENTY-SEVEN

The first time I walked into Finnigan's bookshop, it felt like a kind of homecoming. I breathed in the smell of old and new books and papers and wood and dust. The shelves reached up to the ceiling and ran the length of the ground floor. There was a long table holding old maps and rolled-up parchments, yellow with age and brittle to the touch. At the back of the shop was the children's section. It was full of brightly coloured books, stacked higgledy-piggledy on the shelves, as if someone had thrown them up there. There were a couple of overstuffed chairs pushed back against the wall, inviting the young readers to curl up and while away the afternoon, losing themselves in the wonderful stories that were waiting to be discovered within the pages.

Upstairs was the antiquarian section; old books from writers long gone. Names I had never heard of. Milton, Swift, Pope and many more. Most of the books were leather-bound, in reds and dark greens and creamy yellows. Some of them scuffed from much use and some of them so perfectly preserved that it looked as if they had never been opened. This room smelled different and hard to describe. A mixture of sweetness and decay, like rotting flowers and almonds. It smelled of lives once lived and stories once written. I wished that Grandad Doyle was here beside me to see it.

Miss Berry was amazed that I knew what the word antiquarian meant and I told her I had learned it from my grandad, who was a great reader.

'I can see that you have a love of books, Nora,' she said, smiling at me. 'It will stand you in good stead here at Finnigan's and your enthusiasm for the written word will encourage our younger readers. But for now, you will dust, and let me warn you that it's a thankless task, for as soon as your back is turned, those clever little mites will settle right back to where they were before. Dusting will serve two purposes, Nora: firstly, it will make the shop look loved, and secondly, you will learn where all the different books are kept, so that when a customer comes in and asks for a particular book, you can guide them to the right section. I hope you will be happy with us, Nora, and that you grow to be proud to call yourself a Finnigan's girl.'

Miss Berry was as different to Minnie as she could possibly be. Minnie was small and round and Miss Berry was tall and angular. She was very business-like and at the beginning I was a bit afraid of her, but Josie soon put my mind at rest.

'She's strict, but she's fair. She makes it her business to look out for us all and she has a good heart.'

'Is she married?' I said.

'She keeps her private life very private but I think she lives alone. There has never been any mention of a man.'

I thought it was unusual that both Minnie and Miss Berry were without men in their lives.

'I think she has her head screwed on,' said Josie. 'At least she isn't saddled with a load of kids.'

I missed my family so much that sometimes I ached with the need to hold them and be held by them. At night, as Josie snored gently in her bed, I let my mind wander back to my home. Sitting on the rocks under the lighthouse and listening to the ocean rushing over the sand. In my dreams, I walked along the wood road with Kitty by my side, and I ran up Paradise Alley like I had as a child. Distance had made me feel kindlier towards Ballybun. It began to lay more gently on my mind – I didn't get that awful feeling in my tummy when I thought about it. I still wasn't ready to think about the Brettons, though, and I never let my thoughts go back to the garden, because my last memory was of Caroline Bretton standing by the pond, shouting at me.

Isn't the mind a strange thing? All the wonderful memories I had of me and Eddie working side by side, planting and digging the soft soil. The passing of the seasons, sitting together on the bench as snow fell around us. All those wonderful moments had been tainted by that one moment. Caroline Bretton's cruel face would sometimes have me waking in a cold sweat with my heart thumping out of my chest.

The digs were in Skinners Row, just a couple of streets away from the bookshop. Josie and me had a nice bedroom – there wasn't much furniture in the room, just a wardrobe, a chest of drawers and two single beds, but it was comfortable enough. The room overlooked a busy street that was lined with shops. Dublin reminded me of London – so many people rushing about, carriages and cars passing the door. It was as different to sleepy Ballybun as it was possible to be. Paradise Alley never changed and I knew that however far I travelled from Ballybun, everything there would remain the same always, and that gave me comfort. We shared a kitchen with two sisters who lived on the floor above. They were called Ellis and Molly. You could tell that they were sisters for they had the same colouring; green eyes and the most beautiful coloured hair I had ever seen. It was a deep auburn, streaked with shades of burnt orange and chestnut, russet and burnished copper. It reminded me of an autumn day in the garden, when sunlight filtered through the trees, changing the colour of the leaves as they drifted to the ground. I would have died for hair like that. But although they looked alike, they couldn't have been more different. Molly was loud and full of life while her younger sister Ellis was a shy little thing. They also worked at Finnigan's, so every morning, the four of us walked the short distance to the bookshop and every evening, we walked home together.

Our landlady's name was Mrs Murphy, and the poor soul was as deaf as a post. She lived quietly downstairs and never bothered us.

It was my first week in the flat and I was chatting to Molly and Ellis in the tiny kitchen. 'Jesus, Nora,' said Molly. 'The landlady in the last place would have made the Blessed Virgin Mary herself curse. The slightest squeak out of us would have her running up the stairs like a bloody madwoman – we were frightened to move, she had our brains mashed. Josie let us know that there was a vacant room here, we couldn't get out of the place quick enough.'

'Where are you from?' I said.

'Derry,' said Ellis.

'You're far from home,' I said.

'Not far enough,' said Molly, making a face.

'We come from a big family,' said Ellis softly.

'There are so many kids in the house that I don't know half of them,' said Molly. 'Honest to God, Nora, one day this boy was walking behind me, right up to the front door of my house. I asked him why he was following me and he said that he was my brother and he lived there.'

We all started laughing. 'Forgive my sister,' said Ellis, grinning. 'She has an awful habit of exaggerating, as you will soon find out.'

'I swear on the statue of St Anthony that it's true,' said Molly.

'Well, next time you lose something, Molly Walsh, and you call on him for help, don't be surprised if he ignores you.'

'I'll take me chance – what's the point of a story if you can't embellish it a bit?'

'There's a big difference between embellishing and downright lying.'

'Well, I hope I get an invite to the Vatican when they make you a Saint,' said Molly, grinning.

I wasn't used to this kind of banter and I loved it. Kitty would always be my best friend but this felt different. We were four young girls, far away from our families and enjoying our freedom in this big city. I felt more grown-up somehow, and Ballybun felt a million miles away.

We didn't do anything very exciting; we were all too tired by the time we got home. Ellis had a love of books just as I did and the pair of us were happy to sit on the bed every evening and lose ourselves in the stories. Molly and Josie, on the other hand, liked looking through the magazines that were full of the latest fashions. They also talked a lot about boys.

'Do you have a feller, Nora?' asked Molly.

'No,' I said. 'I don't.'

'What? Never?' said Molly.

I shook my head. 'Never.'

'Well, you're in Dublin now, girl, so maybe it's time to spread your wings.'

'Leave her alone, Molly,' said Ellis. 'I've never had a boyfriend either.'

'That's because you frighten them all away.'

'I'm just not ready for one,' said Ellis.

'What worries me,' said Molly. 'Is if you'll ever be ready.'

'She might surprise us all,' said Josie, smiling.

Molly made a face at Ellis. 'I won't hold my breath.'

I was growing more and more fond of Josie; I had liked her from the moment I saw her flying towards me across the railway station. She'd taken it upon herself to show me around Dublin. We leaned over the Ha'penny Bridge and watched the River Liffey flowing beneath us. Dublin was a beautiful city and I preferred it to London. I think it was because I was in Ireland and home didn't seem so far away. I felt something change in me as I stood next to Josie, looking down at the river. I was a young girl in a big city, I had found new friends and I was doing a job I loved. I felt a kind of freedom that I had never felt before, and I liked it.

We walked up O'Connell Street and stood outside the GPO building. I'd been far too young to remember at the time, but Grandad Doyle had told me about the Easter Rising of 1916 and how the rebels had taken over the GPO building, only to be overcome by the British Army. He told me about the men who had been executed for the cause. 'I thought that James Connolly and Michael Collins would have been spared, but they were shot along with the rest of them,' he'd said. 'Connolly was only forty-seven, Nora, and Collins thirty-two, but they died for a cause they believed in. They chose what they thought was the right path, even though they must have known it could lead to certain death. They were mourned, for they were heroes to many people who believed in the cause. They became martyrs, Nora, and there is nothing us Irish love more than a martyr.'

'Do you think they were right, Grandad? Do you think they were right to rebel?'

'I keep my thoughts to myself, Nora, and I leave politics to the politicians,' he'd said.

As I looked up at the tall building, I felt sad for all those young men who had lost their lives and I wondered if their deaths had actually changed anything.

'Do you think it was all worth it, Josie?' I said.

'A word of advice, Nora – keep your opinions to yourself, for those who believe in the cause are still amongst us, especially in the pubs, where fighting talk continues and rebel songs are still being passed down from father to son.'

'I'll bear that in mind, Josie,' I said. 'And thank you for the warning.'

'The big family wasn't the only reason that Molly and Ellis left home, you know.'

'Why then?'

'Molly said it was like living in the middle of a war zone – they don't talk about it much but I know it affected Ellis very badly and Molly wanted to get her away from the place.'

'What happened?'

'They were on their way to school when a fight broke out between two rival gangs. Shots were fired and they had to run for cover. Neither of them was hurt, but Ellis was never the same again. She wouldn't leave the house – she was terrified of going outside.

Molly said she seemed to go into herself and she knew that as soon as she could, she would leave Derry and take Ellis here to Dublin.'

'But is there not trouble here, too?'

'There's trouble everywhere in Ireland, but you have to live, don't you? You can't shut yourself away for fear that something is going to happen – sure, you could just as easily get knocked down by a bus. This isn't our war, and I won't let it stop me going where I want to go, or doing what I want to do. It doesn't matter to me whether you're a Catholic or a Protestant, it's who you are that counts. I think that Ireland would be better off if it was run by women – they're too busy minding the home and putting food on the table to have time to be fighting each other.'

'So, you think Dublin is safer than Derry?'

'There are places to avoid, alright, but that's just fights between men who are full of the hard stuff and can't even remember what they are fighting for.'

It made me realise that living in a big city like Dublin was going to be different, and I would have to be aware of my surroundings and the people I met.

One evening, we were all in mine and Josie's room, lying on the beds.

'Are you up for a night out on Saturday, Nora?' said Molly.

'Oh, I don't know,' I said.

'Come on, girl, you look as if you could do with a bit of fun after all that dusting.'

I wasn't sure that I was ready to go out on the town. 'Where are you going?' I said.

'The Irish club in O'Connell Street has a dance every Saturday night,' said Josie. 'And the craic is fierce. If you're lucky, you might meet a nice boy who will sweep you off your feet and carry you away to the country.'

I laughed. 'I'm not sure that I'm ready to be swept off my feet.'

'Then just come along and have an orange juice,' said Ellis gently. 'That's what I do.'

'What do you think, Josie?' I said.

'It's a grand place, Nora, and we could all do with getting out a bit more.'

'I suppose we could,' I said, smiling.

'Don't tell Father Patrick though,' said Josie. 'He's dead against the place. He says it's barbaric and a sin against the Holy Virgin. He read out a letter from the Archbishop the other Sunday. Apparently, in the eyes of the Catholic Church, dance halls are dens of iniquity and not to be countenanced. Then he went on about sensuous contortions of the body. Have you ever heard anything so daft in all your life? It's a dance, not an orgy.'

'But shouldn't we mind what the Church is telling us?' asked Ellis.

'Not when they're talking a load of shite,' said Molly. 'Now, what are we going to wear?'

I hadn't thought about what I would wear. I certainly had nothing suitable for a dance. I felt disappointed, because I really wanted to go.

'Sorry, girls,' I said. 'That counts me out.'

'What does?' said Molly.

'Clothes – I haven't got any, not good enough for a dance anyway.'

'Well, if that's all that's stopping you,' said Ellis, 'you don't have to give it another thought, for we have a wardrobe full of the stuff.'

'They have,' said Josie, grinning.

'Come upstairs and take a look,' said Ellis, jumping off the bed.

The four of us ran up the stairs to Molly and Ellis's room. Molly opened the wardrobe door to reveal a row of beautiful dresses in every colour you could imagine. I stood staring at them, hardly able to take it in.

'Have you been and robbed a store?' I said.

'No,' said Molly. 'They were left to us by our Aunty Birdy. She was a bit of a society girl back in the day. My mother said, rumour had it, she frequented the nightclubs of Paris.'

'Paris, France?'

'The very place,' said Molly.

'I've never known anyone who went to Paris,' I said.

'Well, our Aunty Birdy did,' said Ellis. 'And when she passed away from drinking too much cognac and smoking Egyptian cheroots, at least that's what Grandad said killed her, she had the presence of mind to write a will, leaving all her finery to us.'

'Our grandfather was all for burning the lot of it,' said Molly. 'But I told him that I'd cut off his ear while he slept if he so much as breathed on them.'

'Grandad said that Aunty Birdy was a hussy,' said Ellis.

'But I decided that she was really my mother,' said Molly, 'and that one day she would bang on the door, reeking of French perfume and demand to have me back, then we'd spend the rest of our days sitting by the Seine, eating cheese.'

'And where would that have left me, while you were sat eating your cheese?' said Ellis.

'We wouldn't have left you behind, love, we would have taken you with us.'

'Was Birdy her real name?' I said.

'No,' said Molly. 'Her name was Bridget.'

'So how did she end up being called Birdy?'

'She used to like sitting in trees. Grandfather said she was odd, but I thought that she was…'

'Splendid?' I said, smiling.

'The very word,' said Molly. 'I thought she was splendid.'

'Now, Nora,' said Ellis, 'what's your favourite colour?'

'I don't have one,' I said.

The three of them stared into the wardrobe, as if the perfect dress was going to leap out and throw itself on my body.

'Blue,' said Josie, looking me up and down. 'Definitely blue.'

Two blue dresses were laid on the bed. They might have been from an earlier age but they were beautiful and they were what Grandad Doyle would call timeless. 'Try them on, Nora,' said Ellis. 'We'll look away.'

I chose the one with the high neckline – the other one was lovely but a bit on the racy side. The material felt so cool as it slipped like silk over my body. It fell to just below my knees and as I moved, it spread out in a circle and caressed my bare legs. I took a deep breath. 'Okay, you can look now,' I said.

The three of them stared at me for a moment, without saying a word. 'Don't you like it?' I said, disappointed at their reaction.

'It looks as if it was made for you,' said Ellis, softly.

'Well, all I can say is that the rest of us might as well stay home, for we'll have no chance with the lads once they set eyes on you,' said Molly, making a face.

'Don't be daft,' I said. 'For you're all gorgeous, it's me that should be staying home.'

'I wish we had a mirror,' said Ellis. 'Maybe that would convince you.'

'We have one downstairs,' said Josie. 'Come on, girls.'

We ran back down the stairs and into our room, where the three of them jumped on one of the beds.

'Well, go on,' said Molly. 'We're waiting.'

I hardly recognised the young girl in the blue dress whose reflection stared back at me. It fitted like a glove, with its nipped-in waist and full skirt, the colour of a summer sky. I could feel tears stinging the backs of my eyes. I wanted Kitty beside me, in a beautiful dress that had belonged to a little girl who loved to sit in trees.

CHAPTER TWENTY-EIGHT

Saturday night found the four of us squashed round the one mirror, teasing our hair and pinching our cheeks.

'What's with the pinching?' I said.

'Well, unless you have a bit of rouge on you, it's the next best thing if you want to look fresh and alluring,' said Molly.

'Pinching does all that?' I said, smiling.

'Definitely.'

I had never known the pure enjoyment of getting ready for an evening out. It really did feel as if I was leaving childish things behind me. Kitty had been my best friend and we had only ever needed each other but I loved being one of the girls. I loved being silly and giggly, instead of worrying about things I had no control over. I felt young and free for the first time in a long while and I loved it.

Josie was looking in the mirror and scowling at what she saw.

'Jesus,' she said. 'It looks for all the world as if someone had taken a match to my head and set in on fire.'

'Your hair is gorgeous altogether,' I said. 'Mine's a sight for sore eyes.'

'People pay a fortune to get curls like yours, Nora.'

'I just wish it was long and flowing,' I said.

'Like the Liffey?' said Josie, grinning.

We all laughed and I was grateful to these girls for lifting me out of the dark place that I had been in for so long.

It was only a short walk from our house to the Irish club. We'd linked arms and were taking up most of the pavement. A couple of women glared at us as they stepped into the road to get past.

'God, I hope I never get that old and sour-faced,' said Molly.

'Don't be mean, Molly,' said Ellis. 'How would you feel if they got knocked down by a bus?'

'I thank God every day that I have you as my conscience, Ellis,' said Molly, smiling at her. 'Now let's get to this den of iniquity, before Father Patrick turns up and hauls us home.'

As we got close to the club, I could see a long line of people queuing to get in.

'There's an eejit on the door called Paddy Byrne, who delights in keeping us standing outside in the cold for as long as he can,' said Josie. 'May a plague of wasps fly up his nose when he's asleep.'

I laughed as we tagged onto the end of the queue. We were eventually let in and we followed the crowd to the desk, where we paid our entrance fee.

'You and Ellis, find the seats,' said Molly, gesturing at us, 'and we'll get the orange juice. See if there's any room up in the balcony.'

Ellis caught hold of my hand and I followed her up the stairs. 'There's one,' she said, heading towards an empty table. I sat down and leaned over the balcony. The band had started to play and a woman moved up to the microphone. Everything about her was oversized, from her mass of black hair to her large bosom. Her dress was a deep red, cut low on the shoulders to reveal plump white flesh that spilled over the top of the dress and glistened under the bright lights. She swayed back and forth with a lightness that belied her ample size. Her eyes were closed, as if the music had transported her to her own special place. I thought she was magnificent and when she opened her mouth, the sweetest, richest sound filled the room, drawing the dancers onto the floor. I had been nervous about coming here but now I was excited. The music, the people, the smells, had my head and my heart spinning. I took off my coat and in my blue dress I didn't feel out of place – I felt I belonged as much as the next girl and I couldn't stop smiling.

'Glad you came?' said Ellis, grinning at me.

'Oh yes,' I said. 'I'm really glad.'

'Four oranges,' said Josie, putting the drinks down on the table.

'Have you spotted anyone worthy of our attention?' said Molly.

'We've only just sat down,' said Ellis. 'We've hardly settled ourselves in.'

'It will just be the usual lads,' said Josie. 'I didn't spot any strangers at the bar.'

'We should try another dance hall,' said Molly. 'We've been coming here for months and not one date between us.'

Just then, a young boy came up to the table. He was nice-looking, with fair hair and lovely blue eyes. I became aware that I was staring at him and quickly lowered my eyes – I didn't want him to think that I was on the lookout for a feller. 'Good evening, girls,' he said, smiling.

'Hi Joe,' said Molly. 'How are ya?'

'I'm grand, Molly, and yerself?'

'Oh, you know, Joe, nothing out of the usual.'

'And who's this lovely girl?' said the boy, smiling at me.

'This is Nora Doyle, up from the country,' said Josie.

'Would you care to dance?' he said to me.

'Oh, I don't think so,' I said, feeling myself going red in the face. 'But thank you for asking,' I added quickly.

'How about you, Molly? Fancy a spin round the floor?'

'Why not, Joe?' said Molly, standing up.

I watched the pair of them walk away and took a sip of my orange.

'Have you ever been to a dance before?' said Ellis.

I shook my head. 'Never.'

'It's just that if a lad asks you to dance, it's a kind of an unwritten rule that you accept. You see, they might look full of swagger but it takes a lot of courage to ask a girl out onto the floor.'

'I didn't know that,' I said, feeling silly. 'He must have thought me very rude.'

'He'll get over it. I'm sure it's not the first time that Joe Lynch has been turned down and sure, you weren't to know.'

Ellis and Josie were soon asked up to dance and I was left on my own, feeling very foolish and wishing I hadn't turned Joe down. I looked over the balcony at the dance floor, trying to see them, but it was so crowded that I couldn't spot them amongst the swirling bodies that circled the room. There was a glitter ball hanging from the ceiling, casting prisms of light over the heads of the dancers like so many stars. It was all wonderful and I thought again of Kitty and how she would have loved this. I would write and tell her all about it.

I was aware of someone standing next to the table. 'What's a lovely girl like you doing on your own?' said a large man, grinning down at me. I didn't know what to say to him. He was unsteady on his feet and holding onto the edge of the table for support. 'How about the two of us step outside for some air?'

'No, thank you,' I said.

I had no intention of going outside with him. There was a bit of dribble coming from the side of his mouth, the man was four sheets to the wind and he scared me.

'Think you're too good for me, do you?' he slurred.

I was saved by Joe and Molly coming back. 'I think the lady has made her wishes clear,' said Joe. 'Now be a good chap and move along.'

'And who are you to be telling me to be moving on?' said the man, narrowing his eyes.

'I'm her friend, now move along, or do you want to finish this outside?'

'Sod off,' said the man, and lurched away from us.

I shuddered. 'Thank you,' I said.

'You're very welcome. I can't have you getting the wrong idea about us Dublin folk – we're not all eejits.' Joe sat down beside me. 'Where are you from, Nora?'

'I'm from a small town called Ballybun in County Cork,' I said.

'A long way from home then. You must miss your folks.'

'I do, but it's getting easier.'

'I'm Dublin born and bred. I work in my family's bakery, it's all I've ever done.'

I smiled. 'I love making bread,' I said.

'And where in God's name did you learn to do that?'

'I worked in a little café after I left school and the owner taught me. I found it very relaxing.'

'Then we have something in common already, Nora,' he said.

'We do,' I said.

I thought again how good-looking he was. His hair flopped over his eyes and as he spoke, he kept pushing it back. When he smiled, his eyes crinkled up at the edges and when he laughed, I could see he had a fine set of teeth. I suddenly wanted to laugh – I felt as if I was describing a horse.

'Will you share the joke?' said Joe.

'Oh, it's not that funny,' I said, going red.

I was regretting turning him down, for there was nothing to fear here.

'Feeling braver now?' he said, standing up and reaching for my hand.

I looked across at Josie, who nodded and smiled. 'I am,' I said, putting my hand in his.

This was the first time I'd danced with a boy, but it didn't feel strange when Joe put his arm around my waist and guided me onto the floor. We moved slowly to the music and I felt as if I was in another world. As we danced under the glittering lights, I was aware of his hand lightly touching my back and his soft breath on my cheek. I put my head on his shoulder and it felt as natural as if I'd always known him, which was pretty strange, as we'd only just met.

We danced the night away, occasionally joining the others upstairs to chat and drink orange juice. As the evening came to an end, Joe asked if he could see me again the next week. I hardly knew the boy but I liked him and I'd felt comfortable dancing with his arms around me under the twinkling lights. 'I'd like that,' I said.

'That's grand, then,' he said. 'It was lovely meeting you, Nora Doyle.'

'It was lovely meeting you too, Joe Lynch.'

CHAPTER TWENTY-NINE

I could put Ballybun out of my mind during the day, for I had little time to think about anything else than the bookshop. I didn't mind about the endless dusting that had me sneezing my head off every five minutes. I gradually learned where the different genres of books were located. I was often asked to guide a customer to the right shelf and I could see that Miss Berry was pleased with me when I was able to smile and say, 'Of course, sir, if you would like to follow me.' I loved being surrounded by books and I knew how lucky I was to have landed this job. There was a second-hand section that we were allowed to borrow from. I had started to read books by Henry James. Miss Berry noticed that I was bringing the books back to the shop the day after I'd taken them home.

'Either Mr James is not to your taste, Nora, or you are up all night reading,' she said.

'His sentences are so desperate long, Miss Berry, that by the time I get to the end, I can't remember how they began. I've no mind to be reading another one of his stories.'

'Ah well, Mr James is not to everyone's taste. Have you read anything by Jane Austen?'

'No, I've only read the books we have at home.'

Miss Berry went over to the shelf. '*Pride and Prejudice*,' she said, handing me a book. 'I think this might be more to your taste. I have a feeling that there is more than a bit of Elizabeth Bennet in you.'

'I'll give it a go, Miss Berry,' I said.

I devoured the book and read it every spare minute I could. I fell in love with the dashing Mr Darcy and I laughed out loud at Mrs Bennet's urgency to get all her girls married off to men of good fortune. But I failed to see anything of myself in Elizabeth Bennet, and I wondered what comparison Miss Berry could see.

Yes, I could forget about Ballybun during the day. It was at night, when I fell into an exhausted sleep, that Eddie and the garden found its way into my dreams. I could smell the flowers and the wet earth; I could feel the roughness of Eddie's jacket as he comforted me on the day I thought I had killed my baby brother. In my dreams the garden was always bathed in sunshine, the little robin hopped around us as we worked and the tall trees swayed above our heads. When I woke, it felt like a kind of bereavement and I carried the loss of Eddie and the garden with me all day.

I wrote to Kitty and told her all about Dublin and Finnigan's and the dance. A week later, I got a letter.

Dear Nora,

It was so good to hear from you. I've read your letter over and over. I carry it around with me and Minnie had me read every word out to her. It all sounds lovely, the bookshop, the digs and your new friends. They sound nice and I'm trying not to feel jealous. Oh, I wish I could have seen you in that dress, I'm sure you looked beautiful and had all the boys falling at your feet. Talking about boys, I'm walking out with Tommy Nolan – he started coming into the café and we got to talking. Minnie said he only started coming in since I began working there. He's a nice lad, Nora, and we've got close. The whole family has taken to him – even Breda comes out from under the table when he visits the house. The pair of us really have left childish things behind us, haven't we? It seems a long time ago that we sat on the graveyard wall watching funerals. I miss you, Nora, nothing is the same. I understand why you had to go but it's been very hard without you.

*Write to me again, for I love hearing about your grand new
life in Dublin.*
  I gave Eddie your letter.
  Love always,
  Your friend,
  Kitty xxx

I was happy that Kitty had met someone – I knew how lost I
would have been if she had been the one to leave Ballybun. Kitty
was my true soulmate, just as Diana Barry had been to Anne of
Green Gables, and I loved her.

I was looking forward to seeing Joe again. I'd taken to him right
away – he seemed like a nice gentle lad and it helped that he was
also nice to look at.

'You won't go far wrong with Joe Lynch,' said Josie. 'He's a
catch alright, but none of us has ever stood a chance with him.'

'Why not?' I said.

'He was doing a line with a girl called Maeve Flynn for years –
childhood sweethearts, they were. We were all shocked when they
went their separate ways about a year ago.'

'Do you know why they separated?'

'Maeve said that they had just drifted apart and that's all we
could get out of her. As far as I know, neither of them is seeing
anyone else. Until now, that is,' she said, winking at me.

'I'm not exactly seeing him, am I?'

'Not yet, but he looked mighty keen,' said Josie, grinning.

'It must have been the dress,' I said, blushing.

'Or it might just have been *you*, Nora,' said Josie. 'Stranger
things have happened.'

'Oh, you!' I said, laughing.

Saturday came around again and Molly was standing, looking
into the wardrobe.

'You can't wear the blue one again,' she said.

'How about the green?' said Ellis.

'I've already bagged the green one,' said Josie. 'It shows off my magnificent red hair and I have a feeling that I'm going to cop off with a rich feller tonight.'

'Well, I hope it stays fine fer ya,' said Molly, laughing.

'How about red?' said Josie.

Ellis made a face. 'Definitely not, do you want her to look like a scarlet woman?'

'I wouldn't mind looking like a scarlet woman,' sighed Josie. 'The only thing scarlet about me is my head.'

'Will you stop going on about your bloody hair, Josie. I'll be lucky if I have any left by the time I'm forty,' said Molly dramatically.

'What are you on about, girl?' said Josie.

'My mother has barely a hair left on her head and she's only fifty.'

'I'm desperate sorry about that,' said Josie, looking mortified. 'I won't mention my hair again.'

'If you believe that, you'll believe anything, Josie. Our mother has as fine a head as you will ever see,' said Ellis, laughing.

'You!' said Josie, throwing a pillow at Molly.

I loved all the silliness and banter. I smiled at these new friends of mine and felt blessed.

'I'm wearing the blue dress,' I said, making my mind up.

'Sure, he'll think you have nothing else to wear,' said Molly.

'I don't,' I said. 'And it's not even mine.'

'We'll be sure to bequeath it to you in our will,' said Ellis.

'That's mighty decent of you,' I said.

We sat upstairs at the club again and I looked over the balcony. I felt bubbles of excitement in my stomach as I scanned the crowds on the dance floor, looking for Joe. But as the evening wore on, I knew that he wasn't going to come.

'Something must have come up,' said Ellis, gently.

'Or maybe I put him off,' I said.

'And why in Heaven's name would you think that?'

'I might have been a bit forward, Ellis,' I said. 'For I leaned my head on his shoulder.'

'If you'd eaten the face off him in the middle of the dance floor, I might have agreed with you,' said Molly. 'But sure, there's nothing forward in that.'

During the evening the four of us were all asked to dance and the lads were nice enough, but my heart wasn't in it. The music seemed too loud and it hurt my head and worst of all, I felt like a fool. Josie hadn't met her rich feller and I'd been well and truly stood up. On top of all that, when we got outside, it was pouring with rain. It was a sorry little bunch indeed that tramped home to our digs.

CHAPTER THIRTY

I was more put out by Joe Lynch than I cared to admit. I felt like an eejit, thinking I was grand in my blue dress and that people would only die for hair like mine. I'd got carried away by the excitement in the bedroom and the others oohing and aahing and telling me how lovely I looked. I'd believed them and gone into the Irish club thinking I was God's gift to mankind. When all I was, was a little country girl from Paradise Alley, in a borrowed dress.

It would have helped if the girls had said 'Well, you got off lightly there, Nora' or 'Joe Lynch is full of the old blarney and not to be taken seriously'. But none of them had a bad word to say about him. I was therefore left with only one explanation: that I had somehow put him off and that he was too polite to tell me in person. Well, I wouldn't give the boy another thought. From now on I would stick to Jane Austen and get my fill of romance within the pages of a book, where I could be sure of a happy ending. Mr Darcy had not been the nicest of men when Elizabeth Bennet had first met him but then he turned out to be the most chivalrous feller in the world. It had been the other way around with Joe – he started off lovely and turned out to be a coward.

I felt like getting the next train back to Ballybun and licking my wounds in my bedroom at the Grey House. I could pretend that I was sick again and in need of care and comfort, I could go back to work at Minnie's and forget Finnigan's and Dublin. Then I remembered I couldn't go back to Minnie's, could I? For Kitty was working there now. I wouldn't even have Kitty to turn to, because she was walking out with Tommy Nolan. On top of all that, it had been bucketing down with rain for days and my hair now resembled a burst mattress.

By the end of the week I was getting on everyone's nerves with my long face and sour demeanour. Even Miss Berry had noticed. 'Could you please be less energetic with the dusting, Nora,' she said. 'You are in danger of choking any perspective customers out of the shop.'

'She can't help it, Miss Berry,' said Josie, who was stacking shelves next to me. 'She's been let down by a boy.'

'Well, I'm sorry for your loss, Nora, but a bit less enthusiasm would be greatly appreciated.'

'Why did you tell her that, Josie?' I demanded as Miss Berry walked away.

'I thought I was helping.'

'Well, you're not. Perhaps you'd like to take a walk down to the newspaper office – they might be glad of a story for tomorrow's headlines.'

'Ah, Nora,' said Josie. 'Don't be letting on so. Joe Lynch isn't the only eligible lad in Dublin.'

I put down my duster and sighed. 'I haven't been easy to live with, have I?'

'You haven't been a laugh a minute, if that's what you mean.'

'I'm sorry, Josie. I promise I will put the dratted boy out of my mind. His name won't pass these lips again.'

'Does that mean you'll come to the club tonight?'

'It does not. I'll never step foot in that place ever again.'

'But if you're putting the dratted boy out of your mind, then why not?'

'Because I'll either be looking for him all night, or watching him dancing with every girl in Dublin who is daft enough to be taken in by his blarney.'

'It won't be the same without you, Nora.'

'I can't help that, I've been made to look foolish and I won't be putting myself through that again. Now I'd be obliged if you would change the subject.'

Saturday was our busiest day in Finnigan's and I loved it. The children's section was always full of little ones and their parents. Choosing the right book was a very serious thing indeed and they were taken down from the shelf, stared at and then replaced as another one caught their eye. I spent a lot of time tidying up after them, but it was lovely to see the concentration on their little faces as they snuggled up in the comfy chairs and lost themselves in the stories. It also made a pleasant change from the dusting. The day passed quickly and it was soon time to go home. As we all left the shop, we were delighted to find that the rain had stopped.

'My feet are only hanging off me,' said Molly. 'I hate working in the antiquarian section – the only customers that go up there are old men with smelly pipes who want to know the ins and outs of every single book. How the bloody hell am I supposed to know? I wasn't around when they were written. They're nearer to the author's age than I am.'

Just then Ellis nudged me. 'What?' I said.

She pointed across the street and there, leaning against a wall, was Joe Lynch.

'We'll see you at home then?' said Josie, grinning.

I didn't answer. I was staring at Joe as he crossed the road and walked towards me. My heart was thumping as he got closer.

'Hello, Nora,' he said.

'Hello, Joe.'

'I expect you're angry at me,' he said.

I wanted to throw my arms around him, but what came out of my mouth was, 'And why would I be angry at you? I hardly know you.'

'I don't blame you for being angry,' he said.

'I told you, I'm not.'

'I think that perhaps you are,' he said gently.

'Well, what if I am? You made a fool of me, Joe Lynch. You said you'd meet me at the club but you didn't turn up and you didn't bother to let me know. You just let me go there and be shown up in front of my friends.'

'I couldn't let you know, Nora. I didn't know where you lived.'

'I suppose you couldn't,' I said.

'I remembered you saying that you worked in Finnigan's though, so here I am.'

'Well, at least you have found the decency to tell me in person that you made a mistake, leading me on.'

'I didn't make a mistake and I had no intention of leading you on. I really wanted to see you again.'

'Then why didn't you? Why did you make a fool of me?'

'My father was taken ill and I had to take over the bakery. I couldn't get away until now. I'm truly sorry, Nora, for making you feel bad in front of your friends.'

I wanted the ground to open up and swallow me whole. It hadn't been Joe's fault at all. I had been too quick to judge him and all the while his father had been sick.

'Oh Joe, I'm desperate sorry, I just thought that you had changed your mind and you couldn't face me.'

'Let's say no more about it,' he said, taking hold of my hand.

The sun shone as we walked along together. The warm air smelled fresh and new after the rain, as if the whole city had been washed clean, especially for us. I looked up at Joe's lovely face and I thought that Mr Darcy wasn't fit to wipe Joe Lynch's boots.

CHAPTER THIRTY-ONE

It was official. Nora Doyle and Joe Lynch were walking out. During the next four months we spent every moment we could together and I had never been happier. The sky was bluer and autumn had never been more spectacular. Our favourite place to visit was St Stephen's Green, the beautiful park in the middle of the city. When the weather was fine, we would sit beside one of the two small lakes and watch the ducks paddling by.

It was at these times that we got to know each other. I told him all about Ballybun and Paradise Alley and Stevie and Malachi. I told him about Mammy and Daddy and Grandad Doyle who had given me my love of books. I didn't tell him about Eddie or the garden or the Brettons. Maybe one day I would, but for now, there was no need for him to know and I didn't want to be reminded of it. As I watched the ducks swimming by, I thought that perhaps I was a bit like them. Gliding along as calm as you like, but paddling like crazy underneath, at least where the Brettons were concerned.

I loved listening to Joe talking about the city he had grown up in and loved so much.

'This park may look peaceful now,' he said, 'but in 1916, it was the site of the Easter Rising.'

'I thought that took place in the GPO building.'

'Some of it did, but two hundred and fifty insurgents holed up here in the park. It turned out to be a big mistake and many lives were lost.'

'What happened?' I said.

'See that building over there?' he said, pointing across the park to a large imposing structure. 'That's the Sherbourne Hotel, and it was from there that the British army rained bullets down on them – they didn't stand a chance, they were sitting targets.'

I looked around at the beauty of it all. The autumn leaves drifting from the trees in reds and browns and yellows, the last of the summer flowers still bravely showing off their beautiful colours and the green of the grass beneath us. 'It's hard to imagine such carnage going on here, isn't it?' I said.

Joe nodded. 'It was a bad time alright, but even that had its lighter moments.'

'How so?' I said.

'Halfway through the fighting, there was a ceasefire to allow the groundsmen to come into the park to feed the ducks.'

I laughed. 'Really?'

Joe nodded. 'I have always thought that only the Irish could do a thing like that – kill men on the one hand, but allow the ducks to be fed on the other.'

I loved listening to Joe speaking. I loved everything about him. I had never been allowed to mention Eddie at home, but I knew that if I took Joe back to Ballybun everyone would be delighted with him.

Joe took me to meet his family in the flat over the bakery. We entered by an iron staircase at the back. The rooms were bright and airy with long windows that stretched from floor to ceiling. The kitchen seemed to be the heart of the house. It was warm and cosy, with a long wooden table that ran down the centre of the room and a fire burning in the grate.

The first time I had gone there, I was very shy and nervous but they were all so friendly that I was soon at my ease. They teased each other and they laughed a lot. His mother and father welcomed me into their home and couldn't have been nicer. Joe had two younger sisters, Martha and Agnus. They had Joe's fair hair and blue eyes and they asked lots of questions.

'Are you going to marry Joe?' said Agnus.

'What a thing to be asking the poor girl,' said Mrs Lynch.

'If she's going to be my sister, I have a right to know,' said Agnus.

'You have a right to know nothing of the kind,' said Mr Lynch. 'Nora will think you are a very bold girl.'

'*I'm* not bold though, am I, Daddy?' said Martha.

'No,' said Agnus, glaring at her. 'You're like the Angel Gabriel, except that you only ever bring bad news.'

I loved that no one was standing on ceremony on my account. I sat back and just enjoyed being with Joe's family – it was almost as good as being with my own. I started to go there every Sunday for my dinner.

Me and the girls had decided to pool our money to buy food. 'It makes no sense,' said Molly, 'to be cooking different meals in the same kitchen.'

We mostly lived on potatoes, which were cheap and filled us up. On Sundays we treated ourselves to bacon and cabbage. We ate the food that we had grown up with and it felt like a little piece of home.

'If Nora is going to be spending Sundays with the Lynches,' said Ellis, 'she shouldn't have to pay for the bacon and cabbage.'

'I don't mind,' I said. 'I'd rather leave things as they are.'

'You've fallen on your feet alright, Nora Doyle,' said Molly. 'There'll be wedding bells next and then you'll forget all about us and you'll be making your own cabbage and bacon in your own kitchen.'

'Jesus, Molly, we've only been walking out for a few months! You'll have me married off with a tribe of kids at this rate.'

'Don't have any kids, Nora, they'll ruin your life. My poor mother is fifty and she looks ninety – she's been popping them out like peas since she was out of short socks. Ellis and I were glorified babysitters from the minute we were off the breast – we had no childhood.'

I thought about my own childhood in Paradise Alley and how loved I had always been made to feel. Thinking about it made me long for them and I couldn't wait to go home for a visit.

The weeks leading up to Christmas were terrible busy in Finnigan's and it was all hands on deck. Miss Berry promoted me to the shop floor, serving the customers, while someone else took on the dusting. I was delighted with my new position and wrote home about it. I wanted them to know how well I was doing.

The mornings were cold and damp and I shivered. It seemed I had grown since leaving home and the red coat that Mammy had bought me only a year ago was getting too small. My bony wrists hung out of the too-short sleeves.

'You need to buy a new one,' said Josie as we walked the cold streets to work.

I thought about the fortune that Minnie was minding for me. I could buy a whole new wardrobe of clothes if I had a mind to, but the money had never felt like mine and I couldn't bring myself to touch it.

'I can't afford one,' I said.

Molly, who was walking behind us, said, 'Listen, there's a jumble sale at the church hall every Sunday after Mass. Most of it's shite and you wouldn't be seen dead in it, but if you volunteer to sell the stuff, you get early pickings.'

'I got a grand pair of boots there once,' said Josie. 'Let's volunteer and find you a new coat.'

Sunday morning found the four of us standing behind a long table that was piled high with old clothes that smelled like Kitty's pig, Henry.

'Jesus, I'm going to be sick,' said Molly, holding her nose.

'Well, don't be sick over me,' said Josie, moving away.

'Are you ready, ladies?' said Father Patrick.

'As ready as we'll ever be,' said Molly, making a face.

'Gird your loins,' said Josie, as Father Patrick opened the doors.

The stampede of women who swarmed into the hall nearly had me diving under the table. They were like a pack of wild animals as they descended on the clothes, grabbing armfuls of them and thrusting pennies into my hands.

'Aren't they supposed to ask the price?' I said.

'Take what you can,' said Josie. 'Most of them won't offer anything.'

'You mean they'll steal them?' I said.

'If they can get away with it,' said Molly.

At the end of the morning the place looked like a bomb had dropped on it, with clothes scattered all over the floor.

'Holy Mother of God,' said Josie, 'that's the last time I'm volunteering for anything.'

I looked at what was left and there was no warm winter coat in sight.

'Don't look so glum, Nora,' said Ellis. 'I have a fine coat here for you.'

Ellis bent down, lifted a coat out from under the table and handed it to me.

The coat was dark green velvet, with black fur around the collar and the cuffs. I'd never owned anything so stylish.

'It looks about your size,' said Ellis, smiling.

'Well, if it doesn't fit her, I'll have it,' said Molly, grinning.

'Go on,' said Josie, 'put it on.'

I slipped my arms into the coat; the wool was soft and warm and the fur felt like silk around my neck.

'Perfect,' said Ellis, grinning. 'You look lovely and very stylish.'

I didn't have to look in a mirror to know that Ellis was right. I only had to see the look of envy on Molly's face.

*

There was new stock coming into the shop every day and me and Josie were busy arranging it on the shelves. The trouble was that I wanted to read the jacket of every book that came in.

'Jesus, Nora,' said Josie. 'Will you move yourself; we'll be here all day at this rate.'

'Sorry, Josie, but I can't help meself – they all sound so intriguing and I'm itching to read the lot of them.'

'Well, I'd be obliged if you'd read them in your own time and not mine.'

'But don't you feel anything when you look at all these lovely covers? Isn't there something about the smell of a new book that makes you just want to breathe it in?'

'Let me put it like this, Nora – it's not my preferred choice of scent and not one that will have the boys swooning over me, unless of course they are desperate readers like you and Ellis.'

'Okay,' I said, smiling. 'I'll get a move on.'

'I'd be obliged.'

It wasn't an easy task arranging the new books, because customers were still coming into the shop and stepping all over us as if we weren't there. Suddenly Josie let out a blood-curdling scream that had Miss Berry running over to us.

'Whatever's wrong?' she said.

'Yer woman trod on me hand,' said Josie. 'I think it's broken.'

'I'm sure it's not,' said Miss Berry, examining it. 'It's just bruised, Josie.'

The girl who had squashed Josie's hand was kneeling down beside her. 'I'm so sorry,' she was saying.

'No harm done, miss,' said Miss Berry.

'I'm afraid I didn't see you kneeling down there,' said the girl.

'And why would you?' said Miss Berry. 'There's been no real harm done. Go to the kitchen and run it under the tap, Josie.'

Josie made a face as she walked away.

The girl stood up and we stared at each other. 'Dymphna?' I said. 'Dymphna Duffy?'

'Nora Doyle?' she said, grinning. 'And what in God's name are you doing in Dublin?'

'I work here.'

'So, you escaped too?' said Dymphna.

'Something like that,' I said, smiling at her.

'Do you get a lunch break?'

I looked at Miss Berry. 'Off you go,' she said. 'It looks like the two of you have some catching up to do.'

'Thanks, Miss Berry,' I said. 'I'll just get my coat, Dymphna.'

Dymphna and I walked across the road to Dunnes Hotel. We found a table that looked out onto the street and ordered tea and sandwiches.

'It's good to see you, Nora,' said Dymphna. 'You were the last person I expected to see.'

'And I'd forgotten that you were up here training to be a nurse,' I said.

'I packed that in,' said Dymphna. 'I hadn't taken into account the fact that I can't stand the sight of blood, not even my own.'

I laughed. 'So, what are you doing now?'

'I work in an office in Grafton Street.'

'That's close to St Stephen's Green, isn't it?'

'Just along the road. If it's warm enough, I eat my lunch over there.'

'I go there a lot with my friend,' I said.

'Would that be a boyfriend, or a girlfriend?'

'His name's Joe and yes, he's my boyfriend.'

'I'm pleased for you, Nora. So, you don't miss Ballybun?'

'I missed it like mad to start with and I was all for getting the next train home but I've got used to it now. I'm going home for Christmas, I can't wait to see them all.'

'I'm going home too,' said Dymphna. 'We could go together, if you like.'

'I'd like that,' I said.

Dymphna was great company; she was funny and she was clever. I had never given her a chance when we'd been at school – in fact, I may have been guilty of laughing at her along with the others.

'By the way,' she said, 'I've changed my name.'

'You're not Dymphna anymore?'

'I've always hated the name – it's comical and people always made fun of it. I'm known as Erin now – it's my middle name.'

'Erin's a lovely name. Erin Duffy, there's an elegance about it.'

'I never felt like a Dymphna and I was glad to get rid of it.'

'What about when you go home?'

'I shall tell them that my name is now Erin and if they want Christmas presents off me, they'd better remember it.'

I laughed. 'I wish you luck with that.'

Suddenly Dymphna looked serious. 'I've been wanting to say something to you for a long time, Nora.'

'That sounds serious,' I said.

'Nora, I'm sorry I ate the face off you the last time we met – I shouldn't have done that.'

'I think we deserved it.'

'You didn't persecute me like most of them. I always wanted a best friend and maybe I was jealous of you and Kitty. You didn't seem to need anyone else.'

'That doesn't excuse us, and I'm truly sorry, Dymphna.'

Dymphna put on a pretend angry face. 'It's Erin,' she said.

'Sorry,' I said, but I knew that Dymphna Duffy would always be Dymphna Duffy to me.

We finished our tea and sandwiches and hugged each other on the street as we said goodbye. I had a lump in my throat. This was someone from home. I waved to her until she was out of sight. Dymphna Duffy, eh? Who would have thought it?

CHAPTER THIRTY-TWO

When I got home from work the next day, there was a letter on the hall table addressed to me. The writing was unfamiliar, but somehow, I knew that it was from Eddie.

'Would you mind if I read this on my own?' I said to Josie.

'Of course not,' she said. 'I'll go and annoy the girls.'

I'd been in Dublin for months and I'd begun to think that I was never going to hear from him. It had been near on a year since we'd seen each other. I sat on the bed and tore open the envelope, and my hands were shaking as I began to read.

Dear Nora,

I've started this letter so many times but I just couldn't find the right words, so I will write what is in my heart. Before you came into my life, I was lonely. I didn't realise just how lonely until we met. The garden had become my special place, it was where I was happy. I didn't think that I needed anything or anyone else but I was wrong, because sharing the garden with you made everything better and my special place became our special place. In the words of John Donne, 'No man is an island'.

I couldn't understand why you had gone away, I thought I had done something to upset you. I went to the garden every day hoping you would come but you didn't and the garden didn't make up for your loss. When I read your letter it all made sense. To discover that you weren't just my good friend but my sister filled me with joy and in a strange way it has made your leaving easier to bear. I'm sorry that my Aunt Caroline hurt you so much and I can understand why you must think her cruel and unkind, but she is the one person who has been a constant in my life – she couldn't have loved or cared for me more if I had been her own son. I'm not excusing her behaviour, but I just want you to know that she is also kind, at least to me.

We have a connection, you and I, that belongs to us alone and nothing is ever going to change that.

Come next spring, Nora, when the garden is at its best, we will be waiting for you. Until then, keep well and be happy. I shall be thinking of you every day.

Your loving brother,

Eddie. x

There was something else in the envelope – the rose that Eddie had given me. It was flat like a painting and the beautiful, pale-orange petals were as beautiful as the day he had picked it. I would take it back home and place it within the pages of *The Secret Garden*.

As time had gone by with no word from him, I feared that my news had been too much of a shock. I'd even begun to think that he didn't like the idea of having a sister who lived in Paradise Alley. I felt ashamed – I should have known better. I knew the heart of Edward Bretton and it was a good heart. I folded the letter and put it under my pillow. I knew that I would read it many more times but for now I was going to let it lie gently on my mind. Eddie was pleased to know that he was my brother and he didn't mind that I lived in Paradise Alley. I truly felt that I now had three brothers and I felt blessed.

I walked across to the window and looked down onto the busy street below. I watched people going in and out of the shops, carrying bags, holding their children's hands. Some were strolling along as if they had all the time in the world, while others were hurrying, heads down, as if they were late for some important meeting. All of them strangers, whose lives I would never know anything about, whose stories I would never hear. We all have our path to walk and It seemed that mine would always lead me back to the secret garden.

*

On our next day off, Josie and I went Christmas shopping. I'd already put books aside for Stevie, Malachi and Grandad Doyle. They came from the second-hand section but they were good and clean and anyway, the story was the same, even if someone else had read them first. Malachi was still only four years old, so I got him a book filled with pictures of elephants and tigers and giraffes. I bought *Gulliver's Travels* for Stevie and Miss Berry recommended *Three Men in a Boat* by Jerome K. Jerome for Grandad Doyle.

Josie and I were walking down Henry Street on our way to Woolworths, which was the cheapest store in town. It sold everything from pots and pans to fancy goods.

'I'm going to get Mammy an apron,' said Josie. 'The one she has is an afront before God.'

As we entered the store, we were enveloped by the smell of pine coming from a beautiful Christmas tree standing just inside the door. There was a bunch of little kids gazing up in wonder at the brightly coloured baubles hanging from the branches.

'We should get a tree for the room,' said Josie.

'And what would be the point of that?' I said. 'We're all going home for Christmas, it'll be dead by the time we get back.'

'I suppose so,' said Josie. 'It would be nice though.'

'Maybe your mammy will have got one.'

'With all the bloody junk in the place, there's no room to swing a cat, let alone a tree. That's why I have no brothers or sisters – there was only space for one child. It's a wonder they didn't stick me in a glass box along with the stuffed birds.'

Josie always made me laugh.

The counters were piled high with all sorts of lovely things. I needed to get something for Mammy and Granny Collins but I didn't know what to get them.

'I want an apron,' said Josie to the girl behind the counter. 'For my mother,' she added. The girl looked hot and sweaty and harassed.

'Is she a big woman?' said the girl.

'And what's it to you if she is?' said Josie, glaring at her.

'It's nothing to me whatsoever,' snapped the girl. 'But if you want it to fit the woman, then I need to know if she's large or small.'

'Oh, right,' said Josie. 'I'm terrible sorry, I thought you were judging my mother by her appearance.'

'And how in God's name could I be doing that? I've never set eyes on your mother.'

'Of course not,' said Josie. 'Well, I suppose she is a bit on the big side. I'm not saying she's fat, just a bit large around the middle.'

'Rubenesque,' I said.

Josie grinned at me. 'Definitely Rubenesque.'

'That'll be large then,' said the girl. 'Colour?'

'What colours do you have?'

The girl took some aprons out of a drawer and laid them on the counter. There was a woman waving a tea towel at her. 'How much are you wanting for this?' she said.

'Can't you see that I am serving a customer?' said the girl. 'You'll have to wait your turn, I only have one pair of hands.'

'I'm in a desperate hurry,' said the woman. 'I've left a bit of fish on the stove.'

'And is that my fault?' snapped the girl.

'Oh, I'm not blaming you,' said the woman, going red in the face. 'It's just that my husband will eat the face off me if his dinner is burned.'

The girl snatched the tea towel off her and shoved it in a bag, 'That will be two pence,' she said.

'I'll remember you in my prayers on Sunday,' said the woman, hurrying away.

Me and Josie started giggling, thinking of the poor woman running through the streets, trying to save the bit of fish.

'And what are you two being so skitty about?' said the girl.

'Nothing,' said Josie, wiping her eyes.

'Does your mother have a favourite colour?' I said, trying to compose myself.

'She has lovely blue eyes,' said Josie.

'Then I'm sure she'll be delighted with the blue one.'

'I'll take the blue one, please,' said Josie.

We wandered round the store looking for something for Mammy.

'These are nice,' said Josie, picking up some pretty tea cosies.

'Oh, they are,' I said.

Having decided on the yellow cosy for Mammy and a green one for Granny Collins, we left the store and went to a tobacco shop, where I bought some baccy for Daddy and Grandad Collins. Josie bought the same for her daddy. I was pleased with my purchases and couldn't wait for Christmas when I would be back home in Paradise Alley with my family.

'I want to get something for Joe,' I said.

'Now that's a tricky one,' said Josie. 'As you haven't been walking out for long, it can't be too personal, or he'll think you're looking for a commitment.'

'Really?'

'Oh yes, you're diving into choppy waters here.'

'What should I get him then?'

'Something that says I like you but I'm not looking for a ring. Unless of course you *are* looking for a ring.'

'I had no idea it was going to be so difficult.'

'How about a nice tie?'

'Too ordinary.'

'Some hankies?'

'Too boring.'

'You're probably right.'

'Let's go to Finnigan's?' I said.

'On our day off?'

'Then we'll go for a cup of tea and a bun.'

'You're on,' said Josie, linking arms, as we made our way to the bookshop.

'What are you two doing here?' asked Ellis as we entered the shop.

'It's Nora,' said Josie. 'She's looking for a Christmas present for Joe Lynch, the blue-eyed boy.'

'A book?' said Ellis.

I nodded. 'A book of poems.'

'You're in luck, Nora,' she said. 'We had the loveliest second-hand book in only an hour ago. There's not a mark on it. It's not even on the shelf yet, I'll get it.'

While Ellis went to fetch the book, Molly came across. 'Have you no life outside of this place?' she said. 'I wouldn't be seen dead in here on me day off.'

'Neither would I,' said Josie. 'But Nora here wants a book of poetry for lover boy.'

Ellis came back holding the book. '*The Poems of Oscar Wilde,*' she said, handing it to me.

The book felt smooth and solid in my hands. I opened the pages, took a deep breath and inhaled the book's own special smell.

'Jesus, Nora,' said Molly, 'what are you doing?'

'I'm smelling the poems,' I said, smiling.

'Well, I've heard everything now,' said Josie.

'I understand,' said Ellis, softly.

'You would,' said Molly, smiling fondly at her.

'Wrap it up,' I said. 'I'll take it.'

'Right you are, madam,' said Ellis, grinning.

I felt that I had made a good choice and hoped that a book of poems by Oscar Wilde didn't mean that I was pinning Joe down to any commitment that might scare him off. I left the shop, grateful for Josie's advice.

CHAPTER THIRTY-THREE

Christmas Eve at Finnigan's was frantic but there was something special in the air as people crowded into the shop looking for that perfect book to give as a gift. They asked my advice and I was glad to give it. Even if I hadn't read the book, I could tell them that I'd heard the author was a grand writer and very popular. Or I could tell them that the book that they were thinking of buying wasn't suitable for the young person they had in mind.

Me and the girls had decided not to buy gifts for each other, as we were all spent out. We had got very close over the months since I'd been in Dublin and even though we would only be apart for a few days, there were tears in our eyes as we went our separate ways to spend Christmas with our families.

The evening before, me and Joe had said our goodbyes outside the digs. Mrs Murphy didn't allow boys in the house and even if she had, the girls would be in and I'd wanted to be on my own with Joe, so we stood shivering at the bottom of the steps. We'd exchanged presents and it was obvious by the shape of the parcels that we had both chosen to give each other a book.

'I'd like to open it on Christmas Day,' I'd said.

Joe smiled. 'I hope you like it.'

'You gave it to me, Joe, so I know that I will.'

He'd put his arms around me and I leaned into him. 'I wish you weren't going away. I'm going to miss you, my sweet Nora.'

'And I'll miss you too, Joe,' I'd said. 'But I'll be back and I'll be thinking of you.'

His coat had felt rough against my cheek and I felt safe and warm in his arms. There was a strength to Joe, a solidity, that I knew I could always depend on. He carried with him the smell of freshly baked bread and the sharpness of yeast – it was his own particular smell; it was a Joe smell.

He'd held me away from him and we'd stood in silence as we looked into each other's eyes. I'd moved closer, until there was no space between us. As our cold breath mingled and drifted like a white mist into the dark night, it felt as if we were the only two people in the world. Joe smiled and gently touched my face and then we were kissing. His lips were cold and soft and I'd melted into him. I could feel his heart beating against mine as every corner of my body was filled with a yearning that I had never felt before. Is this what everyone whispered about? Is this what Mammy felt when she had kissed Peter Bretton?

I wasn't cold anymore; I'd felt warm in Joe's strong arms. Something had changed in both of us and as the first flurry of snow fell around our shoulders, Joe and I had fallen in love.

I met Dymphna outside the station café and we boarded the train for home. She was a good companion, funny and smart, and I wished again that I had got to know her better when we were at school. We could have been friends. I couldn't wait to tell Kitty all about her. It was nice and warm in the train so we took off our coats and settled back in the seats. As the train got closer to home, I expected to feel that familiar dread in my stomach that had been there for so long, but all I felt was excitement and the need to see everyone. Father Kelly met us off the train and drove us home to Ballybun. We dropped Dymphna at the bottom of Baggot Row.

'Have a great Christmas, Nora,' she said.

'You too, Dymph— I mean, Erin.'

'If *you* can't get your head round it,' she said, grinning, 'I have little hope for those indoors.'

I wanted to walk up Paradise Alley, so I asked Father Kelly to drop me at the stone archway.

'But it's pitch-black, girl, you'll break your neck,' he said.

'Father, I could walk up Paradise Alley with my eyes closed, I know every cobble and stone.'

Father Kelly laughed. 'I'm sure you do. Have a great Christmas, Nora, and remember me to your family.'

I watched him drive away and started to walk up the Alley. It wasn't pitch-black at all, for there were candles burning in the cottage windows, casting a glow of light onto the lane and guiding my footsteps up to the Grey House.

Mammy was the first out of the house, followed by Daddy. I dropped my case and flung myself at them. We were laughing and crying and hugging. I was home and I felt again the rush of love that I'd been wrapped in all my life.

As I entered the house, I dipped my finger in the holy water font that hung on the wall, just inside the door. 'God bless all here,' I said.

'Amen to that,' said Grandad Doyle, getting up from his chair by the fire. 'We are indeed blessed this night, for you have returned to us.' He put his arms around me and I laid my head on his shoulder. 'You've been missed, girl,' he said.

Everything was the same, of course it was, why would I think that it wouldn't be? The turf fire burned brightly in the hearth, the holly berries shone red beneath the lighted candles that stood on the mantlepiece and a sweet-smelling tree stood in the corner. It brought back all those special memories of Christmases past. As I looked around the room, I wondered why I had ever left. This was my home, this was where I belonged. Dublin seemed like a million miles away; Josie, Molly, and Ellis seemed part of some dream, not real people at all, and Joe? Did he feel like a dream too?

'That's a fine coat you have on,' said Mammy, breaking into my thoughts. 'I would never have put you in green, but I have to say the colour suits you, Nora.'

'It was only a few pennies, Mammy, I got it from a church sale.'

'I'd say it came from gentry. Wouldn't you think so, Colm?'

'You look like a Hollywood star, Nora,' he said, smiling.

'Pop in and see Stevie, Nora,' said Mammy. 'He said he was going to stay awake. He's been mithering me all day about what time you would be home.'

'How is he, Mammy?'

Mammy smiled but I saw the sadness behind her eyes. 'We still have him, Nora, we still have him.' She handed me a lighted candle. 'Take this with you,' she said.

I nodded and climbed the stairs before gently pushing open the bedroom door where the boys slept, careful not to wake Malachi. At first, I thought that Stevie was asleep but as I got closer to the bed, I could see that his eyes were open and he was smiling at me. I put the candle down on the dresser and knelt down beside him.

'Hello, Stevie,' I whispered.

'I waited for you,' he said.

I sat down on Stevie's bed and put my arms around him. 'Well, I'm home now.'

I looked across to where Malachi was sleeping. He was making little squeaky noises like a kitten and he'd kicked off all the covers, they were in a tangled heap on the floor. I leaned over and kissed him. His little body was cold to the touch, so I picked up the blankets and tucked them around him.

'I've missed you, Nora,' whispered Stevie. 'Do you have to go back?'

'Don't be worrying about that. Go to sleep now, love,' I said, 'for tomorrow is Christmas Day and I've brought you a fine present all the way from Dublin.'

Stevie rubbed his eyes and yawned. 'Goodnight, Nora,' he said. 'I'll see you in the morning.'

'You will. Goodnight, Stevie.'

CHAPTER THIRTY-FOUR

The family had all gone to Midnight Mass the night before, so on Christmas morning I walked up to the church on my own. You would have thought that I'd been gone for years, the way people were greeting me and hugging me and asking all about Dublin and was it as wicked as they'd heard? And wasn't I relieved to be safe and sound and back in Ballybun?

There were so many people stopping me as I walked along that I feared I was going to be late for Mass and I was meeting Kitty outside. I picked up my pace but was immediately cornered by Mrs Toomey.

'That's a fine coat you have on there, Nora Doyle,' she said. 'They must be paying you a fortune in your grand job in Dublin.' She was stroking the material, as if it was a cat that I was wearing and not a coat. I was just about to tell her that I'd got it in a sale at the church hall when I decided to let her think that I was earning a fortune in my grand job in Dublin. It would do her no harm to be a little green with envy and it would give her something to gossip about with her cronies.

She had a grip on my arm that would have put a heavyweight wrestler to shame. 'I have to go, Mrs Toomey,' I said, trying to pull away. 'I'll be late for Mass.'

'Your poor mother must be pleased to have you home, Nora,' she continued, as if I hadn't spoken.

I could feel myself getting angry. 'Why would you say that she's poor, Mrs Toomey?' I said.

'Well, with her having to struggle with poor Stevie and little Malachi on her own, now that you've run off to the bright lights of Dublin.'

She said all this with a smile on her face. I looked at her sharp little nose that was a perfect match for her sharp little tongue and I had the urge to slap her.

'But that's the young people of today for you,' she continued, sighing. 'They'd rather be off galivanting than staying at home where they're needed.'

I pulled away from her. 'I wish you the Christmas you deserve,' I said, and walked away. *Stupid interfering baggage of a woman*, I thought as I hurried up the hill towards the church. Now I was going to have to confess to Father Kelly that I'd been harbouring mean thoughts about a woman of the parish and I'd only been home five minutes.

Kitty jumped off the wall and ran towards me. 'Oh, Nora,' she said. 'I thought you'd never get here.'

'Neither did I,' I said. 'I swear I was stopped by the entire town; you'd think that I was visiting royalty.'

'You are in a way, girl, for there's not many that have ventured out of the place.'

'And that bloody Mrs Toomey has me blood boiling, eating the face off me for leaving Mammy.'

'Mrs Toomey is a miserable cow,' said Kitty. 'Pay her no mind.'

I smiled at Kitty and put my arms around her. 'Oh, it's good to see you, Kitty.'

'And it's good to see you,' she said, grinning. 'Now let's hurry, Mass will have started.'

We made our way down to the side altar and knelt in front of the nativity scene. There were candles all around the little statues of the Virgin Mary and Joseph and the baby Jesus and there was a silver star glowing over the top of the stable. I looked at my dear friend Kitty and I thanked God for bringing me home this Christmas Day to be with the people I loved.

'I wish we could spend some time together before you go back,' said Kitty, after Mass. 'I'm only dying to hear all your news.'

'Come up to the Grey House after you've had your dinner,' I said.

When I got home, Granny and Grandad Collins were already there.

'Dublin suits you, Nora,' said Granny. 'You're looking lovely.'

'She is, isn't she?' said Mammy.

Malachi was lying flat out on the floor, playing with a toy car that Father Christmas had brought him, and Stevie was sitting beside the fire, opposite Grandad Doyle. I looked around the room at my family and I felt like crying, for tomorrow I would have to leave them again and it would be hard.

After we'd had our dinner and I'd helped Mammy to tidy up, we sat down to open our presents. Mammy and Daddy gave me a medal of Saint Christopher on a little silver chain – it was the loveliest thing I'd ever seen.

'I love it,' I said, hugging them both.

'He'll keep you safe while you are gone from us,' said Daddy, 'for he's the patron saint of travellers.'

Grandad Doyle loved his book. 'Is this from your shop?' he said. I nodded.

'Jerome K. Jerome,' he said. 'I've heard of the feller. I shall look forward to reading this, Nora. No one will be getting a word out of me for the rest of the day, which is a gift for everyone else.' He handed me a parcel. 'Now you won't be surprised to find that we think alike in the present department.'

Grandad had bought me a book called *Peter Pan in Kensington Gardens*.

'I know that we have read Peter Pan together,' he said. 'But I wanted to introduce you to one of life's great illustrators. The man's name is Arthur Rackham and believe me when I say he's a cut above the rest when it comes to drawing.'

I opened the book and breathed in the musty smell.

'What does it smell like?' said Stevie.

I closed my eyes. 'It smells…' I frowned. I couldn't describe it.

'Unique?' said Grandad.

'That's the word,' I said, grinning.

'Will she ever grow out of that silly habit?' said Granny Collins.

'Oh, I do hope not,' said Grandad Doyle, winking at me.

Stevie loved *Gulliver's Travels* and Malachi laughed and imitated all the animals as Mammy turned the pages.

Stevie reached down beside his chair and handed me a flat package. I unwrapped it gently and my eyes filled with tears as I looked at the drawing inside. It was the garden: mine and Eddie's garden. He'd remembered everything I'd told him about it – the pond, the robin, the bench and the swing hanging from the tree. 'Thank you, Stevie,' I said. 'It is perfect, I love it. I shall take it back to Dublin with me.'

'He's been working on it for months, Nora,' said Mammy.

'Aren't you going to let the rest of us see this masterpiece?' asked Granny Collins, smiling.

I passed it over to her. 'Now this is something to behold,' she said. 'A beautiful garden, the like of which I've never seen. Where did you get the idea for this, Stevie? For none of us has a garden like it and probably never will.'

'The lad has a fierce imagination,' said Mammy quickly, coming to the rescue.

'I'd say all that reading has something to do with that,' said Grandad Collins.

'Reading feeds the soul,' Grandad Doyle nodded in agreement. 'And stimulates the brain.'

'And figgy pudding feeds the belly,' said Stevie, grinning and making us all laugh.

Daddy and Grandad Collins were delighted with the baccy and Mammy and Granny Collins loved the tea cosies.

'The one I have is falling apart,' said Mammy. 'I shall throw it away immediately and invite all the neighbours around so that I can show off my new one.'

In the afternoon, Stevie and Grandad Doyle nodded off in front of the fire and Granny and Grandad Collins went back to the farm to see to the animals. Mammy took Malachi down the Alley to the little white cottage to visit Annie and Mrs Fowley.

I wanted to be on my own when I opened Joe's present – for some reason I didn't want the whole family to be asking me questions about him. I went upstairs and sat on my bed. I took off the paper to reveal a book of poetry by Lord Byron. I traced the cover with my finger, then turned to the title page. My eyes filled with tears as I read the words that Joe had written inside.

She walks in beauty, like the night
Of cloudless climes and starry skies;
And all that's best of dark and bright
Meet in her aspect and her eyes.
Lord Byron
To sweet Nora who walks in beauty.
Happy Christmas
Love
Joe xxx

I breathed in the pages and pictured Joe's face. The book smelled of new beginnings. I closed it and gazed at its cover. It showed a picture of a girl with long dark hair, walking along a stony path on a winter's night. Her dress was white and her arms were bare and she was surrounded by a darkness that was deep and oppressive. Trees like skeletons lined the path, their branches reaching up through the mist. How cold the girl looked, how lonely.

Rather than wait for Kitty to come up to the house, I decided to call for her – I had a need to stretch my legs after a dinner that could have fed the five thousand. And I wanted to get out of the house, for there was something I needed to do.

It was bitingly cold outside and my nose was frozen by the time I got to the white cottage. I popped my head around the door and wished Annie and Mrs Fowley a happy Christmas. Mammy opened the door to me.

'Come in for a minute, Nora,' she said. 'And show Annie your new coat.'

The little room was lovely and cosy and I was tempted to warm myself by the fire but I knew that once I did that, I wouldn't have wanted to continue my journey.

'Give us a twirl,' said Annie.

I spun round in the middle of the room and Malachi tried to copy me, making us all laugh.

'The green suits you, Nora,' said Annie, fingering the soft material.

'And it's not a colour I would have chosen for her,' said Mammy. 'It just goes to show that you should try new things and not dismiss them out of hand.'

'Is Mrs Foley not around?' I said.

'She stays in her bed these days,' said Annie. 'She's more comfortable there.'

'I'll go and sit with her for a while,' said Mammy.

Just then, there was a knock on the door and Kitty walked in. 'God bless all here,' she said, dipping her finger in the holy water.

'Amen,' said Annie.

'I've just been up to the house,' said Kitty. 'Your father said you were coming to see me, and as I didn't pass you on the way, I thought you might be here.'

'Are your family all well, Kitty?' said Mammy.

'They're grand, Mrs Doyle. Mammy is expecting another baby.'

'That's a blessing, Kitty. I'm sure you are all delighted.'

'Delighted isn't a word that comes to mind,' said Kitty as we stepped out of the house and started to walk down the Alley. 'The house is only bursting at the seams as it is.'

'Ah, but you'll love it, Kitty.'

'I haven't a choice, have I?' said Kitty, shivering. 'Can we go up to the house now? I'm only frozen.'

'Before we go there, Kitty, I want to see the wall,' I said.

'What wall?' said Kitty.

'The one around Bretton Hall.'

'Jesus, Nora, why would you be wanting to see that? The bloody thing nearly drove you to drink.'

How could I explain to Kitty my need to go back there? I couldn't think of my home without thinking of the wall and it was driving me mad. I had to stop feeling like this and the only way it was going to stop was by going back. Grandad Doyle had once said that it is better to face your demons than to let them fester. 'Chances are,' he had said, 'that they are not as scary as you've imagined them to be.'

'I just need to see it again,' I said.

The wind blowing off the sea would cut the nose off you and Kitty was moaning all the way out to the Strand, but she had agreed to go and it was good to know my friend was by my side.

'We'll end up with frostbite,' she said. 'Our toes will have to be amputated and no one will want to marry us.'

'Let's run,' I said, laughing.

'Aren't we too old to run?'

'I don't think we will ever be too old to run, Kitty.'

As we got closer to Bretton Hall we slowed down. Did I really want to put myself through this again?

'Are you sure you want to do this, Nora?' asked Kitty, seeing the doubt on my face.

I nodded. 'I think so,' I said, uncertainly.

As we turned the corner, I could see the wall, stretching out in front of me, enclosing the grounds of Bretton Hall like an army of guards. I shivered, as if I was standing in front of a living thing, a thing that had the power to destroy me just by being there. I moved away from Kitty and she seemed to understand my need to be alone. I trailed my hand along the cold stone as I walked. I'd built this up in my mind until it had become more than just a wall. It had become an ogre, with Caroline Bretton's face imprinted on every brick. It had made me run from Ballybun and from my family. Caroline Bretton had taken something away from me that day in the garden. I had never been sure what it was. Grandad Doyle would know; he'd have the right word. I had always been proud to be the girl from Paradise Alley but with a few words she had made me feel ashamed of who I was. Why had I let her do that to me? Why had I let myself believe that a pile of bricks could keep me away from Eddie?

As I stared at the wall, a kind of peace washed over me. I might not have been high-born, I might not have the money and status that she had, but that didn't make me any less of a person. One day me and Eddie would come back to the garden. We would dig the soil and we would plant flowers that would blossom and grow. One day we would see each other again, of that I was sure. I walked back to Kitty, smiling.

'Tommy did a grand job, didn't he?' she said, warily.

'It's a fine wall alright,' I said. 'You should be very proud to be walking out with such a craftsman, Kitty. Let's go home.'

'Yes, let's,' said Kitty, catching hold of my hand.

CHAPTER THIRTY-FIVE

'So, tell me everything,' said Kitty. 'I want to know about the girls and the dances and the shop and Joe. You can start with Joe.'

We were cuddled up under the blankets on my bed, but Kitty was still shivering.

'What do you want to know?'

'Is he handsome?'

'Very,' I said, smiling.

'And is he kind?'

'Extremely.'

'And have you kissed?'

'We have.'

'And?'

'And what?'

'What did it feel like? Did it have you shaking in your boots? Did it unleash a passion you never knew you had in you?'

I thought about the kiss. I thought about the coolness of Joe's lips and the way he'd held me close. I remembered the roughness of his jacket against my cold cheeks, and I remembered the silence as the snow fell around us and we fell in love.

'Hello?' said Kitty, grinning.

'Sorry, I was remembering.'

'I was hoping to persuade you to stay, but I can see from that face that I'd be wasting me breath.'

'I fear you would, but now it's your turn. Tell me about you and Tommy.'

Kitty grinned. 'Ah, me and Tommy. I'm not sure it's the fairy-tale romance that you two seem to be having, but we suit each other.'

'That doesn't sound very romantic at all, Kitty.'

'Sure, I've known him all my life, Nora. There are no surprises where Tommy Nolan is concerned.'

I frowned. 'There must be more to it than the fact that you suit each other.'

'I like being with him, it's easy. We're from the same place, we understand each other. He's more than happy to push Sean out in his chair or keep Breda company under the table and Mammy loves the bones of him.'

'As long as you're happy, Kitty,' I said.

'I'm happier than I've ever been. I never expected to fall in love so young. I thought that I'd maybe see a bit of life before I settled down but Tommy is the one for me, so I suppose this will be my life – here in Ballybun. As long as I have Tommy, I won't want for anything else.'

'So, it's true love, then?'

She smiled. 'Oh yes.'

'Then I'm glad for you, Kitty, for all I want is your happiness.'

'Don't forget to write,' she said as we hugged each other goodbye. 'I may never get to Dublin but I get to see it through your eyes.'

The next morning, my family stood dry-eyed at the door as we waited for Father Kelly to arrive. I knew that they were just trying to make it easier for me and that the tears would come later. Stevie had taken it the hardest. He'd sat on my bed, watching me packing my case, making sure that I didn't leave his drawing behind. Seeing the sadness in his eyes made me question why I was leaving everyone I loved and going back to Dublin.

'I'll visit again,' I said. 'I promise I will.'

'But what if I need you?'

'Then I'll come home. Look at me, Stevie, if there is ever a time when you really need me then nothing will keep me away.'

'Not even your grand job?' he said, smiling.

'Not even my grand job.'

'Okay so,' he said, brightening up. 'I'll hold you to that.'

As the train started to move slowly out of Cork, I felt such a confusing mixture of emotions. I was sad to be leaving my family and I was worried about Stevie. And on top of all that, Mrs Bloody Toomey's words kept coming back to me. Was I a selfish girl to leave Mammy? Should I be a dutiful daughter and stay home to help her with the house and Stevie and Malachi? The reasons I had for leaving Ballybun hadn't gone away, they just didn't seem as important anymore. Mammy had said that the people we cared about didn't judge us and those that did weren't our friends. I stared out of the window at the fields and rivers rushing by, every mile taking me further from my home, and yet there was a warm feeling inside me, for every mile was taking me closer to Joe.

He was standing on the platform as the train pulled into Dublin. I pushed down the window and waved to him.

'Joe?' said Dymphna, who was travelling back to Dublin with me.

I turned around and smiled at her. 'I didn't know that he was going to meet me.'

'It must be love,' she said, smiling. 'Oh, that I was that lucky. I have yet to meet a boy that I've wanted to spend more than five minutes with.'

'You haven't met the right boy,' I said. 'Why don't you come to the Irish club with me and the girls one Saturday?'

'Wouldn't they mind?'

'Not a bit of it. They're really nice, all three of them. You never know, Erin, you might meet the love of your life, or at the very least, someone you can spend more than five minutes with.'

'By the way,' she said, 'I'm reverting back to Dymphna. My family thought that the whole thing was hilarious and none of them would call me Erin. To be fair, Mammy did try, but she was mocked for her trouble. There's no point in being Erin here and Dymphna at home.'

'A rose by any other name would smell as sweet,' I said, quoting Mr Shakespeare, who I thought had a very elegant turn of phrase.

'I'll bear that in mind,' said Dymphna, laughing.

We pulled on our coats and lifted the cases down from the rack. 'Call in at the shop,' I said. 'We'll make arrangements for you to meet the girls.'

'Grand so,' she said.

We walked across to Joe. 'This is Dymphna, Joe, I told you about her.'

'Pleased to meet you Dymphna,' said Joe, smiling.

Dymphna gave me a hug. 'See you soon then,' she said. Joe took my case as we walked out of the station. 'I've missed you,' he said, taking hold of my hand.

'I've only been gone a few days.'

'Well, it's been a very long few days.'

I kissed his cheek. 'You really missed me then?'

'Every day. My sisters have been tormenting me about it. They said I've been acting like a love-sick eejit and they're probably right.'

'Well, I'm home now,' I said.

He stopped and smiled down at me. 'Home?' he said.

What had made me say home? Dublin wasn't my home, Ballybun was my home. Paradise Alley was my home.

'I don't know what made me say that,' I said.

'I like that you said it,' said Joe.

We walked slowly back to the digs, our bodies perfectly in step. It was cold but my hand felt warm in his. Maybe home wasn't a place, maybe home was a person. Maybe home was Joe.

CHAPTER THIRTY-SIX

As winter turned to spring, Joe and I grew closer. When we walked out together, I was proud to be seen with him. I rarely thought of home now and pushed any guilty feelings about Mammy and the Grey House to the back of my mind. I didn't know what the future held for me, I only knew that Joe was going to be a part of it.

When I'd come to Dublin, I'd never planned to stay. In fact, I hadn't planned anything at all, I'd just wanted to get away. I'd been sure that one day I would return home and make my life in Ballybun. I hadn't known that I would meet a boy and fall in love. The thought of never going back, never seeing Malachi grow up or Grandad Doyle getting older, made me want to cry – it was something too awful to imagine. Dublin was too far from home and home was too far from Joe. But Joe's future had been mapped out since he was a child; he would take over the bakery, his life would be here and if we married, then my place would be beside him. At night as I lay next to Josie, I turned the problem over and over in my mind. I just couldn't see myself in either place. I decided to talk to the girls about it.

That evening we all crammed into mine and Josie's room. It was a warm night and we opened the window to let some air in.

'Isn't it a bit soon to be thinking about settling down?' said Molly.

'But if she's sure of the feller?' said Ellis.

I smiled at her, I thought she was the wisest of the four of us and I valued her opinion. 'I *am* sure,' I said.

'But what if you change your mind down the road?' said Josie. 'And you're working yourself to death in that bloody bakery, with a crowd of kids hanging off your apron?'

'I'm sure that if I had a crowd of kids, I wouldn't be working in the bakery. I'd be at home minding them.'

'Well, either way you'd be trapped,' said Josie.

'I know what the Bible says on the subject,' said Ellis, gently, 'if that's any help.'

'Of course you do,' said Molly, crossing her eyes.

'I'd like to hear it, Ellis,' I said.

'Well, it says, "A man shall leave his father and mother and be united to his wife and they will become one flesh." So, I suppose that's saying that your Joe should follow where you go and if you have a mind to go to Ballybun, then it's his duty to go with you but I'm not sure that life is that simple. Besides, he might not pay much mind to the teachings of the Bible.'

'But what do *you* think, Ellis?'

'I think that you would need to come to some sort of agreement that will make you both happy.'

'Has Joe asked you to marry him then?' said Molly.

'Not exactly, but we talk about our future and how many children we will have and what we are going to call them. You know, dreams.'

'Well, I don't think you should be making any long-term plans,' said Molly. 'Or be worrying about where you are going to end up. You're only young, for God's sake – you need to live a bit before you settle down.'

'Nora came to us for advice,' said Ellis. 'She knows as well as we do how old she is, but this is worrying her and it's no help for you to be telling her that she's too young to be settling down.'

We all stared at Ellis, who normally said very little but had gone a bit red in the face.

'You're right, love,' said Molly, smiling at Ellis. 'I have too much gob on me.'

Talking to the girls hadn't resolved anything but it had made me realise that I needed to just enjoy being with Joe and that I should leave the rest to fate.

When I wasn't working in Finnigan's and Joe could get away from the bakery, we spent our days wandering around the city. Sometimes we went to the picture house to see a film, or we'd find a café and just sit and talk. We didn't do anything exciting, but we didn't feel the need to. It was enough just to be together. There was no place to be alone but I began to think that maybe that was a good thing, because as our feelings for each other deepened and our kisses became more urgent, the last thing we needed was to be alone. My family were too important to me to bring shame on them. Mammy had enough to worry about without having a wayward daughter as well. She had never wanted me to go through what she had gone through and I would never let her down, however much I loved Joe.

It was Monday morning and Finnigan's was desperate quiet, so we were all trying to keep busy, tidying shelves and dusting books. As the dust flew around the shop, Molly began sneezing.

'I think I might be allergic to books,' she said.

'You're not allergic to books,' said Ellis, 'you're allergic to dust.'

The morning dragged and we were all fed up and couldn't wait for lunchtime when we could escape for an hour. We were just deciding where to go to eat our sandwiches when Miss Berry walked towards me.

'Nora, your parish priest is on the phone.'

I could feel my whole body turn icy cold and the blood drain from my face.

'Is it Stevie?' I said. 'Please don't let it be Stevie.'

'I don't know anything, Nora,' said Miss Berry. 'I only know that he wants to speak to you.'

The girls crowded round me and Ellis handed me a glass of water.

'Are you ready to talk to him?' asked Miss Berry, gently.

I nodded and followed her into the office. It was going to be bad news – why else would Father Kelly be ringing me at the shop? I was shaking as I picked up the phone. It felt heavy and cold in my hand.

'Father?' I said.

'Now I know I'll have given you a fright, Nora, so let me assure you straight away that your family are all safe and well.'

I hadn't realised that I'd been holding my breath until I let out a sigh and felt my body relax. My family were alright and that's all I needed to hear. 'Then why are you calling, Father, if it's not about my family?'

'There's been an accident, Nora, and I thought you would want to know.'

'What sort of accident?'

'A car crash. The Bretton family were travelling to a wedding in Cork. Pat Lamey, who was driving, had a heart attack at the wheel and the car crashed into a tree.'

I couldn't speak.

'Are you still there?' said Father Kelly.

'Who was in the car?' I asked in a whisper.

'All of them, except Caroline – she'd gone up by train the day before. Nora, I have to tell you they all died at the scene. God rest their souls.'

I could feel hot tears burning behind my eyes. I didn't want to ask the question, because once I knew, then nothing would ever be the same again. I took a deep breath. 'Eddie?'

'I'm sorry, Nora.'

I put my head down on the table and cried as if my heart was breaking. I would never see Eddie again, I would never work beside him in the garden, or soar high over the little pond on the swing he made me, or plant bulbs, or cut back the roses or just sit together on the green bench while the snow fell about our shoulders. He couldn't be dead, he couldn't, because he was as alive in my mind as if he was standing in front of me. His sweet smile, the way his hair fell over his eyes, the habit he had of scratching behind his ear, the way the sun glistened on the fine hairs of his arms when he rolled up his sleeves. He couldn't be gone, he just couldn't. Not the Eddie who had shown me a secret garden and taught me the names of the flowers and the birds. It felt as if a light had gone out of my life. I had lost my dear, sweet, gentle friend. I had lost my brother.

This journey home was different in so many ways. When I'd first left for Dublin there had been so many emotions. Sadness to be leaving my family, mixed with relief to be away from the town that had almost broken me. When I'd gone home for Christmas, I had been full of excitement to see my family again and to walk up Paradise Alley and then my return to Dublin to be with Joe, but there was no joy in my heart now as the train sped towards home and all the sadness that awaited me there. My heart was as frozen as the garden in winter.

As the train pulled into Cork, I stood up and pulled my case down from the rack, my feet felt like lead. The first person I saw on the platform was Mammy, searching the crowds of people, stepping down from the train. I ran into her arms and she held me close. Then she took my face in her hands and said, 'He's not dead, Nora. Eddie is not dead.'

CHAPTER THIRTY-SEVEN

The news that had reached Father Kelly was that the whole family had died in the crash, but somehow Eddie had survived. He was badly injured and no one held out much hope for him but he was alive and that was all I needed to know. I could see him and I could hold him and I could give him strength, I could give him *my* strength. If love could make him live then he would live, because I loved him and I wasn't going to let him die. All I knew was that I had to see him, I had to be near him.

All my thoughts had been for Eddie. I'd hardly given a thought to the rest of the family who had died in the crash but now I found myself thinking about Peter Bretton, the man who was my father. I'd never known him. I had never wanted to know him because I already had a daddy and I'd never needed another one. I tried again to bring his face to mind, it suddenly seemed important, but all I could remember was his hair curling over the back of his collar, hair like Eddie's, hair like mine. I remembered that he had seemed kind and that he'd wanted to share a cup of tea with me. Perhaps he'd wanted to get to know me but didn't know how, so he did the only thing he could do – he left me my fortune. Maybe it was his way of saying that he knew who I was, and that in his own way, he cared about me and wanted to make sure that I was happy. I said a silent prayer for the father I would never get the chance to know.

Eddie was in a hospital in Cork but only family could visit him. Well, I *was* his family and if I had to break down the doors of the hospital, no one was going to keep me away. The next day, Father Kelly, Mammy, Daddy and me drove to the hospital.

Father Kelly laid his hand on my shoulder at the doors. 'They might not let us in, Nora,' he said, gently. He went to find a doctor while we sat on chairs and waited.

We watched people coming and going, we watched them being wheeled past on trollies and wheelchairs. Nurses hurried along the corridors. They wore dark navy dresses covered by crisp white aprons that crossed over at the back and white caps covering their hair. The doctors wore white jackets and some wore suits. I watched them come in and out of the rooms, sometimes standing outside to talk to each other. I wondered if one of them was the room that Eddie was in. I wanted to open every door until I found him. A couple sat down beside us – the woman was crying and the man had his arm around her. Mammy touched the woman's arm and she smiled sadly through her tears. I shall never forget the smell of the place. It was an indoor smell, an unnatural smell; cleaning fluid and soap and, faintly, the smell of people; of breath and cigarette smoke, sweat.

It felt like hours before Father Kelly returned with the doctor. Daddy stood up and shook the doctor's hand.

The doctor smiled at me. 'Nora?' he said.

'I have to see him,' I said, urgently. 'I'm his sister, you see, and I have a right to see him.'

'Yes, you have,' he said kindly.

'Can you tell us how badly injured he is, doctor?' asked Daddy.

'Edward's back was broken on impact. He is sedated, and he won't be able to talk to you.'

'But I can talk to *him*,' I said.

'I'll see what I can do,' he said. 'His aunt is with him.'

We watched the doctor going into a room a little way down from where we were sitting and we waited. I didn't care what Caroline said; I wasn't scared of her anymore and she wasn't going to keep me away from Eddie just because she was Caroline Bretton. If Eddie lived, she would never keep me from him again.

We could hear raised voices coming from the room but I didn't care if her voice raised the roof, I was going to be with him. Eventually the door opened and the doctor and Caroline Bretton came out. She stood for a moment and stared at us, then walked away. The doctor shook his head but beckoned us in.

'Do you want to go in on your own?' asked Mammy. 'Or do you want us with you?'

'I'd like to be alone, Mammy.'

Mammy stood up and put her arms around me. 'Go and see your brother,' she said. 'We will be right here if you need us.'

The only bright colour in the room was a vase of red roses – the blooms looked like splashes of blood against the whiteness of the walls and bedsheets. The light that day was blinding, rushing through a window on one wall, illuminating the room like a theatre, glinting off the side of the vase that held the flowers.

In the centre of the room was a narrow bed with the covers neat and straight. Beside it was the kind of chair I remembered from school – wooden, upright and uncomfortable-looking. On the other side was a wooden cabinet with a glass water bottle and a glass. The heart-shaped stone I'd given Eddie for Christmas lay on the top of the cabinet.

Eddie was in the bed. I didn't recognise him at first because I'd never seen him so still. His face was bruised and one arm was in a cast. I reached out and held his hand that lay on the crisp white sheet. It was warm and soft, and I took comfort in the warmth because it meant there was blood running through it. It was warm because however badly injured he was, he was still alive.

'I'm here,' I whispered. 'I've come home.' I looked at his sweet face and gently brushed the hair away from his eyes. 'If you can hear me, I want you to imagine that it's autumn, remember how beautiful the garden is in autumn? Leaves are drifting from the trees and falling around us, browns and greens and yellows, like a shower of rainbows putting on a show just for us. A single golden leaf with crinkled edges lands on my head, making us giggle. Can you hear us, Eddie? Can you hear our laughter dancing across the garden and floating up into the sky above the tall trees?

'The garden is alive, Eddie, it's alive with growing things that we've planted and all the little creatures who have made it their home and it's alive with us. In a hundred years from now, when nature has claimed it once more, our spirits will still be there, our laughter will still echo within those old stone walls and the last rose of summer will still belong to us. Imagine the garden, Eddie, and it will carry you away from this room and this bed and it will take you to our special place. You have to live, my darling brother, because I love you and I need you. You have to live, Eddie, you have to live.'

CHAPTER THIRTY-EIGHT

Father Kelly arranged for me to stay with the nuns at the convent in Cork, just like Mammy had when Stevie was in the hospital. I had to be close to Eddie, even if he didn't know that I was there.

The doctor told me that Caroline visited in the mornings, so I went every day in the afternoons and was able to go straight to his room and not sit in the corridor waiting for her to leave. Slowly, Eddie began to wake up, his eyes opening for a while and then closing again – he seemed peaceful and not in any pain. I held his hand and talked to him about my life since I'd gone away. I told him about Dublin and the new friends that I had made. I described St Stephen's Green and the lovely lake and the ducks. I didn't know whether he could hear me but I kept talking. 'I work in a bookshop, Eddie. It's called Finnigan's, you'd love it. When I first went to work there, I had to do all the dusting, but I didn't mind because it was books that I was dusting. I serve the customers now and I feel like a real shop girl. My friend Molly works in the antiquarian section, I know that you will understand that word because of your schooling. I've discovered writers I'd never heard of before, like Voltaire and Swift and Pope – I expect you have those books up at the Hall but it's all new to me.'

I liked living in the convent, I liked the peace and the gentleness of the sisters who were all very kind to me. In the mornings I helped the nuns. I polished and scrubbed and prepared food in the kitchen – it was the one thing that I could do to pay for my keep and to thank them for their kindness. Sometimes I would sit at the back of the chapel and listen to them singing, their voices blending together, old and young, filling the small space with the hymns of my childhood.

I spent a lot of time in the little chapel, which brought me comfort. It was a small place and plain. The walls were bare, nothing more than whitewash painted over lumpy plaster, and the windows were small, too narrow and high to look out of, but big enough for the sun to shine through. It moved around the chapel at different times of the day. I liked the light best in early afternoon, when shafts of sunlight fell onto the floor at the front of the chapel, making patches of brightness just in front of the simple wooden cross that hung above the small altar. I found it soothing to sit with the shadows behind me and the light in front of me. The chapel was warmest at this time of day too. I'd light a candle and place it amongst the other burned-out candles, the little sea of wax that had melted and solidified again, on the shelf beside the chapel door. The flickering candle flame symbolised life and hope. It was tiny and fragile, the slightest draught would have blown it out, but it was resilient: it wanted to burn, it clung to life.

I visited Eddie every day and lived for those afternoons when I could sit beside him in the silent room and read to him. As long as I could hear him breathing and see his chest rise and fall beneath the white sheet then I was at peace and full of hope.

I prayed to Jesus to let Eddie live. 'You brought Lazarus back from the dead and you turned water into wine, so I know that you can work miracles. Please look kindly on Eddie, because even though he's not a Catholic, he's a good, kind boy and I know you'd like him. He doesn't deserve to die, Jesus, so could you please look down on him in his hour of need and save him.'

One afternoon when I went into Eddie's room, his eyes were open and he looked right at me. 'Oh, Eddie,' I said, 'you're awake.'

'I knew you'd come, Nora,' he said, smiling sadly.

'I've been here every day,' I said. 'But you were always asleep.'

'I heard your voice but I thought that it was just a dream.' Eddie's eyes filled with tears. 'I won't ever walk again, Nora.'

I could hardly bear to think of what Eddie was feeling. To never walk again? To never feel the grass beneath your feet or kneel down in the garden and dig the soil. My heart went out to this dear boy. I held his hand. 'But you're alive, Eddie, and you have to have hope.'

'But I'm no use to anybody.'

'Yes, you are, you are still Eddie and you're loved and needed. *I* need you. I thought you were dead and I was heartbroken, but you're not. You have a lot of living to do and I'll be beside you and we'll visit the garden together and we'll watch the flowers grow. I won't leave you again.'

Eddie turned his head away from me. He didn't speak for a while, then he said, 'And how will I get to the garden?'

'We'll find a way,' I said.

The last thing I'd put in my bag before I'd left home was mine and Eddie's favourite book, *The Secret Garden*. I thought the book might give me comfort. I was so glad that I did, because now I could read to Eddie. The next day I started: '*When Mary Lennox was sent to Misselthwaite Manor to live with her uncle, everybody said she was the most disagreeable-looking child ever seen.*'

Reading seemed to give Eddie some peace; he often fell asleep, but I kept reading. When he woke, he would say, 'What have I missed?' and I'd go back and read it again. We had both read the book before but it was the kind of story that never lost its magic. I'd always felt sorry for Mary, who had lost her parents and her loving home in India, and been transported to a strange cold house on the moors, where she received no love or pity. There had been times when I thought that Eddie was unloved in that big house – Kitty had said that no one seemed to care for him. But it seemed that Caroline cared – maybe Eddie was the only person she *did* care about.

I read to Eddie every day, I poured water for him when he was thirsty and pulled the curtains when the sun was too bright for his eyes. Some days his mood was very low but I kept reading even though he didn't speak to me – the sound of my own voice gave me more comfort than the silent, sterile room.

I tried to write to Joe but I didn't know what to say to him. We had always found it so easy to talk to each other and even our silences were warm and full of love but that easiness had gone. My world had shrunk to the white room and the narrow bed where Eddie lay – I seemed to have no space in my heart for anything or anyone but Eddie.

Dublin, the bookshop, Josie, Molly and Ellis seemed a million years ago. Sometimes I closed my eyes and tried to remember Joe's face but I couldn't quite see it. It became blurred, not solid, no particular feature stood out. I tried to remember the feel of his lips on mine but I couldn't. I knew that I loved him and that he loved me because that is what we had told each other, but in the time that I was away, the actual feeling of that love escaped me and that frightened me, because I had been so sure that Joe was my future. The only worry I had had was where we would live, but now it seemed like a kind of dream, the thoughts of someone else. My place was with Eddie until he didn't need me anymore.

I'd been living at the convent for two weeks when I walked into Eddie's room one afternoon and his bed was empty. The sheets had been removed; the little pebble had gone from the bedside cabinet. My first thought was that he had died and I hadn't been beside him. I could hardly breathe. I ran back into the corridor, sobbing and calling his name, bringing a nurse running towards me.

'Is he dead?' I said. 'Is Eddie dead?'

She led me gently to a chair and sat down beside me. 'Hush now,' she said. 'His aunt took him home this morning.'

CHAPTER THIRTY-NINE

'I have to see him, Mammy,' I said. 'I have to.'

Mammy held my hand. 'Caroline Bretton had no choice but to let you visit Eddie in the hospital but I very much doubt that she will let you anywhere near the house.'

'Isn't there anything I can do?'

'The only thing I can think of is to ask Father Kelly to write to her on your behalf. Although I have to say, I don't think it will move that cold heart of hers. She has her nephew where she wants him and she'll have no interference from the likes of us.'

I knew Mammy was right, I knew that Caroline Bretton would make sure that I never saw Eddie again.

'Will you go back to Dublin?'

'I don't know, Mammy.'

Mammy smiled at me. 'You were happy there, Nora, you could be happy there again.'

'How can I just leave now, when Eddie needs me?'

'Let's hope that a letter from Father Kelly might just soften Caroline's heart and allow you to visit. Stranger things have happened, Nora. I found you, when all my hope had gone, so let's not give up just yet.'

Father Kelly agreed to write to Caroline Bretton, citing that I was, after all, Edward's half-sister and therefore entitled to visit him.

'I don't hold out much hope though, Nora,' he said. 'The Brettons' money gives them power and if she is determined to keep you away, then I fear there is little that anyone can do, but I'll do my best.'

I thanked him and decided to walk out to Minnie's to see Kitty. Minnie and Kitty welcomed me with open arms.

'My sister said that you are an asset to the shop,' said Minnie. 'And a pleasure to be around.'

'I love working there. Your sister allowed me to come home and she told me not to worry about anything. She was very kind to me, Minnie.'

'And why shouldn't she be? You're a grand girl.'

'Could you manage without me for a while, Minnie?' said Kitty.

'Get yourself away, I'd say you have a bit of catching up to do.'

'Thanks, Minnie,' I said.

Minnie opened the glass cabinet and took out two iced buns. She put them in a bag and passed them across the counter.

'Thank you, Minnie,' said Kitty. 'I can always eat a bun.'

'You can always eat anything,' said Minnie. 'It's a wonder you're not the size of a house.'

'I run a lot,' said Kitty, grinning.

We walked across the road to the beach and sat down on the flat rocks.

'Your mammy told me you were in Cork visiting Eddie. How is he doing?'

'His back is broken, Kitty. He will never walk again.'

'That's desperate sad, I'm so sorry, but why have you come home?'

'Caroline has taken him back to Bretton Hall and I know she won't let me see him.'

'Will you go back to Dublin?'

'I don't know. Father Kelly is going to write to her and try to persuade her to let me visit him.'

'I can't see her doing that – she's the spawn of the devil and has no kindness in her heart, especially where you are concerned.'

'That's what I think too, but I don't want to leave him. I promised him I wouldn't.'

We sat on the rocks eating our buns and looking out over the sea. Dublin was a grand city and the Liffy was a fine river but I'd missed this. This was *my* town, the town I'd grown up in. Sitting beside Kitty reminded me of when we were children, when we ran everywhere and attended all the funerals, giving them points out of ten, before we left childish things behind us.

It's a pity we can't give life points out of ten, but we can't, because life is about people, not about whether they are wearing their good shoes or Sunday hat. Life is about love, and how could I compare Kitty to Molly, Josie and Ellis and how could I compare my love for Eddie against my love for Joe? The truth was, I couldn't.

'And what about that lad of yours, Joe? Don't you want to go back to him?'

'That's what's troubling me. Part of me wants to see him but the other part wants to stay close to Eddie. If I run back to Dublin, I'd be leaving Eddie behind.'

'Maybe you don't love Joe the way you thought you did.'

'Sometimes I can't even remember his face,' I said, 'and that worries me as we had become so close.'

'Well, that doesn't sound like true love to me, Nora, and anyway, Eddie's your brother – you can't love him the same as you love Joe.'

'I don't, but…'

'But what?'

'I think that my loyalty lies with Eddie. I think he needs me more than Joe does.'

'Have you explained that to Joe? If he's as nice a lad as you say he is, maybe he'll understand and he'll wait until you're ready to go back to him.'

'That's the problem, Kitty. I haven't really explained anything much to him.'

Kitty finished her bun and stood up. 'Well, you should, or he'll be looking for another girl. How would you feel then?'

I thought about all the lovely things that Joe and I had done together. I remembered how it felt the first time he held me in his arms, when we danced under the twinkling lights and the first time we kissed as the snow fell around us. Then I tried to imagine him in the arms of another girl, taking her home to visit his family above the bakery. Maybe that would be the right thing for him to do – I couldn't just expect him to wait for me when I didn't know myself when, if ever, I would return to Dublin. And yet I wasn't ready to let him go and I knew that that was selfish.

'I don't know how I'd feel,' I said.

'Let's take a walk,' said Kitty. 'You need to clear your head.'

We walked along by the shore; it was good to feel the warm breeze on my face and to hear the waves breaking over the pebbles at the water's edge. The beach was almost empty but a woman was walking alone, with a thin black dog at her side, and two men were pulling a wooden boat up onto the shingle. Above us, seagulls spun and wheeled high in a blue sky threaded with white clouds. It was all so familiar to me; the give of the sand beneath the soles of my feet, the smell of the sea and seaweed, the brightness of the sunlight catching the tips of the waves so that I had to squint my eyes to look out to the horizon. There was a ship out there, dark against the sky, but I couldn't make out any of the details on account of the glare. I wondered if it was going away or coming back. It was impossible to tell.

Strange how two things that were the opposite of each other could, when the sun was in my eyes, look exactly the same.

Maybe that was what love was all about – maybe loving one person didn't diminish your love for another, with or without the sun in your eyes.

CHAPTER FORTY

It was a perfect summer's day; the sky was blue and cloudless and the only sounds were the birds twittering amongst the branches as I walked through the woods. I'd needed to be alone; I'd needed time to think. I kept walking until I came to the bridge that spanned the Blackwater. This place had always given me peace. I sat on the bank and watched the river flowing by and the patchwork of lush green hills on the opposite bank, sloping down to the river's edge. The little cottages scattered about the hills looked like doll's houses, waiting to be played with. This river had been a part of my life for as long as I could remember. I was so used to seeing it that I'd taken its beauty for granted but today, I thought how lucky I was to have grown up in a town that sat at the edge of one of God's most beautiful creations.

I crossed the bridge, skirted Granny and Grandad Collins's house and started to climb the hill. The sun was hot on my back as I climbed and I remembered another day when I'd climbed the hill with Kitty because she wanted to see Finn Casey. It had been summer then too, with a sky as cloudless as today. I wondered for a moment what Finn was doing now. Kitty had never received the longed-for letter, but she was happy and Tommy Nolan had taken Finn's place in her heart.

I was sweating by the time I got to the top of the hill, so I lay down on the soft grass and let the warmth of the sun shine down on my face. I could have stayed there all day. A fly landed on my bare arm, its tiny feet tickling my skin like the softest of feathers. I sat up and watched it fly away, going this way and that, as if it couldn't decide where to go to next, a bit like me really.

I looked down at the Lameys' cottage. I shaded my eyes and watched Rosie cantering around the field, the sun glistening on her back as she ran. I thought about poor Mrs Lamey, who was now a widow, grieving for her dead husband. Part of me thought I should go down and tell her how sorry I was for her loss, but my heart was so full of my own sadness that there was no room left for hers.

Father Kelly had received a letter from Caroline Bretton and as we expected, she had refused to allow me to visit on the grounds that Eddie needed peace and quiet and they had all the help they needed. Caroline Bretton was never going to change her mind and there was nothing I could do about it except think about Eddie and pine and worry.

Today, my mind was full of thoughts of the little garden. It had grown and flourished under Eddie's tender care, but without him there to look after it, what would become of it? Could the flowers survive on their own? I doubted it. There was nobody to make sure they had enough water, or sunlight, or to check that they weren't being eaten by aphids. Without anyone to take care of the beds, weeds would be free to run riot; they'd strangle the more delicate flowers. I imagined the beautiful roses being slowly choked by brambles snaking over the old stone wall, and nettles growing in the gaps between the cornflowers and ivy and hogweed and other invaders sneaking in to take the places of the plants that Eddie had tended so carefully.

And it wasn't just the flowers. Nobody was looking after the bench or the wall or the pond. If the pond became choked with falling leaves, the fish and the newts would suffocate and die. I could hardly bear to think about it: the poor garden, abandoned and desolate and left to its own fate until, in time, it would be as if there had never been a garden there at all.

All the work Eddie and I had done would have been for nothing. I wondered if the little robin missed us as much as I missed us being in the garden together. I wondered if Eddie, or anyone, would ever be in that garden again. It was time for me to leave and go back to Dublin, there was nothing left for me here – only sadness for a young boy who would never walk again.

Mammy was in the kitchen when I got home. She looked at me as I came through the door and smiled. 'You're going back to Dublin?'

I nodded.

'I think that you're doing the right thing, my Nora. Life doesn't take into account how sad we might be, it doesn't stop because we are grieving for someone we love. The sun will keep shining and the flowers will keep growing, and hiding away here isn't going to change that. This will always be your home, but maybe Dublin is your future.'

I went upstairs and started to put some clothes in my case. I was feeling hopeful and remembering the good times, working in Finnigan's and sharing digs with my friends, but most of all I was remembering Joe. I knew that Eddie would be well looked after, even if I couldn't be with him. Not seeing him was something I had to accept – there was no point moping around the house the way I had been. Mammy was right, life would go on and I had to get on with mine.

Stevie came into my room and looked at the bag. 'You're leaving?'

'Sit next to me,' I said.

Stevie sat down and I held his hand. 'I have to start living again, Stevie. There are some things in life that we can't change, however much we want to, otherwise we just go over and over things, all the what ifs. What if I had never gone to Dublin? What if Eddie had never been in that car? I know that's silly, but the mind can play silly tricks on you, and that could drive you mad. So, although I don't want to leave you, I have to get on with my life and know that what happened to Eddie was not my fault or God's, or poor Paddy Lamey's.'

'I've felt the same sometimes, Nora. I've been angry with God for making me the way I am but maybe there's a reason for it all and maybe one day we will find out what the reason is.'

I smiled at him. 'You're a wise boy, Stevie, and you're loved and it's love that's going to help you through this. I hope that Eddie knows that he is loved too.'

'Do you think Dooney will miss his uncle?'

'I think that because God in His wisdom made poor Dooney the way he was, that he has saved him from the pain and suffering that the rest of us feel. I think that Dooney has never really grown up, he's childlike and like a child. He will just accept that the kind man who took him for rides in his car doesn't come anymore.'

'It's sad though, isn't it?' said Stevie.

I nodded.

Just then we heard a knock on the door. Stevie stood up and went across to the window. 'There's a car outside, Nora.'

'Is it Father Kelly?'

'It's too posh to be Father Kelly's.'

I walked down the stairs just as Mammy opened the door to Caroline Bretton. They stood staring at each other.

'I am under no illusion that I am welcome in your house,' said Caroline. Her voice was high-pitched and shaky.

'I have never turned anyone away from this door,' said Mammy, 'so please come inside.'

Caroline looked out of place, standing there in her fine clothes, looking as if she'd rather be anywhere but here. I tried to imagine what she thought of our house, after the luxury she was used to. Even the servants' hall was bigger than our little kitchen. Not that I was ashamed of my home – I wasn't and I wouldn't swap it for all the Bretton Halls in Ireland.

'Please take a seat,' said Mammy.

I was still standing on the stairs, with Stevie on the stair behind me. Caroline looked across at me. 'I would like to speak to Nora,' she said.

'Then you will speak to myself and my husband as well,' said Mammy. 'Stevie, go and fetch your daddy.'

I could never have imagined Caroline Bretton sitting at the table in our kitchen but this was a different woman to the one I had feared and hated – she looked nervous and ill at ease, and there was no sign of the arrogance that I had come to know. We sat in silence waiting for Stevie to return with Daddy.

'Can I get you a sup of tea?' offered Mammy.

'That would be very welcome,' said Caroline.

I watched in fascination as she peeled off her gloves, slowly and deliberately, one finger at a time, and placed them on her lap.

Mammy boiled the kettle and took four cups down from the dresser. 'Do you take sugar?' she asked.

'Just milk, please,' said Caroline.

I'd never known anyone take tea without sugar – maybe it was just something to do with being an Honourable.

Mammy put the tea on the table just as Daddy, Stevie and Malachi came through the door. Daddy nodded at Caroline and went over to the sink to wash his hands. Malachi stood staring at Caroline.

'That your car?' he said.

Caroline looked down at him and actually smiled. 'Yes,' she said.

'S'big,' said Malachi.

'Yes, I suppose it is,' said Caroline.

'Stevie,' said Mammy, 'would you please take Malachi to feed Bonnie?'

'Yes, Mammy,' said Stevie, taking Malachi's hand and going outside.

'Caroline wants to speak to Nora, Colm,' said Mammy.

'Then let's hear what she has to say,' said Daddy, sitting down.

Caroline stared down at the table, she cleared her throat and began to speak.

'I know how you feel about me,' she said. 'But this isn't about me, it's about Edward, my nephew.' She paused. 'He is very unhappy. I have nurses caring for him around the clock and a doctor comes to the house every week.'

'What has all this got to do with Nora?' asked Mammy.

'He won't cooperate with anyone, he won't get out of bed and into a chair, he barely speaks. The doctor says that he is losing the will to live. The only person he wants to see' – she looked directly at me – 'is you, Nora.'

'Nora is going back to Dublin. She can't be at your beck and call,' said Mammy.

'Wait, Mammy,' I said. I turned to Caroline. 'How can I help him?'

'He needs a companion, someone of his own age, and the only one he will agree to have is you, Nora. You owe me nothing, I am aware of that, but I'm not asking for myself. I love my nephew with all my heart and if you can bring some hope back into his life, then I am asking, pleading, that you will consider working at the Hall as a companion for Edward.'

'She will be paid?' asked Daddy. 'I won't have her working for you as a skivvy and I won't have her sleeping in the servants' quarters – she will be no servant to the Bretton family. I have a long memory, Miss Bretton, a very long memory. You tried to have Cissy thrashed when she was just a child, you deliberately tripped her up when she was carrying a tray of glasses. You bullied and humiliated her the whole time she worked at the Hall and when she most needed help, you turned your back on her. If Nora wants this job you are offering her, then we will allow it, because she is your nephew's half-sister and she loves him but let me make this very clear: if you harm one hair on her head, or if you try to humiliate her as you did her mother, she will be out of there and she will never go back. Do I make myself clear?'

Caroline's face had gone red, she twisted the gloves on her lap and stared down at the floor. She didn't speak right away, then she looked at Daddy. 'Her only duty will be to Edward. She will be paid well.'

Daddy reached across the table and held my hand. 'This is your decision, Nora,' he said.

My heart was filled with joy, like seeing a rainbow after a storm. I could be with Eddie, I could help him and somehow, I knew that we would go back to the garden.

'I accept the position,' I said, 'and I will help Eddie in any way I can.'

Caroline stood up. 'Thank you, Nora,' she said.

I nodded. 'I will be there tomorrow morning.'

PART THREE

CHAPTER FORTY-ONE

My bedroom at Bretton Hall was bigger and grander than any room I'd ever slept in before. It was the old nursemaid's room, and had two doors: one leading onto the landing and the other leading into the nursery, the room where Eddie used to play when he was a child. I wasn't up on the top floor, in the eaves, with the other servants, but on the first floor, on the same level as the Honourables, although somewhat removed from Caroline and Eddie.

The landing outside my bedroom was severe. The floorboards were dark wood, polished to a fine shine, and the walls were lined with paintings of long-dead Honourables whose eyes seemed to watch me as I crept along to my room. I was always glad to slip inside, out of the cool gloom of that corridor.

The bedroom had felt strange at first, because it was so different to anything I'd known before, but not in a bad way. The walls were the colour of forget-me-nots and the curtains were of the palest yellow. Against one wall was a dressing table with a gold-edged mirror, and in the corner was a desk with a little chair in front of it. Most of the floor was covered with a large rug of intricate design, in the same blues and yellows. Even when the sky was grey and overcast, the room still looked like a summer's day.

It was such a pretty room, with watercolours on the walls; pictures of flowers and animals and cottages that I assumed had been chosen by the nursemaid. I never knew her, this woman, but she had left lavender bags in the drawers to keep away the moths and to add a sweet scent to the wood, and that was thoughtful of her; she must have been kind. The only other evidence of her that I found was a hairgrip in the bottom of the wardrobe.

The room had a soft shabbiness to it that soon made me feel comfortable. The windows were very old and did not quite fit in their frames, but it was summer and usually I had the windows thrown wide open anyway, to let in the sunshine and the warm air, the sound of birdsong and the smell of hay being cut in the meadows.

The bed was large and soft and had on it the most comfortable sheets I'd ever slept in. And the pillows! I had four pillows to myself and grand pillows they were, in white cotton slips with appliqued hems. Sometimes I put all four pillows behind me and sat up in my bed like a real lady; it was a wonderful feeling.

I remembered the day I had first seen the house; it was the day that me and Kitty had crawled through the broken bit of fence and into the grounds of Bretton Hall some five years ago. I remembered thinking that the bricks were made of gold and what it would feel like to live in such a grand place. Well, now I knew, and it was the very same as I imagined it would be.

In the mornings, my tea was brought to me on a tray and I could drink it in bed or else take it to the dressing table and sit in front of the mirror, staring at my face and the beautiful room behind me, wondering at the twists and turns of fate that had brought me here.

I was glad to wake up in that room every morning, glad to slip out of the bed and walk across the warm floorboards with my bare feet to draw back the curtains. I liked to rest my elbows on the window ledge and gaze out across the grounds, green and lovely in the bright sunlight. It was a far cry from the view from the windows of our house in Paradise Alley. I could see for miles; huge, lovely old trees, acres of meadowland; fields where sheep and cattle grazed. I could see the distant twinkling of the sea.

I was happy to wash at the washstand and then go to the wardrobe and take out my clothes for the day. I was glad to brush my hair at the dressing table and finish my tea and then check that my appearance was neat before I went to the door and turned the handle, ready to go and find Eddie, so that we could eat our breakfast together.

Caroline had kept her promise to Daddy and I was treated with kindness and respect by the servants and staff that worked at the Hall. She visited Eddie every day and was always polite to me. We were united in our love for Eddie, and both took pleasure in the smallest of improvements in his health. I only left his side when the nurses came in to tend to his personal needs, then I walked in the grounds.

I got to know Corny the gardener, and told him that I was worried about the secret garden and how it was going to flourish without me and Eddie to look after it.

'No need to worry yourself about that, Miss Nora,' he said, leaning on his spade. 'I've been keeping an eye on it meself, doing a bit of weeding and stuff. I won't let it die, so don't you be fretting yourself over that. I would be grateful if you would give my best wishes to Master Edward.'

'I will, of course,' I said. 'I'm sure it will give him pleasure to know that you are looking after it.'

I hadn't gone to the garden myself; I would only go back when Eddie was at my side.

Eddie slept a lot, but Dr Kennedy said that sleep was part of the healing process. After several weeks at the Hall, I had long since finished reading *The Secret Garden* to him, as well as some other books that he'd had in his room. It was then that Caroline said that I was welcome to use the library whenever I liked. It was on the ground floor just off the large hallway. The door squeaked as I opened it, as if it hadn't been opened for a long time. The room was dark, but not scary. One wall was taken up by rows and rows of books that reached up to the ceiling, and there was a ladder on a rail leaning against the shelves. The other three walls were of the darkest brown panelling and the windows were draped in heavy brown velvet. The curtains were closed, so that no light came into the room. I walked across and opened them just a little bit. I could see better then and gazed in wonder at the hundreds of books that looked as if they had never been touched. There were more books in this one room than in the whole of Finnigan's. I didn't know where to start looking for a book that Eddie would enjoy.

Just then, the door opened and Caroline walked in. I was surprised to see her and I waited for her to speak.

'Eddie told me that I would find you here,' she said. She didn't speak for a moment, then she said, 'I don't know why we have so many books, my parents were never great readers; I think this room was just for show. It was only my brother, Peter, that loved to read, and he passed his love of reading on to Edward. Even before Edward could walk, he loved being in this room.'

I was still wary of Caroline, and didn't quite trust her – she had hurt my mammy and been nothing but unkind to me before I moved to the Hall. I took a deep breath. 'I want to find a new book to read to him,' I said. 'But I don't know where to start looking.'

Caroline looked along the shelves, her hand trailing along the spines, then reached up and handed me a book. I looked at the cover: *Moby Dick*, by Herman Melville.

I opened it up and smelled the pages.

'What are you doing?' said Caroline.

I felt foolish – I should never have done that, not there and especially not in front of her.

To my horror, tears started to pour down her face. She didn't brush them away, she just let them fall.

'I didn't mean to upset you,' I said, quickly.

Caroline walked across to the window, her back to me, and seemed almost to be speaking to herself. 'It's what my brother Peter used to do, we all made fun of him but he kept doing it.' She turned and faced me. 'He said that every book and every story had its own special smell.'

Suddenly, my father became real to me. I could see the young boy who loved to read books and who smelled the pages just as I did. I started to cry and suddenly Caroline's arms were around me. We stood, holding each other. Caroline cried for her brother who had died and I cried for the father I had never known.

That was the day that Caroline Bretton and the girl from Paradise Alley became friends.

CHAPTER FORTY-TWO

As the summer came to an end, Eddie allowed himself to be lifted from the bed and into a chair by the window, where he could look out over the grounds. He could see the tall trees that edged the bottom of the sweeping lawn. We both knew that beyond those trees was the garden, but Eddie never mentioned it, so neither did I.

We sat side by side, in front of the beautiful windows, and I started to read *Moby Dick* to him. 'Call me Ishmael…' I began. We were both spellbound by the story of Captain Ahab, who sought revenge on the great white whale, Moby Dick, who had bitten off half his leg. We sailed the high seas with him, on his ship called the *Pequod*, searching for the whale. Caroline had chosen well – the story would keep us enthralled until the very last page.

Eddie didn't have much of an appetite. Me and Caroline were worried that he would never get strong if he didn't eat, so as soon as he fancied something, I would go down to the kitchen and ask Mrs Dinny, the cook, if she would make it for him.

'You come down as often as you like, Nora,' she'd said. 'I will make him anything he wants; our hearts are only breaking for the poor boy. We all feel so helpless, but one thing I can do for him is cook and it will be an honour to do it. You come down any time you like, girl.' Her eyes had filled with tears. 'There are only the three of you to cook for now, and I miss the days when I was rushed off my feet and longing for a bit of a rest.'

'My mammy always says "be careful what you wish for",' I'd said.

'And your mammy is right, Nora. Everything has changed, even Miss Caroline. The accident seems to have knocked the rough edges off her.'

'Thank the Lord for that!' Rosie the kitchen maid had said, as she scrubbed down the table.

'And who are you to be judging your betters, Rosie Tierney?' snapped Mrs Dinny.

Rosie had coloured up and went back to scrubbing the table as if her life depended on it.

'Sorry, Mrs Dinny,' she mumbled.

'I should think so as well,' said Mrs Dinny.

Most of the staff had been dismissed after the accident, as there were no grand banquets or balls to cater for. A lot of the rooms had been closed off and white dust sheets covered the furniture. Two housemaids, Kathleen and Alice, were kept on to keep the house clean, and Caroline still had her own lady's maid to see to her needs.

As summer turned to autumn, my thoughts returned to the garden. I knew how beautiful it would be at this time of year and I longed to be there. I longed to sit on the bench with the leaves falling around me and fly high over the pond on the swing that Eddie had made. I longed for the feeling of peace that the garden had always given me and I longed for the days when Eddie and I had worked side by side, a life that had gone forever.

It was easier to write to Joe now, because I had more to tell him about than a white hospital room with a single bed where Eddie had lain. Now I could tell him about Bretton Hall and my beautiful bedroom and the library that held more books than Finnigan's bookshop, but I couldn't tell him what he wanted to know. 'When are you coming back to Dublin, Nora? When will I see you again?'

The Finnigan's girls all wrote to me as well, and all asked the same questions, but they were questions I couldn't answer right now. My only thoughts were for Eddie. Joe felt like someone I had known in a different life, a world away from the life I was living now. I often wondered whether, if the accident that had me hurrying back home had never happened, would Joe and I have got closer? Would he have asked me to marry him by now? And if he had, would I have said yes? I knew that it wasn't fair to leave Joe hanging on and hoping that I would soon return to Dublin, but I was too afraid to just let him go. I remembered Kitty saying, 'You can't love Eddie the way you love Joe, because he's your brother.' I knew that what she had said was true, but right now Eddie needed me more than Joe did. But that didn't mean that I didn't still care for Joe. Everything was so mixed up since I had left Dublin, and I couldn't trust what I was feeling. It made my yearning for the peace of the garden all the stronger.

I didn't have a particular day off, I could come and go whenever I liked, as long as I wasn't needed by Eddie, and today, I'd joined Daddy and Stevie on the milk round. Stevie was now able to fill the jugs with milk that our neighbours brought out to the cart; it made him feel useful and it was good for him to get out and about. It also took some of the load off Grandad Doyle. Daddy paid Stevie every Friday and my little brother was proud to be earning his own money.

'Your mammy used to help on the round when she was a child,' said Daddy. 'That was when she first encountered Miss Caroline Bretton, who threatened to have her thrashed for being rude to her.'

'What had Mammy done?' said Stevie.

'She called her Miss Baggy-knickers.'

'Really?' I said. 'She really called her Miss Baggy-knickers?'

'She did,' said Daddy, grinning, 'and Miss Caroline never let her forget it.'

'She's better now, Daddy,' I said, gently. 'The accident has softened her.'

Daddy nodded. 'Sometimes it takes a tragedy like this for people to appreciate what they had and what they have lost.'

'We've become friends.'

'I imagine it is your love for Eddie that has brought you together. Am I right?'

'That's exactly it.'

'Then I am glad for you both.'

'Miss Baggy-knickers,' said Stevie, giggling, and we giggled all the way home.

Dr Kennedy called at the Hall twice a week and brought news of the town. Eddie and I enjoyed his visits. He was a kind, clever man and we both respected him. Sometimes they played chess together – Eddie had tried to teach me but however often he explained it, I just couldn't get the hang of it, so it was a treat when he could play the game with the doctor. One autumn afternoon, as I was reading to Eddie, there was a tap on the door and Dr Kennedy came into the room.

I closed the book and smiled at him.

'And what thrilling adventures are you reading today?' he said.

I handed him the book. '*David Copperfield*,' I said, 'by Charles Dickens.'

'Good choice,' he said, smiling. 'My favourite book by that gentleman is *Bleak House*, but you can't go wrong with any of them, for he's as fine a writer as you will ever have the pleasure of reading.'

'This isn't your usual day for visiting,' said Eddie.

The doctor pulled up a chair and sat between us. 'I have something I wanted to tell you myself,' he said, 'before you heard it from someone else.'

I couldn't imagine what he had to say.

'The time has come for me to retire,' he continued. 'These old bones need a bit of a rest.'

I could see that Eddie looked shocked by the news; Dr Kennedy had cared for him all his life and given him comfort and friendship since the accident. 'You will be missed,' he said sadly.

'By everyone,' I added. It wasn't just me and my family who would miss him. The whole town would miss this dedicated man, who came out in all weathers to help the sick and troubled. He wasn't just a doctor, he had become a friend to so many people over the years. I thought of all the times he had helped our family, ferrying Mammy and Stevie up to the hospital in Cork and rushing to Mammy's side when I thought that Malachi was dead.

'Ah, they'll soon forget me when they have a young doctor with his finger on the pulse, so to speak. It's what the town needs. Medicine is moving forwards every day and a fresh new brain is just what the doctor ordered.' He chuckled at his own joke.

'You'll still visit us, won't you?' I said.

'Of course, I'll need something to fill my time and who better to visit than yourselves? Besides, Eddie is two games up on me and I'm a sore loser,' he said, grinning.

'But who will take your place, doctor?' said Eddie.

'Well, it just so happens that I brought him with me. Would you like to meet him? He's just outside.'

Eddie nodded.

Dr Kennedy opened the door and Finn Casey walked into the room.

CHAPTER FORTY-THREE

It was Kitty's day off and we were sitting on the wall watching Sean and Malachi playing in the sand. They weren't babies anymore; Sean was six and Malachi was five and they loved each other like brothers. Autumn had always been my favourite season but today felt more like the middle of winter. There was just greyness where the sky met the sea, it was hard to tell where the sky ended and the sea began. There was a bitterly cold wind that would take the nose off you and heavy dark clouds were threatening rain at any minute. Further along the beach the waves were dashing and splashing against the rocks under the lighthouse, throwing white foam up into the air. We were both frozen but the boys didn't seem to mind one bit and they were having such a great time that we didn't want to drag them away. Me and Kitty would rather have been in Minnie's, sitting by the fire, drinking hot tea and eating buns.

I could feel Kitty shivering beside me. 'If it starts to rain, we're going,' she said. We sat on the wall, staring out over the grey choppy sea. 'Are you going to stay in Ballybun forever, Nora?' said Kitty. 'I'd be awful glad if you did, because even though I have Tommy, I've missed you.'

'I've missed you too, Kitty.'

'Even with all your new friends?'

I nodded. 'They are all lovely but they didn't sit on the graveyard wall marking funerals out of ten. They weren't there when we crawled through the fence and met Eddie and they weren't there when Malachi was born. We have a history, you and I, that I will never have with anyone else. A king once said, "Bring me my old slippers, for they know my feet better than the new ones."'

'So, I'm a pair of old slippers now, am I?' said Kitty, laughing.

I slipped my arm through hers. 'I think maybe you are,' I said. 'Just as I hope that's what I am to you.'

Just then we heard the rumble of thunder. Kitty, who was terrified of lightning, jumped down off the wall and dragged an unwilling Sean away from his sandcastle. He set up a wail of protest at this interruption, which started Malachi wailing as well.

'We'll get you both a sticky bun,' promised Kitty, which shut them up immediately.

As the four of us crossed over the road to Minnie's, the heavens opened and we broke into a run. We sat at the table closest to the fire. It was lovely to feel the warmth on our bare legs. Kitty put a couple of logs on it and they spat and hissed in the grate, sending a blast of warmth into the café. Once Sean and Malachi were happily eating their buns, I told Kitty about the new doctor being none other than Finn Casey.

'Finn Casey?' she said, her face lighting up. '*My* Finn Casey?'

'I wouldn't let Tommy hear you say that,' I said, grinning.

'Of course, I won't, but Finn Casey. Is he still as gorgeous as ever?'

'He's an Adonis,' I said.

'Grandad Doyle?'

'The very person. It means a handsome man.'

'And he's the new doctor?'

'He is.'

'How did that happen?'

'Finn has been staying at his aunt's after his uncle died in the car crash and was about to go back to England to look for a job when Doctor Kennedy told him that he was retiring and how did he feel about staying in Ballybun and taking over from him.'

'The only trouble with that,' said Kitty, grinning, 'is that you could only go and see him if you had a problem from the neck up.'

I started giggling. 'I hadn't thought of that,' I said, 'but you're right, so let's pray to God that we don't develop any afflictions lower than that.'

'I suppose a broken leg would be okay,' said Kitty.

'That wouldn't be so bad.'

'I suppose you'll be seeing a lot of him then,' said Kitty, making a 'poor me' face.

I nodded. 'Doctor Kennedy called in a few times a week to check on Eddie, so I suppose Finn will be doing the same.'

'You lucky old thing, Nora Doyle. You'll probably end up falling in love with him and becoming a doctor's wife. Imagine how beautiful your kids will be.'

'For Heaven's sake, Kitty, I've got Joe, so I won't be falling under the spell of Doctor Finn Casey, however gorgeous he is.'

Kitty sighed. 'You say that now, but when he's leaning over Eddie being all doctorly, you might change your mind.'

'Well, I won't,' I said. 'Would you give up Tommy Nolan for Finn Casey if you got the chance?'

A dreamy look came over Kitty's face. 'I wouldn't give up Tommy Nolan for anyone.'

'Well, there you are.'

'What's it like living there?'

'It's like nothing I've ever known before.'

'I hated the place. All those bloody pictures of old men staring down from the walls. They gave me the creeps. I used to have to dust them and I swear to God that their eyes followed me whenever I moved.'

'You have a vivid imagination, Kitty Quinn.'

'I hated working there. Miss Caroline had it in for me, Nora. If she was coming up the stairs and I was going down, I had to go back up again because I wasn't allowed to pass her. She was an awful baggage of a woman, she scared the bejeebers out of me.'

'She scared the bejeebers out of me too, but she's changed, Kitty. The accident has changed her.'

'I suppose it was a terrible sad thing to happen, losing your whole family in one go like that.'

'But she still has Eddie, and however much of a baggage she was, I'm glad that he has her.'

'I still wouldn't trust her,' said Kitty.

'I'm beginning to. There's a softness about her that I'd never seen before and she's so gentle with Eddie.'

'I'll just have to take your word for that, Nora, for I've never seen that side of her.'

'But it's there, Kitty.'

'Is she the owner of Bretton Hall now?'

'I'm not sure, I think that maybe it would have passed down to Eddie.'

'So where do *you* come into it? After all, he was *your* father too and you're the eldest.'

Such a thing had never crossed my mind. How could a girl from Paradise Alley inherit Bretton Hall?

'I wouldn't want it, Kitty. I wasn't born to it, and anyway, what would I do with a place like that?'

'You could live in it with Finn Casey,' said Kitty, grinning.

'And pigs might fly.'

'I wish Henry could fly, that pig smells something rotten.'

'You'd miss him.'

'The only one that would miss him is Breda. If she had her way the pair of them would quite happily live under the table.'

Minnie brought our tea and buns to the table.

'My sister was asking after you, Nora,' said Minnie, sitting down with us. 'She says that everyone is missing you at Finnigan's.'

'That's nice of her, Minnie. I miss them too, I loved working there,' I said.

'Have you any notion of going back to Dublin?'

Mammy and Daddy had been asking me the same question and Kitty had just asked the same thing on the beach.

'Eddie needs me, Minnie,' I said.

'But don't you think that you should be getting on with your own life? What can you do for that poor boy?'

'I read to him, it gives him some peace.'

'You are a kind girl, Nora, but you have your whole life ahead of you and you can't spend it reading to a poor boy who will never walk again. I'm sorry for him, of course I am, but you owe the Brettons nothing and neither does your mammy.'

'Minnie's right, you know, Nora,' said Kitty gently.

'I promised him that I would stay for as long as he needs me.'

'Then I'll say no more,' said Minnie, standing up. 'You're a sensible enough girl and I'm sure you'll make the right decision in the end. The trouble with kindness is that it can be taken advantage of.'

'Don't worry about me, Minnie, for I'm not being taken advantage of, I promise you that.'

'I'm glad to hear it, Nora, for the Brettons have done your family no favours.'

Sean and Malachi had fallen asleep with icing smeared all over their faces. I thought about what Minnie had just said, but my mind was made up. I would stay with Eddie, even if it meant that we would grow old together, reading every book in the library.

CHAPTER FORTY-FOUR

After a week of wind and rain the sun had come out. Eddie was asleep, so me and Finn went outside for some air. The trees were almost bare, the leaves covering the lawn like a patchwork quilt of reds and golds and browns, and gathering in the corners of the steps leading down to the gardens. They were slippery under foot and Finn put his hand under my elbow.

'We don't want you falling,' he said. 'One patient at a time is enough.'

I looked across at the tall trees that hid the garden. 'I wish Eddie could see the garden before autumn ends,' I said. Eddie had told Finn about the secret garden so he knew what I was talking about.

'He could, you know,' said Finn. 'It would do him good to get outside, it's not healthy for him to be cooped up in that bedroom every day.'

'But how could we get him out?'

'A wheelchair. I think Miss Caroline would be alright with that – she wants the best for him and I think that the best thing for him is a change of scenery.'

The thought of Eddie being back in the place he loved filled me with joy. 'What a wonderful idea,' I said, smiling. 'We could take him there every day, we could take him back to the garden.'

'We could,' said Finn, smiling down at me. 'He's lucky to have you, Nora.'

'I'm lucky to have him. I thought I would never see him again after Caroline refused to let me visit him.'

'Love is a strange thing,' said Finn. 'It makes you forget about yourself and put the one you love above everything else, and maybe that is what has happened to her.'

I thought about Joe. I hadn't put him above everything else – did that mean I didn't love him enough? My mind was all over the place when I thought about him but the one thing that I was certain of was that I was where I was supposed to be, and for now that's all I could think about.

'A penny for them,' said Finn softly.

'I have a boy in Dublin, Finn.'

'And you're missing him?'

I didn't answer, because I didn't know what to say that would make any sense.

'It will all come right, Nora. Life has a way of taking you to the right place and maybe for you, right now, this is the place you are meant to be.'

Finn's words comforted me, because I knew he was right – this was where I was meant to be. He seemed to be able to look into my heart and know what I was thinking. I had no regrets, but that didn't mean that I didn't love Joe.

Finn and I walked through the beautiful grounds of Bretton Hall. The sun shone down on the still, wet leaves, turning the lawn into a magical multi-coloured carpet. We didn't speak as we walked, but it was a companionable silence. Finn was a man now, and not the young boy I had spent time with when I was staying at Granny Collins's farm. I had thought about him from time to time since then – something would remind me of that time we'd spent together. Eating lunch under the tree and watching Rosie galloping around the field – it had been a happy time and I'd found myself missing him when he'd returned to England.

We had become friends back then, even though I must have seemed like a child to him. There was something about Finn that made me feel safe – I felt that I could talk to him about anything and he would understand and, even more importantly, Eddie liked him as well.

*

Caroline agreed that the chair would be a great idea and wondered why no one had thought of it before. We didn't tell Eddie about it – we wanted it to be a surprise – and two weeks later, when it arrived, we were standing outside the bedroom door, all of us excited to see Eddie's reaction. We opened the door and Finn wheeled the chair inside.

But Eddie stared at it in horror and shouted, 'Take it away!'

Caroline was at his side in a second. She knelt beside the bed and held his hand. 'What's the matter, darling?'

'I said, take it away!' he shouted again. 'Take the bloody thing away and never bring it back.'

We had got it wrong; something that we thought Eddie would love, he hated.

Caroline fled from the room, tears running down her face. Finn began to follow her with the chair, but I shook my head and he left it where it was, closing the door behind him.

I walked across to the window.

'What are you still doing here?' snapped Eddie. I continued to look out of the window.

'It's my job to look after you,' I said. 'It's what you pay me for.'

'Well, I want to be left alone.'

'Okay,' I said, turning around. Eddie's face was red and angry. 'So, you don't like the chair, but you didn't have to be so rude about it.'

'I didn't ask for it and I don't want it,' he said, glaring at me.

'Do you think we did this to make you unhappy? Do you think that the three of us put our heads together and thought, "I know, we'll get him something he hates," and decided that what you would hate most was a wheelchair. Is that what you think?'

He mumbled something.

'Speak up, Eddie, I can't hear you.'

'No,' he said softly, 'of course I don't think that.'

'Then what is it?'

'I won't be pushed around like a baby.'

'Stevie said that to me once.'

Eddie looked at me. 'Did he?'

'Yes, I'd been telling him about the garden and he wanted to see it but his legs wouldn't carry him that far. I suggested that we used Malachi's pushchair and he said he wouldn't be pushed through the town like a baby for everyone to see.'

'So you understand.'

I walked across to the bed. 'Of course I understand, but look at it, Eddie, just look at it. It's just a chair that happens to have four wheels but those four wheels can take you out of here. There can be more to your life than these four walls. You can feel the sun on your face and the wind in your hair. You created something beautiful and it's going to die without you there. That chair that you hate so much can carry you back to the garden.'

'But what use would I be there?'

'You could teach your aunt or Finn what you've taught me, and between us we could bring the garden back to life.'

Eddie looked across the room at the chair. There were tears in his eyes. 'What would I do without you, Nora?'

'You will never be without me, Eddie,' I said. 'Never.'

CHAPTER FORTY-FIVE

We spent every day in the garden, until the late autumn sun sank behind the tall trees and the days became shorter. Under Eddie's guidance, Finn and I cleared the weeds and brambles that had been allowed to wander at will. We pulled at the bindweed that was choking the roses. We dug the soft soil and planted spring bulbs, before the ground got too hard and waterlogged. Crocuses and narcissi, tulips and snowdrops, hyacinths and winter pansies. Corny had given us a rake and Finn cleared the fallen leaves from the top of the pond. Mrs Dinny provided us with enough food to feed an army, and even Caroline would come to check on our progress. Finn came as often as he could, but as he was now the town's doctor, it was often just me and Eddie, and I cherished the time we spent together.

Caroline always wrapped Eddie in a blanket – she worried about him all the time but I could see the change in him. The colour was coming back into his cheeks and there was a brightness in his eyes that I hadn't seen for a long time. He had something to live for now, he had hope.

Joe's letters had become fewer and fewer and I wasn't surprised, because I'd hardly answered any of his, but one morning there was a letter for me on the hall table. I didn't open it immediately, because I wasn't sure that I wanted to read what he'd written.

The day was cold and grey, much too cold for Eddie to go outside, and anyway, he had the start of a cold and a bit of a cough, so I read to him instead. We were both enjoying the books by Charles Dickens and were halfway through *Little Dorrit*. The whole time I was reading, I was aware of Joe's letter in my pocket.

'What's wrong?' said Eddie.

'There's nothing wrong,' I said.

'Yes, there is,' he said. 'I know you, Nora Doyle. I know you just as well as the books you read to me.'

I sighed. 'I've had a letter from Joe.'

'And it's upset you?'

'I haven't opened it,' I said.

'What are you scared of?'

I closed the book and put it on the table beside Eddie's bed. 'I'm scared that he is going to ask me questions I can't answer.'

'I imagine he wants to know when you are going to go back to Dublin?'

I nodded.

'And when *are* you going back, Nora? You must have thought about it.'

'I don't want to leave you and it's been so long since I saw Joe, I don't know if I still love him.'

'You said to me that there is more to life than these four walls, but doesn't the same apply to you? Don't you want to get on with your life?'

'I *am* getting on with my life. I'm happy here, I'm happy being with you. I don't feel as if I'm losing out on anything. I'm not here out of some kind of duty, I'm here because I want to be here.'

Eddie smiled at me. 'Then you are very easily satisfied, Nora Doyle.'

I smiled back. 'You are right, Edward Bretton, I am. Do you want me to keep reading?' I asked.

Eddie shook his head. 'I'm tired. I think I'll have a sleep.'

I needed some air, so I got my coat and went outside. It was very windy, so I went around the side of the house where it was more sheltered. I sat on a stone bench and took the letter out of my pocket. I felt anxious and a bit sick as I opened the envelope and took out the letter. The thin paper fluttered in the wind as I started to read Joe's familiar writing.

Dearest Nora,

I've started this letter so many times and torn it up but I need to say this to you.

I know that right now your place is with your brother, I understand that, of course I do, but I need to know if your feelings towards me have changed. If you still love me the way I love you, then I will continue to wait for you to come back, however long it takes. But if your feelings have changed, then I need to know. It's not that I want to look for someone else, it's not that. I have never loved anyone the way I love you, Nora, and I thought that we had a future together. You may not be telling me the truth because you don't want to hurt me, but not knowing is hurting even more.

Please think about what I have said, and just tell me the truth.

With all my love, always.

Joe xxx

I folded the letter and put it back in the envelope. I didn't know what to do, or what I could say to him. I had tried so many times to imagine what it was like to be loved by Joe and to love him in return, but I just couldn't make it real, I just couldn't bring those feelings back – they just weren't there anymore. I'd even tried to imagine what life would be like without him if I never saw him again, but even that didn't seem to touch my heart. I needed to talk to someone, I needed to go home. I left a note on the hall table to let Caroline know that Eddie was sleeping and I needed to go home for the afternoon.

The wind coming off the sea was fierce as I walked along the Strand and as I neared the town it started to rain. I hurried past the shops and houses and by the time I got to Paradise Alley, I was soaked and shivering from the cold.

Mammy was in the kitchen when I finally got home. She helped me off with my coat and hung it in front of the fire, then she got a towel and started drying my hair. 'Jesus, child, what are you doing out on a day like this? You'll catch your death! Sit by the fire and I'll get you a nice sup of hot tea.'

'Thank you, Mammy.'

I held my hands out towards the flame and rubbed them together, while Mammy made the tea.

'Something's troubling you, Nora.'

'It's Joe,' I said, sitting down.

'Ah,' she said, spooning sugar into my cup.

I took the letter out of my pocket and pushed it towards her. I drank my tea and waited for her to finish reading.

'I don't know what to say to him,' I said.

'The truth, Nora – that's what he wants to know and it's what he deserves to know.'

'But I don't know what the truth is, Mammy, because I don't know how I feel about him anymore.'

'Then that is what you must tell him.'

'But he won't understand, I don't understand myself.'

'Nora, I nearly lost your daddy because I couldn't tell him what was in my heart. I was as confused as you are now and when I *did* realise that I loved him, I didn't trust him enough to tell him about you, so I ran away. I don't know your Joe, but from what you have told me and from reading this letter, I would say that he is a good man and an understanding man. What I have learned in this life, Nora, is that if truth and kindness are part of everything you say and do, you won't go far wrong.'

'But what if he says he can't wait for me to make up my mind?'

'Then you will either accept it, or realise what you have lost and run back to Dublin as fast as you can.'

I trusted my mammy; she was one of the wisest people I knew. 'I'll write to him,' I said. 'And I will tell him the truth.'

CHAPTER FORTY-SIX

The next afternoon I wrote to Joe. I didn't know whether telling him the truth was going to satisfy him, but I knew that I had to try and make him understand. Joe had started his letter with 'Dearest Nora', but I was afraid that if I started with 'Dearest', it might give him false hope, so I began to write.

Dear Joe,

Thank you for your letter. You have asked me to tell you the truth and that is what I will try to do.

My time in Dublin and my time with you feels like another world, and as the days go on, I am finding it more difficult to bring to mind what we had. You ask if my feelings towards you have changed and it's not an easy question to answer. I think maybe it's my life that has changed. As you know, I live at Bretton Hall now as a companion to my brother Eddie. I know that you need me, Joe, but right now, Eddie needs me more.

Mammy says if I tell you that I don't love you anymore, I would lose you and then regret it and I believe that could be true. I think of our time together and I know how much I cared for you and wanted to be with you. I don't know if you can just stop loving someone, but what I think I know is that life can change, and mine has changed. But that doesn't mean that my feelings for you have changed, I just don't know. Am I being selfish by asking you to wait? I think that perhaps I am.

The truth isn't easy, is it? Especially when I'm not sure what the truth is, but this is my truth as I know it.

I don't want to lose you, Joe, but this is where I have to be
and I don't know if, or even when, I will ever return to Dublin.
Love
Nora x

I folded the letter and put it in an envelope. Eddie still had a cough and was resting, so I decided to walk into town and post it before I had time to change my mind. I had no idea what Joe's reaction would be when he read it but I had told the truth, just like Mammy said I should, and I was prepared to live with the consequences.

Before posting the letter, I decided to visit my namesake. There had been many times in my life when I found myself pouring things out to her that I hadn't been able to tell anyone else and I had always walked away feeling calmer and at peace. I climbed the hill to the workhouse and walked up to the graveyard. Autumn had given way to winter; the trees were bare of the beautiful leaves and the rows of crosses looked as bleak and forbidding as the grey sky above them. I pulled my coat tighter around me and plunged my cold hands deep into the pockets.

Nora Foley's grave was at the top of the slope under a tree. At any other time of the year it would have looked peaceful but today, it just made me feel sad. Nora had only been fourteen years old when she died. She had never known a life outside that great stone building that loomed over the graveyard. She had never fallen in love, or known the feeling of holding her own child in her arms. Mammy said that Holy God in his love and wisdom had taken her up to Heaven, because she had never been strong enough for this world and he wanted to take care of her. I wasn't sure I believed that, because if he loved her that much, why did he make her weak in the first place? Now I would have to go to confession for questioning the ways of the Lord.

I didn't want to lose my faith, but I found myself questioning things that I had never questioned before. Mammy would probably say it was all my book learning but I think it was being with Eddie, who made me see things in a different light.

I knelt down in front of Nora's grave. The ground was damp and cold. I pulled away the weeds that had almost covered her name. Mrs Foley used to keep the little grave neat and tidy but she couldn't do that anymore on account of her health. I promised myself that I would visit more often and tend to the grave myself.

'Am I doing the right thing, Nora?' I said softly. 'Am I going to lose Joe because of Eddie? Am I being mad altogether? I am at an age you didn't even reach. Shouldn't I be dancing with Joe under the twinkling lights, and walking home together hand in hand and being held in his arms? Shouldn't I be working in the bookshop that had always been my dream and having fun with the girls? Shouldn't there be more to my life than sitting beside Eddie every day? And yet there is something holding me there that is stronger than all those things. Maybe it is love, a different kind of love that I can't walk away from. I promised Eddie that I would never leave him; I never gave Joe that promise.'

I sat for a while longer, until drops of icy rain fell onto the grave. 'I'll come again, Nora,' I said, and walked away back down the hill and posted the letter.

When I got back to Bretton Hall, Caroline met me in the hallway. It looked as if she had been crying.

My stomach clenched with dread. 'Is it Eddie?' I said.

Caroline nodded. 'Finn is with him.'

I opened the bedroom door and looked across the room. Eddie's eyes were closed and he was pale, but there were beads of sweat on his forehead. The sheets had been pulled back and Eddie's chest was bare. Finn was sitting beside him, holding his hand, and a nurse was bathing Eddie's body.

'What's wrong with him, Finn?' I said.

'He has a severe chest infection; we are trying to get his temperature down.'

'But he'll be alright, won't he?'

'We'll know in the next twenty-four hours, Nora.'

The nurse left and I sat next to the bed opposite Finn. I stroked Eddie's hand, tears rolling down my cheeks. Finn came around the bed, he held my hand and wiped the tears from my face. 'You have to get better, Eddie,' I whispered. 'Spring will come soon and you have to see the flowers we planted. Remember the garden in the spring? Remember how beautiful it is? You have to be strong, Eddie, you have to live.'

Me, Finn, and Caroline stayed with Eddie all night, taking it in turns to sleep. I watched his chest rise and fall, each breath a struggle. I watched him fighting to live. As the dawn sent shafts of thin wintry sun into the room, Eddie opened his eyes. Caroline was asleep in a chair; I walked across the room and gently touched her arm. She woke immediately and clutched my arm.

'He's awake, Caroline,' I said.

She was at his side in an instant, smoothing his damp hair away from his forehead.

'Have you come back to us, my darling boy?' she said.

Eddie didn't answer, but he smiled and fell back into a peaceful sleep. I looked at Finn, who nodded. The three of us stood beside the bed with our arms around each other. Caroline and I were crying tears of joy and relief; Caroline stepped away first and tucked the sheets around Eddie lovingly. Finn and I stayed where we were and I was aware of him being so close. I closed my eyes and laid my head against his chest and in that moment, I never wanted to let him go. I knew that I had made the right decision in staying.

CHAPTER FORTY-SEVEN

Eddie's recovery was long and worrying and I realised for the first time what a tenuous hold he had on life. I wanted to stay beside him every minute I could, even when he slept, which was more and more often.

One day, as I was reading to him, Caroline came into the room.

'Tell Nora she needs to get some air, she won't listen to me,' said Eddie.

'Well, if you can't persuade her, I'm sure I can't,' said Caroline.

'I'm feeling tired,' said Eddie, 'Go for a walk, the pair of you.'

'And is that an order, Master Bretton?' I asked.

'It is,' said Eddie, grinning.

'Well, Nora,' said Caroline, 'we have our orders, so we'd better do as we're told. The master has spoken.'

We got our coats and went outside. 'Let's go down to the beach,' said Caroline.

We walked down the lawn and took the little path that led us to the shore. The day was chilly but there was a thin wintry sun filtering through the clouds that made walking along the shore pleasant. It was strange to be in this spot with Caroline though, instead of Kitty.

The water was calm and still, little waves gently tipping the shore.

I wanted to ask her something but I didn't know if I should – I didn't know if it was my place to ask. I took a deep breath. 'You never married,' I started.

Caroline smiled. 'I was engaged once, but I realised that he wasn't the right man for me.'

'Was he not kind?'

'It had nothing to do with kindness, Nora. It was Edward.'

'Edward?'

'I imagine that you know his mother died giving birth to him?'
I nodded.

'I'm not saying that my brother never loved the child, he was just never there for him. In fact, he spent so much time travelling that the two were like strangers, and so I became as much a mother to Edward as if I'd given birth to him myself.'

'And what about the feller?'

'Victor was jealous of the time I spent with the baby, and so we parted. I knew then that no man was ever going to be more important to me than Edward, and I haven't regretted it for a minute.'

'Do you not get lonely?'

'I happen to like my own company, and I have Edward.'

I smiled. 'I'm glad you have him.'

Finn Casey came to the Hall as often as he could and we worked together side by side, enjoying the crisp cold air and each other's company. Sometimes I would look up from some task and see him looking at me and I'd smile at him.

I found myself looking forward to his visits, perhaps more than I should. I took more trouble with my appearance, I spent longer deciding what I was going to wear, I wanted to look nice for him. What was I thinking? Finn wasn't going to see me as anything other than a friend, why should he? He was a doctor and I was just… well, I was just Nora Doyle from Paradise Alley, and besides all that, I had Joe, who loved me and was sweet and kind and deserved better than me daydreaming about Finn.

One day, when I knew he was coming, I decided to visit Kitty. It was a kind of test – I wondered if he would miss me as much as I knew I would miss him. I hurried along the Strand towards Minnie's and was glad to get inside out of the wind. There was only one table occupied, right beside the roaring fire. Kitty was standing behind the counter, cleaning the glass case that held the cakes and pies. I walked across to her.

'They'll be gone soon,' she whispered. 'They've had one pot of tea between them and they've been here for a good hour. They haven't even bought a cake. This isn't a bloody hotel!'

'Perhaps they're cold,' I said.

'Well, let them go home to their own fireside and stop taking advantage of ours.'

We stood chatting and eventually the couple left, without a by your leave or a thank you.

'Let's have a cup of tea,' said Kitty. 'Minnie has her feet up and I can hear her snoring.'

I chose a table close to the fire and waited for Kitty to bring the tea. Should I tell her about Finn?

'So,' she said, sitting down, 'what's bothering you now?'

'What do you mean, *now*?'

'Well, there's always something wrong.'

'Is there?'

'Well,' said Kitty, spooning three sugars into her tea, 'maybe not *always*, but you have that look about you.'

'What look?'

'The one that says I need to tell you something but don't know if I should, then I spend the next ten minutes dragging it out of you. So, what's wrong?'

'It's hard to explain.'

'Try. And make sure it's in your own words and not your Grandad Doyle's.'

'You're awful snappy today, Kitty Quinn. I've a mind to keep it to myself.'

'I'm sorry, Nora, but I've been bored senseless all morning. I don't know why Minnie keeps the café open in the winter – I've barely seen a soul all week and I'm sick of my own company.'

'Then it's a good job I came by, isn't it?'

'It is,' said Kitty, grinning. 'And I'm mighty glad to see you. Now tell me what's on your mind.'

'Well…'

'Well, what?'

I knew that if I told Kitty about Finn, it would make it real. It wouldn't be in my head anymore; it would be out of my mouth and I could never take it back. 'I don't know if I should.'

'Jesus, Nora, will you just tell me and get it over with.'

'I've found myself having feelings for someone.'

'Romantic feelings?'

I nodded.

'And it's not Joe?'

'No, it's not Joe.'

'But you never see anyone, you're stuck up in that Hall every day. It's not Eddie, is it?'

'Don't be an eejit, Kitty. Eddie's my brother, for God's sake.'

'Well, I can't think of anyone up there that you could have feelings about.' I stirred my tea, even though it didn't need stirring, and stared at Kitty. 'Oh my God,' she said suddenly. 'It's Finn Casey, isn't it?'

I could feel my face going red.

'It is,' she said. 'It's the Adonis himself.'

I nodded.

'Do you love him?'

'I'm not sure. I don't feel the same way about him as I do for Joe, but maybe what I feel for Joe isn't love at all, maybe I was too young to know what love really is.'

'Jesus, Nora, it wasn't that long ago.'

'But it feels like it, Kitty. It feels as if I've grown up suddenly. Sometimes I feel that there is some meaning in the way Finn looks at me. But I don't know, my feelings for Finn are…'

'Are what?'

'Different.'

'Finn Casey is a doctor, Nora. He'll be after marrying someone of his own station.'

'You make him sound like a train.'

Kitty shook her head. 'You're on to a loser there, girl. There's no way you'll get a feller like that asking you to walk out with him.'

'If I remember rightly, Kitty Quinn, there was a time when you wouldn't have said no to Finn Casey if he asked you to walk out with him.'

'You're right, Nora, but I was just a child then and didn't know my station.'

'For the love of God, will you stop talking about stations. And you weren't a child at all, you were almost fourteen.

'Okay, truce. So, what are you going to do about it? And what about poor Joe?'

'There's nothing I *can* do about it, is there? I just needed to tell someone and you're the only one I can tell.'

'I'm terrible sorry, Nora,' said Kitty. 'You came in here and opened up your heart to me and all I've done is eat the face off you.'

'That's alright, Kitty. I still feel better having told you.'

'Did you have the same feelings when you met Joe?'

I thought about it. 'It was different. Joe made it easy for me to fall in love with him. The feelings I have when I'm around Finn aren't easy at all, they're unsettling. I can't ever remember trying to impress Joe with what clothes I was wearing – none of that mattered, to me, or to him. I knew that he loved me completely just for who I was. I had no need to impress him.'

'Do you think that you might just have taken a fancy to Finn, like I did when we were younger? I can remember telling you that you might, when he was being all doctorly, but you were having none of it.'

'Maybe you're right. Maybe it's just a silly fancy.'

'So, it's helped, talking to me?' said Kitty, looking pleased with herself.

'Yes, I shall put the said doctor right out of my head.'

'Thank the Lord for that,' said Kitty. 'How about a slab of cake?'

'I can't think of anything I'd like better,' I said.

CHAPTER FORTY-EIGHT

I think as time went on, we all knew that Eddie was never going to get better. We didn't say it out loud, but I think that in our hearts we knew that we would soon lose him and he was never left alone. Caroline and I gave each other space, for we both had things to tell him that were personal to us. We didn't know whether he could hear us, but Finn said that hearing was the last thing to go and so we talked, we read to him, we held his hand. If he had to go to that other place, then he would go knowing that he was loved. He took his last breath just before Christmas: our darling boy had gone.

We were all heartbroken and shocked and couldn't take it in. Poor Caroline was grief-stricken. The boy she loved like a son had gone and she was now alone. Finn and I did all we could to help but her grief ran so deep that there was no consoling her. She had loved him all her life; she must have held him in her arms when he was but a baby; she must have sat beside his sick bed when he was a little boy. She would have given him comfort, in a house where there was little comfort to be had.

We buried him in the secret garden because we knew that was where he would want to be. As the snow fell around us, we watched him being lowered into the ground. The Vicar's words echoed around the old stone walls as we silently said our goodbyes to a kind, wonderful boy, who had meant so much to us. The Vicar helped Caroline back to the house but Finn and I stayed by the graveside. I wasn't ready to leave my brother yet. I hadn't cried since his death, because Caroline's grief had been so raw that it somehow left no room for anyone else's. I knelt down on the cold ground and remembered the boy who had jumped out at me and Kitty, the first time we had slipped through the broken fence and into the grounds of Bretton Hall. I remembered his grin, I remembered trusting him, even though Kitty didn't, and I remembered the first time he had shown us the garden – the look of pride on his face as he opened the gate. He wanted us to love it as much as he loved it. And I had.

'Why did he have to go, Finn?' I asked sadly.

'We had him longer than we thought we would. He saw the garden again and he had you. He wouldn't have suffered, Nora.'

'But he's gone and I will never see him again. I will never, never see him again.'

'But he will be in your heart, he will always be in your heart.'

I turned on him angrily. 'I don't want him in my heart!' I shouted. 'I want him alive; I want to see him smile and laugh, I want him here with me, planting and digging, I want him to push me on the swing, I want to sit on the bench beside him. I want him to see the garden change with the seasons. He didn't get the chance to see the flowers we planted. I don't want him buried in the ground. How can I sleep at night, thinking of him here, all alone? Tell me, how can I do that?'

Finn knelt down beside me. 'That isn't Eddie, Nora,' he said gently. 'Eddie is in a far better place.'

'That's just words, Finn, it's just stupid words that are supposed to make me feel better. Well, they don't, okay? They don't make me feel better.'

Finn put his arm around my shoulder but I pushed it away.

'We hadn't finished the book we were reading,' I whispered. 'He will never know the ending.'

That's when the tears came, great gulping sobs that had me fighting for breath, and then I was in Finn's arms, my tears soaking his coat. He held me gently and let me cry, he smoothed my hair back from my face, he held me close to him until there were no tears left.

We stayed like that as the snow fell around us and covered the garden in a blanket of white dust. 'You can still read to him,

Nora. You can finish the book. He will hear you, because he will always be beside you, his spirit will always be here. You will see him in every tree and flower, you will smell him as the roses begin to bloom. He will be here every spring and every autumn, every summer and every winter. He will always be here in the garden that you both loved.'

Finn held me away from him and wiped the tears from my cheeks, then he held my face in his hands. 'Eddie loved you, Nora, and love doesn't just disappear.'

I leaned into him and we stayed like that until our faces and hands became numb with the cold, then we walked out of the garden and back up the hill to the Hall.

There was no place for me here anymore. I wasn't needed now that Eddie had gone but I couldn't leave Caroline alone in that big, empty house.

I remember when Kitty and I used to sit on the graveyard wall watching the funerals. We had never thought about the grief of the mourners as they walked behind the coffin. We hadn't cared enough, as they stood at the graveside and watched a beloved husband, wife, son, or daughter being lowered into the ground.

We had been more concerned about what shoes they had on their feet or whether or not they were wearing their Sunday best hats. We gave them points out of ten for wailing, or for being dignified, when their loss may have been so great that they were beyond tears. When their grief may have been so great that they hadn't cared what they had on their feet or on their heads. If I could go back in time, I would have touched an arm, I would have said that I was sorry for their loss. But we were just children who hadn't known any better.

I spent Christmas morning with my family at the Grey House and then went back to the Hall and ate Christmas dinner with

Caroline. We sat opposite each other, at either end of the long table that ran the length of the dining room. The staff had draped the marble fireplace with holly and winter foliage but that was the only decoration in the house. Mammy used to tell me about the grand parties that were held in the ballroom and the beautiful Christmas tree that stood in the hallway, reaching up to the ceiling, hung with tinsel and baubles and presents. There was no tree this year and there was no grand party, only a deep sadness for the boy we had both loved and would never see again.

As I was leaving to go back to the Hall that morning, Mammy had said, 'You can't stay on there for ever, my love, however sorry you feel for Caroline. She must find her own way, and so must you.'

'But she is broken, Mammy.'

'And she will mend – we have all lost people we love but we make a choice to live or to die and if our choice is to live, then we must live the very best life we can, because that is what they would want for us. That is what Eddie would want for you and for his aunt. That is all you can do for him now, Nora – live your life and make him proud, for he will be with you every step of the way and he will carry you when the hill seems too hard to climb.'

I said goodbye to Eddie in the garden. 'I'm going back to Dublin, Eddie,' I said. 'I don't want to leave you but I have to believe Finn and Mammy, who say that you will be with me. I need so much to believe that. Caroline says she feels you with her, she feels your presence beside her every day and it's giving her comfort. I haven't felt you with me, Eddie, I have only felt your loss. Is Caroline's need for you greater than mine? Or is it all just nonsense, is it just her imagination, because she wants it so much? I need to feel you, Eddie, I need to feel you.'

CHAPTER FORTY-NINE

Finn drove me to Cork, where I would catch the train to Dublin. We barely spoke on the way there. I suppose there was nothing left to say except goodbye and I would leave that until the very last moment, because saying goodbye to Finn felt almost as bad as saying goodbye to Eddie. We had shared something special, the three of us, something that only we would remember.

Finn carried my case as we walked into the station. We were early, so we sat on a long bench under the clock.

'I have something for you, Nora, but before I give it to you, I want you to promise me something.'

'I promise,' I said, without hesitation.

Finn put his hand in his coat pocket and took out a letter. 'I don't want you to open it, Nora.'

'What, never?'

'Perhaps.'

'I don't understand.'

Finn looked directly into my eyes, as if he was almost willing me to read his mind, but I couldn't. Why would he give me a letter that I may never read?

'I want you to be happy, Nora,' he said. 'Always remember that.'

'I will, but I still don't understand.'

'And I'm doing a really bad job of explaining it, aren't I?'

'I'm afraid you are, Finn.'

'I want you to open this letter when your heart tells you to. Not out of curiosity, but because it's the right time and I have a feeling you will know when that time comes. If it never comes, you might come across it one day when you're seventy years old and not even remember who had given it to you.'

'I will never forget,' I said. 'Even when I'm seventy.'

'You might, and if that day comes, just throw it away.'

I stared at Finn's beautiful face; it seemed important that I remembered everything about it. 'I promise,' I said. 'And I always keep my promises.'

We sat together until the train that would take me back to Dublin chugged into the station, leaving a billow of white smoke in its trail.

I picked up my case. 'Goodbye again, Finn Casey,' I said.

Finn leaned over and kissed my cheek. I could feel his warm breath against my hair. I wanted him to hold me just one more time, but he stepped away. 'I want you to remember one more thing, Nora. I want you to trust your heart and not some words written on a page. Sometimes words can get in the way.'

I didn't know what he meant, but I said, 'I'll remember that, Finn.'

'Goodbye, Nora Doyle,' he said.

'Goodbye, Finn Casey.'

Just before I stepped into the carriage, I turned around, but Finn had gone. I was still holding his letter in my hand as the train rolled north. I didn't understand why I couldn't open it, or how I would know when the time came that I could. I trusted Finn and I knew it was important that I did what he asked. I had taken my copy of *The Secret Garden* with me, so I took the book out of my case and put the letter between the pages, next to the last rose of summer.

I had mixed feelings as the train sped towards Dublin. I had written to Miss Berry to tell her that I was coming back – I hadn't expected her to keep my job open for me but she said that there would always be a position for me at Finnigan's. Was I doing the right thing? Could I fit back into that other life that seemed so long ago? I wasn't the same person that had said goodbye to Joe and my friends. Eddie's death had changed me – I could hardly remember the girl who had left Paradise Alley and set out on an adventure, full of hope and excitement. That girl had gone and it was a different girl who was on her way back to Dublin.

I'd hardly slept the night before and when I had, my dreams had been vivid and unsettling. I was sitting on the flat rocks with Kitty and then Kitty turned into Finn and we were eating buns that were covered in bright-red icing that looked like blood. I was running through the rooms of Bretton Hall, asking everyone where Eddie's bedroom was, but no one answered me: it was as if I was invisible.

I had woken up trembling, and scared to go back to sleep, so I got out of bed and stood by the window. The floorboards were cold beneath my bare feet. It was dark outside, the only thing I could see was my own reflection staring back at me. I stayed there until the sun came up over the hill, then I'd washed and dressed, picked up my case and went downstairs.

I'd made myself a cup of tea and sat down at the table. Buddy-two was asleep by the stove – he'd opened one eye and gave a half-hearted attempt at wagging his tail. Grandad Doyle must have heard me moving about and had come downstairs.

'Couldn't sleep?' he'd asked, sitting beside me.

'Am I doing the right thing, Grandad?'

'Only you know that, my love,' he'd said.

'But I don't, that's the trouble. Part of me thinks I'm running away, that if I'm somewhere else, I can forget.'

'You can't run away from grief, Nora, it's something you carry with you. Grief is a natural thing, it has a natural progression, it's something you learn to live with and in time the pain eases. The mind is a great thing, Nora – it has its own way of figuring things out. Go back to Dublin and if it doesn't work out, then you come home, for Paradise Alley will always be your home.'

'Thank you, Grandad.'

'Immerse yourself in those books that you love, for just like those books, everyone has their own story to tell and this is yours. Embrace your grief, Nora, for it is now a part of who you are and will give you a wisdom that you never had before. To truly understand grief, you have to have known it, you have to have felt it. Maybe one day you will be able to reach out to someone who is suffering, because you have walked in their shoes.'

'I hope so,' I'd said.

'Father Kelly, who is himself a great reader, gave me the loan a book of poetry. Now poetry has never really been to my liking, as you know – I favour a good old yarn. But one of the poems was about the Easter Rising, by our very own Mr Yeats. It was a puzzling poem but one line stuck in my head: "A terrible beauty is born." I couldn't relate it to the Rising, but those few words touched my heart and it took me a while to understand why. My little girl Ellen died when she was only nine years old.'

'Yes, Mammy told me, and I'm sorry for your loss.'

'It was indeed a terrible time, for her mammy and me loved her very much. I was angry at God for taking her so young, for she was the sweetest child and as bright as a button. It took a long time to accept that she was gone but when I read those words, they made me think of my Ellen. You see, she would always remain a little child, she would never know the ravages of old age, she would remain as innocent as the day she died and it will be the same for your Eddie – he will always be a young man, he will never age and I think there is a kind of terrible beauty in that.'

I'd smiled at my grandad, who was a wise and clever man, and his words gave me comfort.

As the train pulled into Dublin, I took my case down from the rack above my head and stepped out onto the platform. It was like a re-run of a year ago, as I saw Josie rushing towards me.

We fell into each other's arms, both of us, crying and laughing.

'Oh, I've missed you,' she said. 'Let's go and have a cup of tea and a slice of cake.'

'You haven't changed,' I said, grinning.

'And why would I?' said Josie, laughing. 'Aren't I perfect as I am?'

We linked arms and walked across to the same café that we had gone to when I had first arrived. Josie went to the counter to order our tea and cake. I chose a different table to sit at than the one we had sat at before; I was going to go forwards and not backwards, and a change of table seemed like a good place to start.

Me and Josie had written the odd letter over the time that I had been away, so she knew about Eddie and that I had lived at Bretton Hall.

'I'm desperate sorry about your brother, Nora,' she said, sitting down beside me. 'I hope he didn't suffer.'

'The doctor said that he must have died peacefully.'

'Well, sure, that's a blessing.'

'It is,' I said.

'Are you still terrible sad?'

'I am,' I said.

Josie smiled at me. 'We'll soon have you laughing again,' she said.

'That's what I'm hoping.'

'And you can have your own bed back.'

'Have you had the room to yourself all this time?'

'No such luck. I had to share with this clodhopping baggage from Waterford. She was one of those holier-than-thou types. She said that going to the cinema was a mortal sin and that wearing lipstick was a thorn in the Blessed Virgin's side.'

'So, did you stop wearing it?'

'I did in me eye; I wore the reddest lipstick I could find, she had me head wrecked. She had her comeuppance when she went downstairs and ate the face off Mrs Murphy for hanging her washing out on a Sunday.'

'And what did Mrs Murphy say?' I said, grinning.

'She told her to pack a bag and consider taking Holy Orders.'

I was laughing, really laughing, for the first time since Eddie died. Thank God for darling Josie. I was right to come back; I'd made the right decision. In a world that had been so wrong, I was going to be alright.

CHAPTER FIFTY

Joe's reply to my letter had been short:

> Dear Nora,
>
> They say that absence makes the heart grow fonder but I think that absence has made it more difficult for you to remember what we had. I loved you then and the distance between us hasn't changed that. It hasn't made me love you more, because that isn't possible.
>
> You say that it is your life that has changed and not your feelings for me and that is all I need to know. I will wait for you until you tell me to stop waiting.
>
> My love always.
>
> Joe xxx

I hadn't told him that I was coming back – I wanted it to be a surprise. There was a queue in the bakery, and Joe and his father were serving behind the counter. It was his father who saw me first, he smiled at me and touched Joe's arm. 'I think you might be needed, son,' I heard him say.

If Joe could have leaped over the counter, I think he would, but he finished wrapping a loaf of bread for a customer and then he was at my side.

'You came back,' he said, softly.

I nodded. 'I came back, Joe.'

'Can you manage without me, Daddy?' said Joe.

'Get yourself away, boy. Nice to see you, Nora.'

'It's nice to see you too, Mr Lynch.'

We waited until we were outside the shop before we were in each other's arms and then we were kissing and laughing.

'Aren't we the brazen ones to be kissing in broad daylight for all of Dublin to see?' I said.

'I don't care if the whole world sees,' said Joe. 'For I have the prettiest girl in town in my arms.'

We walked hand in hand to St Stephen's Green and sat on our usual bench by the lake. It was a beautiful winter day. The breeze was sharp but fresh, and the scent of woodsmoke drifted through the air. This beautiful place should have made me happy but all I could think of was the garden and that Eddie had never lived long enough to see the clear blue sky and to smell the flowers. I could feel Joe sitting beside me, I could feel his warmth and his love for me. I tried to shake the feeling off but it was as if a cloud had appeared and distorted everything.

At that moment, Grandad Doyle's words came into my head. '*You can't run away from grief, Nora, it's something you carry with you… Embrace your grief, for it is now a part of who you are.*'

Why had I expected this grief to miraculously disappear, just because I'd come back to Dublin? I had to give it time – Eddie deserved my grief, I was just going to have to live with it.

Joe held my hand, as if he knew what I was thinking. 'We'll just take it slowly, Nora,' he said, gently. 'We have all the time in the world. I never knew Eddie, but I accept that he will always be part of us and that is as it should be. You don't ever have to hide your sadness from me. Talk to me about him, so that I can know him too.'

I leaned into him; he made me feel safe, his sweet words brushed the cloud away so that I could see the beauty of this day. 'Thank you, Joe,' I said.

As I stepped back through the doors of Finnigan's, it felt as if I'd never been away. I was again surrounded by the books that I loved and I was working with Josie, Ellis and Molly. I'd forgotten what it felt like to have fun and be silly, I thought that I would never be truly happy again, but being in the company of my three friends, I realised that I could. It was only at night as I lay beside Josie that my thoughts returned to the garden and Eddie and Finn and I would wake, feeling lost.

Ellis had fallen in love with a boy called Jack. He was studying Archaeology at Trinity College and had come into the shop looking for a book on ancient relics. They didn't have the book, so Ellis had ordered it for him. When he came to collect it, he didn't immediately leave the shop but spent a long time browsing the shelves. Ellis asked if she could help him with anything else. At first, he said, 'No, thank you,' but as she walked away, he said, 'Yes, there is, actually.'

'What is the book called?' Ellis had said.

'It's not about a book,' he'd said. 'I was just wondering if I could take you out one evening. My name is Jack, by the way.'

And that was that, Ellis was in love.

'I thought she'd end up in a convent,' said Molly. 'And instead of that, she's swept off her feet by a scholar at Trinity College, while all we ever seem to meet are clodhopping eejits from the country without a brain cell between them.'

Ellis smiled her sweet smile. 'You'll find someone wonderful one day, Molly, just like I have.'

Molly smiled back at her. 'I'm glad for you, love,' she said. 'For it couldn't happen to a nicer girl. Does he have any brothers?'

'Three sisters, I'm afraid,' said Ellis.

'Isn't that just my luck?' said Molly.

I saw Joe almost every day and as winter gave way to spring, he asked me to marry him. I loved Joe, I did, and all my doubts had gone away – I had just needed to be with him again.

He went down on one knee in the middle of O'Connell Street. I thought at first that he was doing up his shoelace but then he produced a little box from out of his pocket. He opened it and took out a ring.

'Nora Doyle,' he said, 'would you do me the honour of becoming my wife?'

People had stopped and were smiling at us, waiting for my reply.

Suddenly, Finn's face came into my mind, but I pushed it away. It had just been a silly flirtation, nothing more than that. I knew Joe loved me and he would always look after me.

'Of course,' I said, and the crowd started clapping.

When I told the girls, they danced me around the bedroom. I held out my hand so that they could see the pretty ring.

'It's gorgeous,' said Josie.

'You'll need a dress,' said Molly.

'I thought I'd wear the blue one; it was the dress I wore when I first met Joe.'

'You can't be wearing the same bloody dress for your wedding day, he's already seen it.'

'She's right,' said Josie. 'It would bring you bad luck.'

'If you believed in that sort of thing,' said Ellis.

'We'll see what Aunty Birdy has to offer,' said Molly, opening the wardrobe door.

We spread the dresses out on the bed. They were all lovely but none of them were quite right.

'You could wear a costume,' said Ellis.

'And why would she be wanting to stand at the altar in a costume, like some old biddy from up the country?' said Molly. 'It has to be a dress.'

I thought about my fortune, which Minnie was still looking after for me. 'I could buy one,' I said.

'Since when were you in a position to buy a wedding dress?' said Josie.

'Perhaps she's a woman of substance,' said Molly. 'And she hasn't let on.'

'I was left some money by a relative,' I said. 'And I think that it would please him, if I spent it on a wedding dress.'

'Roach's,' said Josie. 'They have the most gorgeous dresses there.'

'You won't need to,' said Molly, holding up a dress.

It was the palest lemon and it had a cream sash around the waist – it was the most beautiful dress that I had ever seen.

'Put it on, put it on,' said Josie.

I slipped the dress over my head – it felt silky and smooth against my skin.

'It's gorgeous,' said Ellis. 'Have you decided when the big day is going to be?'

'We thought in the autumn,' I said, smiling.

'You can't be sure of the weather in autumn,' said Molly. 'Wouldn't a summer wedding be better?'

'This is Ireland,' said Josie. 'You can never be sure of the weather.'

I thought of the garden in autumn. I could see it clearly in my mind. Me and Eddie sitting on the bench, with the brightly coloured leaves drifting about us. I thought of Finn and I walking down the steps of Bretton Hall, with him holding my arm, so that I wouldn't slip on the wet leaves. I remembered his arms around me as we stood beside Eddie's grave.

'Let's go downstairs so you can see yourself in the mirror,' said Josie.

We ran downstairs and the girls sat on the bed as I looked into the mirror – it was indeed the perfect dress. I stared at my reflection and I tried to imagine Joe standing beside me. I tried to picture his sweet face, but it was another face that I saw. I hadn't realised that I was crying until I felt Ellis's arm around me. Josie and Molly, looked confused and worried.

'What's wrong?' said Ellis, gently.

I couldn't answer, I could only shake my head. They sat me down on the bed.

'You *do* want to marry Joe, don't you?' said Molly.

'I don't know.'

'Wedding nerves,' said Josie. 'That's all it is, every bride-to-be has wedding nerves.'

Ellis was staring at me. 'I don't think it is,' she said. 'It's not, is it, Nora?'

As I sat there staring at my three friends, I felt a shift in my heart, a tiny flutter, hardly a feeling at all, but it was there and everything became clear. It felt as if I had been in a dark place and someone had switched a light on.

I was meeting Joe the next evening. I could have just written him a letter but he deserved more than that. I knew I was going to hurt him but better to hurt him now than to go through with something that I knew wasn't right for either of us. He came to the house to collect me – I felt sad but I knew that whatever my future held, it wasn't with this sweet boy.

We had planned to see a film but I asked if we could just go for a walk.

'But I thought you were desperate to see *The Great Gatsby*?'

'I have to talk to you, Joe.'

'I don't like the sound of that.'

My eyes filled with tears as I looked at his sweet face. How could I tell him? I slipped the ring from my finger and held it out to him. 'I'm so sorry, Joe. I'm so very sorry, but I can't marry you.'

He looked angry; I'd never seen him angry before. 'Why, Nora? Is it another feller?'

'There is someone that I have grown very close to, Joe, and I can't marry you feeling as I do. I have no idea what my future holds but you deserve more love than I can give you. I've never betrayed you, you have to believe that. I have never, ever betrayed you, but I can't marry you. I can't marry you, Joe.'

He took the ring, and the anger faded from his eyes. 'If I am not to be the one, Nora, then I hope whoever he is, he deserves you. I shouldn't have asked you to marry me – I have felt myself losing you ever since you left for Ballybun, but I hoped… I love you, Nora, and all I want is your happiness and if that means I have to lose you, then so be it.' He kissed my cheek and walked away.

Tears were running down my cheeks as I watched him go. I knew I'd broken his heart. Part of me wanted to run after him, to tell him I'd made a mistake, but I just stood there until he was out of sight. I had no regrets.

It was awful leaving the girls again and we cried in each other's arms as I boarded the train to Cork.

'Write to us, Nora,' said Josie. 'God only knows what baggage I will be sharing with next.'

I grinned. 'Of course I'll write,' I said.

I pushed down the window and waved to my friends until they were mere dots in the distance – I would miss them, but I knew that I was doing the right thing. I sat down and took Finn's letter out of my pocket. I opened the envelope and took out the single sheet. I was smiling as I remembered his words: *Trust your heart, Nora, and not some words written on a page. Sometimes words can get in the way.* I looked down at the blank piece of paper in my hand. I was still smiling as I watched the fields and rivers rushing by.

I was going home.

EPILOGUE

The summer sun was beginning to drift low in the sky, staining the clouds pink and lengthening the shadows. I gazed around the garden; it had never looked lovelier. The rose bushes were heavy with blooms, yellow irises were opening around the little pond, and clematis and honeysuckle were draped through the trees. The blackbird sang in the cherry tree and a family of squirrels chased through the dappled light of the grass. Finn reached for my hand. I moved a little closer to him and rested my head on his shoulder. We watched as our children picked daisies and scattered them on Eddie's grave.

Katie, at five years old, was beautiful – she was our fairy child, our little daydreamer, who found magic in everything around her. Her two blonde plaits bounced off her thin shoulders as she ran around the garden, looking for the whitest and brightest daisies.

Kieron, at three, was a sturdy little chap, blonde just like his sister and full of fun. He followed her around like a shadow. Katie was the boss and Kieron her faithful servant. They loved each other and we were so proud of them both. I couldn't help but smile as Kieron trotted after Katie, throwing his flowers with a solemn expression on his dear little face, then immediately turning around to find some more. He grabbed them in his fist and tugged, uprooting the flowers.

'No, no, do it like this, Kieron,' Katie explained with the patience of a responsible big sister. 'Pick the daisies like this, at the stalk, and then their petals won't all come off.'

Finn squeezed my hand. We exchanged fond smiles.

It wasn't just us who thought the world of them. Mammy and Caroline adored them and it was through this shared love for the children that they had become friends. Kitty and Tommy were happily married and had two little girls – they visited us often and it was a joy to see our children playing together. Bretton Hall became alive again with the laughter of children running around the grounds. I'd kept in touch with Molly, Ellis, Josie and Dymphna. Ellis had married her college boy, Molly and Josie were courting and Dymphna had found a man she could spend more than five minutes with. They were going to be married in Ballybun.

There were no grand balls at the Hall now, no carriages and shiny cars pulling up in the drive, but every Christmas Eve, Caroline threw a party for the townspeople. To begin with you could see that they felt out of place amongst such grandeur, but it had now become something to look forward to, it became the highlight of the year that was talked about months before the event. A beautiful tree stood in the hallway, just like Mammy used to tell me about, and the house was festooned with candles and decorations. Caroline would always miss Eddie but she wasn't alone anymore – we were her family now, and she was loved.

Grandad Doyle lived long enough to hold Kieron in his arms. We still missed him every day. As I stood watching the children play, his words came into my head.

I think every child should find their own secret garden, whether in reality or within the pages of a book. I hope you find yours, Nora.'
'I've found it, Grandad,' I whispered. 'It's right here.'

The heart will remember,
Though memories may fade
Of that one perfect moment in time
When leaves turned to gold in a garden,
And the last rose of summer was mine.

Nora Doyle

A LETTER FROM SANDY

I want to say a huge thank you for choosing to read *The Girl from Paradise Alley*. If you did enjoy it, and want to keep up to date with all my latest releases, just sign up at the following link. Your email address will never be shared and you can unsubscribe at any time.

www.bookouture.com/sandy-taylor

This has been a sad year for me. I was a third of the way through this book when my beloved son Bo died. Bo read all of my books and he was so proud of my writing. My first thought was that I couldn't finish it, but I knew that he would want me to, as *The Little Orphan Girl* was his favourite and he was looking forward to reading *The Girl from Paradise Alley*.

I have had so many messages of condolence from so many of my readers and I want to take this opportunity to thank you all – they have given me comfort at this sad time. Bo was such a kind, lovely boy, who was loved by so many people.

Thank you also for continuing to support my writing and I do hope that you enjoyed this book. If you did, I would be very grateful if you could write a review. I'd love to hear what you think, and it makes such a difference helping new readers to discover one of my books for the first time. I love hearing from my readers – you can get in touch on my Facebook page, through Twitter or Goodreads.

Love,
Sandy xxx

SandyTaylorAuthor

@SandyTaylorAuth

ACKNOWLEDGEMENTS

To my daughter, Kate, and my son-in-law, Iain, who have given me strength. And my three beautiful grandchildren, Millie, Archie and Emma, who have brought me such joy.

To my friends who have been there for me when I needed them most. Too many to mention but you know who you are and I would be lost without you all. To my brothers and sisters, nieces and nephews. Thank you all.

To Claire Bord, Natasha Harding, Emily Gowers and Kim Nash and to the whole team at Bookouture for allowing me the time to finish this book when I felt able to and for their lovely messages.

To my wonderful agent and friend, Kate Hordern, thank you for just being you, because just being you has been wonderful.

This book is for you, my darling Bo, and I hope that you are sitting on a cloud somewhere reading it.

Lightning Source UK Ltd.
Milton Keynes UK
UKHW011847220120
357431UK00001B/4

9 781786 819086